"Baer Charlton's protagonist Gunnery Sergeant Percival Stone is not unlike the great, silent heroes of American literature, film, and television. Traveling by motorcycle across America following his medical discharge from the Marine Corps, Stone finds connections to richly-drawn individuals whose lives he touched through his long national service."

Richard Rhinehart
Director of Communications
World T.E.A.M. Sports

" *...friend...* – Of all the words, of all the elements of the story, as a Veteran, this is the most important word in the entire book. The story itself tells an all too often tale that touches the lives of many."

Neven L. Gibbs, SSG CAV (Ret.)
Writer, Entertainer and former
Mental Health Counselor

STONEHEART

by

BAER CHARLTON

Dedicated to

All that have, do, and will serve.

01

Being dead is not always about dying.

The death of a soldier comes in many ways. They say, *the one you don't see coming is the one that gets you.*

Gunnery Sergeant Stone lay on the medic's rack still in full battle mufti, as if waiting to go out on patrol. Instead, he lay staring at the top of the tent. The patches on the wind-torn tent, sewn layers thick, made the canvas a stiff board. Who *they* were, did not concern the gunny, but he knew they were right. Stone's vision consisted of a tent on the right, black on the left, evenly split on the pole unless he moved his head.

Another helicopter made the tail-dragging stop onto the pad, creating air currents, which lifted the top of the tent. The stiff canvas would settle back down slowly, almost as if the tent were a great breathing beast. A part of the gunny's mind kept count of the tent lifts, therefore, the count of helicopters arriving or leaving, a sorry excuse of a distraction.

Four tours, and five years before, they had hung a bronze star and a purple heart on the end of his hospital bed in Germany. Meanwhile, the doctors stayed busy removing five inches of his gut, the appendix, and a small part of the liver. Not being a regular drinker, he did not miss the chunk of liver.

The doc claimed the appendix appeared in good shape. However, he was in there anyway, and it was something he could do to make up for the lazy jerk that left it in thirteen years before, during Desert Storm. At that time, they had hung a purple heart on his bed while the medics chased three nine-millimeter rounds and some shrapnel he had collected a few days before, during the *push*. With each conflict around the world, Stone had picked up foreign metal in exchange for tissue.

The removable metal went into a spice jar, along with the slug from the Cuban's AK-47 that his left thigh had stopped during the fiasco of the Spice Island War of Grenada—the war that had never happened, doing what had never been done to save people who had not known they needed saving—even after they had been saved.

The chunks of removed metal, or those still taking their own tour of Stone's body, were not what was in his mind. Nor were the patches on the tent. It was the injury that had cut his career short.

As certain as if Stone had become a body bag stuffing from the IED that had taken out his Humvee and the rest of the team, he was now heading stateside toward a DD-214 and the end of his life. Something he had not personally experienced, but had witnessed up close too many times.

Losing a foot or leg, perhaps even an arm, these would have been honorable reasons for leaving the Corps near the end of thirty-nine years of service. Yet, for the gunny to simply walk out the door on perfectly good legs, leaving his company and squad behind, tore him apart from the very center of his being. Stone had been a Marine as long as he could remember, even before his older brother had not come home from Vietnam.

Three hots and a hop the end of his career, sounded simple. Except for the gunny, it would drag out as they tried to figure out if he was stable, or would regain his sight. It would be more like a few months in a hospital stateside or Germany. He would wait until the medical weenies finished scratching their heads about the hysterical blindness in his left eye. Meanwhile, his blood pressure would have the corpsman waiting for him to blow a valve or just stroke out.

In the near distance, the gunny could hear the waves of Humvees, circling the quad, preparing. The Patrol would run down Blood Alley, left into Rouge's Road, a tour of Bang Town, with a finish sweep on the backstretch of Boom Drive. Then a quick hop back to the compound and a cold soda to top the four-hour day that could strip a month out of your soul, whiten your hair, and turn bright eyes into sunken holes with a hundred-mile stare.

The Afghani heat burned through the tent. Through his right eye, the gunny could watch the slow rise and fall of the tent from the waves of air caused by the Blackhawks coming and going from the base. Slow, rhythmic breathing paced with his. His years as a sniper in Vietnam had taught him about deeper rhythmic breaths, which brought life as well as calm to his body, no matter what was churning through his mind.

Stone remembered all four times he had been shot in Vietnam. He remembered the DC-3 disintegrating on landing and the molten steel flying through his body. The gunny remembered the booby trap that had removed a baby's fist-sized chunk of muscle from his leg and the shrapnel that had dictated he lose another two inches of bowel and the bottom piece of his stomach. He remembered Grenada—the nine-millimeter slugs slamming through his chest, removing his fifth right rib, and the one his leg stopped. He remembered the searing burn on his neck and face in the heat of Africa where the only painkiller was a dirty rag soaked with tepid water. He remembered the elephant sitting on his chest for weeks as he and gallons of antibiotics fought a lung infection from the dust storms in Iraq with Desert I. However, Stone could *not* remember even starting the day before yesterday—the day the IED ended his career as a Marine Gunnery Sergeant. In addition, he could not remember the faces of the team in the Humvee. He had spent ten months with them, patrolling, eating, sleeping, and sharing stories or letters and cookies from home, or Skypes with their girlfriends. He could not remember his men, the ones who had died in that destroyed Hummer.

Stone laid at relaxed attention, in full BDU battle gear, as if he were waiting to move out on patrol. The slow roll of ice in his heart quietly kept repeating, *it's over, it's over, it's over*. The gunny's life, as he knew how to live it, was gone. It was not something he could shoot his way out of with a squad. No helo was on its way to rescue him. Stone now lay in a field med unit, waiting to end his tour, his career, and everything he knew about being. Now he would have to trade out the green or dusty camo for civvies... he did not even think he owned any civvies.

There had been an attempt at the home away from the base back in the summer of 2001. Then 9/11 happened. Everyone had been recalled back onto the bases. Gulf II started soon after. The gunny had packed two bags, one went into storage, and the other stayed on his shoulder. He had no surety of which base the storage unit was located.

"Yo, Stone," someone yelled from the edge of the tent door, "your hop is here."

With a silent groan, Stone swung his boots over the edge of the bunk and planted them on the floor. The gunny's head swam slightly, and then solidified as he stood.

"Right through here, and we'll get you signed out," the Navy captain turned with a flair of his white coat, stethoscope classically draped on his neck.

As he followed the doctor through the door into the office area, Stone's left shoulder squarely smashed into the doorframe. "Shit!"

The doctor barely looked back. "You'll adjust, Sergeant. Eventually, you'll learn to keep your head cocked or swiveling to make up for the monocular vision. The next thing, which will take some time," as Stone stumbled into the back of him, "is that you no longer have depth perception." He turned and put a kind right hand on Stone's left shoulder, just down from half a face and neck of old scar tissue.

Ten minutes later, with his signature in nine places, Stone's boots were on each side of his rucksack, slowly tapping time on the steel plate floor of a Huey. Creedence Clearwater Revival looked out their back door as Stone looked out the side door from two-thousand feet over Dhi Qār, with Hammar Lake off to the west. Since Vietnam, helo pilots always seem to have the best tunes, and the ability to feed them over the intercom.

The blades were still spinning down from the landing in Baghdad. Stone's field boots were already moving across the tarmac in the quirky thirty-four inch gait that could chew up the trail and leave the nineteen-year-old pup Marines panting in his dust. The large Quonset hut sat back from the edge of the landing area. The rounded tin building squatted low and foreboding, the only dark thing on the field. The other tents and buildings had long faded to pastel sand by the heat, sun, and years of war.

A spec sergeant yeoman stepped out of the bunker door with a file in her hand. Slipping the wraparound shades over her eyes, she stopped and almost came to attention as Stone approached. "Gunnery Sergeant Stone," she called, extending her hand toward a waiting Humvee. "Admiral Mike Woodford sends his regards, Gunny."

Stone opened his mouth to ask, but was cut off. "We're on a very tight schedule, Gunny." She pointed to her left. "Latrine is that way, sir. You may want to use it while you have a chance. Your next hop is in a seat for roughly two hours." She reached for his rucksack. "I'll stow your bags in the Hummer." Looking around Stone for another bag, her brow furrowed.

He handed her the bag. "This is all I have, Sergeant. I'll take you up on the latrine offer and be with you in a minute."

They rode in silence as the yeoman drove down the side of the airfield. Finally, Stone could not stand the quiet and glancing again at the driver's nametag, Woodford, same as the admiral. "And how is your—?"

"Uncle, sir," the military voice softened only slightly, "but he might as well have been my dad. He took over raising us after my father died with your brother at Hog Ridge."

Stone swallowed hard, not knowing what to say at a

time like this. "A sad day."

With ease, the yeoman threw the Humvee around a large pothole. "A sad day for the corps, Gunny." She glanced over at Stone. "It's okay, sir. My twin sister and I were only two weeks old at the time. In a way, it was a blessing that we never had any memories of him." She glanced down at the closed file, refreshing her memories about the content and drawing attention to the matter at hand. "The admiral has made arrangements... to speed things along."

Stone looked down the road. A C-130, gray and formidable, hulked at the edge of the tarmac, winding up its engines. The yeoman looked at the C-130 and laughed. "Don't worry—that sky pig is all I would be able to get you on, and it would put you in Germany about midday, day after tomorrow. The admiral had a little more speed in mind." As they swung around the tail of the giant plane, a small fighter jet came into view. "This is why you made the pit stop back there. I hope you don't get airsick easily. These stick jocks get pretty touchy about dirt pounders becoming dirt pukes at Mach 2."

As they pulled up, the Strike Eagle crew stood by the ladder. The flight crew chief took Stone's bag and stowed it in a small hold, then squared the gunny away in the RIO seat behind the pilot. Once settled, the pilot climbed in, and everything became a noisy blur that ended with Stone pushed hard into the back of the seat. They reached thirty-five thousand feet over the Helmand Province, where Stone had just come from. As they reached the Persian Gulf, the plane rose another ten thousand feet and surged ahead as it slowly turned south toward the air base in Bahrain.

The crisp throaty sound of the pilot cut through the static and wind noise. "Are you okay back there? Please don't grab the stick. To talk, press the blue button at the right thumb position on the stick."

Stone studied the randomly moving stick between his legs. A large cluster of many buttons covered the head of the stick. Pressing the blue button lightly, he spoke. "Affirmative, I'm fine... and thanks for the air-conditioning. I haven't felt this refreshed since Adak, Alaska."

The pilot's voice crackled back through the intercom. "No air-conditioning, Gunny. Minus eighteen degrees outside temp right now. If you're too cold, I can roll on more heat. We're an hour and twenty minutes from landing. The flight attendant will be around shortly with a fine selection of nuts and snacks and to take your drink order. Thank you for flying Strike Eagle Express."

Stone chuckled as he looked out the cockpit. the Middle East spread out before him in a way he had never seen it before. He appreciated the bit of stick-jock humor, but even with that, the pilot never introduced himself by even his call sign. Stone gratefully realized there would be no chitchat and assumed he was just as much a curiosity as the entire flight was to him.

Three hours later, and more mysteriously, he slowly drifted off to sleep in a comfortable reclined seat in Business Class bound for Germany, the compulsory first stop on the way stateside. Orders are orders—after thirty-nine years, the gunny had stopped questioning them. It was not in his pay-grade.

STONEHEART

BAER CHARLTON

02

A ceiling fan from a bygone era swept after a single fly turning small patterns near the ceiling. The building hummed with low conversation and a soft static of keyboards. The institutional green of the walls remained the same color they had been since the Eisenhower administration, probably back when Ike had served as a plebe at West Point.

The doctor turned a few pages then grabbed back deeper in the four-inch thick file, looking for clarification of a medical note. Stone watched with the detachment of years waiting for those in control to come to a point where they would share information. The small bronze mantel clock at the end of the large desk ticked softly. The ticking matched the pulse in the gunny's chest—sixty slow beats to the minute. A loud tick-click as the hand registered forward, and the whole cycle started over.

The doctor held his finger in one page. Flipping back, he examined the two-page list of medals that explained the dinner plate-sized field of ribbons on the sergeant's chest. Glancing up, he noted the single Purple Heart ribbon with only a trio of oak clusters. The ribbon was buried in a field that would make a general or an admiral proud, except unlike that other, the doctor knew that every ribbon on this sergeant's chest had been personally earned. This was the kind of soldier that wasn't about to pin a battalion courtesy on his chest.

The doctor returned to the notations in the file that would require far more ribbons and brass on the sergeant's chest than he currently displayed. He thought about the man in front of him: a sergeant that cared more about the job and his men than any personal achievement.

The doctor's eyes ran down the second column. The list was mostly of medals and awards that were bestowed by foreign countries for meritorious service. Most the doctor had only heard of—he had never known a recipient.

The doctor slowly closed the file, lifted his head, removed his reading glasses, and rubbed his eyes. He focused his thoughts.

"I guess the biggest question I have," he began as he eyed Stone, "I'm just wondering why you are even alive."

"I was on the opposite side and farther back in the Humvee."

Frowning in confusion, the doctor then realized the gunny was talking about the IED that had ended his career. He reached out with his index finger and tapping on the very large file,. "I'm sorry, Sergeant, I was talking about things like the four inches of gut they removed in Vietnam, before you went back to pick up— what, four more rounds?"

"Five."

Startled, the fresh-faced doctor stared back up at the gunny. "Excuse me?"

"Five, sir, it was five more rounds, but three that were through-and-through, sir."

The doctor folded his glasses slowly and placed them on the file. Weighing his next words carefully, he pursed his lips then blew them out softly. "How many Purple Hearts do you exactly have?"

"No idea."

"No idea?"

"I stopped counting at nine, sir."

Swallowing slowly, the doctor tried to think of what he was actually doing with this soldier. He was used to dealing with the dozens of men, mostly those younger than Stone, who were missing a leg or an arm. Easily identifiable injuries such as faces half-burned off or heads shaped more like a squash that had fallen off a farm truck.

Here sat a man in sound shape, with all of his digits, eyes, ears, nose, and mouth with combined injuries over more conflicts than the doctor had years in practice. Shrapnel floated around inside him, a total body mass of four-plus pounds of muscle and internal organs missing, and three square feet of burn scar tissue covered his upper body, neck, and face. The only thing now between him, and his returning to the company was being blind in one eye from traumatic brain injury (TBI).

The doctor looked around his desk for an answer that was not there. "I don't know what to tell you, Gunny."

The eternal warhorse growled, and then snapped, "Tell me I can return to my company where I belong, and we'll both sleep better tonight. They said the blindness is only temporary. Today it's gone."

"Or not?" The young Navy captain ran his fingers through his dark, curly hair and stared wide-eyed at the desk. Dropping a hand into his lap, he leaned back. "Look, we don't know what will happen. You could be blind in that eye for the rest of your life, or you could stand up in a minute and see with both eyes. We just don't know. Heck, we don't even know if you might wake up tomorrow and you're blind in both eyes. We just don't know."

The doctor eased forward as he steepled his fingers. Then noticing his actions, he laid them down on the desk. "TBI is kind of a new playground for us new kids. We really don't know how to deal with it, or even diagnose it correctly other than during an autopsy. So because of that, you get a shot at going home and picking up where you left off."

Stone cut him off quietly, through clenched teeth. "My life before the corps was of a seventeen-year-old high school graduate living on Camp Pendleton Marine base, chomping at the bit for boot camp. We put my brother in the ground two years before I joined the corps—a year and two months before my parents were killed in a tornado. It struck them while they slept on the fourth night of my dad's retirement. Now, which part of that were you suggesting I take back up?"

The doctor squirmed in his chair. The knock on the opening door was more of a reprieve than an intrusion. The young yeoman stepped in around the admiral in dress whites. "Sorry, sir, but the admiral insisted."

"Yes I did, son. You've done your job, and now you're dismissed." The admiral glared the yeoman back out of the door. Turning to the now standing doctor, he lowered his temperature to subarctic. "Captain, you've also done your job, and if you wouldn't mind giving the gunny and I a moment..."

The officer straightened his white coat, picked up the large file, and slid toward the door with a quiet, "Admiral."

The door closed with a soft click as the admiral removed his hat from under his arm. Laying it on the desk next to his briefcase, he turned to the sergeant standing at attention. The admiral pursed his lips and then relaxed into a smile as he extended his right hand. "Stone, this meeting is long overdue."

The conflict of remaining at attention in front of a superior officer, or to shake an offered hand was written all over the scarred face. The senior officer sat on the edge of the desk. "This isn't going to work until you start learning how to be a civilian, Stone." Raising his hand just a little bit more, he waited for the gunny to take it.

As they shook with a certain slow curiosity on the pickle suit's side, the admiral chuckled softly, but with no mirth. "Our brothers died together on Hog Ridge. In a really perverse world, that makes us a band of brothers unto ourselves." He motioned toward one of the lounge chairs as he moved the other, farthest from the desk, to block the door.

Now sitting with their privacy guaranteed, the admiral continued. "I was the new executive officer on the Kitty Hawk, fresh out of Annapolis, when they were killed. I wasn't even allowed the time to go to their funerals. Seven of them were buried together that day."

"I know. I was there." the gunny's voice was as distant as the sunny grass on the low slope of the military cemetery in Los Angeles. "We rode up on the train. My mother couldn't stop crying, and dad couldn't stop drinking."

The silence was stunning between the two who still suffered from the loss of their brothers. The old fan turned slow sweeps of humid time, counting the years lost between them and their siblings. The officer picked a small dust mote from the pure white of his right pant leg. "It was too late when I found out that they were interred in Los Angeles instead of Arlington." He let out a deep aching sigh. "I guess it wouldn't have mattered anyway. They had designated burial in LA when they signed up. Kids, I guess."

"What's this all about, sir?" The gunny shifted in

his sitting at attention in the large overstuffed leather chair from the second Roosevelt administration. "At your bidding, I flew first class to Germany, then the same to here. You are based God knows where, but when I'm getting drummed out on my ass, you magically show up and start talking about our brothers."

The admiral gave him a steely look, weighing the man and the circumstances. Quietly, he engaged the gunny. "Scale it back, Stone. There is no opposition here. That temper is what probably made you not only a great sergeant, but also the oldest working gunny. This is about something that is bigger than just the two of us. And I should have reached out to you forty years ago when our brothers died."

The admiral opened his attaché case and fished out a fat packet of old letters bound with rubber bands. Tossing them into the gunny's lap, he explained. "These are the letters my brother wrote to me from camp and then Vietnam. Take them with you. Read them. They're about your brother, too. They were the best of friends from the day they met at their company form-up. They wanted each other to be the godfather of any children they had. They wanted to live next door to each other, and even marry sisters. Identical twins would have even made it better."

He and the gunny laughed. They both knew comrades in arms who had bonded that way. Some had successfully moved on as lifelong friends; others had not been as lucky. The nature of military life and war can form strong bonds, the kind of bonds beyond the understanding of anyone non-military. The strength of a bond like this often proves even stronger than the bonds of matrimony. It is the good news/bad news about the military, and the two old warhorses sat steeped in this understanding.

The admiral softened. "I watched your career from

a distance. I even came to see you in the hospital in Yokahama, but you were pretty much still out of commission."

The gunny protested as he started to lean back into the chair. He pointed his finger at the officer. "No, I do remember. It was in the middle of the night. I thought it was strange that a doc would be in his khakis and no white gown." The officer nodded and Stone continued. "You stood in the door for a few minutes then left."

The admiral ran his finger around the back of his starched collar. "I didn't know you were awake. I didn't want to disturb you."

The gunny sat up. "When I was at Bethesda, during Desert Storm, the nurse told me that a Navy officer came in every night shortly before midnight to check on me."

The white clad arm rose. "Guilty as charged. I usually left the Pentagon around eight or so and went to dinner, then stopped in."

"But you never came and introduced yourself. Why?"

The admiral picked at his manicured nails then looked up. "By that time, I just didn't know where to begin. We had both lost our brothers. That put us on level footing... but by the time they dragged you back from the first Sandbox, I had suffered an inflamed appendix, and two hemorrhoids." He waved at the salad of ribbons on Stone's Class A uniform. "You had seen action in nine places and we're working on your third bronze star, a Navy Cross, and sixth Purple Heart. Hell, I was waiting for you to push it all into the middle of the pile and spin one more time for a Medal of Honor. I had nothing. You were already out of my league. I barely had a third rail on my chest, and they were welding extenders on your dinner plate."

"Being an admiral is at least a full house at the

table."

"Not where it counts." The two locked eyes in the arena of truth. Both knew that in the hierarchy of price paid in the world of war, the gunny had the higher ground. They both slowly relaxed in their chairs.

The gunny ran his right palm over his brush cut. "So, this is really it. I'm out."

The admiral's lips curled into tight rolls over his teeth as he nodded. "I'm afraid so."

The gunny stood up, walked to the window, and looked down on the quad where a small company of soldiers marched past. The green buds of a false early spring were on a few of the trees that had bought into a few almost warmish days. Asking more as a mental rhetorical than an actual question, the gunny spoke at the scene outside. "So where do I go from here?"

He heard the officer stand up and step to the desk. "I can't tell you that, but I do have a few items you need to take with you."

The gunny turned to see the admiral pulling a thick manila envelope from his case. "If that's money—"

The admiral chuckled. "Gunny, one thing I do know, is you don't have a need for any small amount of money I could provide you." The gunny stared at him, perplexed.

"You never really lived off base. You owned maybe a dozen t-shirts or bowling shirts over your career. Always ate at the commissary, base doctors, and banked almost all of your pay with a financial adviser. Don't ask. He's my adviser, too. Dan Whitewater, one of only eleven to survive Hog Ridge." The admiral looked up and settled his shoulders. "Like I said, a perverse band of brothers." Pouring the contents out of the envelope, he started to explain each one, starting with the cell phone. "This is an iPhone—"

"I don't need a phone."

"Shut up, Stone. You do, and you need to listen."
The admiral shot him a hard parental look. Stone
shrugged and closed his mouth. "Good. Now, I won't
go through all the functions of the phone. The ensign
outside, that looks like she's only thirteen? She will go
over everything that's in it. Suffice it to say, there were
many people who worked long hard hours pulling
together what is on the phone. Oh, and just between us
men... don't even *try* to get on the ensign's bad side."

Putting the phone aside, he picked up a small address
book. "All the phone numbers, names, addresses and
information that are in the phone are also in this book, just
in case you are more of a Luddite than I think you are...
but also, this makes for some good reading, for you to
know your resources. Everyone is listed by their last name
and by the rank you knew them by."

Flipping the book open and pointing to his name, he
continued. "So, I'm listed in the 'W's, but also in the 'A's
as just Admiral. I took the pleasure of finding out that I'm
the only admiral you know." The officer pointed back to
his main listing. "So there is my home phone, cell phone,
and my office phone. If I don't answer, and you need me,
just call my office. The ensign will always know how to
contact me if there are any questions that she can't
answer."

The admiral turned to the back pages of the book.
"This is something we couldn't put in the phone. Each
contact is listed by the state they live in. The code behind
the state is what quarter. Like here, NB – SE, Nelson,
Richard 'Sparks' Corporal, he's in Nebraska in the
southeast quadrant. Then you can look him up under his
name, and find out what he is doing for work, or how he
can help." He continued flipping the pages and found
another entry. "Ah, says he has some homemade root beer
waiting when you get there." Looking up, the officer
smiled with teeth that were as straight and white as his

uniform.

Closing the book, he opened a pocket-sized map atlas. "Wherever you see this little purple star, you know someone."

Putting the items back in the envelope, he picked up the last item, which was a business card, and handed the card to Stone. "This is Poco. He was the best executive officer I ever had aboard ship, until he caught a bullet from an angry husband. He'll set you up with a car or truck."

Handing the envelope to Stone, he said, "Don't worry about the phone bill; it's assigned to my office. Just make sure you use the thing." Extending his right hand, they shook. "I would have you over to the BOQ for dinner, but I'm due on a carrier in Hawaii in a little over twelve hours."

Stone stared at the envelope in his hand then back up to the admiral. "I don't know what to say."

Looking at him, the admiral stated with sincerity, "You don't have to say anything, Stone. I would say welcome home, but I have a feeling that is something you will have to go look for. I will be out with the fleet off and on for the next few months, but if you—"

Stone groaned. "I know, call your secretary."

The officer moved the chair and opened the door, and turned. "I've got to fly, but when they kick you to the curb in the morning, call Poco. He'll come pick you up."

"Thanks again, sir."

The officer smiled. "I'd tell you to call me Mike, but I have a feeling it wouldn't do any good." They shook again, and the admiral walked down the hall.

Stone called, "We'll talk later... Mike."

The admiral waved his right hand over his head without turning around, but called, "That's a start, Stone. That's a start."

"Sir," the voice did sound like a young girl. "Mr. Stone, sir?"

Stone turned to find the young ensign standing casually as her right hand waved toward the two seats along the wall. "Shall we work on your phone skills?"

Stone looked at the chestnut haired ensign who could have been his granddaughter if he had ever stopped to have a life. The gruff voice of a sergeant in command of hundreds of young lives no older than she was came easily. "Thank you, but I don't need help." He turned to leave.

The little girl's voice was crisp with an officer's edge. "Excuse the impudence, sir, but how will you know when your phone is ringing?"

Turning back, Stone stared at the young woman, trying to make heads or tails of what she had asked. Instead, he was caught in a war with her youth, and the brass of her question, as well as its honesty.

She pointed at the large envelope. "That is what is vibrating in the envelope, sir."

Stone looked down at the offending item as the tension wiped out the vision in his left eye. The manila container shook again like a small rattlesnake, only more deadly, in Stone's opinion. Slowly, he extended the envelope and surrendered it to the ensign.

Fishing out the vibrating phone, she deftly answered it. "Yes, Admiral." She nodded as she studied Stone's face. "Yes, sir, I believe we have reached an accord, sir." She listened and finished the call. "Yes, sir, will do, sir. Mace's would be my guess, sir. Yes, sir, I'll let him know, sir. See you in nine days, sir." With a flourish of her hand, she hung up and powered down the phone.

Looking at the elder gunny, the ensign smiled. "It would appear, sir, that I am to teach you about your phone over steak and lobster on the admiral's expense account."

"On one condition," the gunny growled.

"That would be...?"

"You stop calling me sir."

"Because you work for a living," the ensign finished. "Yes, sir, my father drilled that into me too, sir." She smiled at the two sirs she had just slipped in. "How about you call me Julie, and I'll call you?"

"Stone," The gunny clamped down on the word to end the conversation. Glancing at the brass nametag on her whites, he finished with, "and let's just stick with what I'm used to... Ski." The reference to almost all Yeomen in the Navy and Marines having the Polish or Russian name that ended in the letters 's-k-i or s-k-y' both pronounced like the winter sport, and name tags that contained nothing more than the three letters.

Looking at him with a slow measuring eye, she slipped the phone back into the envelope and reached for her cap. Turning, she asked brightly, "Well, Stone, are you ready for dinner?"

He stuck his hand out for the envelope.

She pulled it closer to her. "Oh, no. I'll just hang on to this until I can trust you enough to answer the phone." The smile played across her face, and Stone recognized for the first time that she had some freckles to go with the chestnut hair.

His stomach rolled like a lazy sturgeon in the sun, reminding him that he was hungry. "Fair enough, Ski, fair enough. I'm at your lead."

STONEHEART

BAER CHARLTON

03

Stone had felt drawn to the old style railcar diner. It smelled clean and felt cheery. With quilted stainless steel on the outside, these diners had been a common sight across America in the early 1950s, but had died against a tide of much larger chain restaurants by the end of the Vietnam War. Stone figured he had subconsciously chosen the older mom & pop style coffee shop in an effort to recapture his childhood. The only problem, he could not remember having ever stepped foot into a coffee shop as a young boy, much less a railcar diner.

As Stone sipped on his coffee, washing the occasional bite of toast down his throat, he played with his phone. The marvel of a huge phone book available at the touch of his finger felt amazing, and took some getting used to. Stone was overwhelmed that it contained hundreds of people he thought he had forgotten over the years, yet so cleverly arranged (last name first, then rank, nickname, real first name), he found himself instantly remembering.

Stone swept the names and memories up and down in a two-way waterfall. Every once in a sweep, there would be a name he had to think about. Soon, however, he found by touching the name, a fuller catalog card would appear with an address, number, and where they had served together. There was even a pop-up suggestion box to explain why he might want to contact them. Somebody he suspected as a certain little freckled ensign had logged many hundreds of hours compiling these addresses and numbers for the phone book. Everyone had an email address as well, but Stone had no idea when he might have access, or want to have access, to a computer.

Stone turned his head, raised the coffee mug to his mouth as the phone vibrated in the other hand... chirping a fast revelry. He jumped and dropped the phone on the counter in alarm, spilling coffee. Stone glared in anger at the offender lying on the Formica countertop. He heard a husky chuckle and then, "Yeah, scares the hell out of me too, when they do that."

Stone looked up to see a beefy woman with a graying reddish butch haircut and T-shirt sleeves rolled up past tattoos. She was not an ugly woman, but ruggedly handsome in a more mannish sort of way. Stone shrugged inwardly. He had seen and heard worse in the corps. "It's only my eighth day of ownership." Stone glanced down and glared at the hunk of plastic and metal as it chirped again. "It took me three days to figure out how to turn it back on." He looked at the screen. There was something written there from Ski. Confused, he scooped it up and showed it to the woman. "What does that mean?"

The woman read it as the waitress sauntered down the long counter with coffee in one hand and a donut in the other. The woman's lips moved as she read the message over a second time. Looking up she recognized the waitress. "Good morning, Candy. The donut is a great start, but the build starts today, so I'll need an omelet to go with it."

Putting the coffee and donut down, Candy asked, "What kind?" Stone had not even seen where she had produced the order book and pen from, and figured it was one of the older waitress's super powers.

"Anything Sparky wants to make with a lot of meat and stuff in it. Tell him to choke the horse with it." The redhead's voice rattled like rocks in an old lead pipe.

"You've got it, Rusty." The waitress swiveled and headed toward the cook's station as the other woman watched her walk away.

Quietly, Rusty muttered more to herself, but within Stone's hearing, "Man I wish I had an ass like that." Shaking her head, she turned back around to see the stunned look on Stone's face. "What?" she exclaimed, while rising slightly and slapping her right hand on her haunch and laughing. "Mine's as big as a tank car."

Stone was disarmed and smiled. There might have even been a slight chuckle, but not one that he would admit to.

Sliding her eyes from studying Stone's reaction, Rusty pulled the phone over to her, and poked and swept it alive. One more poke and she was back at the text message. "Someone named Ski says you are within seven miles of a corporal named John 'Tweeter' Shay and should go look him up." Rusty pushed the phone back toward Stone.

Stone looked at it as if it were the devil himself. "How does she know?"

"Know what?"

"Where I'm at."

"Maybe you told her?"

Stone shook his head ever so slightly. "I don't even know where I am."

"Oh, I can help you there," offered Rusty. "You're in Maysburg, North Carolina. Claim to fame until now was that Davey Crockett came through here before there was a town."

Stone asked, "And now?"

"Ten homes in ten days, starting in," glancing at her watch, "about forty minutes."

"*What* are ten homes and ten days?" Stone was confused.

"Habitat for Humanity," Rusty leaned back astounded as the waitress set down an omelet that a twenty year old Marine would be proud to get himself around. "You're not here to volunteer for the building?"

Stone shook his head. "Didn't know about it."

She explained as she cut out her first bite of the omelet. "Well, over the next ten days, or two-hundred and forty hours, we're going to build ten homes ready for occupancy. Move-in will be the eleventh day, along with a huge barbeque."

"I have the time. I just don't have any tools."

"If you have the time, I have more than enough tools in my RV." Rusty stared at Stone's face for signs of insincerity.

Stone felt the examination, and was one-step ahead. Looking around Rusty, he called down to the waitress. "Candy, it looks like I'll need one of these also," as he circled his finger at the omelet, "except, I'll take whole wheat toast instead of the donut."

Candy and Rusty harmonized with, "You don't know what you're missing."

The toast arrived with a homemade donut sitting on top. They had been right. He had never eaten a whole wheat and bran donut before. This was Candy's own creation. This civilian stuff was going to take some time getting used to.

A few short hours later, Stone felt a bit out of place with a utility belt. The hammer seemed to hunt out his crotch or butt crack to hang down. The tape measure was a completely new, 'chicken or beef thing' as Rusty put it. However, the physical labor of lifting, moving, hammering, and just doing something with a company of people felt good for his soul.

Rusty took him under her wing when they tried to assign work details. She had been doing nothing but build-outs around the country since retiring about eight years before. The intricacies of a build-out, which was happening at lightning speed, were hard-wired into her nature, and taking command seemed her forte. Rusty kept Stone close by until she figured out what he knew and where he was a good fit. Before long, Stone found himself with a clipboard and a white hard hat as the much-maligned hammer hung where the sun did not shine.

A large truck full of more studs rumbled down the street toward Stone when a balding guy with glasses leaned out of the support trailer and yelled at Stone. "Hey, Gunny," pointing down the road. "That load needs to go around to the back side of number nine and ten. They have their decks down, and are ready for walls."

Stone gave him the thumbs-up and walked to the far side of the street to talk to the truck driver. As he started to step up onto the running board, his pocket vibrated. He yelled up at the driver as he pointed the direction to go. Reaching in with his left hand, he fished out the phone.

From Ski:
If you do not call them, they will come find you.
Enjoy the build-out

Oh great, he thought, *now she even knows what I'm doing.* Stuffing the phone back in his pants, Stone looked down the road for his next truck. As he stepped toward the line of blue plastic outhouses, he thought of the phone and hesitated. "Screw her, she's Navy," he chuffed under his breath. Coffee is only on a short-term loan.

The light filtered blue through the tough plastic of the portable as Stone sat thinking. It felt good to be doing something that mattered. It felt even better to be doing it with a great group of people. He ran his right hand over his short hair. Thinking it was about time he got his forest logged down to a respectable—and then it hit him. The bald guy with the glasses had called him Gunny, short for Gunnery Sergeant. It was a title rank like no other term or nickname, and it did not exist outside the military.

Stone fished down into the pants gathered around his ankles and pulled out the phone. Turning it on, he stared at the message, which was still there. His eyes slid shut in a slow burn.

With eyes open to see what he was doing, Stone thumbed out to his contacts, found the right number, and pressed to dial. It had better be a short call as he could hear the next truck coming down the street.

"Gunny," the chipper voice answered, "you wouldn't

call a girl while sitting in a field latrine would you?" The ensign was answered by silence. Understanding she may have pushed a boundary, she quickly added, "Don't you dare drop that phone in the toilet, Stone, or I'll have to come down there and make you dig it out. It's government property."

The measured voice rumbled up from the depths of many purgatories. "You have three seconds to tell me who is in the trailer, Ski." Shifting the phone to his left hand, Stone reached out for the toilet paper with his right, wishing there was a toilet to flush at that moment.

"John Shay, 'Tweeter' to you, but he asked that you not call him that." She was peddling backwards fast. "Please."

Stone thought about it for almost a second, but the sound of the diesel truck ended the conversation and he hung up.

Stepping back out into the sunlight, Stone was greeted by not just one truck but four, slowly contracting on the street like a caterpillar halting. Looking at his clipboard, he realized nothing matched. He stuck his index finger up for the drivers to wait a minute as he stalked off toward the trailer, muttering under his breath, *What a FUBAR this is!*

Yanking the trailer door open, he growled, "Tweeter!" and ran into a fresh clipboard with an inch of sheets.

"Gotcha covered, Gunny. These will take you out past dinner... and it's Reverend Tweeter to you." The slightly underweight gentleman lounged back in the rolling desk chair smiling as if he had just gotten the last canary. The bald head, glasses, and the small basketball tummy, did not fit Stone's memory of the gawky kid that had been his radioman in Vietnam. But the smile and white blotch shaped like Europe spreading across the dark face was still all 'Tweeter'—the fastest bird caller in the country—for finding a helo evacuation in the dead of night, or some bored jet-jockeys ready to pickle off some bombs when the company was in need.

Stone traded the clipboards and turned back out the door. "Your shoelace is untied, Padre," slamming the door.

Tweeter looked at the Velcro tennis shoes, and called through the door, "Good to see you too, Gunny."

Walking back to the trucks, Stone smiled softly. It was good seeing the little twerp again. *Reverend, huh... that has to be a story,* he thought while climbing up on the running board of the first truck. He looked down at the top sheet on his clipboard.

STONEHEART

BAER CHARLTON

04

The first three days of the build-out had been a whirlwind for Stone. In addition to settling into a new, somewhat unsettling friendship with Rusty, he was renewing his relationship with Tweeter. Some habits were too hard to break, while other things took some getting used to.

The three sat around Rusty's large motor home throwing back root beers. Rusty was sixteen years sober, Tweeter had never touched alcohol because of his religious beliefs, and although Stone liked the occasional Scotch, it was not in the offering, and the root beers were tasting the best, anyway. The conversation slowed as Rusty noticed Stone staring at the top of his root beer bottle. "Where'd you go, Stone?"

He looked up as if from a distance. Focusing, he tried to give a weak smile. "I was just wondering if it were possible to become a root-beer-a-holic."

Tweeter cleared his throat with a forced, "Bullshit." Stone slowly looked over to him. "Man, you left the track almost five minutes ago, you just never saw it come or go."

Stone looked at him with a total lack of

understanding. Rusty asked what the others were thinking. "What are you saying, John?"

"Traumatic Brain Injury and maybe some accumulated Post-traumatic Stress Disorder." The reverend sat up, and took the floor. "I've been seeing both more and more lately. This war produced more walking wounded than all the others combined. The worst part of it, we don't know enough about TBI to treat it properly, and the military is denying there's a problem."

He turned back to Stone. "You have vision in both eyes?" Stone nodded. "How often do you find you're waking up from a daydream, but you don't know where your mind went?"

Stone had to stop and think, pursing his mouth before quietly hazarding a guess. "Occasionally, maybe a few times a week. Why?"

Tweeter was not finished. "I've seen you brought to a halt by things that other people let slide or never even pay attention to, and then in the span of a few minutes, I watch you exhibit the patience of a saint explaining something to someone new. Take that woman who wanted to use a hammer because growing up, her father didn't think it was right for a girl to do manly stuff. Did she give you the hammer back?"

Stone chuckled. "Nah, I gave her the whole belt. It felt stupid to wear a work belt while pounding the pavement and driving a clipboard."

Rusty was lost. "So what are you saying, John?"

"They can't really see into your brain as well as when they autopsy you." He turned back to Stone. "You did get an MRI in Germany when they pulled you out, right?"

"Bethesda."

John nodded his head. "Better yet, but it really doesn't matter. The little tiny lesions that occur in the brain don't really show up like a tumor would. So everything is subjective in diagnosing TBI."

Stone frowned. "But I didn't hit my head."

Tweeter walked carefully through the mental mine field. "No, no, you didn't. Except your head hits your head, or more correctly, your brain hits the inside of your skull."

"Where it's very rough."

"Right... the front... and that roughness cut up the brain with small lesions."

Rusty leaned forward. "Why wouldn't the inside of the skull be smooth?"

Holding up his left index finger, Tweeter's eyes opened to match his dramatically arched eyebrows. "Ah, very good question." He leaned forward to the coffee table in front of him as he quickly rearranged the books, cigarette packs, and other stuff, and then he explained. "The top, sides, and back are smooth. In the front of the braincase where the eye and sinus penetrate, the bone ridges, and nodes that project into the braincase elevate the brain up off the skull. This is how the brain cools off. The sinuses move the air that reduces the temperature. The lower temperature of the bones radiate back to the ridges causing..." pausing, he wiggled his fingers between the cigarette packs under the books, "ventilation, so to speak."

He then placed a soft pack of cigarettes on a cooking knife that he stood on edge and laid a book on top of it to steady the pile. "But when we get hit hard, even when it's not to the head, such as the gunny's getting thrown around the inside of a Humvee from a bomb," his hand smacked down on the book, then pulling the book back, he revealed the cigarette pack, which was now half cut in two, "we get a lesion that leaks, sometimes a little, like the gunny, and sometimes a lot. The ones that leak a lot come home in a box."

He leaned back against the cushions of the couch taking another sip of root beer before he continued. "In a boxer, the knockout along with hundreds of hits, slowly take their toll—look at Ali. Now, his problem is mostly from Parkinson's, but it is masking the insidious disease that plagues the sport, or even football—many of the linemen, with thousands of tiny concussions built up over their short careers, end up either dead or walking dead."

Rusty scratched at the bottom of her bare foot. "So Stone here is a true walking wounded?" She looked over at the man as he patently ignored her and sipped on his bottle of root beer. "But the question is… does he know it?"

"I'm right here," the subject growled.

"Yes, but are you listening to Tweeter?"

Stone looked up at the woman he had come to uncomfortably respect. "Am I aware that several times a day, in the middle of saying something, I hit a blank for a stupidly simple word I've used a thousand times, but I just can't see? Yeah. Am I aware that, at any given moment, the vision in my left eye might go black? Vividly... Am I aware of certain transitory aches and pains related to no injury in that area but is really my brain misfiring?" He pulled a long draw from the bottle. Putting it down, he looked up at the waiting faces. "What?"

"Gunny, you just stopped."

"I finished, damn it." He flushed red.

Rusty looked long at him. "Look, it's getting late, and we might have to take on the dawn before it stops being black out... Let's just call it a night, ladies..." Rising, she turned to collect the empty bottles. As she leaned over Stone, she added, "and if some idiot pounds on the door at two a.m., it's your turn." Calling after the retreating other man, "Good night, John, and thank you for the root beers."

A hand waved back from the darkness beyond the door as it slid shut.

The woman turned from placing the bottles on the sideboard of the sink and stood looking at the unmoving activity behind the scarred face of the man in her parlor. She leaned against the counter.

Stone looked up. "What?" The whisper was more of a croak.

Rusty pulled the dishtowel off the counter hook and slowly wiped the counter as she watched Stone's eyes. "I was just thinking about everything John was saying about the brain thing and the post trauma stuff." She hung the towel and moved back to sit down. "That must be a real bitch to adjust to... but losing your temper with friends that care about you isn't the way to go."

"If this is the mom talk about getting along with—"

Rusty leaned in with concern on her face. The hard pulse of her work face softened. "This isn't the mom talk. We both know that I don't have *mom* in me—but even if I were still a man, I would advise you to relax and let your friends care about you for once. You're not their gunny nursemaid anymore. You're just Stone... and from what John said, you have a phone full of people you took care of, and now they get to just be your friend with a root beer or some other helping hand. All you have to do is let them."

He looked up at her, and his face tattled on him that

he knew she was right. "Yah, I've been told it killed my advancements for some time now."

They both looked at the motor home's door as they heard a truck pull up outside the church parking lot. Stone looked at his watch. "He's three hours early. It must be a doozy."

Rusty put her hand on his shoulder as she headed for the back bedroom. "Give me four hours of beauty sleep, and I'll relieve you."

Stone knew he had just gotten the better end of the deal and rose to attend to the knocking at the door as he thought *this volunteer stuff is almost as bad as real work.* Sniffing under his left arm, he wondered if he would get time to shower.

"Hey, Stone," Rusty had stopped and turned half way in the small hallway.

"Yeah?"

She looked at the faux paneling and reached over to stroke one finger slowly down the wall, thinking. Quietly, she shared, "I may not have that woman's intuition that our mothers had, but I made a good living at reading people and situations." She looked at him standing at the door. "If half of what John says is true, someone went to a lot of trouble tracking down a lot of people where you meant something in their lives, and who now want you in theirs. Look at John—you haven't seen him in, what, maybe thirty years?"

"Thirty-six, Nook base in Vietnam."

"And he has been waiting for you to call." Stone could hear the rock catch in her throat. "Maybe he's found closure in his life, and maybe he hasn't. I do know that some of us have to go halfway around the world, and beyond, in order to find peace in our own skin, but it doesn't mean we get closure."

She knocked a knuckle silently on the opposite wall as she leaned with exhaustion against the other. "I know you aren't too sure about this guy becoming a woman thing, but you will, I think, understand over time as you ride around the country on that motorcycle of yours, looking for some place to call home.

"For me, it was a long road and some painful surgery, and then I still wasn't there until I retired, bought my first RV, and discovered that I could be a nomad and build homes for other people who didn't know me before. To them, I'm just a chunky lady with a raspy voice who can really swing a hammer. That's all they care about me, and it's enough. At the end of the week, we can hug and share our memories. Then they move into their home, and I move on to the next one.

"I found my family, and they are different every single job. I'm comfortable with this skin... well, maybe if I could lose a little weight, but I am who I know I am. This is my home," waving her hand at the building site, "and they are my family."

Stone shifted at the door. Whoever knocked before was either gone or patient. He pointed at the door.

"I know you need to go, but I think this is important. You may not know it yet, but someone put your family in that phone and in the red book, so you would learn that you didn't lose all of your family in Vietnam or in a tornado in the middle of the night. The people in that book and your phone aren't there just for you—you're here for them, too. Somewhere in that phone is an answer to a question, and when you answer that one, there will be more.

"I know I'm rattling on here, but what I'm trying to say is, home isn't always a place, it's the family you have. And yours is like mine, all over the place—out there. Only unlike mine, you've met yours before, and now they're in that phone. Now you just need to figure out how to go home."

The silence between them was a volume of unspoken camaraderie. Stone had not stopped to think how similar they were. He had only seen their differences.

The light tap on the door jarred them both, and Rusty mumbled a good night and repeated her charge of four hours as she filled the hall, headed for bed. Stone opened the door to find a smiling face on a goofy looking young black man with ears twice the size his head needed. Stone smiled, not from amusement, but from another kid in a different land engaged in a different war.

Stone flipped the white hard-hat onto his head. He pulled the rain jacket on as he stepped out into the light drizzle and the night.

"What do we have coming in, boss?" Stone asked, and it made the kid beam to be respected.

The work lights were flickering as dark slicker-draped workers moved about the subdued work site. Hammers seemed quieter in the dark, and compressors and pneumatic guns less a reminder of past conflicts in Stone's mind. He felt comfortable with the dark night and glaring lights. It was almost like a desensitizing therapy for him. He turned as a large truck turned around the corner four blocks away. A shadow detached from the larger shadow of a tree and became the person who had been assigned to wait for the supply truck. Stone smiled. This person knew their post, and the world was right.

Some hours later, Stone stood in the street waiting for the three trucks of the early morning reload making their way toward the build-out. The sky was about one shade lighter, but still more than an hour away from full sun-up.

"I looked for the crappiest old coffee I could find. I mixed in a little dirt, a shot of concrete, and then stirred it with an old rusty nail."

Stone smiled as he turned and took the short coffee with two heat sleeves that Rusty held out. "Good morning, sunshine. Those *four hours* did you some good. You almost look human."

Rusty laughed with a hoarse rasp. "Yeah, well, nobody ever confused this gal with beauty sleep. I just do it because there's food at the end of the rest, or should be," she said as she looked around at the site.

"I think I saw Rose and Jim headed over toward Letha and the kid's place. With the rain, they set up a large tent for the chow tables, so at least there will be donuts for you."

Rusty shot Stone a wry grin and slapped her left butt cheek. "You know where this girl lives, you silver-tongued devil you." She headed toward the area that Stone had mentioned, and she called back, "And I made up the couch for you. As soon as I get back, I'll relieve you, and you can sleep till noon, unless Johnny boy needs you sooner."

"Hey, Rusty," Stone called after her as he turned to take in the new headlights four blocks away. "Grab me an apple fritter or bear claw if they have any."

The wave over her white hard hat was all Stone needed as he watched the truck with the last load of trusses slowly thumping down and back up as it crossed the last street and entered the build-out blocks. Stepping up onto the running boards, Stone pointed as he gave directions for the trucker to get lined up to be off loaded.

The days ground under the wheel of progress like the rotation of the big mud ball under the sun and moon. The work crews of volunteers came and dissolved away in cars, trucks, and by the busloads. Some days, only a couple of hundred, and on others over a thousand workers crawling over the project, until that final day—move in day.

"Did you see that little scrawny guy laying the sod?" Rusty laughed so hard she fell into the chair. The three of them were so tired that even the cheap cans of root beer were enough to get them giddy, if not high.

Stone sucked on the last of the can and threw it across the motor coach's living area into the garbage can full of cans for a three point long shot. "We had a tunnel rat in 'Nam that was that same way. Point him into one hole and he would pop out another. He would then walk over a few dozen feet, kick off a cover, and dive back down into another hole. He was like a good hunting dog—he just loved what he did."

"I hired him." John laughed. The other two looked at him and busted out laughing.

"The sod laying guy?" Stone laughed. "For what?"

"You ought to stop by the place tomorrow. I have two acres of lawn that have been prairie dogged and gophered to death for as long as we've lived there." John popped the top on another root beer. "Gino used to be a horticulturist in Argentina. He says that he knows how to get rid of the monsters and restore my lawn. My wife said she'd kill me or at least cut my nuts off," holding his palm out toward the only female in the room, "no offense, Rusty," and turning back to Stone, "if I didn't hire him."

Rusty laughed a hearty deep-throated manly laugh. "I think I love this woman."

John gave her a stern look but with a twinkle in his eye. "Back off there, woman, I had dibs on her first." They all laughed.

"So how long have you been married, Tweeter?"

The man became serious as he looked down into the top of his root beer can... and a million miles away. "Shortly after Da Nang, I sent her a letter from the hospital in Tokyo. I explained how being shot in the ass had also destroyed my chances of being a father. I figured she probably wouldn't want me anymore if that were the case, and I wanted to hear it in a place where I could maybe do something about it."

Quietly, Rusty was nodding her head at something she was hearing for the first and fiftieth times. "Drugs or a scalpel?"

Tweeter nodded. "Or both."

"Well, obviously that didn't happen." Stone pulled him along to better thoughts.

Tweeter shook himself and returned to the motor home. "About two weeks later, she showed up in Tokyo at the hospital with a minister she had found by trolling the halls." He laughed at the memory. "Heck, she hadn't been any farther away from home than Natchez or up Maryland way." He looked up with clear, but wet eyes. "She was on a mission to get me married one way or another. After the padre married us, right there in the physical therapy room with about twenty other guys and fifty nurses, and stuff, she kissed me and told me to hurry up and get my ass home because the lawn was getting deep and needed mowing."

Fighting back some squelched speech, Stone croaked out, "Quite a woman."

"Yeah," he shook his head slowly. "She hasn't let up on me since."

Several hours later, long after the root beers had run out, Rusty woke up in the easy chair to find Stone sitting in the driver's side with the captain's chair turned sideways, and his feet up on the center ottoman, looking out the window. She could tell he was not asleep by the smallest of sparkle off the wet of his eyeball that was set in a million mile stare, which had nothing to do with today, or what was in front of him.

Quietly, she got up. "I'm going to make some chamomile tea. Are you in, Stone?"

The nod was not from close but not as far as the look had been before, so she filled the pot and got down the tea. As the water heated, she disappeared back into the rear of the coach. Returning, she made up the two large mugs and gave one to Stone. As he took it, Rusty also dropped an old-fashioned red leatherette locket-style travel picture frame into his lap.

Stone sipped the hot tea as he picked up the palm-sized frame. Squeezing the button with his thumb, the case fell open in his hand as if it had a million times before. There was only one picture, and in the other side was a lock of blonde hair tied around a lock of chestnut and gray hair.

The picture was of better times. The young couple stood leaning against a Lincoln Town car. By the bell-bottoms, Stone guessed at the mid-seventies. The mini-skirt was the micro of the late sixties, but still looked good on the young woman with the long dark hair. Her head leaned on the shoulder of the blonde with curls just touching the bottom of his ears. The only resemblance was the quirky smile.

Stone focused on the tilt of the head, and the woman's mouth looked like she was soft spoken. His eyes traced the way her body molded into the man's and vice versa. He cleared his throat, and took a sip of the tea. "You really loved each other a lot."

Rusty nodded, not really looking at Stone, but many years before. "She wasn't hard to love. She was one hell of a woman."

"Did she know?"

Rusty thought a moment about the depth of the dark pool, and waded in. "Probably, but you just didn't talk about things like that in those days. Heck, even gays weren't gay then."

"So what happened?"

"She passed away January ninth, nineteen-eighty-four of leukemia." Rusty's eyes rose toward the ceiling as she gently lay back against the cushion. "It had snowed a light dusting that night. She lay there in the hospital bed looking out the window. She asked me to move the bed one day, and nobody ever thought to move it back away from the window. It just made so much sense. She stared at the snow, and she finally said, 'Rusty, God has prepared the way,' and she was gone."

Rusty wiped at her eyes with the back of her sweatshirt sleeve. "That is when I realized life is just that way. In the blink of an eye, you can be gone. Six months later, I started hormone therapy."

"And you still miss her?"

Rusty's voice had extra gravel in the mix. "Every

single day."

"Ever dated anyone else?"

Rusty chuckled wetly. "You're the closest thing to dating I have ever done since. It wasn't ever a sexual thing with me. I was always in love and lust with her. We were high school sweethearts. It was just a genetic thing within me, and that was all."

Stone looked back at the photo then back up at Rusty. "But you weren't from around these parts."

"No, Southern California, Hermosa Beach to be exact." She reclaimed the frame from Stone and closed it reverently. "That is why I won't do any Habitat work in California."

Stone frowned. "Someone might recognize you from before."

Rusty shrugged noncommittally. "It's just not me anymore."

Stone nodded his head. "Makes sense." He sipped more of the tea as he thought about himself and who he now needed to be. "So where do you go from here?"

"Operations? They're all done," and then she blushed as she realized what Stone had actually asked, but laughed as she saw a glow around his face, too. "Oh, you weren't talking... about... crap. You meant with Habitat." Stone nodded and smiled into his tea mug. Rusty shifted in the passenger seat and looked into the darkness outside the large front window. "Fort Lauderdale. They're doing a slow build for a family of a mother and her three kids. I figured it would be good to relax with a slow build for a while. Get to know the family and maybe a little about the area. I haven't been to Fort Lauderdale yet. What about you and that wild-bunch motorcycle of yours?"

Stone looked out the window at the dark punctuated by a few work lights still burning as a final prep continued. The nail guns were silent, no more trucks, just calm with the occasional person moving from here to there. Stone thought about the aftershock, which occurs when there is a hot battle, and then it suddenly stops with no place to put the still-rushing adrenaline. He sipped at his tea. Looking back at Rusty, he remembered what she had asked. "I was thinking about Blue Mountain Parkway. A few days ago, a guy was telling me that it's one of the roads motorcyclists travel all the way from California just to ride on." He took another sip and watched a darkened figure carry a large something from a truck into one of the houses—drapes or maybe carpeting. He looked back at Rusty. "I figured that was as good of a reason as any to do something."

She nodded. "Anybody down that way in your phone?"

Stone shrugged. "I don't know how to look people up by the state they're in."

"What about the book they gave you?"

He raised his eyebrows. "Man, I had completely forgotten about that. Sure, I'll bet there is someone or two to stop in and see."

Rusty smirked. "Just don't forget to stop in at John's place on your way south, or he might just track you down, and it wouldn't be pretty."

Stone and Rusty both gave it a halfhearted chuckle. The two warhorses from different wars both recognized the truth to the statement. The silence spun out, both lost in their own thoughts as the adrenaline crash swept them away.

The morning light found Stone drooling onto his T-shirt, still in the driver's seat, and with Rusty's crooked smile looking down on him. She nudged his leg with hers and he startled awake. Slowly realizing where he was, he focused on the proffered mug of steaming coffee. "Give me ten minutes in the water locker, and then you can have it while I whip us up some traveling grub." She turned and headed toward the back.

True to her word, she bustled about the small kitchenette while Stone grabbed his shower. The bacon crackled, and the toaster was still down as she rested against the counter.

She sipped at her coffee then put the mug on the counter as she lifted up Stone's phone. Quickly, she typed in simply *Rusty* and her cell phone number. Then thinking twice, she listened for the sound of the water still running, and looked up a number. She smiled, and thought she would probably like this girl. It listed her as simply *Ski*. She typed in a text message.

> *From Stone:*
> *Ski, U don't know me, but my name is Rusty*
> *U can ask Tweeter @ me*
> *Stone is doing fine for now*
> *I put my # in his phone,*
> *Thought U should have it 2*
> *–R–*

STONEHEART

BAER CHARLTON

O5

The rain had been light when Stone had first decided to get up and push west. The small field tent had been an easy five-minute job to break down and pack on the back of the motorcycle while pulling out the foul-weather gear. Rubber booties protected the leather boots, and weather-tight mittens encased Stone's gloves and partly up over his jacket. Only a small dribble of cold rain had found its way up into the helmet and onto his neck. A tiny smirk crossed Stone's flash-scarred face as he thought of the tiny intruder as just another insurgent in his life. As long as it did not bring an IED with it, Stone would allow for it.

The flats in Arkansas rode out straight and dull as the shining black freeway led forward into the even darker night. The amber lights glowed next to the green on the speedometer of the older Honda Gold Wing that Stone had bought from Poco. The tires bit onto the rain-glistened highway exactly the way the former Navy officer had described they would—in his typical motor pool lingo that Stone had become familiar with during one of his tours of Vietnam.

Stone eyed the 187,426 miles on the odometer with a jaundiced eye. All the while, Poco reassured him that the engine and transmission were perfectly sound for another fifty thousand miles or more—at least enough to get Stone *home,* wherever that was. Stone did not want to start a conversation about being homeless. That could only end with the insistence of a place to stay with an old buddy-of-a-buddy, and a wife Stone had never met. Stone was sure if Poco were married, his wife would not want him dragging any old buddies back from a far distant past. The tires hissed in the black rain of Arkansas as Stone thought about the confusing new world since the last IED had upset his old world.

At least the returned vision in his left eye had been steady these last few weeks as he swung a hammer and directed traffic at yet another Habitat for Humanity build-out in the Smokey Mountains, and as strange as that felt without Rusty.

With the slight movement of his eyes, Stone watched the large truck framed in the dark of the left mirror, and a thousand yellow marking lights slowly gaining on him in the fast lane. Someone had warned him to watch out for some of the new trucks with three trailers, but with the cold rain, highballing doubles like these were bad enough.

Stone subconsciously counted the wheels and tires as they passed with their wave of spray, waiting for the end and relief. The space under the trailers between the tires gave off what seemed like a wave of built-up heat from the tires. Stone knew it was just the relief from the fire hose of the icy spray. Confirming the last tire was the vision of padded stainless steel doors and rows of yellow lights. The last of the spray spread out in front of the motorcycle, and

Stone questioned the sanity of his riding at night in a storm. The Christmas cheer of yellow and red lights began to shrink as the truck pulled away from the slower motorcycle. The twin grounding chains, which hung from the back of the trailer, were dully lit by the tiny sparks chipping off as the chains bounced and jumped about on the highway, protecting against lightning strikes across the flat planes.

The yellow and red lights advanced into the black of night as a replacement of tiny white lights appeared in the motorcycle's mirrors. A never-ending stream of humanity going from here to there, some headed out, while others headed home.

The tiny white lights in Stone's mirrors grew to a brooch of diamond-white lights set in a pavé of yellow, much like every other truck on the highway that night. Another truck with another company painted on the side, followed by a set of double trailers, and then followed by more peace in the black night with tiny lights in the rearview mirrors, and the rear of the trailer just cleared Stone. The spray in front of him, a lighter black against the wetter black, and then the entire scene turned suddenly into a searing white light as lightning struck the back end of the trailer.

Almost losing his balance, Stone wrestled with the bike as he braked hard while waiting for his vision to return. Finally, standing at a stop on what Stone hoped was the shoulder of the highway, the night black crept back into his eyes.

Either it existed as a black stormy night or Stone was now blind in both eyes.

Sitting on the motorcycle, his hands rested impotently

in his lap. Stone closed his eyes, not caring where he was on the highway. The war inside raged over four decades—too many gunshots, too many bombs, and too much that was not where he was now.

Stone did not know how long he had been sitting with eyes closed when a flash of light to his left was followed a second later by the crash of thunder. Stone flinched slightly, opening his eyes. The instrument cluster glowed brightly, closer than the headlight that struggled to reach out into the night. The motor purred with the tiny tick that Stone had come to accept as a quirk instead of a problem.

A set of lights in the mirrors brought Stone back to awareness. He was parked in the middle of the two lanes. Quickly grabbing at the clutch and gas, a shift, and he was racing to avoid a rude midnight end to a wet ride. Another lightning strike off to his right reminded him that he stood out as the highest point in several hundred yards in the middle of a storm.

The overpass loomed up out of the night, and Stone braked hard as he eased over to the shoulder under the cover of concrete. The width of the overpass was just a narrow country road, but still an overpass.

Stone maneuvered the large motorcycle to the small patch of semi-dry asphalt. The relief from the rain pounding on the windshield, his facemask, the helmet, and his rain suit, added to the quiet of the retreating diesel truck, and the almost silence of the cooling motorcycle engine. The soft ticking finally died away.

Stone sat on the seat in the silence. It was deafening.

Thinking about finding a better place, he looked up the concrete slope to the pocket where it met the roadbed above. The large black area would provide a place out of the light wind, and maybe even a place to nap. The part of his mind taking over at the moment was looking for a place that was easily defendable.

As the old warrior slid his back down the bridge's cold stanchion, the fragile mind let go of today and reality...

The heat of the steel plates, which were the landing field, came and went as the young soldier stood waiting for the DC-3 to let down from the sky. They said it had a landing speed of a hundred and twenty miles per hour, but as he watched for the seventeenth time that day, the big silver bird just hung in the air. The heat of the jungle, full of Charlie, disturbed the air below the plane as it hung in the stifling heat, which did not affect Stone. In fact, he felt cold.

Stone stood half-naked at the side of the steel-sheeted jungle runway, the hole-punched steel plates a blast furnace on his searing flesh. The steel in the air, falling... smoking... burning... dying.

The stench of rotting Vietnam raked his nose and stung the back of Stone's throat.

He stood rooted in the middle of the oil-canned steel.

The heat seared his body, turning muscle and bone to sandy disconnected mush.

Stone heard the large smoking airplane letting down, looming death from the air. He could not turn his head—only hear—hear its destruction coming on death's leathery wings.

The second giant engine was coughing and choking in its own smoking death. Finally, the death is complete and absolute along with its twin floating silently—unheard release.

Stone's head strained to turn and his feet tensed to run. All was as solid steel, welded in place on the steel airstrip. Finding unmoving flesh, the hand of death met no resistance reaching in for the heart, talons for fingers, caging the beating muscle of life. Does it scythe the meat where it is turning it to dust, or does it grab with piercing talons, and rip it from the chest still beating? The freezing thin steel blade of fear slides in smoothly, through and back out of the heart, stitching the kind of fear that only the invincible can feel. The icy drizzle, which runs down the last of the spine, and into the white-hot sphincter below, scorching the only last hope of life untouched... before the end.

The reality of the cold concrete burned Stone's back. His racing heart was more of a hum than individual beats. His chest heaved at the breaths his frozen lungs could take. His body felt his bowel turn liquid as yesterday's meal searched to become today's embarrassment.

Unbidden in his mind, the large rotary engine exploded as the prop touched the steel runway. The sun-scorched steel pounded the air while waves of deadly heat turned the flying fuel into the blossoming flower of a deadly fireball—unfolding petal after deadly petal. The young soldier could not turn his head—only hear. As the movement in the air slowed, the sound became a white silence and slipped into the tinny, ringing silence of gray silver.

The giant steel bird of death, with its landing gear shot away, crushed to the ground with a great thud, felt only in the heart, not heard. The fragile cage wrapped around a crew, gone long ahead of Stone, and began to unwrap with silent orange and black fingers of flame, guiding and following the enveloped steel satellites.

The steel satellites moved out in all directions in search of destruction—jungles to burn, fires to start, people to kill... and the one hot steel spoon of death whiffled its way through Stone's back and continued out his front, dragging muscle and gut as he crumpled to the fire-scorched steel. Stone knew this was the single spot where the planes came to die—the oil, the blacked warped steel—this is ground-zero of death. The shearing metal-on-metal roared the requiem from hell as the fire consumed all before it. Now, it came for Stone. Like naked running footsteps, the clock of time quietly ticked down the end of his days.

The plane was suddenly on the ground, and Stone felt as much as heard the painful screaming of the tires. The plane skidded sideways as the entire side and tail exploded. The fireball of hot orange gas, white-hot steel, and aluminum skin raced across the perforated steel field, reaching out with searing death.

Stone was frozen in his memories, in the unthinkable displays before his mind's eye. He knew the nine shards of superheated steel were heading toward him, to remove chunks of his—

Stone jerked awake. The smell of burned rubber seared his nose and the echoes of the screaming tires resounded off the concrete overpass. Shaking from the cold, as much as the memories come to life, Stone remained frozen in place trying to understand where he was and what was happening.

The short memory rolled back, a metal door had slammed, and Stone looked out into the night at the stopped truck. A halo of layers and layers of yellow marking lights and pulsing red flashers gave the running figure the appearance of being there, and yet not being there. Only the scuffling of boots striking the wet highway gave credence that the approaching wraith could be real.

Stone waited.

The figure came under the overpass. "Hey, is anybody here?" The voice showed concern but not panic. "If y'all own this here motorcycle, sing out." The figure walked slowly about the bike, looking, trying to figure out maybehow long it had been there. "Leastwise, tell me if you're okay or not," now straining to see up into the black of the concrete pockets of the overpass.

"I'm okay." Stone was not sure if he wanted to let the guy know his identity or even if he were there. Yet, he had a feeling the guy would not go away without answers.

Shifting, he rose stiffly. Passing his legs over the edge, he levered himself out onto the decline and slowly sidestepped down, warily watching the dark figure. "I'm okay. I just stopped to get out of the rain and away from the lightning."

A truck's headlights dimly lit up the figure as it approached from the west. The man's meaty right hand stretched out. "Tom. Tom Talbot... but most people just calls me Slim."

Stone sized the man at well over six feet and pushing somewhere near the size of a forward tackle or three. He took the man's hand. "Gunnery Ser– um, Stone, sir, Stone."

The man hesitated at the sound of a single name, and then shook. Not letting go, he pressed for more. "When did you get out, Sergeant?"

Uncomfortable with his hand being held, but figured

he would wait it out. "About a month, sir." The lights of another truck were revealing a man about his age, and with as much silver in the hair. The face appeared worn from hard living, but still kind. Stone also felt the man examining the scars and patchwork of his face.

Letting the hand drop, Slim's face pulled back in a one-sided smile. "You must have seen a rig get hit, didn't ya?" Stone nodded shyly. "Well, about three miles up the road," jerking his sausage sized thumb over his shoulder, "there is a truck stop. You stay close to the side of my trailer, and we'll go see if they still make anything worth eating. Sound fair?"

Stone nodded. "I appreciate the escort, sir."

Slim laughed. "Escort, hell, I just hate eating alone. Besides, it will let you dry out a bit, and I haven't bought a soldier a meal in a long time." Turning, he pointed at the bike. "And don't dilly dally none, I'm in a hurry because I need the bathroom."

Stone stayed just behind the spray, but the main force of the storm had moved on, and there was just a light patter of what was left of the rain.

Stone parked up close to the restaurant front door. As he took off his helmet and put away his rubbers and slicker, he could hear more than a few voices across the giant parking lot calling out to Slim. The object of the attention walked up to the bike as the man called back to another driver with a warning to keep it safe. Stone was pretty sure Slim was talking about something other than driving.

"Think we ought to try this joint?" The giant man asked with an equally large smile.

"My guess is that you *try* this joint all the time."

The deep laugh rolled free and easy from the man. "Only about two or four times a month," Slim opened the glass door and waving Stone in, "and maybe sometimes more."

The heat hit Stone and warmed his bones on its way to toasting his backside as well. It felt like he had stepped out of the great north and right into Vietnam all over again, but this time, it felt homey.

"Slim." The bottle brunette with four large platters balanced on one arm and a coffee pot in the other flashed by. "You're late."

Slim smiled at Stone. "Sorry, Ellie, I had to stop and pick me up a paramedic to make sure I don't choke on that horse meat you've been serving me." He winked at Stone as they headed for the counter.

"No such luck, sweet cheeks. You were so late, I done already run out of the good stuff. We've been down to possum and road kill for the last ten minutes." Placing the large plates in front of a family of customers who were staring at her with very large eyes, all the blood drained from their faces. She placed her left hand on the woman's right shoulder, and quietly reassured her. "It's okay, honey, you done got the good stuff. I gave the possum to your husband, but it's fresh this week at least. The young'uns got the road kill." Giving the kids a big smile and a wink, "You young'uns let me know if it's any good. If so, we'll start going down that patch of highway more often." She poured the woman some more coffee. "Relax, honey, we are all just fun. The beef is all from my brother's ranch, and the eggs are from my Uncle Stan's place. It's just the bacon that's road kill."

Spinning, Ellie left the wary mother to follow her

children's lead. Muttering to herself, she smiled evilly, "Yankees! Serves them right coming down here and stopping into a truck stop like it was some Piggly Wiggly back home." Sliding around the counter end, and looming up in front of Slim and Stone, she placed the coffee pot on the counter, stepped up on the ledge and leaned over and grabbed Slim's face as she gave him a large kiss on the lips.

"Hey now," one of the cooks called out mechanically.

She patted Slim on the cheek as she stepped down. "Shut up, Harold," she called back to the cook with equal amount of old routines. She turned to Stone. "Hi, I'm Ellie. You only get that greeting when I see you more than I want to see my husband."

Stone smiled. "The name is Stone. I take it that the cook is your husband?"

She glanced toward the cook station at the man working there. "Harold? Nah, he's just a guy I sleep with on occasion. My husband is a suave Italian guy with loads of money and fancy cars. I only work here because the villa in Monte Carlo is boring this time of year, and besides, I get to see Slim." She stared at Stone with a straight face, as if it were nothing but the biggest truth. She blinked once.

Stone was not sure what to make of it, except Slim was either having a heart attack, or he was laughing so hard he could not make any noise. Slim was rocking back and forth, as he held onto his chest.

The stone-faced waitress poked her pen backwards toward him as she never broke eye-lock with Stone. "Where did you get him?"

Stone started to chuckle. "He scraped me up off the

highway."

"Were you road kill? Do I have to serve you to Yankees that don't know better?"

Stone started to worry about Slim who was turning purple in the face from laughing. Ellie slowly broke eye contact and watched Slim for a moment. "Slim," she oozed in a calming voice, "honey, stop it before you stroke-out or fart. I don't want none of either in here. You hear?" She looked back at Stone. "Look, sugar, I'd love to spend the whole morning looking into your baby blues, but I have a mess of people to feed. What y'all havin'?"

Stone had not even seen evidence of anything that might resemble a menu, but he snuck a peek at the well-fed Slim and turned to the waitress. "I'll have what he's having."

She blew a bubble with her gum and popped it as she let one eyelid slide half shut in a look of pure stupid. She cocked her hip and looked at Stone with the half eye. "No you don't."

"Why not?" He jammed his left thumb at the body of the now blue faced man with beet red showing through the sparse white of a flattop. "He looks well-fed."

The silence stretched out as she did not flinch or even move except for the slow rhythmic chewing of her gum. Finally, she yelled out, still without moving, "Order in. Two roadside fresh-kills, double down, boxcars with a mud slide, run the pigs, and stack them high."

Harold, without even a heartbeat from her finish echoed back, "Double down on a heart attack alley, triple the bypass and round up the coroner."

She blinked only the whole eye once. "You probably didn't want the tall glass of buttermilk though, did ya?"

She looked over at Slim who was now almost catatonic. "I gotta go now before he drops dead. Now you know why he only comes to see his sister once in a blue moon." She finally smiled a large warm glow. "It's been good meeting you, Stone, and playing with ya." She moved off like a fast attack destroyer seeking out other targets of opportunity. "Hustle up on that road kill, Harold, Slim is on the clock, and I want him out of here before he has that stroke."

Slim's color had long returned to the usual pink of a man who spends his life in the shade of a truck cab. They tucked into their meals: one-pound steaks, three eggs, and two biscuits with some of the best sausage gravy Stone had ever tasted. Sausage covered with a half rasher of lean country bacon topped off by a half-done dill pickle. The large meal was then all but washed away by the sea of coffee provided by the very attentive Ellie, who said not a word while the men ate.

Stone dumped decorum and spoke through a mouth half-full of perfectly cooked steak. "I think this is the best meal I have enjoyed in at least a few decades."

Slim wiped his mouth with the left hand and a napkin as he pointed the fork with his right. "Sis and Harold put up the best food on the line. I once had to take a contract running Boston to LA for six months. I ended up in the hospital and lost almost a hundred pounds. I was anemic, malnourished, and homesick."

Stone looked at the serious face on the man and realized the talent for telling a deadpan joke ran in the family.

Ellie had snuck up on them. "You telling him about that time you lost half your body weight?" Turning to Stone, she continued, "No joke, it was a whole lot of some kind of ugly." She splashed the two mugs of coffee as she moved on. "That divorce was just plain ugly."

Stone shook his head, knowing he had been had from both barrels.

The plates were gone, and only a half mug of coffee remained between them. The cracks of dawn were beginning to knife through the trucks in the lot. Stone twisted his mug nervously as another of the dozens of truckers walked past and slapped Slim on the back. They asked about him or just told Slim it was good to see the ugly side of the family.

Staring into his mug, Stone asked quietly, "It wasn't about eating alone, was it? I mean, you seem to be anything but alone here, and I'm guessing it's like that no matter where you go. So, why? Stone looked up, and then at the man. "Why stop? Why buy me breakfast? And don't get me wrong, I'm not complaining."

The man was silent, but Stone knew this would not be another straight-faced joke. The answer could come from a very raw place down deep in the man. "I have a son."

Slim looked up and around the large busy diner, and finally facing Stone. "He was in the National Guard." The pain was very close to the surface, and the man had to swallow twice to continue. "It was only so he could stay in school and become a horticulture specialist. Then there was the call up after 9/11. They took everyone in the county under the age of seventy. We lost many good guys and a couple of gals, too."

Stone nodded. He had heard the story too many times.

Slim looked at him. "It's not what you think. He came back. He just never made it home." The man slowly worked the mug in a circle as he studied the coffee inside.

"He tried to get his head back in the game with school and all. I told him he didn't have to work. I'd support him the whole way—just focus on studying. Some nights I could hear him in his room crying. Other times, he would just leave the house and go walk all night. He tried to talk to the people at the VA in Little Rock, but they had no way to understand him. He didn't come home missing a leg or something you can see and fix. He was damaged goods on the inside. They call it PTSD, but the VA said that it was just malingering or trying to milk the system." Stone could see the vein on the man's forehead bulging, and the color was getting close to beet red.

Stone put his hand on the man's forearm.

Slim wiped at his eyes, and his voice cracked as he croaked, "I'm alright." The silence was almost terminal. Stone noticed Ellie leaning against the corner of the back counter, the concern on her face told Stone that she knew exactly what Slim was saying. The pain was raw in both of them.

Slim sniffed long and deeply. "One day, we had a stupid yelling match, and before I knew what was going on, he had packed a bag and was taking off on his Kawasaki. The last thing I said to my boy was mean and hurtful." He looked up at nothing in particular, just staring off into space. "Somewhere, he's out there on that dumb motorcycle... and maybe if I buy you breakfast... someone out there will look out for my boy." The shoulders started shaking as the man buried his face in his hands.

Ellie's face rose as she slowly spun out and walked away, and Stone knew that it was a private hell. Everyone suffered all around, and it was the man who everyone knew and was a friend to all, who suffered the worst. There is the hell of being MIA in war, but worse is being the same when you are supposed to be home.

The trumpets quietly blew revelry in Stone's pocket. He took out the phone to look at the text message from Washington.

From Ski:
Huge storm last night - - U dry?

"Message from home?"

Stone looked up to see the red eyes of a caring man who was curious. "Sort of, but I still don't get how to tell her to stop doing that."

"Doing what?"

"Somehow, she knows where I am. And then she sends these messages, and I don't know how to do the same back... and I don't want to call her."

Slim chuckled deep from his heart and belly. "Well, first, she's tracking your GPS in the phone. You're screwed if she has you on Nanny Map. Parents use it to see if their kids are in school or over at Johnny's doing homework or worse, or at the mall when they're not supposed to be. As for the texting, just text her back," Slim stuck out his hand and took the phone. "First, open the phone, and you see that icon?" Stone nodded. "That is your message. Only—" The man laughed, "I'm assuming this is not a wife."

"Worse, she's a young yeoman to an admiral."

"Okay, so we poke that, and open the message center, and now what do you want to tell her?" He looked at Stone, smiled, and said, "No, you can't tell a young lady that."

Stone chuckled. "How about 'I'm dry and mind your own business?'"

Slim poked at the represented keyboard and turned it to show Stone. "See, there is your message, and for numbers and other stuff, just poke these buttons and toggle back and forth to the other screens. When it's what you want to say, just poke the little blue send button." His right thumb slipped down and the message was gone.

"But that isn't what I wanted to say."

"Sergeant, be nice. Telling her to butt out isn't what you tell someone at five in the morning. Telling her you are dry and fine, having a great breakfast with a friend, and thank you for caring, is what you say."

The horn tooted in his hand. He read the text and laughed as he showed it to Stone.

From Ski:
This is NOT Stone,
what have you done with the old reprobate?

Stone reached for the phone. "Here, let me try."
"Be nice there, son."

From Stone:
Gee, reprobate sure is a mighty
big word for such a little girl.

Stone showed it to Slim who laughed. "You do like to push it don't you."

From Ski:
OK, now I know its U

Admiral back tomorrow—
U want 2 talk?

Stone typed *no,* turned the phone off, and started to slip it into his pocket.

Slim rested his hand on Stone's arm. "You might want to stick my info in there."

Stone froze and looked in the man's eyes.

"You don't know how, do you?"

Stone slowly unfroze and withdrew the phone and handed it back to the man. Painfully, Slim explained how to add a contact and everything related to the address book. Then having another thought, he scanned quickly though the apps and explained as he downloaded things he thought would help Stone, such as a weather app. "Maybe next time you'll only get wet instead of struck by lightning."

Stone slipped the phone back in his pocket with just a little more care and respect. "I want to thank you for breakfast... and..." Stone started to drift while looking for the word.

"The phone," Slim chuckled then sobered. "I was going to explain that even though it looks more like a slab of liver, it's still a phone. But I don't think that was the problem, was it?"

"No." Stone shook his head. "That wasn't the problem." He wove his finger in the air in front of him as he searched to explain what he did not really have a great grasp on. "It's like I'm talking, and the string of words just ends, and I look at the teleprompter in my head, and there is just a blank. I try to think of what the word is that I know I've said a thousand times before means, or what it looks like... but it's just a blank."

70

"It's that PTSD thing." Slim looked Stone square in the eyes. "I saw that going on with my boy." He reached out with his right hand and gently grabbed the gunny's shoulder. "If you ever need anything, you just give old Slim a holler, you hear?"

Stone swallowed. The man was only a few years older than he was, but it was something he imagined his father would have said. "I will, Slim, I promise."

They held the tableau for a few beats of the hearts, and then Slim's hand slid down the arm and gave Stone's bicep a friendly squeeze. "I'll hold you to that, son. I surely will." Looking up at the oversized Mack truck clock on the diner's wall, he slapped Stone's arm. "I gotta highball it on down the road and deliver these chickens before they defrost and start laying eggs."

Turning around and shouting at his sister, "Ellie, wrap this soldier up some lunch so he don't starve or nothing over there in Oklahoma. You know they don't have any food worth eating." She waved, and the whirlwind known as Slim was nothing more than a breeze of the door swinging shut.

Stone watched him stride across the tarmac. If one arm was not up waving to someone, both were—a king in his kingdom loved by his people and peers alike. Stone recognized something there, but he could not quite grab hold of it to see.

Stone felt more than he heard the woman beside him. "There goes the saddest clown in town. That smile is on his face, but I wish it was in his heart."

Stone turned. "His boy?"

She nodded as she watched her brother climb into his steel world. Her head leaned more than turned to look at

Stone. "That was just the icing on the cake." The big diesel fired up, and the black smoke belched from the twin-stacked pipes. "The week after Osiel left for Afghanistan," she nodded at the rolling truck, "his Carmen dropped dead of a massive stroke right there in the canned goods aisle of the supermarket. Slim's birthday cake was in the basket."

"That's awful." Stone was stunned.

The waitress harrumphed. "That was just the start. Their daughter was driving down from Boston for the funeral, and fell asleep at the wheel, drove straight into a freight train at eighty miles per hour." She turned to look full on at Stone, "You all being here tonight, and him joking around and all... that was the first time I've seen him laugh like that in more than a few years."

Stone just stood and stared at her. He was so used to horrific stories of war, he had no idea there could be ones to match or worse in the peace of America.

"Well, enough of this long face stuff. Let's see what Harold packed for a picnic."

As Ellie stuffed enough food for a patrol into a paper sack, Stone asked her for a piece of paper to write something on. Ellie grabbed a second bag and laid it flat on the counter. Stone pushed it back at her. "Could you write down the kid's full name, and if you remember it, his company and service info, please."

Ellie looked at him and her eyes turned watery, she nodded. "If you can find him, Stone, you will have my heart forever." She bent down and wrote between wiping her face. She muttered more to herself, "An angel on the side of the road, that's surely what you are, a guardian angel just standing there waiting for our Slim." Stone noticed Harold just standing behind the cook station looking after the love of his life.

As she hugged him at the door, Harold did not say a word, but just came up and shook Stone's hand. No words were necessary.

BAER CHARLTON

06

A wispy distant voice came from the phone. "Hello?"

"Hello," Stone snapped with as much kindness as he could muster for being disturbed. "This is Stone. Who is this?" The phone had read Mario 'Bugs' Bugatti. This was not even a close second to the squeaky voice Stone knew from a few years back. Bugs had been a quiet kid who had only talked about growing food and flowers; and yet, he had been the best driver in the company. If a ride were needed through Bang Town, littered as it was with mines or IEDs, Bugs drove. He seemed to be able to sense the hidden dangers. He never lost a Hummer, never lost a convoy or a patrol.

The quiet on the other end of the phone was starting to unnerve Stone. "Hello? Bugs, arr..."

The wispy voice wafted from Stone's phone like a fog. "Is this Gunnery Sergeant Stone?"

"Yes, who's this?" He looked across Grand Lake at the sunset he had been waiting for, almost as if by staring he could see the person so distantly on the phone. "Hello?"

The voice shattered into a million pieces as it became half a step away from a cry from a wounded animal. "I'm

Trina. Katrina Bugatti—Bugs' wife."

Stone had always hated crying. It didn't matter if it were a child or a three hundred-pound Ranger with his guts on the battlefield crying for his mother—it unnerved him. "Carina, I need you to take a deep breath. Just breathe."

There was quiet on the phone, and then the voice pulled together from the years of correcting people about her name. "It's Katrina, just like the hurricane."

"That's better," Stone sighed, "but I really don't think the reference to a very destructive storm fits you somehow. I think I'll just call you Trina. Okay, Trina?" The years of assigning nicknames were also years of defusing bad situations, and the gunny had become an expert at it.

"Just don't get on my wrong side, Gunny, or you'll find that the hurricane was only a shadow of an angry Polish girl." Stone could hear the steel he hoped would stay in her voice and help her through whatever had spawned the call.

"I think we have a deal, Trina. Now what can I do for you?"

"It's Bugs."

Stone slowly got up and prepared to break his fresh made camp. He listened as the young wife relayed her story. Her husband Bugs, soon to be the father of their first child, had been in a small accident and was now in the hospital fighting for his life.

"Trina?"

"Yes, sir?"

"Are you at the hospital now?"

"Yes, sir."

"I need you to find the charge nurse. She or he will be at the nurse's station."

"And then what?"

"I need to talk to them, please. So, can you go there now?"

"Just a minute..." Stone could hear her asking someone, "I need to talk to the charge nurse, please."

The phone was a soft hiss of electronic silence. Stone pinched the phone between his head and shoulder as he now worked rapidly to stuff the sleeping bag and vapor barrier into the stuff bag. Popping open the side bag he shoved the bag and tent in and closed it. Opening the main rear boot, he started pulling out the rain and cold riding gear with the electrically heated vest and chaps.

"Trina?"

"I'm here, Gunny. Here's the charge nurse, her name's Pam."

"Hello, ah, Gunny?"

"Gunnery Sergeant Stone, ma'am, but just Stone now, ma'am."

"How can I help you, Stone?"

Stone ran his left hand over his face as he thought. "I'm in eastern Oklahoma right now, at a place called Grand Lake, but I'm leaving as soon as I figure the fastest way to get to you. It sounds like Trina is in a very fragile place right now, and I gather Bugs... I mean, Mario, is all she has other than the child on the way. If you could look after—"

"We've got her covered, Gunny," the nurse interjected. "We'll keep her on the other bed there in the room. We're in the ICU ward, but I'll make sure she's an exception. When you get here, you ask for me, my name is Pam Harm, as in *First, do no harm*. If I'm off duty, you make sure they call me. I'll leave a note with the charge station."

"Thanks. I'll be there as fast as I can."

"Gunny?"

"Yes, ma'am?"

"First, I work for a living, the name is Pam. Second, you're near Tulsa, get west to the I-35 and go north. Don't take the turn-off at Wichita—it's slow with a lot of local cops who would rather throw you in jail for going ten over, don'tcha know. Keep all the way up to the I-75. During the night, you can roll with the truckers, if you can keep up. Take the turn-off for Colorado Springs and Pueblo. When you see the sign for Pueblo, start speeding. Ninety should get some attention. Tell them to call us. Ya, and then they'll escort you straight here, so you don't have to look at a map. Other than that, stay safe, and we'll see you tomorrow."

Stone could hear the phone passed as he zipped his jacket.

"Gunny?"

"Yeah, Trina."

"Thanks."

"Get some sleep, sweetheart. I'll be there tomorrow."

"Thank you, Gunny."

The constriction of his throat stopped him from answering, so he hung up and shoved the phone in his jacket pocket. Then thinking, he retrieved it. Swiping the face, he poked the address book, then Ski.

From Stone:
Bugs in hospital.
I may need your help.
Stand by.

Stone shoved the phone in his jacket, pulled on his chaps, and smoothed the Velcro tabs down as the phone vibrated. He pulled the phone out, looking at the front. He smiled and stuck it back in the pocket.

From Ski:
B safe.

Slinging his leg over the saddle of the motorcycle, he turned the key and pushed the starter button as he toe kicked the kickstand into place.

The night was settling down around the red taillight as the deep-throated drone of the motorcycle disappeared into the west. The temperature was still nice, but Stone knew he would be turning on the electrically heated chaps and vest later that night as the temperature would drop and the wind-chill would have its way with his core body temperature.

Later, as the sun tried to warm the cold earth, Stone stopped for the fourth tank of gas. The microwaved bean burrito might have passed for warm, but unsatisfying. The coffee was tepid to nasty. Half of the burrito lay on the cooling seat as Stone sipped the coffee while topping off the gas tank. His mind, as numb as his feet, took more than a few seconds to realize he was looking at a state patrol car door. The silver car with blue and black stripes sat meaningless to him. The emblem he had never seen before. It took a third reading of the small words in the emblem to remember that Colorado... something about Colorado...

His gas tank overflowed.

"Damn!" Stone stepped back as he withdrew the nozzle, noting the rest of the burrito was history.

The trooper looked over with a bit of curiosity as he watched an old guy having a bad beginning to his day. The police mind cataloged everything going on: the gas overflow, the burrito on the seat, the coffee in the off hand, and the guy becoming distracted when he noticed the car. *The only thing missing,* he thought, *is a cell phone.*

As if on command, there was a very distinctive sound of a trumpet playing revelry and played by a very small speaker. Hanging up the nozzle and grabbing paper towels, Stone fished the phone out of his jacket pocket. *Doesn't this woman ever sleep?*

Stone's voice was a cold gravel bark. "What do you need, Ski? I'm kind of busy right now."

"How're you doing this morning?"

"I'm tired, I'm grumpy, and I just lost my breakfast." Exasperated at the moment, but also at losing his temper, Stone stepped away from the motorcycle to look east into the morning sun. Maybe to draw a bead on whom he was talking with.

"You're in Colorado."

"Yes, I'm in Colorado, but where, I'm not sure."

"You're about forty-three miles from the hospital."

Stone's shoulders slumped. "Hold on a moment, Ski." He walked over to the officer who was about to get back into his patrol car. "Excuse me, sir."

"Yes?"

"Is Pueblo part of your patrol area?"

"Not usually, why?"

Stone searched for the reason. Only gray blank fogged his mind. It was not the first time it had happened, but it was increasing. Not thinking of any other thing to do, he held the phone out to the officer.

"Hello?" The officer answered timidly.

"Who is this?" Ski demanded, then catching herself, "please."

"Officer Jeff Bridges of the Colorado State Patrol, and who am I speaking to?"

"Ski, sir. Yeoman Juliet Bronislovski, sir. I am aide-de-camp to Admiral Woodford at the Pentagon, sir."

"Well, aide-de-camp Ski, I have a half frozen man standing here next to a pneumonia horse. What can I do for you two?" He smiled and winked at Stone, but worried about the lack of response.

"Sir, he's headed to the hospital in Pueblo where one of his former company mates from Iraq is fighting for his life. The man's wife is about eight and a half months pregnant, and they have no other relatives. Gunnery Sergeant Stone left Tulsa Oklahoma last night at sundown."

"What can I do to help, Ski?"

"I think Stone's motorcycle could keep up with about a hundred miles per hour, but that would be up to your judgment, sir. He doesn't know where he is going, but if he could follow you..."

"Done," He poked the red image with his thumb and handed it back to a stunned Stone. "Gunny, we're burning precious daylight."

Stone stowed the phone, handed the gas attendant a twenty, put on his helmet, and was just sliding his leg over the seat when the officer called from his open window, "And Gunny?" Stone looked over. "Keep up."

Stone nodded.

The flashing lights lit up halfway across the gas station's apron, and the siren started as the car bounced across the street and powered up the on-ramp. Stone followed close behind.

STONEHEART

BAER CHARLTON

07

The hospital seemed the usual structure Stone collectively referred to as *St. Hallways*. Not even close to a labyrinth like Bethesda or the hospital in Germany, but nevertheless, the kind of large building Stone tended to associate with the terms obfuscation and confusion. The nurse at the front gave him concise directions, however, and the layout turned out to be more straightforward than Stone had expected.

His biggest fear, in a sort of way only a marine would understand, was the very large tummy on the cute young woman on the other side of the glass wall. Stone stood taking in the long dull brown hair and shoulders that did not come with being nine months pregnant. The sweatshirt appeared to say Georgetown, most likely to have come from Goodwill or a hometown rather than the university. The only surprise for Stone was the bare feet and nearby flip-flops.

He had seen hundreds, if not thousands, of Trinas at every base where the spouses had housing. Usually chosen last at team sports at school, also the last chosen on Friday nights. When the fresh shave-tail came home from boot camp, the attention turned into a plump tummy and marriage.

The small girl raised her arm, wiping snot and eyes. She focused on her bare left foot, resting on her right knee, as she picked at it. Stone watched the small shudders of her shoulders. They told him everything. She rivaled Bugs for bad shape, but she needed to hold it all together for the sake of the new family.

Quietly, Stone stepped back and turned to face the nurses' station. An older nurse had been watching him, slowly shaking her head, a commentary on the situation. She muttered something to the other, much younger nurse, and then rose. The younger nurse nodded then looked up to see Stone for the first time. Softly, she said something and nodded down the hall.

The older nurse approached Stone and asked quietly, "You must be the gunny she's been talking about?"

Stone extended his hand. "Stone, ma'am, just Stone now."

The older nurse shook his hand and registered the deep core cold. "Barbara Pinier, I'm the charge nurse. You're on a motorcycle?"

"Yes ma'am, all night."

Decades of no-nonsense nursing took charge of his arm and spun him around as they headed back down the hall he had just come up. "First we're going to get something warm into you."

Stone liked the firm, but gentle way of this woman. His mother maintained a house full of testosterone the same way, or a backyard full of Cub or Boy Scouts. They all came from marine base families. Besides, the hand resting gently in the crook of his leather clad arm felt good and comforting.

The half swallow of tepid coffee sat next to the dirty empty plate that an hour before had been heaped with a hearty breakfast. Inwardly, Stone smiled to think Rusty would have liked the meal, but Slim would have just seen it as the first course.

The crystal hazel-gray eyes watched him. Stone had stopped talking a couple of minutes before, in mid-sentence. As the woman had waited for him to finish his thought, the critical care nurse had superseded and was now watching his tracking.

"Stone?" The question was soft, more a wafting breeze than a demand for an answer.

"Mmm?" His eyes and thoughts came back from a long way ago. The here and now was almost alien to him, yet he blinked a few times slowly and returned.

"Gunny, we have a crisis here, but you have one that you need to also address."

"The TBI? Yeah, I know." He looked down at his finger, picking at his thumb, a nervous habit he had not remembered doing since seventh grade when they lived on Guam. Folding the offending hands together, he looked up. "It's not something that I can take a pill for and be good. I'll have to work on it, and it will take a long time. But, as you said, we have a situation here. What can you share with me?"

The older nurse sighed. "All of it. Those two kids don't have anyone else. They're both orphans from a local orphanage, and they were placed in a few foster homes together. So, you're family, so to speak. If you can think of any other avenues of help that would be available to them,

I think they're open to hearing it, especially the girl, Trina."

"So, what is the deal on Bugs?"

"Bugs? He doesn't have bugs." She scrunched her face from not understanding.

Stone smiled, thinking of the strange nicknames that collected in the services. "Sorry, Mario. His call sign in the Sandbox was Bugs. His last name is Bugatti, but he was the kind of guy that could hear things. Ears to the ground, rumors, traffic—whatever it was, Bugs was your source of intel on it."

"Okay, now I get you. Mario." The nurse looked slightly over Stone's left ear and a hundred miles away as she mentally called up a complete extensive medical file.

Returning her focus on Stone, the nurse continued. "Mario came back from a tour of duty about a year ago. He had gotten a cut on his leg that he didn't really think much about, except it didn't heal like it should. He had a simple cold last fall, and three weeks later, he was checked in here when he could not breathe. His immune system has all but shut down."

"HIV?" Stone grasped at meaning as he battled sleep and a still frozen brain.

The nurse duck-lipped and shook her head slightly. "We thought of that. It was ruled out along with a couple of dozen other things. Last week, he cut his hand while pruning a tree limb and the hand became infected overnight, and in the morning, he was having trouble breathing again. We were at a loss, until Trina said that he had started losing hair, body hair especially, about a month ago. That is when we thought to look at radiation poisoning. Mario has a very rare disease that comes from long exposure to depleted uranium. Most of the time, he will physically be fine, but then something like this injury to his hand will happen, and he's fighting for his life. The best we can do is make him comfortable and help him ride it out. We're treating him now as we would for any other radiation exposure. But, it's not like he was recently exposed, so you might say it's deep-rooted. So we're taking it day by day."

Stone stretched and yawned. "Why isn't he at a VA hospital?"

"Like many, these guys that were National Guard, it wasn't in his exit package."

Stone leaned forward as he rubbed his face. "Insurance?"

The nurse rolled her lips in against her teeth and shook her head.

"So, what's the long term answer?"

She shrugged and leaned back in her seat. "We don't know." She draped one arm across the other chair back as she slowly spun her coffee cup around. "There are so many strange things coming back with you guys that everyone is taking shots in the dark. Most probably he will soon be developing colon cancer or worse—pancreatic and liver. We just don't know. We don't know if Mario will live to see his daughter walk, or talk, or even long enough to walk her down the aisle. But there is one thing we do know."

"And that is?"

"He needs to get away from Colorado.'

"Why away from Colorado?" Stone frowned in confusion.

"He needs to find a place that has very low background radiation. The higher the altitude, the higher the rad count. We're still in that Rocky Mountain high."

Ever the gunny, Stone wanted a plan of attack. "What can we do right now?"

The older nurse had seen her share of health issues. She glanced out at a person walking by in the hall, and then continued. "Well, you saw how close they are to becoming a family. He probably won't be out of here in the next month, and from what Pam told me this morning, he hasn't had a job since the first of the year, and they are about to get thrown out of their apartment."

Stone washed his face in his hands. Being in the corps had made things so much easier. This civilian life was going to take a whole lot of getting used to. His eyes wandered about on the floor as Stone's mind kept hearing his original boot commander yelling about there not being any answers on the ground. The gunny raised his eyes and head and looked at the nurse.

Stone cleared his throat. "Give me a few minutes, Barbara, and I'll be back up there. Let Trina know I'm here, and I'll be along soon."

The older nurse rose and rested her right hand on his shoulder. "Take your time. Get some more coffee," and she was gone. As Stone watched her go, the self-assured gait reminded him of someone else, and that name reminded him of something else. He pulled the small red book out of his inside breast pocket.

About twenty minutes later, the worried young woman waddled barefooted into the room, holding her hands flat on the sides of her very large tummy. She stopped just inside the doorway and looked askance at Stone. The large brown eyes were crushing.

"Thanks, Stell, I've gotta go." Pushing the end button

on his phone, Stone looked at the girl, just barely a woman.

"Hi," he sighed softly. Every question was in that one word, and he did not need to hear anything back to have all of his answers.

Trina swayed over to him as he rose to his feet. The tears dribbling at the corners of her eyes were soon beyond stopping as she raised her arms forward and sank into Stone's chest. The two large arms wrapped her head in, and they stood there as she drenched his shirt.

Stone just held her. There was not a thing he could say—not that he knew what to say.

Later, a tall blonde nurse with cartoon dogs on her scrubs stuck her head in the break room. Her eyes were soft delft blue that went well with the two large braids woven back and forth across the top of her head in the Norwegian style of the north plains farming region where she had grown up.

She watched the gentle rise and fall of the young girl's head on a large man's chest as they both slept. Exhaustion masked both faces. Smiling at something making her happy, the blonde nurse withdrew, returning to the nurses' desk where the nun stood.

"Sister, they are in the break room, but right now, they are sleeping. Could I get you some coffee, and we can talk? I think both of them need more rest than they will be getting, but some is better than none, don'tcha know?"

The nun smiled. "Where ya from?"

The Norwegian nurse smiled broadly. "Sheboygan and you?"

"Ah, ya, Sheboygan—boys in the front, and girls in the back." The nun laughed. "I grew up near Lake Geneva, cows and corn, ya know."

They laughed at the commonality. The younger blonde chuckled. "Uff da, who woulda thought two Nordy girls from cheese land, would wind up in Colorado?"

The nun elbowed her. "Well, don'tcha know, now that I can trust that you know how to make good coffee, it's sounding pretty good, ya?"

The nurse started to head toward the break room out of habit, and then turned. "On second thought, let's just go on down to the cafeteria and get a Svenhard while we're at it. I'll fill you in on the situation, and you can fill me in on the mysterious Mr. Stone." Taking the nun's arm in hers, they walked off down the hall like a couple of school girls fresh off the farm.

Stone found them an hour later in the cafeteria among a few dirty dishes looking like they may have contained something good. His stomach growled as he walked up.

The nun looked up at the movement. "Well, there is the cheery young boy I used to know."

Stone leaned over, kissing her cheek as he gave her a hug around the shoulders. "Thank you for coming, Stell." Looking at the blonde nurse, he stuck his hand out. "Hello, my name—"

She took his hand in both of hers, "Is Stone. Ya, we spoke last night or sometime. I'm Pam, Pamela Yoder." She smiled at her new friend Stella. "It was Yoder, it's Pam Yoder Harm now." She pushed out a chair with a practiced foot. "Please, join us. This concerns you too."

As he waved his finger back and forth between the women, he began, "How much—"

The graying nun laughed. "Percy, we are so far out in front of you."

Stone glared at the use of his given name. "So where

are we at?"

The nun reached out and covered his hand with hers. "I made a couple of phone calls. For right now, there is nothing we can do for Bugs. He needs to stay here. But, Trina is going to pop any day now, so she's the focus now. We also can't separate the two of them. They are the only support system for each other with the depth that they will need."

"So what happ—"

Pam laughed and pointed a finger at him. "He was always this way, ya?"

"Hmm," the nun fluted her lips, "we couldn't make him stay in the bed. He kept wandering down the hall, checking his men."

Stella turned back to Stone, and smiling at the memories, patted his hand. "For right now, I will stay with Trina. We have some funds available to pay her rent for a few more months. I will have to go back to the school next week, but I'm setting up a rotation of other nuns to come and stay with Trina. I think she might like the help learning how to be a new mom. Most of these nuns have worked in the trauma wards in third world countries. The change of looking after only one mom and a baby will be like a vacation to them.

"When Mario is stable enough to transport, we will move him back to Des Moines. We have a small four-bed clinic at the convent next to the school, and we can care for him there. When he is able, I think it's about time there is a groundskeeper living in the old caretaker's cottage. Pam says that Trina didn't finish high school, so we can take care of that, too. I'm sure we can find something for her to do, as well."

Stone sat quietly looking at her face, remembering the serenity he had awoken to twenty years before as she looked down on him lying on a makeshift bed hidden in a corner of a bombed out school. Four of them had been wounded, and she had been taking care of them while the rest of the squad had held off the rebels until help arrived. When they finally pulled out, the nuns with some children in tow had retreated with them. Sister Stella had ended up working in the hospital. The pain on his face, unrelieved by their earnest but ineffectual ministrations, had kept Stone awake, and they had become good friends, talking in the dark quiet of the hospital ward. Over the years, she and Stone had kept in touch.

The sister patted his hand as she leaned back, watching the healed flash-burned face. "It's been many years, Gunny, many long years." She turned her head to include the nurse. "If it wasn't for Stone insisting that his squad search for shelter, finding refuge in that small school, I wouldn't be alive today. The boys paid dearly for their care and kindness, but we have kept them in our prayers since then."

The three looked up to see Trina padding her way into the cafeteria while rubbing the sleep from her eyes. "I woke up, and my pillow was gone."

Stone chuckled as he turned in his seat and offered out his knee. The small, very pregnant girl plopped down on it and cuddled into his shoulder like she had been doing it all her life. Her left thumb hesitated only a moment at the mouth, before sliding in. Content, her eyes slid closed, as her mouth softly suckled at the solace.

Stone looked at the nun and shrugged as if to say, *who knew?* He stroked the motionless sleepyhead. The quiet of the four was of tired content. The ice machine in the corner gurgled with a rattle of chunky fresh ice, which harmonized with the hum from one of the large glass fronted refrigerators.

Once again, Stone thought, *it's the middle of the night, and I'm in a hospital talking with the nun.* Things had not felt so right in a long time. The girl on his lap yawned and smacked her lips in the way that only little kids can do, or so he had thought, as the chubby hand fell softly into her lap.

A muffled electronic trumpet tooted, and Stone reached into his pocket, only slightly shifting the sleeping girl on his lap.

From Ski:
R U OK?

He looked at the nun whose eyebrow lifted in a soft sleepy question. Stone thought about where he was now, weighing it against his past. The broken smile drew softly across his patchy face. He winked a slow friendship wink at his old friend.

From Stone:
For now— perfect.

He laid the phone on the table in front of him so Sister Stella could read the conversation. She smiled softly as her eyes crinkled into happy slits. Stone's left hand stroked the young girl's head. *Perfect.*

BAER CHARLTON

08

The directions were pretty straightforward, and Stone found that Des Moines was not a complicated city to navigate. The high ivy-covered wall stuck out against the gray of the neighborhood, even from three blocks away. The two openings were only obvious when he was almost on top of them. Stone took the second driveway as directed and slowly motored along the side of the two-story brick building. Finding the parking place exactly where Stella had told him, he parked the Gold Wing and let it shudder into silence.

As he removed his helmet, the evening birds were beginning to twitter in the peaceful gardens and small field of the compound. Behind him, through the open windows of the second story, he could hear the nuns at their prayers. The gray gauze of the humid twilight descended softly, filtering the field as Stone's mind played old videos of past jungle clearings, fading with time, hopefully to stay that way.

A door creaked softly to his left and his head swiveled. The young nun with her black hair pulled back instead of hooded, stepped out and quietly closed the screen door. Turning, she walked quickly across the parking area with her walnut colored hands clutched in front. As she reached him, her arms spread and her dark brown eyes danced above a field of black-on-brown freckles. "You must be Stone. I'm Sister Mary Margaret." Admiring the motorcycle, she continued. "Amazing, Sister Estella Frank said you rode a motorcycle, but I had no idea it would be so large and formidable." Her speech revealed French-like accents that were familiar, and yet not, to Stone.

Stone chuckled and stuck out his hand and took hers. "I'm happy to meet you, Sister Mary Margaret. Stella said I would be met by a sister, but I expected some withered up old crone, not a smile and face of spring."

She blushed and laughed. "She also warned us about the silver-tongued devil that hid in the breast of the Stone." She waved him off the bike. "Come, you must be hungry. We will be breaking our fast shortly. I hope you like tough mutton and hardtack bread." The two smiled at the measure of teasing.

As they walked toward the convent, the sister sobered. "Sister Stella said you were in Mogadishu." Feeling as much as seeing his slow nod, she qualified their connection. "I was in the second tent city until the raiders drove us out. We hid out on the veldt for almost five years. I lost my mother and five siblings to the marauders."

Stone looked sidelong at the slender young sister and realized that she had not been a nun working in the camps, but a small girl in refuge. She had witnessed the horror of war, but on a far more personal scale than he had. He made a mental note to ask Stella if Mary Margaret had been one of the students who had evacuated with them.

At the screen door, she stopped and turned to him. "I

just wanted to let you know." She spread her arms around him and leaned like a feather into his body, almost whispering, "Merci, merci beaucoup." As she pulled back, she spoke, "I just wanted you to know there are those of us who are alive because of men like you." Turning, she opened the door, and Stone was certain that what he smelled was not old mutton and hardtack bread.

Sister Mary Margaret explained as they ate that the convent was not the quiet gathering of subdued sisters living out their lives in somber reflection, as some would think. Looking around the table at the few dozen animated women in habits and street clothes alike, Stone could guess the noisy table of that night was the normal state of the day's end for this collection of nuns.

The boisterous husky sister on his other side laughed and spoke with an exotic French-infused California accent. With a butter knife in her right hand, she stabbed the air as she pointed out a sister and her calling. The identified sister would pause in her conversation to raise her hand slightly to acknowledge the introduction.

"Sister Joseph Michael teaches the deaf advanced sign language skills at the community center," where the sister did not even look at them and finger spelled a set of signs that Stone recognized as *hi* or *hello*. Sister Mary Frank continued with a flourish of silverware. "And the twin redheads are Sisters Teresa and Ruth." Twin heads turned to beam headlight intense smiles and mirror image hand waves with finger wiggles. "They are working at the local hospital. Teresa is an RN and Ruth is a medical transcriber. In their spare time, they tend to our little flock's needs for care and office work."

A deep bass voice called out as the front door of the

building closed. "Hello. I hope dinner is ready. I'm starving, and I could eat a horse." Stone watched the door where nothing appeared. His eyes dropped two feet lower as a smiling older gentleman slid around the corner and entered the common room on silent wheels.

One of the older nuns, brash with age, teased the man in the wheelchair. "Paul, as usual, you are so late that we and our guest have eaten everything. There is not even a morsel that would satisfy a church mouse, much less a bottomless pit of a beggar such as you."

Wheeling up to the space made at the end of the table for him, the man continued the quid pro quo. "Well, that being the case, my dear Mary Peter, I will be nothing short of forced to go have my way with the sacrificial wine." He then turned to his left where a full plate of food was gliding to his place setting. "Ah, and here is a kind soul from the land of my heart, the bosom of all that I hold dear, and the fountain of all things wonderful. And how are things back home in Toledo, Sister Elisabeth?"

The elder nun, who standing was barely taller than the seated man, blushed, and then laid her arm along his shoulder. "The same as it was that spring morning in 1958 when I took leave of the city limits and have never thought of the city again." She gave him a hound-dog face and then turned to face the rest of the table and winked with a smile at Stone to reveal that what she had said was not necessarily the truth.

Sister Mary Margaret leaned over and in a low voice, filled Stone in on the joke. "Sister Elisabeth comes from one of the more traditional Catholic families in Toledo. She has about a dozen nieces and nephews, and maybe three dozen grandnieces and nephews. She spends the most time of all of us on the Skype." She looked down the table to check if she was overheard. "So much so," she continued, "that we got her a laptop all her own."

From down the table, the tiny nun chided, "Don't forget to tell him about the three great-grandchildren and my new great-great-grandniece." The table all nodded in concurrence, and Stone was sure the nun shared her family liberally among the others.

The quiet of the room was thick, yet soothing. Just moments before, after all the dishes were cleared, the sisters had quietly left to go into their chapel for Vespers, leaving Stone and the man in the wheelchair at the end of the table. Paul quietly sipped his water as he watched Stone adjust in the abrupt transformation that was a part of the daily routine in this convent.

Finally, Stone gradually let out a breath that ended with a *wow*. He blinked and thought as he stared at the table for an answer that was not there. Looking up to the end of the table, he was about to say something but did not know what it was.

"It takes some getting used to, Stone." Paul sipped more water as he studied the gunny in the man sitting before him. "Speaking of getting used to, how are you doing?"

Stone looked at the man, not understanding.

"I think you have some issues... TBI and PTSD, yes?"

"How did you..." A blank space rose in Stone's mind blocking the simple word *know*. His mind froze. He could not see the next word in his script. He had only recently begun to realize this had actually been happening for many years, but never frequently enough to get in his way.

"Know?" The man pushed on his wheels and turned to glide silently down the long table. "Let's start over, shall we?" Reaching Stone, he stopped and held out his hand. "Hi. I'm Doctor Paul Hollis. In 1973, I removed about four inches of shot-up gut from a young marine. I would like to say that I remember you, but you were only one more gut on a never ending line of blood, guts, bones, and tortured tissue." They shook hands. "I don't recognize you, and I'm pretty sure you wouldn't have recognized me either. You would have seen a dashing young man who was tall, insanely good-looking, square-jawed, with twinkling eyes, and fresh scrubs." Paul held out his arms with the palms up, and shrugged his shoulders. "At least they let me keep the twinkling eyes."

Stone swallowed. "What happened?"

"The chair? Oh, this was only about seven, almost eight, years ago. A drunk decided because he was bulletproof and as he had driven home drunk hundreds of times before that it was safe to do it again, one more time. I guess you might say number 347 was my wake-up call that I was an alcoholic and had a problem. Well, more like problems, I needed to address. Of course, a year before the divorce became final on marriage number three, which also coincided with my surgical privileges being suspended for the fourth time."

Stone sat in amazement as the man spooled out his demons without so much as a hint of hesitation. "So how can you... I mean...?"

"Do surgery?" the doctor interjected. "I can't. Not from a seated position."

The doctor put his coffee mug down. "Oh, I'm sure there is someone out there who has figured out that I could do maybe maxillofacial work, but the truth is I would need to be able to climb up on a table to do much of the work. So, these days I sit."

The doctor looked at his hands that no longer performed surgery. Looking back up, he reconnected himself with the subject at hand. "While I was recovering, I met many vets having a hard time adjusting to coming back. Everything was supposed to be the same. They were just supposed to slip back into being that guy they were a few years before... and it just wasn't that way. Home hadn't changed, they had. And so had I."

The man adjusted in his wheelchair. "I knew I was never going to be a surgeon again, so I went back to school while I was physically rehabbing and got my Marriage, Family, and Child Counseling certificate and hung out a shingle to help other vets adjust."

Stone cleared his throat. "So how did you end up here, and I'm assuming that you're working with Sister Stella?" Stone scratched at his flattop. "I mean this is kind of weird meeting like this, what... forty years later?"

Paul grabbed his left pant leg, lifted the leg up, and rested it on his right thigh. Leaning back into the short backrest he continued. "It is kind of 'Small World'-ish, but you have to admit, there really aren't that many military soldiers or docs. It's not like me saying, 'Wow, you're from Los Angeles, do you know my uncle Felix Smartsky?' To which you look stunned and say something like, 'Wow, he's my neighbor across the street.'"

Stone chuckled at the analogy. "But you do have to admit..."

"A little 'Freaky Friday'?" Paul slid his palms along the wheels' push rings. "I'd say it was more than just a little. Once I found out who you were, Stella and I did talk about it, and Stella being Stella, you know, was open to it as being one of those strange ways that her God works. Me, I'm more of a Jedi kind of guy... there is a purpose, but we just haven't seen it yet. So, back to my question, how are you adjusting?"

Stone thought about what he could say, and what he did not want to say. Then thought about how Paul had approached his own fragility with a straightforward thrust.

"It's not a hard question, Stone. It's just a simple one. Let's take it one step at a time. I saw the motorcycle, so you're getting around okay?" Stone nodded. "Good, and the highways and streets aren't giving you any trouble?"

"Why would they?" Half of Stone's face crinkled in a questioning frown.

Paul put his palms up in front of him. "I didn't say they would, I'm just asking questions here. Some guys find stoplights can be... well, confusing or even confrontational. We're just talking here, okay?"

"Sure." Stone washed his palms over his head while leaning his elbows on the table.

Paul watched the movements. "Tired, long day?"

Stone's face sank slowly into his hands, and he blew out a tired sigh of exasperation. Looking over with semi-blurred eyes, he refocused on the man. "Yeah, but more like a long week that started further back."

"Stella filled me in about the kid and his wife. Now there is a tough break."

Stone thought through the week's series of events. "Well, maybe when we get them over here, things will settle down for them." The light switch was thrown somewhere in Stone's head, and a dim bulb struggled to light up. "That's what you're here for." The doc nodded and shrugged as if to say, *among other things.*

The gunny chuckled. "Mary Margaret said that Bugs was the help in the gardens that she has been so selfishly praying for. I'd just be happy to see the young couple settle in where they have a good support system as well as thirty some built-in eager babysitters."

Stone smiled at the thought of the small warm bundle of little girl, softly snoring in his ear as he and Stella had talked into the night. Occasionally, a light thump had reminded Stone there was a second party in his lap, too. A distant trumpet sounded, and Stone fished the phone from its hiding place. "Stella mentioned, the sisters would enjoy having someone to look after…"

Holding the phone up, he interjected, "Excuse me. Duty calls, so to speak."

The paraplegic held up his hand. "I understand. In fact, I think I'm in there."

Stone looked back up at him with one eye, and then looking down, his one-sided smile tugging at his cheek as he muttered, "I wouldn't be surprised."

From Ski:
I see you're in DM with Sisters
 Say hi to Dr. Hollis.
Tell him I love his music.
Some progress on your request --
will know more in a week or so.
Get some sleep. ;-)

Stone chuckled. "She says she likes your music." He started typing back.

The doctor asked, "The admiral's secretary? She has good taste in music."

Stone absentmindedly nodded as he typed, musing, "I suspect she's more than just his secretary. I'm thinking more like an XO."

Stone looked up and smiled. The joke Paul had made earlier with Sister Mary Peter finally hit home. The old band of Peter, Paul and Mary *was* good music.

From Stone:
Safe here
Kids arrive next week
Paul and Sister Mary Peter thank you
Keep on request
Thanks

STONEHEART

BAER CHARLTON

09

The morning dew on the flowers was just evaporating, leaving tiny tidal rings of city *schmutz* as the drops dried. The hazy pall hung heavy over the downtown area in the distance as the runner plodded flat-footed along the asphalt. The dark stain of sweat drew a 'Y' down the front of the gray sweatshirt, and an almost matching 'I' between the shoulder blades.

The rhythmic plop, plop, plop was slowly altering by the sound of another set of feet coming around the corner of the last block. The woman rapidly closed in on the runner in front of her as his companion leaned forward in an effort to increase the speed he was putting out to the racing wheels of the chair. The three closed in on the last block before the stone wall which was overhung with wisteria and only broken by two driveways.

As Sister Mary Margaret pulled alongside Stone and Paul, she smiled while panting only slightly as she easily challenged the two men. "Shall we race to the back door; loser does the dishes?"

"And here," the doctor huffed, "I was going," and puffed, "to offer you a ride."

Stone just laughed and did not even try to speak. The gunny knew what he sounded like after running the first couple of miles he had run since leaving Germany. It would be all he could do to make it to the back door, much less race against a much younger woman who appeared to run long miles regularly.

"Silly old doctor, you know us black girls can outrun you white boys any day." Laughing, she bolted ahead and proved her point by turning into the driveway just as the other two had passed the first corner of the block. "Breakfast in thirty minutes, gentlemen, and don't be late—we have guests." They heard her lilting voice carry back over the wisteria just before the screen door slammed.

Out of the corner of his eye, Stone saw the doctor stop pushing and gliding to a halt. Hitting the asphalt flat-footed, Stone came to the same halt and started walking around to cool down.

The doctor was breathing almost as hard as Stone. "Don't let her get to you, Stone. Sister Mary Margaret runs ten miles every morning. She runs about eight or nine marathons every summer and last year raised almost a quarter of a million dollars for different charities. She's a running machine, and an even bigger donation machine. When she runs for the relief funds, she shows her photos of running in the little shorts and running bra. She's not bashful about her body as it tells her story well, and she figures it brings in about one to ten dollars a scar from each person."

Stone leaned with his hands on his knees. He drizzled with sweat from the unscarred side of his head. "I was there. I don't think those scars begin to tell her story." Standing up, he blew out his lips and cheeks in a flutter.

The sun was striking across the city and many of the windows were already sparkling with the morning heat. Turning, he looked at the doctor who was slowly massaging his upper arms. "From the looks of that chair, it wasn't made to just be in an office."

The doctor held one eye closed as he cocked his head and looked up at the younger man, studying him for a moment. "Who's the counselor here, you or me?"

"I'm just saying."

"It's not. It was the plan to get out and be active… but the opposite is a very seductive mistress."

Stone noticed he had hit a deep-rooted nerve and tried to make amends. "I'm here for a few weeks, it would do us both some good to get out each morning."

The older man laughed as he looked down at his legs bound in the chair. "And then what? You turn me over to the hot-shoed wonder and let her have her way with me? I'd be dead on the side of the road within the week."

"No, but for the first mile or so, she runs slower… actually almost walking. You could run with her until she kicks in and leaves you in the dust, and then make your way back. It's better than just sitting there doing nothing, waiting to die."

The older man turned red in the face as the vein in his forehead started to thump. Pushing off, he turned his back to Stone. As he made it to the driveway and looked back at Stone still standing at the corner, he knew the gunny had been right. "Who's the counselor, Stone? Who's the counselor?" As Paul pushed through the break in the wall, he could smell the wisteria, a scent that always reminded him of his first wife. He pushed harder, building up speed as he called back loudly, "And, it looks like you have to do the dishes… loser." The doc could hear the, *oh shit* and the pounding of the track shoes. Paul pushed harder in hopes that he had timed his win correctly.

Taking his hand from the wheel he was pushing, Paul reached for the ramp's rail. He watched the rail suddenly retreating.

"Gotcha!" Stone hooted.

Paul had cleared the large table, as Sister Mary Margaret rinsed the dishes, and Stone loaded the racks and ran them through the commercial washer he had fixed the week before. It was still considered Stone's personal territory since he already captured and nursed it back into the land of the living. Half the sisters sang many hosannas in his name that night at Mass. The others gave lighthearted thanks for being saved from the dishpan hands. No one here was shy of being in service to the rest.

Paul sipped on his coffee as he watched Stone and Mary Margaret wash the dishes. The flow between the two in unspoken language was a dynamic he had not really watched before. "So the vision comes and goes still?"

Stone looked at the young nun, then back at the doctor. Thinking, he turned to the last tray to load through the dishwasher, pushed it into the large maw, pulled down the lever that drew the doors closed, and started the wash. Wiping his hands on his apron, he turned, and thought through the answer. "Not for about two weeks, I guess." He smoothed out the apron and glanced out the window toward the caretaker's quarters where they had moved the young couple to stay two days before. "There was a loss for a couple of hours in Colorado."

"Was anything going on?"

Stone wagged his head. "Nothing really, we were just

working out the logistics of getting Mario over here without incurring the cost of an ambulance."

The nun quietly removed her apron and folded it onto the counter. Placing her right hand on Stone's upper arm, she thanked him, and made her excuse to leave. "I have devotions, and I'll leave you men to talk."

The two watched her leave as the doc said softly, "Thank you, Sister." Mary Margaret barely turned her head back as she nodded, and was gone. The quiet was crushing. Stone squirmed inside, and then lifted his head. "What is it you really want to ask, doc?"

The man studied him standing at the counter. Stone's body appeared almost at ease, not combative, but also not relaxed. The eyes gazed at the floor, counter, and out the window, everywhere but on the man trying to help. "Sit down, Stone," the man asked quietly. "Please," as he rolled over to the small kitchen table.

"I see you making a lot of motion, but not the settling in." Paul set his coffee mug on the table as Stone folded his hands casually in front of himself. "It's like you're a bird. You will fly all over to gather the twigs. You'll even stick the twigs with bits of yarn and grass into the nest. Yet you won't sit in the nest or sleep in the nest. You hover just outside the nest, like it's not yours to own, even though you built it."

Stone stared at his hands, and then started picking at one of the cuticles, thinking. The doctor knew Stone was mulling over what he said, but the Paul side of him wanted to scream because it was not a hardball question, merely an observation. Hence, Paul waited, with all the serenity he could gather, for the man who was becoming a good friend.

Stone took in a deep breath through his nose, held it, and let it out slowly. Laying his hands down flat, he looked up into the other man's eyes, solid and not wavering. "I guess it might be because I really don't know if it's my nest to sit in."

The hardened marine drew his upper lip into and between his teeth and bit down. The scar tissue drew taut and white. "All of my life, my dad was a marine, just like his dad before him. Even when my brother and I were little, we knew and talked in our dark bedroom about when we grew up and that we would be marines, as well. There was never any doubt.

"Because my father was a rifle instructor, among other things, we always lived on the base he was stationed. When mom took us shopping, it was at the Base Exchange, the PX. When we went to school, it was on the base. When we dated, it was some marine's daughter. We went to the base theater for the movies, or the PX for a soda, or down to the rifle range to watch the night shooting."

Paul snickered naughtily. "Really?"

Stone frowned. "Really, what?"

"Night shooting? Or…"

The gunny shrugged with one eye half open and raised eyebrows. His smile reflected the hand caught in the cookie jar. "Kind of, but mostly not, there really was night practice as things got uglier in Vietnam, and there was a lot more emphasis put on sniper training, and that entailed night shooting, as well."

The doctor arched his eyebrows in a mental *huh*, and then leaned back in the chair and rolled his hand and finger in the air as if to say *continue*.

"In 1966, my brother graduated from high school and

114

enlisted the next morning. Fifty-nine weeks later, he was a sniper headed for Vietnam. Forty-seven weeks and three days later, he headed home in a box with most of his platoon. We buried him in Westwood, near Los Angeles, the summer before my senior year. Forty-eight weeks later, I repeated the cycle. My mother wasn't happy, but she had married a second-generation marine, and she understood.

"Shortly after I landed in Cam Rahm Bay, my father was injured in a training accident. He had cracked his spine in four places. They fused the disks, but he was retired medically. It almost killed him to go out that way."

The doc raised a finger. "Do you see any correlation to the medical your father got and the one you got?"

Stone shook his head. "Dad was a good soldier. He never complained. He did his job, and he was very good at what he did. He also understood just how valuable he was in training excellent snipers and shooters who didn't waste resources. But I know down deep, Dad resented the fact that he had never seen combat himself. He enlisted between the second war, and Korea. By the time Korea rolled in, Dad had already been established as a superior trainer, so he never got called. Even though I'm sure he asked."

"And you?"

"I never spent much time in the rear echelon. I was one-hundred percent FirGo, so I saw it all."

"FirGo?"

"First to Go, always lived on base, and always had a Go-bag packed."

The doc rolled back his head with a smile and mouthed his new word, "*FirGo.*" Nodding, he mentally logged the term for future use. Paul frowned with half his face, unsure if he wanted to ask the question. "And where are your folks now?"

"Gone," Stone glanced down at his hands, then back up. "When they left the corps, he contacted an old buddy who owned an auto parts store in a small town named Festus, Missouri, about an hour outside St. Louis. Just after I got back in-country... Vietnam, for my second tour... a tornado struck in the middle of the night." Stone looked back at his hands, and swallowed a few times, softly, still hurting. "I like to think that they never knew what hit them. Folks said that they didn't even find so much as a toilet or photographs. It was as if God came and took them lock, stock, and barrel."

Looking up after a moment of thought, Stone continued. "So after that, any sort of nest that I thought I could call mine was gone. My nests were always the bases or where I was stationed. But with most of those, you knew you would be moving your nest within a week or three, so why put down twigs, so to speak."

The doc now understood a lot more about the problem. Stone really did not have a place to go back to because it had never been there.

"So have you thought about where to go from here?"

Stone harrumphed sardonically. "Well, I was starting to think about that when I was down in Oklahoma. There was a little cabin on a big lake. The rent was right, and about the time I was looking out over the lake at the sunset, my phone rang."

"And so you rushed to help another comrade in arms, and now you're here."

The soft female voice interjected, "Still helping."

The doc looked up as a gentle hand smoothed its way

along the top of Stone's shoulders and came to rest as the ample hip rested against his other shoulder. "Speaking of helping, we need to start preparing for lunch, and if those dishes are all clean, you can help by setting the table."

Stone smiled as he leaned his head into the padded rib cage of the older nun. "Sister Stella, you always had a way with words to make me do your bidding."

She chuckled. "It is not my bidding that I have always had you do, it was His."

Stone laughed and pointed at the doc. The doc crossed his two index fingers and hissed like Dracula, and they laughed as Stella bopped Stone on the head lightly. "Always with the little boy stuff."

Stone laughed, rose up, and slipped his arms around his favorite sister. "It's good to have you back here, Stella. You have no idea how bad this one and Sister Mary Margaret have been picking on me."

Stella started pounding on his back in mock protest. Finally released, but laughing too hard to talk, she just dusted the backs of her hands at them and chuckled her way back out of the kitchen. Four novices rubbed their backsides along the wall passing her to get into the kitchen and start the food prep.

Paul chuckled as he counted out the silverware. "Do you think she'll regain her composure before she has to say the blessing?"

Stone looked back down the hallway, then at the four novices who tried hard not to listen to the conversation in which did not concern them, and then smiled back at the doc. "I rather doubt it. She'll probably have a novice say the grace and even lead the evening, evening…"

"Vespers," the little redhead at the sink stated, then

117

turned as red as the beets she was preparing to wash. She took in a sharp gulp of air, and crossed herself.

Stone almost could not control himself. "Thank you, Sister, you are most helpful. Maybe you can help Sister Stella at dinner with the blessing."

Paul pushed all the harder as he zoomed past the dangerous man and down the hallway with all the silverware. Without counting the large stack of plates, Stone grabbed the whole pile and moved with haste after his comrade in arms and mirth. As Stone turned the corner, he could hear the four novices loosen their control in peels of young laughter.

Stone thought as he rounded the corner into the dining hall, *oh jeez, now what have I started?*

The distant trumpet sounded in his pocket.

From Ski:
Can you talk?

Stone looked at the table and knew the time schedule, and it was inflexible.

From Stone:
No

He put the phone back in his pocket and began to set the table under the watchful eye of the doctor who was laying out the silverware.

Paul grinned about the phone. "The XO?"

Stone nodded.

The trumpet sounded, and Stone continued laying out plates.

"She sounds persistent."

Stone gave him a hard look, and continued with the plates.

"I'm just saying," the doc continued around the table as he shrugged off the hard look Stone was trying to drive through his back.

The trumpet sounded again.

Stone laid down the last plate and pulled the phone from his pocket.

From Ski:
No – seriously

From Admiral:
Stone, we may have a situation
When can we talk?

Stone was not ready to deal with the admiral, but he also knew the admiral understood that, too. He looked at the doctor who glanced up from quietly setting the table as if to say, *I'm not part of that, so leave me out.* Stone started typing.

From Stone:
Give me an hour.

BAER CHARLTON

10

Even in First Class, Stone felt cramped inside of the airplane after the few short months of riding on a motorcycle. The cabin air smelled stagnated and fetid compared to open breathing in the helmet behind the windscreen. Stone would have preferred to put in some long hours on the bike, but the admiral had insisted that time was not a luxury they could afford.

As Stone leaned his head back into the reclined seat, he thought about the last time he had seen the young sergeant Jimmy "Spuds" Spalding. With his first run at the Sandbox, he had arrived as a pink-skinned college kid. Along with thousands of others, he was trying to pay the bills by joining the National Guard. Like most, he never expected to see any kind of action beyond helping with a flood or a search and rescue event that would make for some great girl chasing stories back at college. By the time his boots hit the sand on his second callback, he had rapidly faded out to a gray five-o'clock shadow of living in the face of death, matched with the grueling grind of mind-numbing heat. The gawky college kid had been replaced by a gaunt specter with an all-too-familiar distant stare and wire-tight tension in his jaw.

In another place and time, his last patrol to clear a small neighborhood would have been routine. The one-thousandth of a second it takes to go from standing on two legs, to having only one knee left was a constant reminder that, in a war, nothing is routine. Luckily or unluckily, Spuds was still living proof of this dilemma. Stone's unit had been the call-out to rescue the downed team. Four hours, three-hundred pounds of ammo, and a drone strike later, they pulled the unit out of hell with the help of three body bags, one which Stone had personally packed, and eight months later Stone visited the BAR man's folks in rural New Hampshire.

The boy's parents had taken Stone around for what seemed like all four-hundred and eighty residents of the small farm community. The peaceful green of the tidy lawns, the intense colors in the gardens, and the openness of the parents, proved an almost alien landscape to Stone.

Instead of every day subsisting as a humming wire of *do I live out the day, or is this it,* which had become the normal for Stone, this lack of tension unnerved him. Just the idea of stepping out the front door and walking down the road without so much as a glance over your shoulder was in itself so intense that Stone realized he had not slept either of the two nights at their farmhouse.

Three days later, he made a phone call and volunteered to return to the Sandbox for his third tour.

The father, also a product of Vietnam, recognized the signs in Stone. Therefore, when Stone made his excuses to leave a day early, the man had stopped his wife at the door and walked the gunny out to his rental car alone. As they shook hands goodbye, the man had held his hand. "I know what I see in your eyes. You're going back over there. It's more comfortable for you. It's what you know. When you come back, if you ever feel like you can stand the quiet, we'd like you to come and stay again... As long as you want... there's no lock on the door, and you know where we keep the coffee."

"Sir," the attendant touched Stone's shoulder. "Sir," as he jerked awake, he looked at her. The vision in the left eye momentarily clouded in a dark gloom, and then cleared as he focused. "Please put your seat in the upright position. We'll be landing in just a few minutes," and then she was moving to the next row. "Sir, please turn-off your computer, and stow it under your seat as we will be landing in just a few minutes."

Stone looked out the window staring at as much as he could see from the aisle row seat. The wet night was stippled with a wash of lights, marking the city of Portland, or the city of Vancouver, Washington just across the large Columbia River. The dark of the cabin and the distant lights slowly sparkled like the specks of color Stone saw when holding the heels of his hands against his closed eyes. While listening to the whine of the flaps being lowered in preparation for landing, the gunny realized his headache was back. Barely perceptible, the plane slowed and Stone's stomach clenched dully, a reminder of how much he did not trust flying.

As the plane let down over the city, the twinkling lights became buildings, streets, and open grassy areas of schools, parks, or just undeveloped areas. Stone realized he never asked what Spuds was doing in Oregon. In fact, true to Stone's nature, he had not asked what he was doing here, either. The wheels chirped into contact with the runway, and the entire plane jolted as the nose gear hit. *Too late to question it now*, Stone thought.

Two, almost three years had passed since Stone put Spuds and the other three on the medical flight. At the time, he thought it would be the last time he saw the kid. Now, as the plane shut down and the bell dinged, Stone unclipped his seat belt and rose with everyone else, and wondered what would be waiting for him in the terminal.

What he did not expect was a six-foot Spuds standing tall and smiling, once again pink skinned though somewhat older than Stone had remembered. Could this be the same kid who had shown up in the Sandbox on his first tour so scared and nervous? But Stone remembered he had also been excited, and he could not stop talking about cooking, although the closest Stone saw him to cooking was heating up MREs. Spuds seemed to be an endless chatterbox about grilling and barbecues, or what kind of vegetables should go with what meats, plus the cooking. It always entailed the intricacies of the cooking. Everything but potatoes—it turned out that Spuds hated potatoes. So, the other guys in the company, being guys, just were not going to let it go.

"Spuds," shaking the young man's hand, "I think you've grown some since I last saw you." Stone could not help but smile in admiration at the two gleaming legs pimped out with flames and pin striping, along with a matching cane.

The kid reached out and poked Stone in the rock hard stomach. "It looks like civilian life doesn't agree with you, Gunny. You're just wasting away to skin and bones." They both chuckled at Spud's same old line from the Sandbox. "Isn't anyone feeding you?"

Stone reached over to tousle the young man's unruly

head of sandy blond hair.

Laughing, Spuds ducked and stepped back, surprisingly nimble on his aluminum legs. "Hey, that isn't the only bag you're traveling with, is it?" Spuds chimed as he pointed at the small go bag. "I mean, after all, you're a civilian now. You need more than two shirts."

"I brought five." Stone nodded seriously, and the kid stopped goofing around. "I even brought some formal wear."

The kid's mouth opened to speak, but there was nothing connecting. Stone delivered the punch line. "I bought the high-end stuff. It came with a front pocket and a hood."

As the kid started to giggle, he bent over to beat Stone from snatching the bag off the floor. "A hoodie... yeah, you're going to fit right in out here in Oregon." Turning to the exit of the terminal, he added, "We just might have to go buy you your first tattoo."

"Never gonna happen, squirt," Stone growled.

"Well, at least let me take you to a titty bar while we're here in Portland. Titty bar capital of the world, along with tattoo parlors, nuts, and freaks."

"I thought I was here on business."

"Not here. Downstate and that will be tomorrow." The kid pushed through the glass door and into the cool evening drizzle. "Right now, it's time to get us fed, and then maybe some rack time."

The evening was balmy under the enormous glass canopy protecting eight lanes of traffic and extending from the terminal building to the short-term parking structure. Stone watched as the young man navigated across the expanse on two aluminum legs. His gait was almost normal, only slightly stiff. Stone also marveled how, at moments, the cane became almost an afterthought. The two laughed when Spuds became aware that Stone had fallen back a few yards. Knowing he was watching the shiny sticks, he called back over his shoulder, "You're not checking out my ass, are you?"

An hour later, the waitress silently removed Stone's plate as he carefully wiped his already clean mouth on the cloth napkin. Looking around the bar restaurant and hotel, which had once been one of the last whorehouses in Portland, his eyes slowly bounced from artifact to artifact that made up the décor of the White Eagle.

Carefully folding the napkin and placing it on the table at his elbow, Stone laced his fingers and squared his elbows on the tablecloth. "Okay, I'm fed. Now what is this all about?" He watched as the other man finished chewing his last bite of a smallish dinner and shoved the plate forward an inch. "If all you wanted to do was buy me dinner, you could have come to Des Moines. The nuns put up a great meal."

Laying the pulled napkin out in front of him, Spuds looked into Stone's mangled face for the friend who had pulled his ass out of the fire in the Sandbox. "It's my uncle, my mother's baby brother." Leaning back, Spuds rested his one hand in his lap, and the other draped high along the booth's back.

Spuds closed his eyelids then rolled his eyes as he thought about how to talk to the gunny who was here to help as more than just a friend. Opening his eyes, Spuds nodded forward, looking for the answers in his lap or hand. "We live down west of the Medford area at the bottom of the state." He looked up and toward the window that was now gray-orange with the last of the evening color. "He has cancer, cancer from his days of being bombed with Agent Orange and other crap Uncle Sugar and the chemical companies, like Dow and Monsanto, decided to dump out of airplanes onto the jungles."

Spuds finally looked up at the open and waiting face of his former sergeant. "He qualifies for VA benefits, but the only hospital is up here in Portland."

"So what's the problem? Just have him come up here."

"It's not that simple." Spuds' hand came up out of his lap and absently started drawing scratches on the tablecloth. "In 1969, when he came home, he stayed almost the whole night in the house. In the early dawn, he moved out into the forest. Over the years, he got used to at least living in a house. Well, it's a shed really, but it's out in the forest. That is as close to people or society that he can stand.

"The family bought about eighty acres of forest so he would never feel hemmed in, and that's where he is now. We can't even get him into the small town where we live. If we need to buy him some new boots, see a doctor, or dentist, they have to come to him, out there in the forest."

"Then how do you know he has cancer?" Stone stretched his arms out along the top of the booth.

"Our family doctor came out and examined him, and took blood samples. He said, 'There probably is a good chance that with treatment, he could have another eight or ten years.' But we have to get him up here for treatment." Spuds replied.

Stone leaned his head back against the booth. His eyes appeared to be looking at the stuffed owl over the bar, but

Stone's view and thoughts were thousands of miles and years away. Finally, he refocused on the young man and leaned in. "So, let me get this straight and very clear. The reason I am here is to convince another old warhorse he needs to come to a city he's afraid of, so some VA weenie doctors can stick a bunch more crap in his body and make him feel like dying. All so he can live a tiny bit longer in the forest." Stone's face did not even flicker, and his stare was blank.

Spuds did not squirm. Both had paid the price of entrance into this special club, and he understood what Stone was saying. He also knew that it would kill his uncle to come to the huge city of Portland—but there were other circumstances. "It's my mother." He looked down at his hands on the table. The slight tremor in the fingers would have been on the lips of a lesser man. His lips curled into the biting teeth. Blinking in resolve, Spuds looked back up. "Since he came home, it's been hard on her. About twenty years ago, my dad was killed in the forest while logging a steep hillside. Then I went over to the Sandbox, and came home this way. She's just afraid of losing any more pieces of the family, and I don't blame her."

Stone thought about the piecemeal way he lost his own family. The other side of his brain was thinking about the people he had been gathering lately that were becoming, in a loose way, another family. He thought about Sister Mary Margaret losing her family, but not her faith in people. Things were circles with people—as you lose here, you gather there. Like Rusty, losing everything, but then getting her own self in the bargain, and now getting a new family on her own terms. Something many people are never given a chance to accomplish or possess.

"Okay, we'll see what we can do."

As the waitress laid the bill on the table, Stone reached for it but Spuds grabbed it faster. Stone started to protest, but the sound of a distant horn blew, and Stone reached in his pocket and pulled out his phone.

From Ski:
How's Portland?

Stone poked back at the screen and hit send. Spuds looked up questioningly as he handed the waitress the bill folder and his credit card. Stone just shook his head.

From Stone:
Not as easy as it sounds
Talk tomorrow
Past your bedtime

The horn blew and Stone peeked and chuckled. He slid out of the booth as he holstered the phone back into his pocket.

From Ski:
Yes Uncle Grumpy

BAER CHARLTON

11

The morning had started in near silence, other than the usual grunts, points, and few words used between two marines to get the job done. Stone recognized the kid felt worried and he was working on staying cool as the day of driving would take its toll on the only person who could drive the specially adapted van. Over breakfast, Spuds pointed out their destination on a map—the small bend in the river three hundred miles to the south end of the state.

The sun began to rise as they stopped in the capitol city of Salem to grab a fast breakfast at the only place open. The waitress looked cute in a country horsey sort of way, but even she could not bring the attention of the company's Casanova to the present, so Stone was not even going to try.

As the curves of the freeway graced their way through hills covered with trees and scrub brush, Stone experienced an uneasiness he had not felt since the Sandbox. The hills seemed different. He knew there were no Taliban fighters lying in wait on the ridges, yet nonetheless, the feeling still crawled in his gut. Anything would be a distraction.

"So what happened over there?"

Spuds swerved slightly from the sudden noise.

"Where?"

"Nam."

The kid glanced over at Stone, then back at the road. When Spuds looked back at Stone during a straight part of the road, Stone was deep in thought, Spuds found himself studying the man with the mangled face and more gray hair than his father would have had, had he remained alive. This man, who had pulled the last remnants of his body out of hell and stuck him on a chopper to salvation, but a man he hardly knew. As Spuds pushed the levers, which could be either the gas pedal or brakes, he thought about the strange mix of a man. First to growl and kick your ass when you needed it, and then in Stone's own way, he would also tuck you in at night, so you felt safe or at least watched over.

"What do you want to know?"

Stone considered the questions. What did he need to know, and could it be the same as what he might choose to know? "Let's start with what did he do over there?"

The kid glided the van through a few curves as he thought. Then his eyes sort-of slid almost shut, and a smile pulled back his cheek. "I remember my mother telling me about the many letters she received after Unc got in-country. They all started the same way… *'I got up this morning and started burning more shit in the barrels.'* It really cracked her up.

"He was a support person on a rear echelon artillery base, one-fifty-fives mostly. He would talk about the cannons when I was a kid. He would point at the ridge a few miles away and say, Polly…" Spuds blushed slightly and looked over at Stone for approval. "He used to call me pollywog." Stone nodded and Spuds continued. 'Polly, our cannons could throw a shell as big as you all the way over that there ridge.'"

He looked over at the gunny. "It wasn't until I got to the Sandbox that I found out the howitzer could throw it a full fifteen country miles."

The gunny smiled and nodded with somewhat mixed but fond memories of the large cannons. "And damn accurate too, when you needed it," while looking out the side window at a break in the hills into a protected valley, and then he added, "and they were a lot safer than a B-52 carpet bombing or some stick-humping sky jockey pickling off a set of twin napalms." His left hand subconsciously reached up and softly stroked the nerve dead facial scarring.

Spuds caught the touch. "Is that where you picked up the face?"

Absently, Stone looked at the hand he had not known was there. Returning it to his lap, he looked over at the kid. "Nah, that was in Somalia. A different country, a different continent, a different decade, but much the same war."

They both studied the highway. Each lost in their own wars.

"So he was burning the camp's shit. What else was he doing?"

Spuds nodded. "Unc was driving the supply truck for a while, then one day he hit a pedestrian, and so he asked to be transferred."

"Did they?"

Spuds shook his head. "The base commander told him the Viet Cong or their sympathizers were the only ones who didn't get out of the way, and that he had done what he was supposed to do—kill Charlie. It still screwed him up, but the commander finally let him go do something else. That's when he was attached to the Seabees laying down steel landing strips in the jungle.

"That's where he got sprayed by the Orange?"

The kid nodded. "After a while, it got a little too hot for even the Seabees, and they were pulled out and the helos took over. By that time, Unc was short, down to about twenty-eight cots and hop, so they had him fill in as an orderly at a MASH unit.

"He was running back and forth into the operating room with supplies and sterile stuff, and he had just left the room when Charlie lit off about five rounds of mortar. The door into the operating room hit him square in the back and carried him out into the yard. Unc was the only one in the tent that survived that day. Sixty days later, he was let go from the hospital in San Francisco."

Stone remembered. "Letterman, Letterman Hospital. It's just under the Golden Gate Bridge."

Spuds continued. "He remembered the orderly telling him, on a quiet night, they could hear the suicide jumpers scream all the way to the water. It never happened. The orderly developed into the only person Unc wanted to actually kill, just for being so cruel."

"So he came home, and never left." Stone looked over at the kid, nodding.

"I don't even think I ever remember him going to the coast, much less going into Medford or Grants Pass. Unc just wouldn't go. Not even in the seventies when there was nothing in GP. He just wouldn't go.

"When I was about twelve, his appendix ruptured. He made the big animal veterinarian in the next little town come take it out, right there in his teepee. He stayed awake the whole time with his hand on a service forty-five. Scared the hell out of my mom, but afterward, she offered to cook the vet dinner. The doc looked at her and said what he really could use is a stiff drink. My mom is a Bible thumper, but she didn't even blink. The next thing we all knew, she was pulling up one of the boards in the kitchen, and there was a bottle of something. She told the doc he could have only half of it or he'd go blind. The doctor took one sip and said that it was the best moonshine he had ever tasted. I think it was maybe my grandpa's mashing. But no, he never left. Never drove, either. Just lived out there in the forest."

"Did he ever talk about Nam?"

"No." The kid eased the van onto the off-ramp for Grants Pass. "Everything I know about Unc being over there was reading all the letters my mom saved and talking to a couple of buddies that lived here in GP or around. But pretty much, nobody talks about being over there."

Stone nodded as he watched the rural community pass his window. Rolling down the glass, he stuck his elbow out and rested it on the door, smelling the pine and fir mixed with people and civilization.

"I think that is what I miss the most about my legs."

Stone looked over at the kid who nudged his chin at the open window. "Rolling down the window and hanging one arm out, and driving with the other draped over the steering wheel."

Stone looked at the window then at the kid driving with one hand and with the other controlling the lever pushing the accelerator and brake. He thought about all the injuries and how everyone makes assumptions about the guy with two hooks. They wonder about him getting dressed, but not about going to the bathroom and wiping himself. It was the little things like hanging your arm out of the window, or feeling the sand between your toes, it's never the big ones like seeing your child's face as they grow up or being able to even hold a child or make love to your spouse. It is always the littlest things that affect you the most. Stone's right hand rose to the left side of his face. He could not smile, or sense feeling, or ever get a date on a Saturday night. It was the small things that make your life take a stumble.

Spuds worked the lever, and the van rolled with the green light. "There's a good burger joint down here on the strip. We can stop for some lunch, and I can get one to go for Unc. He always liked these, but he only gets them when we come to town and bring him back some."

"No burger joints in your town?"

The kid laughed as he worked his legs and slid out of the van. "We have a gas station that is the post office and a small grocery store. Willie is also a notary and can marry you between pumping gas."

The kid had not been joking. They sat giggling about it as Willie pumped their gas a couple of hours later. Stone watched the old man with a cane hanging hooked in the side of his bib overalls, bouncing against the man's bad leg. As the gas pumped on the first low click of the nozzle, the man carefully made his way around the van washing every single window and side mirror. Not a streak remained, all of the last week's bug splatter taken away. Spuds explained. "Willie knows every vet in these counties from Brookings to Lincoln City. He never could serve because of his clubbed foot, so he says thank you by cleaning all the windows."

"And pumping the gas," Stone added.

"Nah, that's a state law. It keeps several thousand people employed for at least minimum wage." Spuds laughed. "Every once in a while, some idiot tries to get the law overturned saying the gas prices would go down if everyone could pump their own. I think the last time it went to the voters, it was shot down by ninety-seven percent. Oregon people are like that. We like to think of the little guy with no other chance at a job."

"So if you're a vet, you can get your windows washed and your gas pumped, but if you need medical treatment, you have to drive a whole day away?"

"Pretty much," the kid's lips sucked in tight to his teeth as he nodded and looked out toward the distant ridgeline of trees.

The silence broke with the muffled sound of Willie calling out something, and then slapping his hand on the side of the van. Spuds rolled down his window. "Yeah, Willie, What's up?" The old man limped back around the rear of the van.

"I said, I think the deputy wants to talk with you."

Spuds looked in the rearview mirror where he watched the very young deputy parking his cruiser and getting out. Stone could see the kid sink into himself. Spud's head dropped down to his chest. He swore quietly as his hands wound into fists and gently pumped the meat between the bones of his fingers. It was a pressure reflex Stone witnessed in the Sandbox with many guys.

The deputy walked up to the driver's side door. "James."

Spuds looked at the steering wheel as if it would save his life or soul. "Harold."

The deputy was not comfortable and looked across the road at the distant ridge, the trees, and a passing car. "Um, I didn't... well, I don't..."

Spuds let him off the hook. "My uncle is dead, isn't he?"

The kid deputy was on the verge of losing it as the tears welled up in his eyes, and he looked back at the highway. "Las... last night," he choked. He wiped at the un-deputy-like tears streaming down his still pink cheeks.

Spuds' face was a stone tableau except for the trace of wet that ran to his chin and dripped into his lap. "His gun?"

The deputy could only nod. Stone could tell this was the worst thing the kid had ever had to do in his life. He was unprepared for this sort of duty.

"Where's my mom?" Spuds finally looked up at the kid in the uniform.

The kid tried to speak, but only squeaked. Instead, he pointed in a general direction to the right down the highway. He was crumbling before their eyes.

"Miller's Feed?" The deputy could only nod, and Spuds reached out his left hand. "Harold, you need to just go home. You can't work, and Taylor should understand that." The kid nodded and walked back to the police car.

Willie stepped up to the window and even his eyes were red but not rheumy. "I'm sorry, James. I should have told you when you drove up. I'm such a coward about these things."

Spuds looked at the man. "It's okay, Pop. You did fine. We all knew it was coming. How much do I owe you?"

The old man rested his hand on Spuds' arm. "Don't worry about it, son. I'll put this one on the Sheriff's bill.

That asshole Taylor will probably make little Harry answer phones for the rest of the day. You go help your mama."

"Thanks, Pop, you know you are always our hero." He started the van.

As they pulled out, Spuds glanced at Stone. "Harold?" Stone nodded. "He was born next door to us. His real daddy up and runs off when his momma was about six months along. Unc was the closest he and I had for a father, since my dad died when I was two. Logging takes a lot of the men around here."

"So what's the story about the feed store?"

"Miller's? It's kind of like Willie, a little of this and a little of that, and hopefully, at the end of the month, you have a living." The kid looked over to see that Stone still was not getting the picture. "They're what pass around these parts as the local mortuary. If you get cremated, you never know if you get some horse, dog, or elk ash mixed in with yours."

Needing levity, Stone observed, "Quaint," and looked back out the window.

BAER CHARLTON

12

"Are you sure?" Spuds continued to drive Stone to the big town of Medford to a car rental location. "Just give me a couple of days and I'll drive you back up to Portland."

Stone studied the kid as he focused on driving the narrow country road. He could imagine, in Spuds' younger days, driving the same stretch of road slouched behind the wheel, with his right arm around a girl, and the left index finger guiding the car with his elbow resting out the window as the tunes played on the radio. Now he was a man, and driving became a serious business demanding one hand on the steering wheel, and the other on the control for the gas and brakes. No extra room for anything else, much the way Stone sensed the situation after observing quietly as Spuds and his mother went about the time-honored tradition of washing their kin, and preparing them for burial.

The burial had been too close to Stone's *home* for comfort. In the last light of the day, they had laid the canvas wrapped body into a grave in the middle of the forest. It had been his uncle's home and universe since coming home shattered from his country's war. Stone knew he had not returned to respite but had ended the term of one war to start an even longer battle within him. The canvas form on the ground immediately brought home Stone's own battle he needed to deal with... and staying with Spuds would only be a distraction.

"I appreciate the offer, Spuds, and your mother is a kind person to put up with me, but I really need some time alone. I also think you and your mother need some time to work out where you go from here."

"I just feel like an ass to have you come out here, and then turn around and leave."

"You're not an ass, kid. You did the right thing for your uncle and for your mother. Unfortunately, it was about forty years too late." Stone drew his lips in against his teeth and studied the canyon going by with all the care of some gnat thinking about celestial physics. The sting in his eyes mirrored the hardness in his throat. The silence in the van continued until they came to the first light in Grants Pass.

With little consideration, Stone asked what he thought was a throwaway question. "What is between here and Portland that isn't the freeway?"

The kid thought about it for a few minutes as he turned right and drove toward the freeway on-ramp. "It's pretty much a consistent eighty or so miles from the I-5 to the coast. In some places, there are back roads winding through the terrain. Lots of choke points, but also, lots of small clusters of locals. The total fly over is just short of three-hundred miles."

Stone smiled at the kind of sit-rep he would have gotten in the last thirty-eight years when he was in a country that was hostile. The kid was rereading the area he grew up in to match what he knew Stone would understand.

"Do you have any maps?"

"No, but I have an auto club membership, and we can stop off and get you everything you would want and then some." The kid glanced over and flashed the kind of smart-assed smile Stone had seen in the Sandbox.

"Topos with lays and quads marked out?" Stone smirked back, asking about the topographic maps that were marked up with all the information a military maneuver would need.

"Hooyah." The kid laughed. "They even have the A&W drive-ins marked in root beer colors." He looked over at Stone with a more serious face. "You were thinking about a foray?"

Stone scanned the valley as Medford spread out before them. "Thinking about it." Then he looked back over at the young man. "I already know what the freeway looks like. I thought I'd see what the other part looks like. Maybe even engage the natives."

"I could highlight—"

"Not what I was thinking," Stone snapped and added gently, "but I know you meant well."

As they pulled into the auto club's parking lot, Stone finished his thought. "I think I need to slow down and just be with myself for a little while, think about where I go from here... I mean, I can't just wander around from day to day like a bum."

They slipped out of the van, and as Spuds adjusted his legs, he looked up at Stone through the cab. "I understand. I know in my mind and heart why I came home, and that I am home... but somehow..." the kid drifted off.

Closing the door, Stone said quietly, more to himself, "I understand kid. I really do. And I think your uncle understood that too."

A while later, as they stood next to Stone's rental, Stone continued. "You asked me if I'm going to be okay, but let me ask you the same thing."

The shrugged shoulder told Stone more than words could have conveyed. Spuds looked at his legs that did not kick at the dirt uncontrollably as his own feet did for so many years. He drew his lips in, looked up then off to one side at nothing, and anything which was not Stone—the gunnery sergeant who could read any grunt in the company as if they were the Sunday comics.

Finally facing his reality, he met Stone's gaze. "I haven't really had any chance to think about it since I got home and was dealing with Unc. My guess is that I'm getting better by not dealing with it all, but then... maybe I'm not."

"So what are you going to do now?" Stone opened the trunk and placed his go-bag into the rental's trunk. Closing the lid, he continued. "Your uncle is no longer the issue. So what does Spuds do for Spuds now?"

"Right now," he looked at the ground between his shoes, "I think I need to be the glue that holds my mom together. This morning, I saw that she had laid out the poles for the teepee near the burial, so I guess we will be sleeping out there until at least fall."

"I didn't know you were Indian."

"Part, well, mom is. I don't know how much, and that makes me even less." Spuds ran his fingers through his blond hair. "Sometime back when I was a kid, we built the teepee. Unc had split a whole bunch of hides from deer he had taken, and so we made a real one. More summers than I can remember, we slept in the teepee. It became more of a family bonding and ritual kind of thing with no TV, no radio, and no phone... just us. I guess that is why we're such a tight family."

The gunny nodded "So, now it will be for healing."

"I guess so." The kid looked up, squinting into the sun as he faced Stone. "And maybe this is what I need to finally feel like I'm home."

Stone thought about the power of a simple touchstone, then reached out his hand to shake goodbye.

Spuds looked at the hand and chuckled. "Dude, when you were my superior, I saluted you, but now we're equals and both civilians. Plus, this is Oregon..." He stepped the small step and hugged the larger man.

The younger guy could feel the older man stiffen, but he didn't let go. Instead, he quietly reassured, "It's just the way it is, dude, so you better get used to it."

They broke away, and Stone stumbled for a way to address the subject or avoid it. He chose a safer path, for him. "You... uh, we have spent over four days together, and you have not talked about cooking food, not even once. What gives? Are you giving up on eating good food?"

Spuds just laughed. "In the Sand, there wasn't anything worth eating, much less talking about. Here, we eat good food every night. When I got home, mom threw up her hands and said 'I'm glad you're home, I'm starved.' I've been cooking ever since. Even Unc would come into the house for dinner."

"So why don't you get a job as a cook? You can stand on those for a whole shift, can't you?"

"I don't know." He looked at the aluminum tubes. "I guess I should try to stand around all day for a few weeks, but then, where to get work? The unemployment down here is close to twenty-some percent, and for returning vets it is almost a solid one-hundred percent."

"Ouch."

"Yeah."

They shook hands. "Thanks for coming, Gunny. It means a lot that you were here."

"Kid, looking back, I wouldn't have missed a second of it and don't roll up the welcome mat just yet. I will come back sometime," he said as he slid into the car.

"Don't stay away too long. Some of the best fishing is in this part of the country, and I know at least seventy-three great ways to cook salmon."

Stone started the car, laughing. "You've got a deal."

The days were warm, and the locals a mix of temperatures. The five nights sleeping in the car had led him to a small roadside motel of originally eight rooms, but two being taken over by an owner's obsession with quilting. She had seemed startled when Stone walked in the door, and she explained the summer season was over, but the hunters were not due for another week. She sized him up and said up-front, "The room is forty dollars, unless you want to drive up the road before the liquor store closes and get a girl a pint of Jack, then the room is just a twenty in cash."

Stone nursed his small glass of Jack, and enjoyed the company. LaLonnie had lived in the area all of her sixty-eight years and knew more history, and where all the bones were buried, than most teachers or politicians. She carried no animosity toward a soul, her only religion being her faith in the distiller back east, but her heart broke from the region's condition. Once robust with King Timber, southwest Oregon now stood broken by cruel poverty. Not only the VA ignored the population of vets, it was the economy beating on people who could least afford it, and they had nowhere else to go. It's the dust bowl all over, but a soul doesn't have to even move or travel to become part of it.

The early morning light still filtered weakly through the trees as the sound of distant trumpets made Stone stand back up from climbing into his rental car. He had not thought about Ski in the past week of silence. He watched what had been a Model A, before its back end was chopped to accommodate a truck bed, rattle down the road. *Dust bowl all over,* Stone thought as he fished the phone out of his pocket.

From Ski:
How are you doing?
How was the Black Hog Inn last night?

Stone thought about the first question, ignoring the second, *how was he doing?* He looked about him in the tall stands of fir trees, an old run-down motel, a life battered woman with a happy smile for any and all, an open-ended rental car, and no idea which way he was going to turn once he drove to the end of the parking lot.

From Stone:
Adrift

He laid the phone on the seat beside him as he started

the car and watched the tiny edge of frosting wash away with the first blast of the defroster. As he eased the car away from the cabin, LaLonnie came out of the office and padded barefooted to the edge of the concrete apron.

"After last night, I kind of figured you for an early riser." Her smile appeared infectious, but it had a special glow this morning for Stone. She held out the twenty he had paid her for the room. "You must have dropped this last night." Her eyes twinkled as the laugh lines appeared to double the number of her chins. "Most folks never even give you more than the time of day when they stay here. Last night, sitting with you was worth a year of vacation." Shoving the twenty into the window, she continued. "I don't know if you were really interested in my prattling on, or just deaf and sleeping with your eyes open like my Chet used to do before he turned in for the final sleep. But this morning, I woke up the rooster and cleaned the office before the sun even hit the tips of the Dougs."

Stone put his hand up to stop the offered bill and gently pushed it back. "I was listening to every word. I now know more about this state than I know about the other forty-nine combined." Slowly and gently, he closed his hand around her hand and the bill and moved it back out the window. "Consider it a down payment on a reservation in the future. I think I have to come back and get more education about these parts, and the company is enjoyable, too."

She blushed, but the hand only hesitated a moment before the bill was secreted away in some hidden pocket in the muumuu that had seen better days. Stone did not notice the other twenty that fell softly onto his lap. "You're a kind man, Stone, and you are welcome here any day or night.

I'd even throw a couple of hunters out of here to make room for you."

He smiled. "I might just have to help you do that."

She laughed. "I'd let you, too." Snapping her fingers, she wagged her finger at him. "I know y'all will be needin' a good breakfast." Pointing down the highway to the right toward the coast, she directed, "Twelve miles, you can't miss it, Mom and Pop's. Tell Molly that LaLonnie sent ya. If I had a daughter, she's what I would have wanted her to turn out like. Say hi to Hank and Ruby, too." She stood up and patted the top of the car.

"Thank you, LaLonnie. You've been the best, and I'll come back sometime. I promise."

Stone eased out onto the empty rural two-lane highway—a gray path cutting through the deep forest of tall trees that reached up and almost met over the road, well over a hundred feet in the air. The fresh breeze reminded Stone that summer was gone in these parts and would be replaced soon by rain and maybe snow. He glanced down at the phone as he tapped the face to see the text message.

From Ski:
That is what civilians call a vacation
Head 4 coast
Go north

Stone pulled off to the side of the road. As the gunny scooped up the phone, he chuckled, and looked in the rearview mirror as he picked up the folded twenty from his lap.

BAER CHARLTON

From Stone:
Where have you been?
The horns blew.

From Ski:
On vacation
Admiral style
Talk soon

STONEHEART

BAER CHARLTON

13

'Welcome to Fall, Oregon' the sign read. The next, more official one read, *'Fall, Pop 248'*, or at least with the bullet holes Stone thought that's what it spelled out. Stone was also thinking is should read *'Welcome to the home of people who don't respect anything they can shoot and have more guns than teeth'*. He crunched the car onto the gravel parking lot of the Mom & Pop's EAT. He would have thought that the name *Fall* was strange for a community, but he had been studying the maps, and compared with some of the other names like Drain, Sink, Boring, Butt, Skid and No, it was simply poetic.

The three trucks in the parking lot contained about nine dogs between them. One ruled as the winner with five of those dogs. Stone knew from LaLonnie that all the trucks should have as many chainsaws as dogs, as well as other logging equipment; except the five local mills now sat shuttered or long gone. The hills and forest were hurting for any income that they could obtain. None of the dogs looked like they were good for hunting and most had the serious looks of guard dogs. Stone did not think the property they guarded had anything to do with the word *legal* attached to it, and it was none of his business. Besides, the smell of home baked biscuits brought back much better memories than any thoughts of trying to figure out the source of money for the owners of three battered trucks.

The floorboards of the diner revealed the same Douglas fir of the front porch. The only difference being the inside floor was cleaner, less worn and boasted many coats of wax. The walls, just slightly lighter, glowed from the same wood. The ceiling, Stone noticed, was sheet-rocked or plastered, depending on when the building was constructed. The other customers sat quietly in three separated booths, frozen in a tableau of conversations, and stopped mid-sentence. Nine pair of eyes watching Stone's every move.

"Hi, welcome to Mom and Dad's Café," the cheery voice took Stone by surprise as the young woman approached from behind him as he sat down at the counter. The flat tone in the delivery was explained as the young woman with Down's syndrome turned to face Stone as he sat. "Would you like coffee? It's the best in four counties." Her eyes twinkled and matched her smile.

Turning over the cup on the counter to receive the best coffee the four counties had to offer, he smiled back. "Why yes, please."

As she poured the coffee with focused intent, and Stone studied her face. "You must be Molly."

The coffee hesitated as the young woman looked up at Stone, then finished. She placed the coffee pot on the counter. "Yes. Yes, I am." Her face almost frowned as she thought hard. "Do I know you?"

Stone smiled, he hoped in what would pass for kindly. "No. No, you don't. But I stayed at LaLonnie's place last night, and she said to say hi."

The smile snapped back to the beaming face. "I love my aunt LaLonnie. She's not a real aunt, but I like to call her that because I don't have any real aunts."

"She would make a great aunt to have, and I think she loves you like a niece, too."

Shifting mental gears, which seemed to have a random control, Molly asked, "Do I need to know you, or are you just passing through?"

A thought flashed through his head of a husky gal in a big bus RV—*what would Rusty say?* The thought and feeling of a new friend becoming so special, it made him laugh. Maybe just a little more than the occasion may have called for, but the young woman's surprised look at him laughing made him laugh all the harder. To cover any misunderstandings, Stone stuck out his large paw of a hand. "Hi, Molly, I'm really glad I got to meet you. My name is Stone, just like the rock, but I hope not as hard."

She took his hand, and her smile grew. Stone noticed the freckles that hid under her tan skin and her dark hair. The glitter sparkled in her eyes of innocence. As she shook his hand, she leaned in to Stone and conspiratorially whispered, "You have a nice smile. You shouldn't hide it so much under that burn stuff."

Taken back by her openness, he laughed again. "I'll try to remember that, Molly." It is only doctors and children that are not afraid to comment on his face or other people's abnormalities. Now add a cute young woman in Southern Oregon. *What is my world coming to?* Stone thought. It was going to take some time getting used to this *civilian* world.

"Hey, Molls," one of the loggers across the room called. "Our coffee mugs have holes in the bottom."

Molly winked a conspiratorial grin at Stone as she called, but without turning around, "Stick a finger in it, Harold, you too, Alex," stopping the other man in mid-open mouth. Turning to attend to the now-chastised men, she advised a chuckling Stone. "Mom baked the biscuits at five this morning. The sausage gravy grew up three miles from here, and the eggs are free-range natural from about a half mile away. Just stay clear of the picante sauce because it's from New York City." Changing out the coffee pots for a full, she turned to the giggling men. "Hold your pants on boys. I have heaven in my hand." Stone was sure the teasing was a nonstop merry-go-round with Molly and the men, similar to the pokes and jibes among a company of men. Growing up, Stone had no memories of even light teasing in his home life. It had not been tolerated.

A while later, as he mopped up the last of the gravy, he heard, "How was your breakfast?" Stone looked right and into the face two seats down—the woman's hair was a tumble of curls pulled loosely up into a large bun at the crest of her head, with a dusting of what looked like flour caked in the front where a hardworking arm had wiped a brow. The face was tired, but as warm as the soft seasonal light filtering through the tall trees of the area outside. "Were the biscuits still soft this late in the morning?"

Stone thought about the teasing nature of Molly, and guessed the same held true for the rest of the family. "Actually, the whole meal was awful." He waited for the slow count of three. "I had to work hard to hide the evidence." He smiled as her shocked face broke into a quick smile and a laugh to match his.

"Well, then, certainly remind me next time to make your job harder and serve you an extra-large Logger's Load. We don't want to go easy on you." She laughed as she sipped from her coffee mug. Stone smiled and sipped his coffee, too.

The foursome of forest-roughened workers gathered their things from the far corner booth and nodded at or patted the woman on the shoulder as they filed past. "Great breakfast as usual, Ruby." The oldest patted and rubbed her shoulder and then nodded at Stone.

"Thanks, Trent. You know it means a lot to hear that coming from you." As she turned her head to address her husband in the kitchen pass-through, "Cookie, once again you forgot to put enough poison in Trent's eggs." The cook and husband just smiled and waved a friendly hand at their longtime friend. She smiled and confided in Stone, "I dated Trent all four years of high school, even went to all of the dances with him, but I came home from the Senior Prom with Hank. We walked down the graduation aisle together in a class of fourteen students, and seven years later, we walked down the aisle again for the last time. Six months later, Molly was born."

Stone looked over where the men were paying. Molly was carefully counting the change back. Softly there was a mixed count of numbers from one of the men. "Seventeen… four… twenty-one… twelve—" which caused Molly to stop, surround all the change by banging her arms down on the counter inside a curved closed wall. Through theatrically gritted teeth, she cursed softly, "Dammit all, Trent, stop that." Then the men started chuckling as she drew the change back and started over. She lowered her head to hide her own quiet smile and chuckle, another facet of the game of teasing.

Turning to her mother with a half-smile, Stone asked, "All the time?"

"Oh, just about every day for the last ten years. Trent is her godfather and surrogate uncle. She's the daughter he could never have."

"You know to the day when it started?"

"Well, not exactly but just about, shortly after her sixteenth birthday." Ruby watched her daughter for a few minutes with a softening in her eyes, before turning back toward Stone. "We made a huge mistake, but we thought we were doing the best thing for her." She picked up a fork and used it to scratch at the back of her head under the bun. "We sent her off to a school for children with Down's Syndrome. The school was in Pennsylvania. She hated it, but we didn't know because she never told us. A couple of days after she turned sixteen, she packed her bag, left the school and got on the bus. Nobody had ever told her how. She had figured it out all by herself.

"Three days later, the school finally figured out that she was missing. They were afraid something bad happened and had the local cops out searching for her. On the sixth day, just before the lunch rush, on a day our only waitress was down with the flu, Molly walked through the door. She walked into the kitchen and kissed her father, went to the lockers, got out an apron and went to work like every summer since she was six."

"Just like that?"

Ruby nodded. "Just like that, pouring coffee and getting waters, just like nothing was out of the ordinary. I was in the back office, and the school finally got the balls to call the crazy woman way out in the Wild West. As I'm listening to this ineffectual mealy-mouthed man stumble about explaining how they had misplaced my daughter, I'm watching her move through the diner as if she had fifty years of running the show under her apron.

"Finally I stopped the whining man and told him flat... well, seeing how you misplaced my child, I will be watching the mail for your check refunding all of my tuition I trusted you with."

Stone laughed. "What did he say?"

Ruby laughed with a sinister hitch. "He asked, 'Don't you care about your daughter?' But, I replied that I needed the money more right then and that I expected him to have it in my hands within seven days, or I would start writing letters to every Down's syndrome society, organization, or group that I could. I also told him I would be filling my Senator in on this event over Sunday supper. The childless Senator, who just happens to love our daughter like a favorite niece and taught her how to swim and fish."

"And the Senator's take on this event?"

"Oh, yeah, right. Like someone in the government really cares about us out here in the forest fire country? Our representatives in Salem barely know we exist, much less back in Washington. Nah, things never came to that. They refunded us for all ten years of her schooling. They lost my baby, and I never saw fit to let them know she was here. They were just happy that I never called again. But there are those mornings I get an evil mean-streak in me and reach for the phone, but I have never dialed. But it does put a smile on my face for a few days."

Stone looked at the young woman making change.

"And so you never sent her away again."

"Have you gone into a fast-food chain lately? They only give you the change the machine tells them to do. They don't know why you get such and such amount; just that the machine told them to give you so much. The day she came back, I walked out of the office to find her making change. Even I don't count the change back. That night Hank and I counted the draw, and it was three cents off. I made change during breakfast. Most days, I could be a buck or ten up or down, we didn't care, it all works out. I haven't made change since, and her drawer is always to the penny, always, even with Trent tormenting her, bless his cold hard little pea-picking heart."

She startled from watching her daughter. "Oh my gosh, your cup has a hole in it," rising from the counter. "Let me get you some more coffee."

Stone raised his napkin, dabbed at his mouth, and standing up, cautioned, "No ma'am, I need to be getting down the road. But I can guarantee you this—I will be back for more of those biscuits and gravy to wash down with your great coffee." Pulling a folded twenty from his front pocket, he laid it on the counter. "I don't need to have change counted back, I got a lot more out of this visit than I bargained for when I took LaLonnie's advice and stopped."

"Ah, so you're her new knight in shining armor. If I had known your name was Stone, I wouldn't have let you even reach for your wallet."

"It was the twenty LaLonnie wouldn't let me pay for the room with. She distracted me with another one while she dropped this one in my lap. Consider it a case of good will going around. If you want, you can buy her the next bottle," pointing over his shoulder at Molly gliding through the tables. "But now I can see why she has such a tender spot for Molly."

Ruby took his hand and held it in a slow warm shake. "Well, Mr. Stone, we will look forward to your return, and I might just let you pay for your meal again... or not."

Distant trumpets sounded as he passed through the rough-hewn door out into the parking lot. Stone fished the phone from his pocket.

From Ski:
Are you on the coast?

Stone poked at the phone, and then got in the rental car.

From Stone:
I'm getting there. I'm retired, you know.

From Ski:
Not today

Pushy, Stone thought, as he turned right onto the highway among the tall pines.

BAER CHARLTON

14

The older man, standing with a cane on the side of the road, looked angrily at the car that had betrayed him. The shredded tire that he had driven on, instead of stopping, smelt in accusation. The man hit his cane against the shreds of tire as he remembered having thought he could make it home and away from the busybodies from the small town. Success had not even been close.

The green sedan eased over onto the shoulder with the crunching of tires on gravel and leftover sand mixed with some rock salt. The old man watched as the engine shuddered to a stop and the forest quiet resumed its cacophony of birdcalls with a general forest white noise. The door creaked only slightly with a newer car complaint as the man with the brush cut hair stepped onto the road and stood.

Stone stood behind the door as a shield against an unknown situation as he asked, "Do you need some help?" His eyes were busy sizing up the car with a lone person on the side of a road. The tall green forest had long disappeared from his mind's eye, replaced by intense heat and tan sand. His eyes and brain were on two different channels.

"I guess I ran over a nail or something. I tried to limp it home but…"

Stone's brain was processing words, but not the content. The message was in a language the gunny knew he should understand, but the mind told him that it was not the right language for the situation. His hearing became a slow incoming tide of white static. The static surged to fill his hearing with an accompanying drum of his heartbeat. Then it washed away leaving the birds twittering in the tall pines and a man looking at him and Stone unsure of which existed as real.

The man took a step in his direction. "Are you alright?" He leaned a bit more toward his cane and rolled his hip to lift and move the leg forward in another step.

Stone shook his head slightly and stepped from behind the door as he closed it out of the way. Walking toward the man, Stone had trouble getting back to the scene in front of him instead of the vision of two years before. Stone apologized, "No, no, I'm fine. Just a little touch of vertigo or something." Nodding toward the lame car, he continued. "Looks like you could use a little muscle on a tire iron. Do you have a spare?"

The man took in the burned face and the military cadence of Stone's walk. Deciding it was not his business, he turned toward the car. "In the trunk, if you don't mind. I can pay you."

Stone stopped as his hand touched the trunk lid of the large luxury car. Looking down the highway then back at the man for a moment silently, and then asking, "Do you find you have to pay everyone to help you?"

The man mentally chewed on the question. Finally, he admitted, "Yeah, well, when you're the richest man in the parts, it seems to go with the territory."

Stone studied him and figured there was no sarcasm in the man's words. Then he paused, looking up the highway as if waiting for an answer that might come around the bend in the road. With no answer, he opened the trunk and started taking out the spare tire. "That's a sad commentary on either the people around here, or you... Either way, it's a sad thing to say."

The man watched silently as Stone replaced the tire that was little more than a shred or three on the rim. Stone fingered the lack of remaining tire and took it as evidence of the man's opinion of himself and the people in the area. A lot can be ascertained about a man standing on the side of the road with no cell phone, a broken down car, and that nobody had stopped to ask him if he could use some help.

Closing the trunk and dusting his hands together, Stone turned to the man. "You can't drive very far on that tire. It's little more than a half-baked muffin of used rubber. You need to get a new tire and stop driving them to the metal."

The man stuck his hand out. "Thank you for your kindness." As they shook, he added, "The name is Mynhoffer, Bernard... Bernie Mynhoffer."

"Stone."

"Just Stone, like Cher and that other little girl?"

"It used to be Gunnery Sergeant Stone, but now... I guess it's just Stone." He studied the man's face for a pause. "Percival."

Bernie's eyebrow raised a fraction of an inch. "As in the Holy Grail... or as cruel as kids can be, Percy." Stone nodded. "Yes, I see... Stone is a fine name, so Stone it is." They finished shaking hands. "Are you just passing through, Stone, or have you moved to our slice of heaven?"

Looking about at the forest, Stone shrugged. "Just passing through on my way back to Portland."

"The interstate is faster."

"Probably, but definitely not as interesting, Bernie, and it lacks any chances to be a knight in shining armor," He smiled at the shared information. "Besides, I believe the ocean is this way," as he pointed up the highway.

The older man shrugged and frowned to one side of his face. "And a lot of traffic, and people."

Stone laughed. "I think they kind of go together."

With a back wave of his right hand, he inserted, "You can have my share of both of them."

"Well, I seem to be headed to a meeting out on the coast, and maybe that person will be cute and not quite as grumpy," Stone teased.

"Hmm, good luck on that one," the man grumped with a smile.

"Oh, they're around if you look. Maybe you should go get yourself a nice lunch down at the diner," pushing his thumb back down the highway.

The man's eyes widened as his face darkened. "Mom and Pop's? Not flipping likely in my lifetime." He turned and opened his door as he more fell into his seat than a stepped. "Thanks again, Stone," he snapped as he slammed the door and started the car. Putting it in gear, he redistributed much of the gravel from the shoulder onto the shoes of a stunned Stone.

Stone's face darkened as he spoke to the empty road, "There has to be a story behind that much anger." Shrugging his shoulders, he fished out the trumpeting phone.

166

From Ski:
What are you doing?
You've been stopped in the
middle of nowhere for an hour.

Stone thought about it, and tossed the phone back on the seat while climbing into the rental car, feeling his own form of grumpy as he thought, *nosey busybody.*

The drive almost made up for the dark mood brewing off in Stone's distant mind. Somehow, he felt the old feeling that there was an ambush around the turn in the trail, or down the path and out into the opening. Gradually, the green and scent of forest worked its magic as there were no openings, no ambushes, not even another nosey lieutenant following his every little movement.

The ocean he had smelled for the last few miles exploded into view as he broke out of the marine forest, and only the windshield and a few cars on the coastal highway obstructed his view. The diamond pavé strewn across the undulating deep blue sea, glittered under the early afternoon sun and reminded Stone of the sprinkles on the top of a birthday cupcake at some child's party. The sound of a child screaming with excitement reinforced the illusion as he rolled to the stop sign.

The screaming wail was joined by another cry and then another as the seagulls circled the fishermen casting into the surf. One pulled heavily on the thick rod as he paused the reeling, and then pointing the rod out to sea, reeled in the line like a whirling dervish. Stone sat and watched the two fishermen, one calmly watching the other feverishly working the rod and line. The two were

167

surrounded by the dispassionate chaos of nature. A calm sea surged a flat mountain of water to wash around their boots in foamy life-packed wavelets. With barely moving wings, the gulls wheeled overhead, riding up the wash of displaced air at the edge of the surf. Stone knew the seemingly unmoving sand became enriched in a constantly moving biological mass. This mass was equal to, or even greater than, all the people standing or walking along the stretch of beach. Everything within the sweep of Stone's vision was both agitated and calmed by the yin and yang of life. It was almost hard to believe that there could be so much going on in such a peaceful scene.

As Stone looked left and turned right onto the coastal highway, he glanced one last time at the anglers. The one, now holding a fish that seemed as long as his forearm, was animated as he held the fish out for the other to see. The picture of camaraderie on a lazy afternoon in the surf and sun, Stone hoped his mind would save this snapshot. *Maybe I should try fishing someday.* The rental car surged north along the highway as he mashed a bit hard on the pedal. He knew if he were to take up fishing, he would have to slow down long enough to put down some roots, something that had eluded him for almost fifty-eight years.

The sound of trumpets interrupted his thoughts. They sounded much louder than usual and Stone looked around, expecting to see a band along the highway. Then seeing the lit screen on the phone, he picked it up.

From Ski:
6 miles — on left — red building

Stone dropped the phone back onto the seat. *Six miles*

from what, Stone thought, and a red building tells him nothing. She must be having one of those paper-pusher days where it's more fun to screw with the enlisted than doing real work like the rear echelon pussies in Vietnam. They would spend their days down at the local café sipping brews and then rushing back to the office. To justify their existence, they would call in a *sortie,* which would have the grunts humping through the jungle all night, hunting Charlie in a place that even Charlie would not go. *Desk weenies, they're all alike.*

A scattering of buildings whipped by as Stone drove a little fast through the thirty-five mile-per-hour zone. A siren and lights were not Stone's awakening, but the phone actually ringing was. Now fully enmeshed in his emotional memories, he thumbed the phone's screen and growled into the phone.

"What?"

The calm male voice almost had an edge of laughter to it as it explained the facts of life. "I don't care what kind of day you think you are having, but a state trooper who just left here, watched you blow through his town like you were a green fire truck. I would suggest that you calm down, turn around, and get your mangled ass back here to the crab shack before he catches up to you. I may be able to talk him down off his high horse and save you a ticket, Gunny."

Stone realized he was about to talk into a now dead phone. Placing it back on the seat, he slowed and made a U-turn on the highway. A couple of miles back, the trooper passed him like a wraith trying to catch a soul fleeing from hell. It was an outside chance he had not realized there had been only one green car on the highway that day.

Stone took his chances and turned in toward a building, which gave the impression of more weather-beaten rust than red. The blob of a sign with three intact legs, two half legs, and a few places where there might have been some legs at one time or another, could be the crab shack the admiral had referred to.

Stone was the only car in the parking lot, except an old beat-up truck. Its running condition was questionable, but it was parked near the back door. Looking about as he stood up from the car, Stone confirmed no other cars. The hill, covered by only some kind of ice plant or ivy, fell off to the boulder-strewn beach below.

"We're in here, Gunny," the little girl voice that did not fit her rank called, and Stone spun around his body. In the doorway stood a little girl in jeans, tennis shoes, and a sweatshirt from Annapolis. Stone waved, and she retreated. The glint of silver lieutenant's bars on the collar of her sweatshirt had not escaped his notice.

Gently closing the car door, Stone commented to no one, "I'll be go to hell. She's a full fucking LT now." He snickered to himself, but *she still looks only thirteen*. He was still shaking his head as he stepped through the door.

The admiral dressed in no military except for the flight jacket hanging on the coat hooks next to a jean jacket with appliquéd letters, which spelled the same color they were made from, pink. Stone paused for a second, and then decided he did not need to know the reasoning behind such an anomalous declaration. Nevertheless, he smiled at the incongruous railroad tracks of the silver bars on the collar.

"I was looking for your car." Stone slid into the other side of the booth, until he realized that the side was set for two, and the lieutenant stood looking at him. He rose back up and let the little girl in first. "Sorry, sir."

She looked back at him and smiled with an impish grin. "We tried to get one of the chow hall tables to make you feel more at home, but they said we needed at least a party of forty." She ignored his acknowledgement of her new rank.

Stone studied her for almost a full minute before realizing what a grumpy ass he was being, and he started to laugh. He looked at the amused admiral. "She keeps you on your toes much?"

The man put down the coffee mug he had been manhandling Navy style with two protective hands. Smiling, he burped a soft half chuckle. "You have no idea." He looked for confirmation from his assistant. "She's in my life 24/7. I wake up in the middle of the ocean in a cold sweat. I check my phone for a message, then I will step down into the bridge where someone will inevitably hand me a note from her."

BAER CHARLTON

15

Sliding into the booth next to the lieutenant, Stone thought about the whole idea of randomly meeting the other two on the wrong coast in the middle of nowhere. "Okay, so you've tracked me everywhere I go. You know where I sleep and whom I sleep with, what I eat. Hell, she probably knows whether I just use the urinal or—"

The admiral held up his hand as he leaned back. "I have it from a higher pay grade than you, or I, that she cannot do such things." He leaned forward and gave a glaring look at the small girl of a woman. *"Yet."*

Putting her hands up in the football sign for time-out, she injected, "And just for the record here, I do not know if you are sleeping with someone or not. It's not like I have cameras everywhere. It's just a GPS thing."

Stone squinted with his left eye as he looked to his right. "Just a GPS thing?"

She squirmed slightly. "Okay, a very real-time state of the art GPS thing."

The admiral leaned back with a satisfied open-mouthed grin. "Ah," with a soft chuckle, "you put him on the same leash you have me on." His right index finger hovering in the air seemed to pin her to the back of the booth. The silent conversation between the two with just their eyes turned into an amazing thing for Stone to watch.

"So... I'm to guess that..."

The admiral lowered his eyelids for a last comment directed at his subordinate, then looked over at Stone. "Basically, we are more brothers than even we knew." He looked back at the lieutenant. "We will have a talk, but pretty much, you have a quasi-niece that is quite literally looking over your shoulder."

A young Eurasian woman, wearing a long black apron, sauntered over to the table with the kind of attitude slouch, which Stone was still trying to get used to seeing stateside. He suppressed his urge to start barking commands to stand up straight. Cracking her gum, she slowed to a stop as she spoke. "I take it that this is the person you've been waiting for?"

The redheaded aide-de-camp jumped in before either of the men could take control. "Yes, miss," pointing toward Stone, "he'll need coffee with cream, so you may as well just bring a carafe," as she rose slightly to peek at the admiral's mostly empty mug, "and for lunch, we may as well have the family platter."

The girl just stared at the woman who was barely her senior. "You realize the family platter is enough food to feed six people," stating the obvious with complete disdain.

"Obviously, you have never tried to feed a marine who left half his guts in Vietnam, another half in Somalia, and even more in Grenada. it's like the food never gets to all of the parts. So, if we have to order more, we'll let you know." Ski ignored the server's attitude. "Oh, and I almost forgot, do you have an apple pie for desert? He gets really grumpy when there is no apple pie for desert." Stone just looked at the little cherubic face as she ran intellectual tractor trails all over the poor waitress.

The waitress could not put her finger on what was wrong with what she had just heard. However, the server knew she had one order for the family platter. "No, ma'am. We don't have any deserts here at the shack, but if you are all headed north, you can get some pie at the Safeway in Lincoln City." Turning to Stone as if he were a potential ax murderer, she added, "I'll get you that pot of coffee right away, sir."

Stone pointed at the admiral and the lieutenant. "They are the sirs. I work for a living."

The waitress gave him a double take and left, scratching her pencil in her long black ponytail, which bounced about her tiny peanut butt. The admiral hid his face in his hands. Only his shaking shoulders revealed his mirth. Stone closed one eye and looked hard at the lieutenant. "Your math, for such a smart little girl, leaves a lot to be desired."

The lieutenant looked back at her own mug, pulling the string on the tea bag up and down as she pouted. "She deserved it."

Stone looked at the admiral.

As the waitress rushed back with the carafe and a clean mug, the admiral looked at the fresh coffee in his mug. He finally looked up first at Ski and then at Stone. "It all goes back to our brothers and Hog Ridge. Our brothers shared hooch with the company clown and yeoman. This yeoman was one of the few who survived that week. After several years of rehab and settling back into civilian life, that man married a nurse he had met at the local VA.

Twenty-six years later, we have their bouncing baby girl in our midst. And, if you haven't noticed, she has great talent for all things electronic and computer, like her father."

Stone sipped on his coffee. "So, like taking in your brother's family, you collected the rest of the company's family, as well?"

"I like to think of it more as making my own family… my way."

"Which leads me to the question," as Stone put down his mug, "why didn't you ever get married and make a family of your own?"

The lieutenant looked down at her mug, as the admiral squirmed, barely perceptible. "After I moved my brother's girlfriend and their twins in with me, I didn't need any more of a family." His finger slowly traced around the rim of his mug, clearly uncomfortable with the direct question. "Becky was my girl at any function where I needed an escort or spouse." The lieutenant seemed to shrink deeper into the corner, a fly on the wall who did not want to be there.

"But that is not the question, is it?"

The admiral looked at Stone in the same meaningful blank stare as someone swearing an oath in a court of law. "That is the only question I am prepared to allow to be asked at this time." The man bit his lip, and then softened as he looked at the other half of his team. "Maybe someday after I retire, we can sit around a backyard, pet the dog, and talk some more. But for right now, I'm a very busy man, and I have the family I want, and they know they are my family because I love them and want them there."

Stone held the look then nodded as he looked at Ski who was still watching the mug in front of her. "So you're family, too." Ski nodded, leaned back, and with her lips pulling in and out of her teeth, she looked at Stone with a slightly defiant look. Stone finally nodded. "Well, I guess it's good to know it's family that has my back." Stone mirrored the same bashful smile, which gently grew across her face.

Stone snapped his fingers. "Which reminds me... family, I gave you a mission."

Ski sat up, now in her element. "I looked for the years bracketing what you gave me for a name of Talbot, spelled six different ways from the nine states surrounding Kentucky. There was not a single Navy Seal with a last name of Talbot, separated, or attached. There was a Thomson, but he died of wounds received in battle five days after being shipped stateside."

"Seal? Where did you get that he was a Navy Seal?"

"That's what you said, a Seal named Talbot."

Stone thought a moment and let his face fall into his left palm. Rising, he looked at the Lieutenant, and he breathed a sign of exasperation. "I said, 'Osiel, O-S-I-E-L. That is his first name—it's just pronounced like it was the three letters O-C-L.'"

"Osiel got it. I'll get on it later today."

The admiral cleared his throat. "We're on vacation."

She looked at him and laughed. "Right, and we're on a 989 foot-long cruise ship, and that's a rental car parked across the street."

Stone looked through the windows and realized that across the street and on a small rise sat a Navy Seahorse helicopter. The things you are so used to seeing, are the things that can end up sitting right in front of you, unseen. He silently chuckled. *Of course, that's where they parked the... um, car.*

"One family platter for a family of... oh," the large black man's soft yet booming voice drizzled off to almost a whisper, "three."

The admiral pointed at the respective men. "Stone, I'd like you to meet Chief Dickens. More commonly known as The Chief Dick and we aren't talking about what he may have tried in port." His eyelids lowered and his eyes rolled out to the side. "You two are in the same fraternity. He would have been a master chief except for the two or three runs at being a chief got in the way. Chief, Gunnery Sergeant Stone."

The man laid down the oversized platter of fries, along with what looked more like tempura than the usual breaded and deep-fried fish. Extending his beefy hand, he greeted with, "Great to know you, Gunny, and if I knew there were three of you, especially a jarhead, I would have cooked double."

Ski muttered at her tea, "I tried to tell the twit that you have working for you." Shoes from both sides nudged her toes.

Stone shook his hand as he noticed the pair of dragons tattooed on the insides of his arms. "No problem, Chief, I don't eat like the young guys do." He pointed to the tattoos. "I take it you're a shellback?"

Pulling a chair over, the man sat unasked at the end of the table and started in on the large platter of food. "Double Shellback and an Emerald Dragon, all time zones, all meridians, and all of the seas, and oceans, and then when there was nothing left to do, I retired."

The admiral smiled at Stone watching the retired chief helping himself to their food. "The chief here was boson's mate on three of my ships. He sometimes ate with the crew, but mostly with the officers... We never did figure out who gave him permission, but after a while, we found his outlook on running the ship to be of more value than adhering to protocol."

Wiping his hands on a napkin before lifting another piece of fish, the boats harrumphed. "Like I ever needed permission. It was you weenies that needed guidance. I just liked to eat with other people, never did like eating alone. Besides, it was a strange time of the Civil Rights." He turned to explain to Stone, "So nobody knew what to tell a little black man like myself."

The admiral shrugged and nodded with raised eyebrows and a full mouth. The lieutenant just picked choice pieces from around the edges and ate quietly. Stone figured she needed to be teased. "Jeez, Ski, do you have to talk so much?" As she blushed and looked at him from the side of her eyes, he took his first bite of the fish, and joined the silence.

The waitress, quiet as a ghost, refilled the waters and dropped a fresh coffee carafe. At some time, she silently placed a much larger mug of coffee beside the chief's right hand as she stole a small chunk of his fish and danced away from his hand aimed at her small behind. The dance of a father and daughter that were used to a more physical game of teasing, Stone thought. Nothing was escaping his review, leastwise the light crust on the even lighter fish.

Finally, Stone could not eat another bite and leaned back to mirror the admiral and lieutenant. The chief was noticeably slowing down as well, which seemed just as well with just scraps and a couple of small piles of fries remaining on the large platter. Wiping his mouth and folding the napkin to place on the table, Stone turned to the chief. "That was not the kind of fried fish I'm used to getting. I'm embarrassed to think about how many pieces I had."

Grabbing the large mug with the dragons embossed on the side, the chief rinsed his mouth with a slug of what Stone assumed was coffee. "I was stationed in Yokohama for almost seven years." He jerked his thumb behind him to indicate the taciturn young waitress. "Midgie's mom is a Eurasian product of a rape during the post war occupation in the late forties. That brought shame to her household, and nobody would date her. So, she was willing to at least talk to me, a black man. She learned English and swearing, and I learned Japanese and cooking, and we both learned about love." The man looked through the window but saw something other than the helicopter across the street. "Her folks were grateful that I brought her back here. They since have learned to love their daughter and granddaughters, and I think the mama-san even might have a soft spot for this big guy, but I know it's tough on all of them in their culture."

He looked up at Stone, who was waiting with a quiet face. The chief's eyes opened wide. "Oh, that's not... The fish, it's not cod. I get halibut only. The tourists get cod, rock cod from about a hundred miles from here, but local. But only family gets the halibut, done tempura style." He smiled with pride about his food. "You might have wondered about the shorter French fries. I use the Oregon grown reds instead of the big pithy things which go to the food chains."

"The extra care shows and tastes good, too."

Standing up, the large chief cleared the dishes onto

the large platter. "Well, back to the salt mine, and I know you folks have some business to conduct without me." He nodded to the admiral and lieutenant. "Nice to see you again, Captain, and always glad to see your daughters when you bring them along. Stone, it was nice to meet you." The chief nodded and moved off like a destroyer on a mission.

Stone watched with admiration as the big man wove deftly through the tables and chairs of the empty restaurant. Turning his attention, and a raised eyebrow toward the admiral, Stone asked, "Business?"

The admiral just opened his clasped hands in an open supplication and a shrug that mirrored on his face with semi-closed eyelids under raised eyebrows. His right index finger pointed at the now fidgeting lieutenant.

"Um, yes. First I need your credit card and your debit card." Reaching into her small leather portfolio, she extracted an envelope. Taking Stone's cards, she gave him back new ones. "These came last week. They are your new accounts. The debit is still accessed by your same pin number, but the credit card is drawn against your travel expense account with the office. It is a DOD account, so please don't abuse it. If you're going to have a wild night in Las Vegas with women and booze, please hit up an ATM. The daily limit is one-thousand dollars, so it should keep a modest leash on any wanton lifestyle you may want to whip up."

"Excuse me? What DOD account? I'm... ah, retired."

The admiral cleared his throat as he looked for salvation in his coffee mug. "Not exactly, we... um," sucking in his teeth and looking over his coffee mug at the lieutenant...

"We optioned your retirement," she continued. "You work for... um, no better word for it, The Family." She batted her eyelashes in a cute little girl fashion Stone found to be almost working. "Actually, you are attached to the admiral's office as a Post-Service Civilian Liaison between the admiral and post-service vets."

Turning on the admiral and with a slight verbal edge, asked, "What is that supposed to mean?"

"It means, I need to know what is wrong out here, and you needed a job."

"Thanks for telling me," Stone growled and gave a glare to Ski.

"Don't jump on her," the officer barked back. "It was my doing," and after screwing his mouth sideways, he admitted, "It was just her idea."

The lieutenant jumped back in as an equal partner in the fight. "Look, Gunny, I asked over a month ago if we could talk. You just blew me off. I was ready to fly to wherever you were located and explain your unique situation." She pointed at the pocket where he kept his phone. "In that little device, you have over a thousand people you served with. They go back four decades. No other consultant in DC can lay claim to this kind of access. I spent almost the entire three months when you were in Germany, calling and talking to these people. Not one of them said 'Yeah, whatever.' Only a few just hung up on me, but everyone in your phone is waiting for you to call. If you are within five hundred miles of them, they will either come to you, or expect you for Sunday dinner."

Her mouth opened and her mind caught up with her jaw, and it closed. Her arm on the table slumped. "Look, I'm sorry for the outcome of Spud's uncle, but it is that kind of thing we need to know about. It's those kinds of people who never write letters, and if they ever did, they stopped a long time ago. Nobody would listen. Well, we are…we will… but we don't want letters. We want you to go visit them."

The admiral moved his hand across the table with his index finger making a point on the table. "Look, Gunny, you went and saw that kid in Colorado, let's start there. What is going on with that situation? All we could find out is he served with you, and he has some kind of cancer, but it's not covered by the VA."

Stone hunched his shoulders as he engaged. "Bugs has cancer, or at least precancerous symptoms, caused by radiation poisoning based on long-term low to mid-level exposure. It didn't help that where he was living had a high rad count. And when he served in the Sandbox, the place he used as an office was a secured area, which was also used to store munitions."

Stone stopped to think and sip his coffee. "We never saw what was inside those crates. They came and went, and they were always under the Need-to-Know basis. What we did know was that some other sensitive materials were irradiated by the close proximity.

"When the spring came, Bugs started getting nosebleeds. He just chalked it up to hay fever, but we were nowhere near anything that resembled agriculture or gardens. A few of the other guys who used the access and quiet for either Skyping home or sleeping were also complaining about nausea or nose bleeds. But when you're worried about worse bleeding from being shot, who stops to think about a little nosebleed or even waking up with a blood trail coming from your ears?"

"Wait, from the ears?" The lieutenant had been listening with a pen in her hand. "Do you remember anyone specifically who had bled from their ears?"

"Check with Bugs, but I think his name was Taylor. The kid's wife had twins just before he deployed for the third time. He spent a lot of time just staring at the Skype monitor, and his wife held their laptop on the edge of the crib with both kids. It was kind of cute sometimes. The grunt laid there snoring with drool running out of his mouth, and the kids sounded just like him. I have no idea how his wife kept from laughing, unless she was asleep also."

"So, where are we with Mario, er, Bugs now?"

"I called the sisters, and when we could, we moved them over to Des Moines. They needed a groundskeeper to help the sisters with their five acres, and the sisters are getting a little mom and baby to watch. Most of their work is out in the city, but they are thinking about raising funds to build some apartments and a school building on the site to have their own shelter for battered women and children."

Ski pointed the back of her pen at Stone. "Yeah, about the good sisters, you know them from where? Because I spoke to everyone, and I certainly don't remember talking to any nuns."

"Do you remember talking to a nurse named Estella Yoder?"

"Right, she was working in a hospital or something in Somalia, and you were guarding the hospital."

Stone smiled. "Good try, you even got the country right. The nuns worked in a refugee camp, and ended up on the run into a small village. They found us holed up and shot up in what had been a church school of some kind. Later, they spirited us over to the mausoleum because the Muslim fighters wouldn't go near the cemetery. They saved our lives, not the other way around."

"But she never mentioned anything about being a nun."

"And if you ever see Sister Mary Margaret run a marathon, you would never know that she was a nun either. It took me almost three weeks to realize that she hadn't been a nun when they saved us, she was the young girl who kept holding the bowl of water when they washed us and redressed our bandages." Stone blew his lips out. "She had seen more human evil and hatred by the time she was nine than you might ever see in your lifetime."

"Let's get back to helping people." The admiral brushed his hands over his short hair. "So for now, Bugs is taken care of?"

"Yes and no. Yes, the sisters have taken them in and they will look after him, but no, he needs to be available for VA benefits. But until the military," Stone points his open hand at the admiral, "the Pentagon acknowledges some of the things like depleted uranium tank shells and other nasty things we'll have stuff like those guys who got ignored with Agent Orange."

"Which brings us to Spuds," the admiral finished.

Stone nodded. "And a whole lot of other guys who are stashed out in the country, and would rather die than travel into a population center like Portland or Medford to get the treatment they need, even if you generals and admirals would sign off on it."

Ski leaned against the booth wall. "So, do you have any answers?"

"Maybe, but what I do know after talking to a few guys that Spuds knew there is no help in the country. They don't need a whole lot. Some do, but mostly they are like Spuds. James needs to see a specialist in amputees about once or twice a year. But it's a whole day of hard driving each way, so it's a minimum of three days for a half hour doctor visit."

The admiral put down his coffee mug. "So do we have the doctor come to Spuds and any other guys? Say, he sees them at a hotel or even a local hospital?"

"Why not just let the local hospital do the work, and bill the VA? It's got to be cheaper."

Ski's right eyebrow rose as he leaned forward to see if there was any tea left. "Yes, but it also opens up the avenue for billing abuse and..."

"And guys like Unc eating their service sidearm because some weenie in DC thinks we might pay for a few guys who didn't get service." Stone leaned forward. "Boy, the chief is right, you guys are a bunch of whining weenies." He fell back with body language he knew would send the message that he washed his hands of the whole conversation.

"And we answer to even bigger whiners in Congress who never served, and never will," the admiral barked back.

"Boys..." the voice of a young mother hen stopped the tone, "Look, Gunny, that is exactly why we need you out here. It's why we need these talks. The weenies can have their focus groups, studies, and polls. What they don't have is you. You've been there, and you've met with the biggest focus group with thousands of years of personal knowledge about how the system is broken or what works.

We need both of that—nothing special, just you, being Gunny out there on your white charger, flashing a lance if you need to, or lending a hand or just an ear."

"All we need," the admiral continued, "is for you to meet us, and let us know what's going on."

"And if you can fix something along the way." Ski shrugged with a palm up. "Go for it, and just let me know ahead of time if it's going to be expensive." She smiled in a large self-satisfied smirk, first at Stone and then the admiral.

"Yeah, just remember there are three hundred million bosses that I have to answer to." A boson's whistle tweeted shrilly, and the admiral's head whipped around.

"Time's up, Captain. The guys are back at the whirlybird, and I can hear them warming the engines." The chief wound his finger in a circular motion in the air by his head.

As the three hustled out of the booth, the admiral grabbed Stone's hand and shook it as he growled, "Don't you dare give me a salute. It is I that should be saluting you." He nodded at the little redhead already headed for the door. "And you don't get to hug my girl until the third date."

The two men smiled knowing the measure of their newfound relationship. "Have a great cruise, sir, just don't run her aground."

"We'll have to work on the rank thing, Gunny, but that's for another day." Three long strides and he went out the closing door, running after the little redhead who was already in the middle of the street. The blades on the helicopter began to turn slowly as Stone watched. The waitress came and stood beside him, watching as they climbed in and shut the door. The blades became a horizontal blur and soon the hulking form lifted into the air and passed over the crab shack as it headed somewhere out to sea.

The waitress looked up at Stone. "I'd resent his form of coming ashore, but he is my godfather, so I guess I have to cut him some slack, but someone has to pay the bill." Handing the food bill to Stone, she smirked. "Looks like you're the one holding the check today."

The distant trumpets harmonized with the fading beat of the helicopter blades as Stone fished the phone out of his pocket.

From Ski:
PTL Thanks

Stone looked at the message and half of his face frowned. The waitress's hand eased the phone to roll where she could read it and she laughed. "'Pay the lady, thanks.' Yeah, you're screwed."

STONEHEART

BAER CHARLTON

16

The dark slender hands calmly rested in the lap of the black dress. The dark eyes were not as calm as they scanned the last thin crowd of travelers coming through the security checkpoint. Sister Mary Margaret did not mind the late hour. Rarely could she sleep before one or two in the morning, when she would drift off from sheer exhaustion.

The convent, built with thick brick walls surrounded by high walls covered with foliage, absorbed noise. However, even there, she could still hear the city. It breathed a jumble of sounds that stirred the pot of her memories as a little girl. Loud noises, even blocks away, turned into gunfire, and it was coming her way.

Even the blender could betray her even though it remained her favorite tool in the kitchen. It could make frozen fruit into ice cream in a couple of minutes. Nevertheless, in her memories or during a rare nap in the office, it could become automatic weapons fire.

The sounds of happy people coming and going made sounds she never mistook for anything but happy people. Therefore, for her, going to the small Des Moines airport remained an occasion of her own joy, no matter what the

BAER CHARLTON

hour of the day or night. Even though she was an hour early for Stone's flight, the extra time was just a simple selfish pleasure of time she cherished to quietly sit and think and people watch.

Sister Mary Margaret waited peacefully as Stone made his way to her from Portland. The night was quiet for both.

Remembering the day's events put a smile on half of Stone's face in the darkness of the First Class cabin. He might have smiled even more if he had known the flight attendant was peeking around the edge of the galley door, strangely drawn to the kind handsome man, with the badly scarred face, in seat 2C.

Stone could still smell the river and grass from the morning run. He had woken up shortly after six o'clock in a small bed and breakfast which been recommended to him by a nice couple in Tillamook where he took an ice cream break after the tour of the cheese factory. The small Victorian home provided everything the couple promised. The beds, as guaranteed, were just short enough for his feet to hang out the end, something Stone had been used to on military cots all of his life.

As he rose, Stone could smell coffee, but without food, so he asked about running. The husband standing in the kitchen, still drenched in his own sweat from his twelve-mile run, directed Stone to the large park of Oaks Bottom.

The park had been easy to find and gave the bonus of running along the Willamette River. The morning was still hanging on the trees and bushes, the air redolent with a mixture of crisp greenery and the muddy pungency of rotting vegetation. The first three miles cleared his head,

192

and the next two woke up his body. About the time Stone started to awaken his appetite, he realized he had a partner in his run.

The Doberman weighed maybe eighty pounds. Even without being a real dog person, Stone could see there was still some puppy left to grow into the large paws, which were almost silently keeping pace with Stone's running shoes. The dog looked like he just started running because he had not worked up to strong breathing. Stone knew the Doberman had awareness of him by the way he was pacing him. Testing the dog's attention, Stone veered slightly left onto an ancillary path. The dog kept up even without breaking stride, pacing Stone as if he expected the move.

"He's going to run you into the ground. Elvis," the female voice called from several yards behind. "He thinks you're headed for the parking lot on the other side of the fence instead of the south exit."

Stone slowed until the cute young blonde in the form-hugging white sports bra and tiny powder-blue running shorts caught up to the two males. "I take it that Elvis here is your Dobie?"

She smiled a large friendly smile. "Well, I don't know anymore... after running off with a strange good-looking man." They slowed and stopped as she ruffled the top of the dog's head. "Do you think I should take him back? Give him another chance?" She easily bent and grabbing the dog's face in her two hands, kissed him on the lips.

"I think you better. He wouldn't fit on the back of my motorcycle."

Her head popped up as she stretched her arms in a swan dive move, and then stood up. "What kind of motorcycle do you ride?" She pulled her arm across her breasts as she stretched the shoulders, one of the hallmarks of distance runners.

"Just an old Goldwing with a billion miles on it, but it gets me around." He did not know why he felt like a goofy kid when the girl was obviously young enough to be his daughter, if not granddaughter. He stuck his hand out. "Stone, my name is Stone."

She shook with a gentle strength that showed more than the athletic body. "Jeannie." Leaning down and grabbing an ear. "And you've met my main man, Elvis." The dog leaned into her leg and nosed her crotch. "Hey, I've told you before, not in public." Stone liked that she goofed with the dog without blushing.

Stone glanced at his watch. He did not want to leave such a pleasant face and even more pleasant presence, but Stone knew the food would taste better for all at the table if he got a shower before breakfast. "As much as I would love to spend more time with you," and looking down to deflect any misconception, "and Elvis, I need to hunt down and kill some food."

Her blue eyes sparkled as she saw through his almost slip. "Where are you having breakfast? Because I can recommend a few places."

"I stayed at the Blue Iris last night."

Jeannie rolled her eyes. "Oh, well, Steve and Irma put on a good feed. Smart idea, going for a long run before breakfast, because you won't want to move after you eat."

Stone snorted. "Thanks for the warning." He rubbed his growling stomach. "I have a hard enough time keeping all of this laced into my corset as it is."

Jeannie laughed and jabbed him in the shoulder as if he were a brother. "You're funny, Stone, we need to run together more often."

Stone caught the guilt-free flirting. "Yes, well, unfortunately, I fly back to Des Moines this evening."

"Too bad, you'd probably look cute in a pair of real running shorts, and I bet you could put in a good showing in any of the 10k runs we have around here."

"Hey," he paused as he placed a hand lightly on her shoulder, "I didn't say I wasn't coming back."

"Well, okay. When you're in town, we three can run together." Snapping her fingers, she asked, "What time is your flight?"

"7:40, why?"

"I start work at two at the Dockside. Come by for an early dinner, because you know they won't feed you on the flight."

"Where's the Dockside?"

She started running back the way they had come. "Ask at the Iris, we've been around since 1921. You won't regret it, Stone." The blond angel in running gear and the big Dobie were gone around the large hedge of rhododendrons. Stone was left wondering if she had been real. *I guess I'll have to find the Dockside and find out,* Stone thought as he resumed his run back up towards breakfast.

True to both recommendations, he was not disappointed by either meal. It was just the company at the second which became the superior, with just the right amount of take-no-prisoners and sass because it kept Stone looking forward to running again with the new name and number in his phone.

"Sir, we'll be landing in a few minutes if you could please bring your seat to an upright position."

Stone had not realized he drifted off into a restful sleep. *Hmm, I should fly First Class more often.*

The nun sat quietly in the waiting area. There were no flights left to arrive. Her eyes seemed to be watching the arrival area, but as Stone silently stood off to one side and watched her, he guessed her focus flew thousands of miles and many years away. He had never noticed little twitches before, movements of no more than a quarter inch or just a spasm of the muscles in her jaw. Stone had seen it all before, in others as well as in himself.

Moving in on the seat next to the nun, he silently drifted down into the seat like a whisper of smoke in the morning coolness. "I don't think you come to pick people up as much as you come for the quiet," Stone spoke softly to the air in front of them. "The quiet is where there is no evil, no hurt, and no pain, but the quiet is also where the torture of memories can go to reach relief."

The dark hand with four large long keloid scars raised and came to rest on the much lighter also scarred hand. The quiet sounds of lowered voices from the security area and echoes from down the hallways hummed and gently thrummed in the night as the clock slowly slid past the midnight hour. The voice was like a memory of a soft spring breeze coming across the green grasslands of the upper central east Africa plane.

"The fighters and marauders only came during the daylight. In the dark under the silent moon, we were safe. It became the only time we could ever sleep or let our guard down. One night, my little sister walked out onto the grassland to see the crescent moon that was just a tiny thread rising over the plain. I left my sister sitting on a rock, and I went to a bush a few meters away to go to the bathroom. A lioness had been hiding in the short grass..."

Stone placed his other hand on hers. "Ni sawa," (*It's okay,*) he almost whispered in her native Swahili.

"It only took a second, she was so small. She never even cried out." She fell silent, and they sat watching the slow midnight movements of a cleaning staff, the TSA closing down for the night, and a silent zombie passed by driving a sweeper. The nun leaned a little closer. "I have told myself since then the lioness's swiftness was a blessing that she didn't have to endure the marauders... or even the men and boys in the camps." She looked up at Stone and he turned. "But I come here, because I still have doubts. If only I had taken her with me to the bush..."

Stone gently squeezed and then softly patted her hand. There was nothing that he could tell her; he had no special magical insight or he would have used it for himself years ago.

The zombie returned riding the carpet sweeper, and the TSA agents withdrew with soft 'Goodnights.' Stone blinked at the tears that stung his eyes but would not flow. In his pocket, the phone vibrated once and stopped. He would check it in the morning.

BAER CHARLTON

17

Stone had suffered with the hard winter. The running became an on again, off again thing between shoveling snow and subzero mornings. Between runs, there had been more flights as people in his phone book checked in as to his current location. Ski also found other places and people Stone needed to visit. The flights were tough as he walked into uncharted territory with every new travel. His life had become an education of former buddies dealing with TBI or PTSD, adjusting to less than four limbs or more often than not, a combo pack of some or all of the above. The hardest part for Stone was riding in cars. Not because he had become claustrophobic, but because during the few short months of last summer, Stone had become comforted by the openness of his motorcycle.

As Stone plodded along behind the blue sweat suit with 'St. Mary's' incongruously stenciled in an arch over the small rear-end of the nun, he thought maybe he was truly addicted to motorcycles, or at least the open air.

"If you have any hope of keeping up with a 10k runner that is half your age, you had better pick up the pace there, Gunny."

Stone laughed as he dialed up his pace to pass Mary

Margaret. "Whoever thought that a sweet little nun from Somalia could be such an evil sadistic taskmaster?" He pulled even with the smiling nun, and paced off her, the experienced racer.

She smiled gently at the older man whom she had watched get in better shape than he had probably been in a decade. "The desert burns the hell into our soul, but the convent teaches us how to swing the ruler." She looked at Stone as he glanced over, and she grew her eyes huge and laughed with the Halloween laugh, "Bwahahaha." As they turned the final corner, she saw their other racer already a full football field ahead of his usual mark. The race was now in earnest. "Short line or we have to be wash and dry this morning." The two exploded into a heart-bursting race to reach the convent's back driveway and the door before the man in the wheelchair.

The two runners stood hip to hip as the man in the wheelchair enjoyed his third cup of coffee. Paul sipped as he poured over letters and forms. Looking up, he thought aloud, "So if we can't get the VA to do an outreach in the backwoods, what do you think would happen if we find other funding, like through Catholic Charities, and open it as a free clinic for everyone or something?"

Stone looked out the large window at the protected yard. Snow still remained in the shaded areas, but there were tiny dots of green that would soon be buds. Spring was on the shortlist, and his eyes slid to the corner of the building and the hulking mound of a tarp that covered what he really yearned for. Grabbing one of the larger towels, he carefully removed the large serving platter from the drying rack and slowly polished the high glaze as he turned and rested his butt against the large sink. "If we opened it up to the whole community, there would be a lot of good that could happen." He traded the dry platter for the next damp stoneware dish. "Spuds said the forest takes many men, and that has to work hard on the families, and even on the loggers who do survive, but I think you'd be talking about more than just counseling." The towel slowed to a stop as Stone rested the large platter against his flat belly just above his belt. "They need medical too. Not just general practice doctors, but ones that are trained to deal with the amputations, the TBI and PTSD. These are all alien concepts for most doctors. They also need dental and vision, too. Spuds said that the last dentist he saw was in the Sandbox, and I'll bet his mother hasn't seen one since Spuds was in high school."

Mary Margaret deftly rescued the forgotten platter and towel from the hands she recognized were doing battle with their own TBI war. The large platters were becoming expensive to replace. She pointed out softly, "Where you have young men, you have women. There is probably a need for prenatal care and education. Many young women have no idea what it will take to be a mother. They only knew how to become a mother."

Paul laid the pen on the table in exasperation and leaned back in his wheelchair with his arms and hands outstretched in a show of the size of the problem. "Well, there you go. This little community of less than a thousand people needs at least a hundred highly-trained expensive professionals who make a whole lot more in a large city hospital."

"And that's why they have nobody," concluded Stone.

"And nobody gives a tear," the sister finished as she folded the towels on the counter.

"'Rip', Sister. The saying is nobody gives a rip." The ins and outs of English for the sister, with Paul's corrections, were an on-going process.

She turned and leaned into the corner of the large stone counter. "Nobody cries for their plight?" Her mouth hung open, but her deep dark eyes danced with the playful fire she brought to the serious conversations the three had been having during the long Iowa winter.

A familiar trumpet sounded and brought the conversation to a hold. Paul looked at Stone's pocket. "It's been very busy lately." Stone hummed agreeing as he fished the phone from its pocket holster.

From Ski:
How soon to airport?

From Stone:
Where – what?

From Ski:
Here – few days

Stone thought a moment and smiled almost evilly. "Paul, how fast can you type a brief on all of that stuff with a proposal of what is needed? Just a short form," he asked while waving his open hand at the table strewn with paperwork.

Mary Margaret raised her index finger and dashed out of the room and down the hall towards the offices. Returning a few seconds later with a thin sheaf of papers stapled together. "I took the liberty of pulling together what we have been talking about all winter. I just didn't know how to bring it up." Stone stared at this strong resolute nun and still saw the small child hiding in a bush in the middle of a cold desert night.

Taking the brief, Stone scanned over the points. Everything was gathered there, laid out in a step-by-step process which proved clear and concise. There were no extras or hyperbole to muddy the water. He looked back up at the little girl waiting and needing. Quietly, he reached out and gathered her into his arms. No words could come to his lips for the grace he felt that had been bestowed on him.

After a long minute, and just before the embrace became awkward, he let her go. He looked down at the papers. "Thank you. This is exactly what I need." Looking up with a shy smile, he added, "along with a ride to the airport."

"Which one"

"Let me find out."

From Stone:
I can leave now, which airport?

From Ski:
Strike Eagle standing by

Stone looked up as he put the phone away. "Air National Guard base. I'll grab my bag."

"Do you want any of this?" Paul indicated the paperwork.

Stone smirked. "Let's leave the sucker punch for later."

BAER CHARLTON

18

The hotel room was black except for the tiny crack of light that glowed from the phone, which was face down. The chirping crickets called for Stone again. Groggily, he noted the 2:48 a.m. as well as the name of the caller. He swiped his thumb across the glass and growled into the phone with his worst grumpy gunnery sergeant voice, "This better be good, Ski. It's oh three-hundred. I don't wake up for another two hours."

"The fog is rolling in. I'm on my way to pick up the admiral now. We're going up to the Memorial in Arlington, and the admiral wants to know if you're in."

Stone sat up. Even with the fog of sleep, he knew this was not just a whim. Vets did not just go to the Vietnam Memorial like other tourists. Stone ran his hand over his face while trying to think of what could possibly be the reason to get the admiral out of bed and up to the Memorial at this hour. It sure as hell would not be just because of the fog.

The gunny was wrong. The fog brought the vets out of the night. The fog provided concealing shadows, softened sound while providing cover for the attending group, who were there for painful personal atonement. The vets' highly personal communication precluded any public display or observation of their care or suffering. The deep fog, combined with the night, gave them that circumstance for a communion like no other. They, the survivors, stood in the fog. One or both hands seemed only to touch the cold stone, but it was so much more.

"Gunny? Hello?" The phone hung limp in his left hand between his knees. "Did I lose you? Gunny?"

Stone raised the phone woodenly, his eyes focused just enough on the glowing numbers and words. A few months prior, one of his former squad members reprogrammed the phone to read not only the constant time, but also the date. It took almost a full three heartbeats to realize why the admiral planned to go up the hill this morning, and why he would invite Stone to join him.

"I'll be out front." He put the phone down. Vietnam and his brother—a lifetime away and yet so near. Stone rose and padded his way to the bathroom.

Even though Stone knew in his head that his brother had been buried in Los Angeles for forty years, his heart told him it was finally time to say goodbye, and this time with a much deeper level of understanding.

STONEHEART

BAER CHARLTON

19

Jeannie's bell bright voice resonated from Stone's phone. "Okay, sweet butt, Elvis and I will meet you in front of the Oaks roller rink at the crack of dawn. Don't forget to wear those cute nylon running shorts. It's always very warm on that day, and I'm gonna smoke your old man butt too."

"Shorts and a chopped down T-shirt, just like you ordered. Oh, and I couldn't borrow a dog, so I'll bring a friend or two."

"Great, honey! The more runners the more funners."

"Okay, Jeannie, we'll see you next month. I'll get the pacemaker tuned up."

The laughter jingled out of his cell phone. "Okey dokey artichokie, but save room for that TCBT after your nap, old man."

"Oh, that is a real date. Soon... darlin'." Stone laughed at her infectious verbal endearments. Turning to the others, he smiled. "Okay, she's in."

The older nun stood quietly at the door watching the three conspirators and smiled to see how much they all three had blossomed during the winter in their supportive friendships, not the least of which, her surrogate child, Mary Margaret. At the urging of both Paul and Stone, she had finished her course work to become a Registered Nurse and was continuing on to earn a certification in the care of amputees, so when Paul needed assistance, there would be someone knowledgeable at hand, as well as a friend.

Sister Estella also realized that between the young sister's professional growth and her growing friendships with these two men, she would soon be leaving the safe haven of the convent. She had no surety as to their future life in southern Oregon, but she felt confident in the support system the new friends provided Sister Mary Margaret. The three running companions were a side blessing that the older nun had given thanks for on many nights.

Deciding she wanted in on the fun, Stella pushed off from the door jam and entered the large institutional sized kitchen, the domain of the three. She offered a coach's voice. "So, you think you'll smoke this girl's shoes?"

Stone chuckled at his old friend cleaning up the cruder competitive term. "As far as we can tell, it's only a 5k sprint, and we're running some pretty competitive times, now that we don't have to worry about slush," he said as he gave a side-glance to a blushing young lady at his side.

"Hey." She jabbed at his arm. "We didn't have all of this snow and slippery slushy stuff in the desert."

Paul chimed into the teasing from his chair. "Yes, but if you think slush is slippery, remember that you're going to run in a race with a few thousand dogs, and you know what they do."

"Yeah, they don't call it Doggie Dash for nothing..." Stone doubled down, "and the word dash is a slang term for the dog stuff you will be trying to avoid."

"Stone, that's horrible. It's not a term for poop. Ya, you terrible boys," the older sister feigned exasperation.

Trying not to laugh at the Mother Superior's mock defense, Mary Margaret pleaded dramatically. "Oh, Sister, where for art thou as I fend off these oafs on our fair city's rough streets? Yea, verily, but the question doth beg, be it better to run away from or run with the pack of animals tearing at the very soul like jackals to the carrion?"

As they stopped laughing, Stella held her right side. "Okay, Sister, that was just too far over the top. You owe me five Hail Marys and ten Our Fathers, and I will have you lead the singing tonight." She tried to act the punisher, all the while secretly admiring the young girl's mastering of not only English but also her new love of Shakespeare.

"But I lead the singing every night."

"Okay, then you need to set the table. The other sisters need to get in here and cook some mean gruel and hard tack so that we doth not starve and they can't do it with you three camped out." She turned to Stone. "Speaking of camping, have you set up your new tent yet?"

"Was just headed that way, sister, did you want to come along and help?"

She glanced at the window sheeted with early spring rain. "I guess we could set it up in the rectory. It's a Wednesday, so nothing will be going on in there this afternoon. Sure."

Several days later, Stone remembered the familiar vibration through his thighs and hands. The motorcycle had been gone over thoroughly in the last week as the temperature rose to become a true Iowa spring. The morning had threatened a small shower, but the afternoon had become almost warm. The final preparation for Stone to leave had ground down to the stalling motions of playing with Bugs and Trina's bubbling baby girl aptly named Grace. The gardens had been held off until Bugs was able to get around and take care of them. Trina had taken to the books so well that everyone wondered why she had done so poorly in school before. Stone had his theories, but held his tongue.

The spare helmet rested firmly against his left shoulder, and the spare body seemed to cover barely more than his spine as Mary Margaret lay against his back, experiencing her first motorcycle ride. "If you don't stop smiling, you'll get bugs in your teeth," he teased her.

"I have a toothbrush just in case." She was enjoying all of the new sensations. Sister Stella told her that if she were going to the forests of Oregon, she would need to have guns, boots, and a flannel shirt, and had taken her shopping at a farm store. The leather jacket had taken both Stella and Stone by surprise. Mary Margaret prayed her God would forgive her coveting such a sensible article of clothing that also felt so good to wear. The motorcycle ride was Stone's idea, but Mary Margaret rejoiced that he was so observant.

"Are you sure you have to leave tomorrow?"

Stone thought about how comfortable the sister had become by the second mile of streets. Smiling, he turned right and headed for the freeway. "I need to be in Salt Lake by next week, and I want to swing south to do it. There are a couple of people I want to check in on."

"Oh." She slumped against his back ever so slightly,

but Stone felt it. "It's just that the weather is turning good now."

Stone almost laughed at the small child in the young woman, and addressed her in Swahili. "Pole qwa kazi," as he apologized for the work, "but I need to do what is needed of me. I think you can understand that."

The small voice acquiesced, "Ndiyo mjomba." (*Yes, uncle.*)

Stone threw her hope, however. "When you come out to Oregon, we'll get you a helmet, and the weather will be warmer." He rolled the throttle back as they roared up the on-ramp, and he felt the two hands dig into his ribs as he heard a laughing squeal from the back seat. *Oh yes,* he thought with a smile, *probably many rides in Oregon.* He thought about the curving forest highways and back roads of southern Oregon and smiled contentedly, *pure motorcycle country.*

Three days later, he passed the city limit sign into the world center of Mormonism. As he drove through the downtown area, he marveled at the enormous width of the avenues and boulevards. The bag attached to the top of the gas tank had a clear pocket on the face. Stone glanced down at the address and his new GPS that was secured in the watertight envelope. He took the right that the digital map was showing, and pulled over into the parking lot of the motorcycle dealership.

Pulling into the back area, Stone nosed the bike into the mechanics' shop door. A lanky mechanic with a long ponytail stood up from behind a Harley. Her frown at the sight of a 'Rice Burner' or a classic '1200cc Gold Wing,' defined the mechanic's loyalties. Stone snickered as he slowly pulled his right leg across the seat. He fumbled with the key and bag on the tank, stalling for time. He watched the tall mechanic slowly wipe her hands in the ubiquitous red shop rag as she also took her time approaching. The rider and bike were obviously lost. The Honda dealership was over a mile away.

As she got closer, without taking off the helmet and blackout face shield, Stone asked, "Do you work on anything but road trash here?"

The mechanic lost a slight half step in her awkward gait. Her head turned ever so slightly as she looked out of an eye half closed with a shading lid of suspicion. Her voice was more the case of gravel thrown on a tin roof than a mockingbird trill in the field, a testament to the old scar tissue that flared across the right side of her neck. "On Wednesdays, we do run a special on castrations and neutering of old Navy seamen. But this is only Tuesday, so you're probably safe or already taken care of."

Stone could barely finger the latch on his helmet from laughing so hard. "Max, I would have thought spending a year in the VA would have given those Navy surgeons enough opportunities to cut hate and vindictiveness out of your sorry ass." He offered his right hand, but she just stepped in for a long hug, longer than most would have been comfortable with, and much longer than Stone would have stood for a short year before, but one that he now understood fully.

She hung into his body as if she were a battery being recharged, and in a way, Stone thought, she was. He was coming to understand how we draw our life's energy from those with whom we choose to associate. As Stone was learning from the bits and pieces of each person, it is the larger picture of whom we are, and whom we call family.

"Oh God, Gunny." The mechanic took a deep sigh and finally pushed off and held Stone at arm's length. "It has been way too long." She moved a little sideways and examined the flash burn scarring on the side of his neck and face. "I think mine looks sexier. Looks like your face healed a little too tight around the mouth. You get any tearing or ripping?" Stone quirked his mouth and shrugged.

Stone, no longer uncomfortable about his own disfigured face, openly examined hers as well. "So you're saying that yours is getting you laid on Saturday nights?"

The gray-hazel eyes of the woman flashed with challenge that quickly became amusement. "Hell, Gunny, I stopped going into bars before I went to Somalia." She grew a little smile as she shied her head and looked at him from the side of her eyes. "Too many bar fights and circumstances that the MPs couldn't ask about, and I couldn't tell."

Stone gently jabbed his fist at her shoulder. "I kind of figured, but it was none of my business, and I didn't care anyway. Just as long as you made it back to base in one piece and kept the Hawks in the air."

She smiled shyly, a glimpse of a little girl showing through. "Thanks, Gunny. That means a lot to hear you say that." She thought a moment and fished in her back pocket for a phone. Thumbing through the phone, she stood silent, with the tiny tip of her tongue sticking out of the right corner of her mouth. Stone remembered her signature mark of concentration. If she were sitting in the chow hall with her tongue cocked in the corner of her mouth, Stone knew she was worrying out a detail that would keep the Blackhawks in the air.

Her face lit up. "Got it." She handed the phone to

Stone. "That's my girl and our two daughters."

Stone looked at the picture of an Asian woman with her arms up around the necks of two very large horses. "Holy crap, Max, what the hell are those things?"

She laughed. "That's Hee and Haw, a matched set of grand champion Belgium Greys. Peanut enters them in dray pulling competitions. They do pretty good in the dead drags, so it somewhat offsets them eating us out of house and home. Peanut's a big animal vet, so we also write them off as publicity as well."

He handed the phone and picture back to the mechanic. "Nice looking family. You look happy, and it suits you."

"Thanks." She slipped the phone back into her back pocket. "But you didn't come cross country just to shoot the shit about my girls."

Stone's lower lip slowly bunched up as he thought about what he needed. He had been working on how to ask for over a thousand miles, and it still did not sound in his head like anything he wanted to say. In his thoughts, he would start slow, easy, and work up to the hard stuff. "Well, first, it's about this Rice Burner..."

The hard bags were not as large as the ones on the old Gold Wing, but Stone was sure he did not need any more room than allowed there. The vibration and noise was a little unsettling at first, but Stone was also pretty sure they would both work hard on him and somewhere down the road, end up seducing him into getting a speeding ticket or three. The radio was still something he had no use for, but it was coming with the bike, so he figured he had to take it or leave a gaping hole in the front wind fairing. At least the patch on the back of his leather jacket did not need to be changed. The same Corps Globe and Anchor, which had been on there for the last twenty years, was still good enough to bury him in. He just got more use out of it this last year than all of the nineteen years before combined.

"We'll fob the old Rice Burner off on some unsuspecting swabby for you. Just remember, this engine only has about six-hundred miles on her, so stop in Boise, and let Peter do the oil and check it out." Stone laughed at the Max the Mother Hen, which he had known in Somalia.

He leaned in and met the full body hug. "Thanks, Max, for everything."

She talked into his neck, "It's the least I can do… fuck it, I'm never going to get used to you as a Master Sergeant. You're just going to have to screw up so you can stay Gunny, Gunny. As for the other thing, consider it done. No man left behind."

They broke, and Stone wiped at his eye that was starting to weep. Between wipes, he noticed the mirror image in Max. "It will mean a great deal to several people if we can get it done…"

"Say nothing more, Gunny. I'm all over it." Max smiled with one last wipe at her eyes and a backhand pass across the snot drip at the tip of her nose. "And when you see Sister Stella again, tell her… aw heck… just give her a big hug for me."

The mention of the sisters reminded Stone of one other thing. "Remember that little Somali girl that was helping take care of us, the one that would brave going out at night to the well for water?"

"Sure, we called her Twiga because she was slender and peaceful like a giraffe."

"Well, she's coming out to run in the race in Portland

with me. She's a nun, but you wouldn't know it when she puts on her tiny running shorts and top and smokes some serious road-burning times." He slowly wagged his head in admiration. "We had some good runners in the corps, but I think, in a marathon, she could smoke any one of their shoes."

Max laughed. "Shoes? Is that the new jargon for asses?"

Stone smiled lopsidedly as he put his helmet on. "It is when the good sisters are talking, or in earshot. And I'm beginning to think that when it comes to Stella, there is nowhere she can't hear my swearing."

The trumpets tooted from the new bag on the gas tank. Stone pulled his helmet back off and looked at the text.

From Ski:
You have been stationary for the last five hours
RU all right?

Max leaned over to peek. "Oh God, did she catch us?"

He pulled the phone out of the clear pocket. "Nah, this is my other minder, the young ensign that you spoke to last year, Ski. Only now they made her a full louie—and a pain in the ass."

They both rolled their eyes in a mutual disrespect for the brass.

From Stone:
Bike problem. Fixed. On road now.

From Ski:
Hustle – UR burning daylight

From Stone:
Go to dinner or something
I'm trying to drive here

Phone stowed, he pulled the helmet back on. "Thanks again, Max. I'd better be on the road before she comes after me again."

The tall mechanic with the gentle smile raised her hand as he fired up the motorcycle. "Anytime you're in the country, we have a very comfortable barn."

"Will do." Stone kicked the shifter into first gear and let out the clutch as the GPS lit up and spoke to him through his new helmet. The Gunny looked both ways as he eased out on the large boulevard and thinking about the GPS—*Oh, now that is going to take some serious getting used to.*

The tall mechanic laughed as she spun back to the shop. Her long ponytail whipping around and catching over her shoulder as a vehicle crashed in her hip pocket. Smiling, she drew the phone out, knowing who was probably texting her.

From Ski:
Is he gone?

From Road Rash:
Just left
Where U at?

From Ski:
Bus around corner

BAER CHARLTON

From Road Rash:
Give it about 10 to be safe

From Ski:
He suspects?

From Road Rash:
Clueless

From Ski:
Standing by

From Road Rash:
Peanut due at 5
Will make coffee

From Ski:
Roger

STONEHEART

BAER CHARLTON

20

"Elvis, hide your eyes. There's an ugly bunch of old man sweat pants over there."

Bent over, Stone started laughing so hard he could not tie his shoe or stand up straight. He continued laughing, bent over, with his butt in the air, while the bubbly voice wafted across the open lawn of the Oaks Park. "Someone is looking to be turned over a knee and paddled for elder abuse," he growled.

Jeannie took the last step, "You mean you, old man?" She ground her crotch against his hip, which just made him laugh harder, and even more defenseless. "Because," as she started mock humping his hip, "you seem like the one turned over something." She bent down as she laughed. "What are you doing down there, old man? Looking for grubs like a bear in the woods?" Jeannie started laughing, and then neither of them could stand up. So she pushed and they both fell over on the grass, leaving them easy prey for the wild tongue and cold nose of the large brown and black flash of Elvis dancing from one under-defended face to the other.

"Elvis, stop," and she begged. "Enough already?" The two lay holding their sides from laughing. Finally, she squirmed around and gave Stone a big hug as they lay on the ground. "It's so good to see you again, old man."

"Good thing I had the pacemaker stepped up." He was still breathing a little hard. "I don't know if I've ever laughed that hard."

Jeannie slapped him on his firm belly as she jumped up. "Hard? Hard is what you're going to need to try to keep up today." She reached down and gave him a hand up, snarling at the beat-up Marine Corps PT sweats. "And I told you to wear sexy running shorts. You're going to die in that wigwam suit."

He smiled slyly. "Oh, I have shorts on, too."

Looking around, Jeannie teased, "I thought you said you were bringing a couple of friends." She turned back around on him with her sparkling smile and flaring eyes. "You didn't lie to me about having friends, did you? You do have friends, don't you? Or are you one of those guys that has friends, but only when he rents them?"

Stone stood smiling and chuckling at the nonstop smart-mouthed, fun-poking young woman. He had missed Jeannie after only experiencing her for a single day before.

Jeannie noticed him quietly watching her with his lopsided smile. She ratcheted down her harangue a notch in tone, but no less having fun at his expense. "I mean, if you are, I'm okay. This is Portland after all, and we have all sorts of demented people here, and most of them work in City Hall. So you can tell me." They both turned to watch a large tour bus pull into the far end of the parking lot and slowly make its way to where they were standing. "I can get used... to..." Jeannie noticed the short pixie looking woman waving like mad from the front seat of the bus. She turned around to face Stone who was smiling like a goofball. "Do you know these people?" She pointed at the now stopping bus.

Stone chuckled. "Yeah, I think I do... Well, maybe I just thought I knew them." Stone started to see more faces and realized who was on the bus as he started moving toward the opening door. "They said they were bringing a van-full, not a bus."

"We picked up a few people along the way, Gunny." Ski bounced off the bus and reached out a hand to Jeannie. "You must be Jeannie, Elvis's mom." She shook her hand, and said, "I'm Ski, Stone's surrogate mother hen." As each person stepped off the bus and first hugged or shook the Gunny's hand, Ski continued, "This is Max, his new motorcycle doctor, and this is Peanut or Patty, her partner and just in case Elvis is in need of a doctor." A mother with a babe in arms stepped down and gave Stone a deep hug and a kiss on the cheek. "Trina and Grace will be playing water support, as will the other third of their family, Bugs..." Ski stood on her tiptoes and looked back into the bus, "who is back there... uh... somewhere?"

Jeannie laughed. "Who are all of you people? Good lord, I was just harassing Stone for having to rent friends... is he this rich? Maybe I should overlook his white hair and slow speech and just marry him." She reached over, and as she took a right jab at his arm, she noticed the sign on the side of the bus. Grabbing and turning the Gunny to face the sign. "That is the best! Did you do this?" Looking for her dog, she hollered, "Elvis, Elvis," she whistled, and as he ran up, she grabbed him and pointed at the large banner taped along the entire side of the bus. "Look, honey, you have an army." They all looked with pride at the ad hoc name of the group in large block letters that ran the length of the bus: The King's Army. The flood of runners continued out of the bus.

Soon enough, their attention broke as a horn sounded from an approaching van. The ten-thousand watt smile of Spuds, driving, was matched by the smile of Sister Mary Margaret in the passenger seat.

Jeannie leaned over toward Ski, and quietly asked again, "Who are all of you people?"

Ski just smiled as the admiral helped Paul get out of the van and into his racing chair. "You might say that someday, Stone is going to realize that, this is his family, as well as several hundred more people in his phone." She turned to face Jeannie. "So you might say," as she reached up and hugged the other woman, "welcome to the family."

An air-horn sounded the twenty-minute warning signal as they all began stripping down to their running gear. The bus was controlled chaos, rapidly becoming more hysterical as people shucked out of their street clothes, and Jeannie saw all the team's running gear. Every single one was white with brown and black paw prints on them. *The King's Army* in blue suede letters graced the backside of all the shorts and chests of all the tank tops and running bras. Stone thought for sure Jeannie was going to wet her shorts and was laughing with the spirit of the event, winking at a self-satisfied smiling little elf named Ski, who winked back, mouthing the words *You're welcome.*

Ski stepped over to Jeannie, offering out a small bag. "We had to guess at your size. Actually, I called and talked to a Kathy at the Dockside, so I hope they fit."

As the bus arrived near the drop-off site, the runners all attached the last details that earmarked them as the team running for Elvis—large black sideburns and long floppy hound dog ears.

BAER CHARLTON

21

The post-race invasion of the Dockside was complete. Kathy took in the mass of fake black mutton-chop sideburns and turned to Terry and just said, "Go lock the door. We're done for the afternoon." Adding, "And I don't think Jeannie is coming in to work today." The room was wall-to-wall white running togs with brown and black paw prints. The jukebox played nothing but Elvis, mostly his "Hound Dog" song. The decibels were close to an intimate rock concert, but the attitude of the revelers vibrated anything but passive viewing. The runners who had just run a good 5k for a great cause and some early finishers just ran it again for fun.

Stone looked glassy-eyed at Paul and wondered if maybe doing the second round had been in his best interest. Paul had the same silly rum-punch look on his face, even though he shorted the second round when he made a sharp left and followed a pair of yellow shorts up onto the grassy area at Tom McCall Park. The same person wearing yellow shorts walked beside the American flag shorts as she and Jeannie carried two trays of full shot glasses to the main table where Stone sat.

"Okay, everyone grab a shot. We need a toast." The

BAER CHARLTON

chaos receded as the military training of lines and orderliness took hold.

Quietly, the company of men, women, full bodied, in wheelchairs and on aluminum, stood or sat-up straight as one. Jeannie looked from one to the next, taking in all the people she had never known before and now felt like family. Slowly, she raised her glass and held it out. "I don't make speeches but you guys are incredible. I know you're all here for my dog, and the dogs that still need adoption. I also know you're all here because of this one man. I didn't know it that day last year, but I felt blessed the day Elvis and I track... tracked... him down."

Sister Mary Margaret stepped up and slid her arm around her new sister's waist. Quietly, she confided to the now crying blonde, "It's okay, sister, I'll finish for you. I've been waiting to say this for over twenty years." She turned to the group and raised the glass higher, and from deep in the belly of her heart and soul, she belched out, "Hoorah!"

"Hoorah!" They answered loudly, and they all threw their drinks down the hatch as one.

STONEHEART

BAER CHARLTON

22

The oncoming lane went black.

It had been a warm wonderful three-day ride down along the coast from Portland. The noisy high, generated by forty-three of Stone's 'family' came to a sudden stop. The left turn-off, the Pacific Coast Highway, was the same left turn he had taken the previous year. The trees, which grew tall and seemed to encroach over and onto the road, were still the same. Then a short two miles into the forest, it all disappeared.

The squalid aftermath of a desert engagement, the shot up and burned out villages in Somalia and Bosnia and other places he preferred not to remember could not have prepared his mind for the utter devastation he saw in every direction.

Stone barely managed to pull the large bike to the side of the road. His heart was racing, and the flood of blood hissed in his ears. The deep-throated banging of the big V-twin engine transported a large emotional part of his mind and body back to a valley in Vietnam. A silent, invisible B-52 laid in a carpet-bombing, which made the entire valley, village, rice paddies, and people to light up, throw-up, and turn to mere scrap in the roiling hell of fire and evil black smoke. Seconds behind the larger plane came a squadron of fighters pickling off tumblers of napalm and turning anything left to burn to ash.

The man sat on the motorcycle as his body shook with the emotion that had gripped the nineteen-year-old that day, and now thundered back through the same man thirty-seven years later. Less distance than a thin piece of paper separated the two men—a separation that would never go away, only hopefully diminish.

It was not the call of a bird or the step of an animal that brought Stone back to the present—it was the absolute silence. The kind of silence that only a valley filled with two feet of ash can produce. No trees stood past four feet tall—rocks as large as a man or a horse or even a car pushed through the ash as if to say *only we can survive.*

Stone's stomach rolled and flopped. He did not know if he were hungry, had lost his appetite, or just needed to throw up. The last won out, bringing him to his knees in the ash, his mind frozen. No thought, no justification, no explanation, would right the vision that was consuming him at that moment. No scene on a television, or pictures in a newspaper, could ever convey what he was breathing in, taking in, living, and dying in that moment. The acrid stench seared the back of his nose and throat and burned his eyes. The lack of noise became as deafening as the moments after an IED destroys your vehicle... In a flash, Stone could see the last few seconds of his final ride in the Humvee, as well as the previous ten months: the faces, the laughter, the shared hopes and dreams... and in a second, it was all gone.

The empty stomach searched and found just dry

spasms. The few water drops in the ash near his vomit made no sense to Stone. The wet emerged only on the skin that could not feel the anguish, only rigidly stand guard. The stone face of a life-long marine. The face of a Gunnery Sergeant—forever frozen.

The ticking of the cooling engine counted the slow meter of the man on his knees. Slowly ticking, counting, and measuring as the mind stumbled back, still wounded, from the abyss of the past to the black hole of the present. Summoning concentration, intentions, plans. Taking care of business and pushing the rock of Sisyphus.

The foot moved sluggishly under the knee, and the body rose stiffly. Almost as a zombie, the body becoming more in control as the mind and eyes scanned for miles. Less than a year before, Stone could not have seen even a hundred yards through the lush forest.

Listlessly swinging his right leg over the motorcycle seat, Stone sat down. His hands hung motionless as his mind raced in a gray void. The little hamster was spinning the wheel but going nowhere. He finally summoned the strength to reach out and turn the key. Stone thumbed the starter as he pulled the kickstand in with his heel. The straps on his helmet hung unused and unnoticed as he chunked the transmission into first gear and rolled slowly back onto the highway.

Stone had never seen the aftermath of a Pacific Northwest forest fire that is fed by fuel-rich undergrowth, pushed by sea winds, and turbocharged by six years of drought. The lack of rain, snowmelt, or even moisture from coastal mists, resulted in trees that were nothing short of Roman candles waiting for a spark. Paper and wood ignite at the low temperature of 451° Fahrenheit. At around 900°, the trees start to burn, and the fire spreads; with a little wind to fan the fire, the temperature easily reaches 1,600° by which time the forest fire has usually expanded much larger than a thousand acres. By the time the fire starts to crown, race, and spread through the tops of the trees, the temperature is over 2,000° and begins to create its own windstorm.

A fire like this can hit the bottom of a mountainside, and then crest the mountain four thousand feet later, in less than five minutes. With a major storm pushing down from the Gulf of Alaska, and winds coming ashore between forty to sixty miles per hour, it does not matter if the fire started in the fall or spring. Anything in its path becomes ash as the fire spreads by the mile, not by the acre. Stone rode through the hellish world left behind by such a fire. Miles of black and gray ash, and then an anomaly—three small trees and a bush, green with no apparent singeing. The sky was overcast and gray, matching the ground. There were no birds. The deep throat of the Harley pounded the air but the ash absorbed all sound, creating an eerie sensory deprivation.

As Stone rounded a slow curve, a flitting light sparkled across his dashboard and gas tank. The gunny turned his head to see with his right eye. A car had run off the road and crashed into an apparently still solid burned snag.

Parking the bike on the side of the highway, Stone double-timed through the calf-deep ash to the side of the car. The gunny thought he recognized the car, and the old man slumped into the deflated air bag confirmed it. "Hey!" He jerked at the door. "Bernie. Bernie, can you talk?" He jerked again at the door, and it cracked open a couple of inches with a protesting groan.

Pulling on the window frame, Stone put his right boot against the rear door and pried the front door open. "Bernie? Bernie Mynhoffer? Can you hear me?" Stone hesitated then felt the man's neck for a pulse. He finally found the beats, but they seemed thin and soft.

Stone looked around at the sound of an engine. Rushing back to the road, he stood in the middle and waved his arms to stop the beat-up red truck coming from the southeast. With a squeal of bad brakes, the truck shuddered to a stop. Stone stood in a staring contest with three pair of eyes set in rough dirty faces. The driver asked through the windshield, "What?"

"There's a man hurt over there in the car, he needs help," Stone explained as he walked to the open window on the driver's side. "I need some help getting him out and we need to call 911." He put his hands on the windowsill as the three men looked in the direction of the green car and tree trunk, then looked back at Stone.

The driver moved the wad of chew from his lip to the side of his mouth. "That car is Bernie Mynhoffer's car." He spit out the window and barely missed Stone's arm.

"That's right, it's Bernie. And I'm going to need some help getting him out of there."

The man on the passenger side also spit and then calmly stated, "Nope... Not going to do that."

Stone was incredulous. "Why not?"

The middle man with no chew in his mouth grumbled, "Cuz it's Bernie." The three giggled like schoolgirls saying their first swear words.

Stone stared at the three loggers. The gaunt look of the dust bowl had become a genetic trait where Stone could not tell if they were related or just friends. The noses turned in unison as if attached to a rod as they looked from Stone to the car crumpled in the tree.

"Well, if you won't help him, help me by calling 911."

"Can't," the driver spat another meteor of tobacco juice.

"Can't or won't?" Stone growled and half-turned back to help the unconscious man.

"Can't," the passenger with the window said as his door screeched open. "No phone."

Stone fished his cell out of his pocket. "Then use mine."

The driver harrumphed, "Look at your bars, smart ass."

Coming around the nose of the truck, the passenger explained as his arm waved slowly at the expanse of waste, "There's no cell tower standing in the Biscuit Burn area. That asshole you're trying to save… it was his gypsy show that lit up the forest. It took out jobs, homes, businesses, roads, and over a hundred million harvestable board feet of trees. Not to speak of the protected old growth forest, the spotted owl, and probably a million pounds of walking dinner for the folks struggling to make ends meet around here." He came up close and poked Stone in the chest. "So that's why we don't give a shit if big Bernie dies on the side of a tree that he burned down. That asshole never cared about anybody else. Why should we, or even you, care about him?" The sudden proximity put the man's week of stubble and lack of grooming well within the sensory range of Stone's nose. It surprised him that the one thing he did not smell on the man's breath was booze.

"There's nothing I can do about your jobs, or trees, or anything else you hold against this man, but he is another human being." Stone stepped in closer in the way that only a drill instructor and sergeant knows how to do. "He's never done any wrong that I know of. So, I'm going to do everything I can to help save his life. You can either help me, or you can walk away. But, if you walk away and he dies, how long do you really think it will take me to find you three?" The cold stares of the two men could have tempered global warming.

"We'll help you get him on your motorcycle but then it ends there."

Stone nodded. "Where's the nearest emergency room?"

"Newport."

Stone did the mental calculations. "When will I get cell service?"

The man pointed. "Out on the coast and north about four miles."

Stone turned back toward the car, tree, and Bernie. "Then time is ticking."

The man turned back toward the other two and jerked his head, and they reluctantly piled out of the beat-up truck. The eight boots stomped up small clouds of ash as they headed for the car.

Stone pulled out his pocketknife and handed it to the driver. "Cut out the seat belts, as long as you can. We'll tie him to me on the bike."

Five minutes later, Stone was roaring back toward the coast highway as the other three stood on the road. The one spat chew and juice onto the shoulder. "Sure as hell has no air conditioning, no good will come of this."

The middle logger scratched at his chest through his T-shirt and mumbled, "Should have just let him die."

Stone ran the stop sign at the Coast Highway and carefully leaned into the right turn as he felt the dead weight of the man tied to his back. Rolling on the power, the big engine gracefully moved the needle past the 80 mph mark as Stone felt time drifting away.

It took a moment for Stone to realize that with his left eye he had caught the flicker of a single bar on his cell phone lying in the special envelope. He closed his right eye and watched the road with the vision now returned in his left. *Hmm,* he thought, *good to know.*

Stone pushed the button on the control cluster. At the beep, he stated loudly, "Call... Ski." The phone searched and there was the familiar buzz of a ring.

"Stone, what are you doing? It says that you're moving faster than a car and slower than a plane... and you're calling me?"

"Ski, I need help."

"I can barely understand you. Are you on your motorcycle?"

"I have a dying man strapped to my back. I need a medical evac ASAP."

"Hold on."

Stone rolled north another four miles before she returned. "Stone, I'm tracking you. I have a Medi-Flight Jet Ranger coming at you. A paramedic is on board and they will meet you in about twelve minutes. Keep heading north. If a state trooper shows up, do not stop."

In five more minutes, the trooper with lights and siren was in his rearview mirror and then in front of the motorcycle leading the way. Seven minutes more, and the helicopter was letting the wheels down as it flew over the top of a low rise ahead of them and began to lower crosswise onto the highway. Stone stopped beside the trooper car just outside the rotor wash.

As the paramedics ran toward them, Stone cut the belts as he yelled, "Car crash, maybe an hour or so ago. He's in his late sixties, I don't know if he has any next of kin. He was knocked out when I found him face down in his airbag."

The medics carefully pulled the man off Stone's back and laid him down on the stretcher. "We'll take it from here, sir."

"Where are you taking him?"

"The closest crisis with a helipad is Medford Medical."

The trooper turned to Stone. "I'll get you the address."

"Thanks." Stone watched as the medics stowed the man and lifted off. He could feel the first tickle of the wave of unused adrenaline and knew what was coming. He turned back to the trooper. "Thanks, I'd appreciate that." The butterflies were starting to fill his stomach as the slugs dragging coals started to invade his muscles. "How far to Newport?"

The trooper turned back from his car with the microphone in his hand. "About ten minutes if you don't want a speeding ticket." He smiled as his cheeks crinkled up. In understanding what Stone was about to go through, he added, "But if you keep close, we can probably be sitting down with coffee by that time. Can I buy you some lunch, Gunny?"

BAER CHARLTON

23

"No, there's nothing left there. The fire took out much of the good in the counties, Mom and Dad's was just part of it." The state trooper pushed his coffee mug around, stalling as he swallowed hard. "Hank died trying to save LaLonnie's place, and from what I heard, when she heard about him, she went right down—died before she hit the floor. Call it a heart attack, but most people around here would say it was a broken heart."

Stone watched the man who obviously knew everyone in the area. "Any ideas about where Ruby and Molly landed?"

"I think they are still in Medford. I understand some family, friend, or something took them in. The fire changed the family dynamics of many people. You just met three of them. I don't think Bernie will be getting any candles lit for his recovery in these counties." The trooper slowly rotated his coffee cup left then right with his finger and thumb as he stared at the empty mug and the heart of a region.

"So where does all of that anger come from? I mean, I've seen hatred before but not like that."

The light reflected dully off the brass nametag that

said Johnson as the trooper leaned back and looked at the ceiling, The deep voice rumbled like it should have been coming from a man twice his size "Oh, where to start?" Leaning back in, he looked at Stone. "It all goes back to his father in the early years. At the peak, when logging was king, his father ran three or four shows."

"Shows?"

"A show is a logging camp or company. Any company that does business in timber and hires loggers is a show. Big Max had three main ones along the coast range and one that floated over in the Cascades to the east." Stone watched the index finger scribe lazy figure eights on the nicked tabletop. "Max became successful, because he dealt fairly. You do a day's job—you get paid a day's pay. If you produced more, you made more. He also knew all of his men and their families. My dad said Max waited with him while Mom labored with me for nineteen hours. Max only left to get them food from the cafeteria, and at the end, he even had two cigars with the right color of wrapper"

"And then?"

Trooper Johnson looked up and smiled at the waitress refilling their coffee. He looked back at Stone. "Sons aren't always their fathers." He raised his eyebrows and grimaced. Looking up, "If they were, I would be a logger, also. Instead, I can't swing an ax to save my life. I have propane heat in the house, and splitting propane is as close to splitting logs as I come."

"Okay, Bernie wasn't the same man as his father. So if he was such a mean-spirited person, how did Bernie become so successful?"

The trooper looked out the window and watched the

traffic flow, gathering his memories and sorting them for accurate time line. Turning back to Stone and taking a sip of coffee, he seemed more resolved than eager to let the story unfold. "He didn't start as an asshole. He just seemed to grow into it. Dad said that, in school, he was a nice guy. He didn't play ball and wasn't really a ladies man or player, but he hung out with everyone at Bud's Drive-in Burger Shack and always helped with the dance decorations and all. Bernie was just one of the nice guys that get kind of overlooked but always there. When Vietnam came along, but before the draft, he went and came back, nothing even there.

"I guess things started changing in the eighties. By that time, he was running the shows and buying up land in the valleys. With him, it didn't seem to matter what kind of land, timberland or commercial. If it was cheap, he snapped it up. That's how he got the land Mom and Dad's sat on. Actually, it's that whole strip that runs down to the Chevron station, almost a mile or more of commercial or residential mix, and it's acres deep. He just never developed any of it. I suspect he probably owns most of the valley."

Stone rested his left arm along the back of the booth. "What about Mom and Dad's?"

The trooper smiled as he remembered local history he grew up with. "That was a restaurant since the old days when it was a camp canteen, back about the turn of the last century. In those days, a show could be running upwards of two hundred loggers that needed to be fed twice a day with bucket lunches for out in the forest. The original building probably stood two or three times that size. Long tables with huge boards used as serving dishes. Those were the wild days."

"So when did Bernie start to change?"

The waitress stopped to pick up the dirty plates and recharge the coffees.

Leaning back, the trooper looked at the table with wide eyes. "I guess when Madeline ran off down to California or somewhere a lot more glamorous."

Stone frowned, "Madeline?"

"I don't know if they got married or not. One day he's a bachelor, the next his old high school sweetheart is back in the picture and in his house and driving his car. She would have been my first successful speeding ticket— except it was thrown out by the judge." The trooper picked some imagined lint from his uniform sleeve, and then leaned to the side and relaxed. These were his memories, personal, and Stone could see the change come over the trooper.

"So you were on the force then?"

"I had just started. I got my training up in Corvallis on the old water pads and all, and they asked where I wanted to post. We had real money back then and probably over six hundred troopers. Drugs were our favorite busts, because they usually came with some great cars that we got to keep and use under cover. I got a Corvette for a short while until the night shift splintered it all over a tree at a hundred and twenty miles per hour. Sexy car, but a piece of crap back in the winding turns. The Porsche was a better car. Nobody wanted it because it was just a plain Jane 911T. No turbo, no whale tail, no tubbed-out wide ass-end, just a fast car made for the curves like a slot car."

"So Madeline moved out…"

Breaking his reverie of old memories, the trooper

grimaced and leaned forward into a cup of other facts. "No move. She decamped. From what I heard, she just packed a couple of bags and left. I guess that's when things started getting ugly around here. Looking back, it looked like he had been hurt more than anyone guessed, and he seemed to take his anger out on whoever was standing close at the moment. Sad, really."

"How so?"

"It stirred up a lot of bad feelings among everyone. Timber prices were down, so the loggers got laid off, and then they went home and took it out on the wife and kids, or they headed for the bar and took it out by breaking furniture on each other.

"The more people lose their jobs, fewer taxes collected. Then you have kids coming to school, and the food bill goes way up, except... no money for food. When kids are hungry, the worse they do at schoolwork. The worse the grades on the report card, the more beatings on the kids and wives. Eventually, you get to shootings." The trooper just kind of hung in the bench of the booth, drained.

"And," Stone continued for him, "the worse the local condition, the more they blamed Bernie, and the more they blamed him, the worse he became until he became a bitter old man who lashes out first and never apologizes."

The trooper thought about that, and then with a frown pulled to one side, he nodded. "Yeah... that about sums it up."

"So now we have three loggers who would rather drive on and let him die." Stone looked down at his phone and the little trumpets.

BAER CHARLTON

From Ski:
OK?

He thought and replied that he was and then put the phone away. He did not want any meddling from three thousand miles away at the moment. He needed to think.

The trooper looked with a question on his face. "So, what now?"

Stone pursed his lips and thought a moment. "I guess, I'll get a place here tonight and go see what's what tomorrow in Medford."

The trooper fished his wallet out as Stone started to protest. "It's okay. I'll get the bill. Our afternoon has probably been worth a few months with a therapist. A lunch tab is cheap. I probably got more out of today than you did." Fishing a business card out of his wallet, he handed it to Stone. "My cell phone is on the back. I'd like it if you could keep me posted on Mr. Mynhoffer." The trooper stopped. Stone could see the emotion in his tense stance. "Bernie... Bernie took me out to lunch after the judge tore up his wife's ticket. He told me to never take a ticket personal, it was just business. Down deep, I think that nice guy is still in that mean body. It's just trapped, for some reason, and can't get out."

Stone looked at the trooper's card and they shook hands. "I will, and thanks for lunch, Vern."

The deep rumbling voice that seemed to echo on its own, laughed. "Semper Fi, Gunny, Semper Fi."

STONEHEART

BAER CHARLTON

24

Stone sat watching the man's chest slowly rise and fall. A soft beep pulsed in harmony from the machine as the heartbeats jagged their way across the screen, and then as they faded, started a fresh line of hills and valleys. The yellowish afternoon sunlight glowed through the filtering drapes drawn across the large window. The gentle warmth felt good on Stone's neck as he sat reading in the lounge chair. His eyes standing duty—reading a few lines, watching the chest rise and fall, reading a page, and watching Bernie sleep as the afternoon dragged on.

Stone chuckled inwardly as he thought about what he had become. A man's man, now sitting in a hospital room with no care to go elsewhere, reading what had first seemed to be a children's book but turned out to be a story that was speaking directly to him. Even though he did not see himself as small, or a dragon, it was about being or feeling different from everyone else. Somehow, now hooked, Stone was slowly turning the page and noticed it was page 104. He looked at the orange faced Doxa watch.

"Where did the day go?"

Stone marked his place with a dog-eared page, stood up, and stretched as he headed for the bathroom. Maybe he would go down and get some coffee, too. As he dried his hands on the paper towel, he opened the door and walked out. Bending, he tossed the wet towel in the trash.

"You were here yesterday, too," the soft voice croaked dry and unused. Stone looked up at the man in the bed. The eyes were barely slits but Stone could see a tiny glint of wet reflecting the light.

"And the three days before," Stone answered as he unhurriedly walked the seven feet of space to the side of the bed. "How are you feeling, Bernie?"

"I should have died." Bernie coughed with all the strength he could muster.

"You tried." Stone looked at the monitor as he thumbed the plunger on the call button. "Do you remember anything?"

The man thought for a while, and then his eyes slid sideways as he lied, "No."

"Liar," Stone moved to that side of the bed. "Okay, so you don't want to talk about why you tried to kill yourself, so let's talk about the fire." The man glared at him, but remained silent. "So it would appear that one of your crew somehow set the fire. Why?"

"It wasn't my crew." His last ounce of determination burned in the man's eyes. A certain iron edge still traced through what passed for a voice. "It was a Sunday, and my crew doesn't work on Sunday. They never have and never will. It may have started on one of my cuts but it wasn't my show." Bernie rolled his head away from Stone. "I'm tired, go away."

Stone waited a few minutes in silence. Finally, the man's head rolled back. "Who are you, anyway? You're not a cop, and you're not a ranger."

Stone stepped closer, watching the man. "No, no, I'm not. But I'm probably the only guy in Oregon right now that cares if you live or die."

"Then you might as well go away. I'm dying."

"Maybe, but before you die, I want some answers. How about we start with Madeline."

A megawatt of electricity galvanized through the man as Bernie snapped his head to look at Stone. "How dare you?" The gravel voice through the clenched teeth drove the point home, "Get out. Get out!"

Stone stared him down, but did not budge—the man seemed used up.

"Sir." The nurse coming through the door looked at the man in the bed, and then at Stone standing by the foot. "Sir, you'll have to leave."

Stone nodded as he turned. "I'm not done here." He disappeared. The monitor in the room was making angry noises of warning that echoed the strident sound of the boots marching down the hall that nobody would want to challenge.

Stone pulled his helmet on, and as he sat on the thumping motorcycle, he checked his phone. The address next on his list was only a few miles away. Stone inserted it into his GPS and swung his leg out to catch the kickstand and swing it in just as the trumpets blew.

From Road Rash:
He'll talk
But only to you

From Stone:
Soon

Stone drew the steel arm in from the asphalt and kicked at first gear. The sun was heading for the western hills, and he headed south. The gunny assessed the geography and stopped for gas. Where he had been going could wait. He could be in Salt Lake City by tomorrow night with a short night in Reno. After all, the bike did need to see the doctor for a check-up.

A full tank and a pocket full of jerky, Stone punched at the phone.

From Stone:
Tomorrow night late

Eight days, and over a thousand miles later, the motorcycle had taken its toll on Stone, but it had also given back. Big rigs pushing him about on the windswept reaches across Nevada and Utah had hardened his steely resolve. The week had been long but productive. As he rode the elevator, Stone rubbed his butt and wondered if the workout videotape from the eighties referred to the steel that his buns were rapidly becoming. The linoleum hall glistened with fresh wax as he strolled toward the room. He thought about the man in the room. *Let's hope I'm productive with him, too.* Stone turned the corner through the door. *At least he's sitting up now.*

"Oh, Christ on a rubber crutch. Why can't you leave me alone?"

"Because you're not alone, Bernie, and you don't get

that."

"Look, you changed my tire, and you saved my life, thank you. I've got nothing else for you, not a thing."

Stone quietly took the straight chair and spun it around, sat backwards, and straddle-legged like it was a motorcycle. "You burned up four-million acres of forest and countryside, Bernie... but that wasn't what's been tearing this area apart. It was just the last bullet through the wounded heart. The cancer has been going on for over twenty years and it's time for it to stop."

The man rolled his head and looked out the window through the partially drawn drapes. Almost wistfully, Bernie conceded, "There is nothing left." The oxygen tube hissed quietly at his upper lip.

Stone studied the man. He was truly crushed. Dead, except the breathing part. "There is hope, Bernie. There is still good left in the area. Some things fire can't burn out of the human spirit—I know. I have firsthand experience. Some people in this area work hard every day at seeing the good. They pull it out of others. They rub it on others and generally work to create a world where kindness and goodness are the two warring factors for the day instead of hate and despair."

Bernie croaked in a whisper, "What do you know? You're not even from around here."

"All my life, I have been where I'm not from. So I learned to read people, recognize things about them. Like you being an asshole. Okay, I get it. You like being an asshole because you think it protects you. But, from what—someone hurting you? No. Maybe from people getting too close to you? Sure. But that's not protection. It's just isolation. New York is loud, confusing, and the

people stink… so you just don't go. You live in Central
Park, so to speak, but you won't move or deal with your
problem."

Stone took a deep breath and sighed. He started again,
but softer. "Okay, you're an asshole and a crotchety old
man, so what. You drive through an area where you own
half the land or more, and you're afraid to stop because
someone might shoot you—because someone might want
something from you or because they might just say hi? No.
You're afraid to stop just because you're afraid. I don't
know when it started or why, but I have a gut feeling that it
had to do with Madeline."

"What the hell do you know?" Bernie dismissed
Stone. However, Stone inwardly smiled seeing a lot more
energy, even though it was coming from a bad fire burning
in Bernie's belly.

"I understand a lot more now than a week ago. I know
you turned your back on everything you grew up loving—
everything. No student body would have ever voted an
asshole like you to be student body president, much less
voted him to be prom king. But it wasn't Madeline back
then standing by your side, it was LaLonnie, wasn't it?"

Bernie rolled his head to look out the window staring
at a long time ago. Finally, he rolled his head back to look
at the quiet man waiting at the side of his hospital bed. The
memories tempered his words. "I was dating Madeline, she
wore my ring. LaLonnie and I weren't a couple. They
voted for each of us."

Stone nodded. "Because you two were the most ready
to help, most fun-loving people of your class. It didn't
matter that you two weren't a couple. You two were good
friends. In fact, everybody I spoke to said that all eighteen

students of the graduating class were good friends. A guy named Bill Dermot said that if you didn't help him every lunch with his math and French, he wouldn't have graduated. An asshole doesn't do that. So what happened?"

The man just rolled his head back to face the window, looking far away and years before. The monitor, busy before, now stood silent and dark. Stone waited. The sniper in him slowed the heart, smoothed out the breathing and waited.

The afternoon shadows changed on the floor as Stone wondered if the man had drifted into sleep, but the rhythm of his breathing was of a person awake and thinking, and not the steady even pace of a sleeper.

"I never knew," the voice could have been someone walking by on the sidewalk two floors below, or a memory from somewhere else. Stone waited.

Almost as if in a dream, the head turned and looked at Stone, clear-eyed. "I never knew why she left. I guess that's what made me the angriest... and lost. I came home from a business trip to an empty house. Everything *Madeline* was simply gone. I never realized how little... not a picture of us... nothing we had bought as a couple. She had packed a couple of bags, pretty much everything. She left some winter clothes, just stuff she wouldn't need or want. Anything that alleged we were a couple had vanished. It was as if she had never happened. Just someone I made up. There was no letter, no phone call, nothing. She just ceased to exist."

Half of Stone's face frowned. "What about..."

"Private detective," he asked and then harrumphed, "Sure, I spent thousands looking for her. Every month I would get a report. It would say something to the effect of *'no further developments to report and your balance due is another five thousand dollars.'"*

"But they never found a trace," Stone finished for him.

The old man just gently wagged his head. "When the Internet came along, I kept hearing about people finding old friends and skip tracers tracking down people that didn't want to be traced." He shrugged and blew out his lips in a puff.

He looked up from the sheets over his knees and studied Stone's face. "If we're kicking painful pasts, let's share. What happened to your face?"

Stone laughed. "That, my friend, is the worst trade you will ever make, although Molly said it in a nicer light." Stone notice the pained wince at the mention of the young woman. "I crawled out of a downed Black Hawk, dragging some of my men. Just when I thought we were safe, the fuel tanks blew up. I didn't realize we had crashed into a gas station with dozens of fifty-five gallon drums full of fuel. When it went up, we lost five of our squads. We would have all died except for a small group of nuns and orphans."

Bernie's right eyebrow rose in question. "Where?"

"Somalia, in the bad days before it got worse," the gunny's lips curled in tight rolls against his teeth.

"You stay in touch with anybody?"

Stone fished out his phone. "The head nun and I have been close ever since. She's now the mother superior of a shelter for battered women and children in Iowa. But one of her nuns, then a little girl they rescued there in Somalia, is coming out here to Southern Oregon." Remembering Max, he continued. "And the mechanic who was filling in for the copilot. She's now a motorcycle mechanic in Salt Lake."

Bernie plucked at the sheet over his legs. "Why here?"

"Mary Margaret? Because some vets here need help and can't go elsewhere."

"But there's already a VA in—"

Stone was holding up his index finger. "Actually, Bernie, you got a twofer on that one. Now it's my turn." He waited for the man to sink back and nod. "What do you have against Molly?"

A flush began on the man's neck but stopped short of coloring his face, and the expected vein never started pulsing. He stayed stiff, and then went soft, giving up. "Ah hell, let's just rip the band aid off the old wound."

The old man held up his one finger, and yelled weakly, "Nurse. Nurse, I'm dying in here." He smiled at Stone and wiggled his eyebrows.

Stone could hear the starched dress and scissor shearing sound of large thighs in panty hose. The sound is as distinctive as a pump shotgun or an AK-47 being shot at you. Once you hear it, never forget it.

"Mister Mynhoffer," the voice started before she rounded the door. "I told you before that we do not serve Scotch in this hospital." The black nurse stood at the end of the bed, arms akimbo. Between her body and her attitude, any defensive coach in the NFL would have been happy to have her.

"Nurse Butterfly, this is Gunnery Sergeant Stone."

Stone coughed into his fist. "Actually it's Master Sergeant now."

She nodded at Stone and returned her gaze to the

patient. "What do you need, Bernie? I have paperwork that needs to be done."

He pointed at the full canister of water. "I have plenty of water but no ice, could you be a real sweetheart and get us a couple of glasses of ice, pretty please?"

She held one eye half shut as she opened the other wider, giving both men *the eye*. "I won't tolerate any hanky-panky in here, you two."

"No, ma'am," Bernie said soberly. "Never think of it, uh-uh, not on your watch, never."

She gave him a stronger look but still returned a few minutes later with the glasses of ice. Placing both on the tray hovering over his feet, Butterfly turned to leave, before slipping through the door, she added, "No more than two fingers, Bernie. You're on thinners and he's driving."

Bernie watched the door until they could not hear Butterfly's feet or panty hose anymore. A few seconds later, they could hear a chair protest as she sat down and wheeled to the desk. Bernie smiled at Stone and pointed at the three drawers set into the wall. "Bottom drawer, under my clothes."

Stone fished the half-pint of Scotch out of the drawer and held it up with a question on his face.

Bernie snickered softly as he tossed his head toward the general direction of the nurse's station. "Her son is the janitor in the middle of the night."

"Butterfly?"

Bernie nodded. "She married one of the local Indians... Excuse me, First Nation men, who used to work for me until he lost a leg. He was getting state disability but I paid for her to get her RN up in Portland." Bernie looked at Stone who had stopped pouring. "What? You didn't think I had any redeeming side left?" He took the larger of the two pours and held it up. "It was either forty-thousand dollars' worth of education or a quarter million for wrongful injury. The lawyers would have sucked up at least half of the latter, so I opted to teach her how to fish instead. It also helps that her husband drives a box van down to the Bay area now."

Stone returned the bottle to the drawer and held his glass out. "Still the asshole but doing some good anyway." Clinking their glasses together, Stone sat back down.

Bernie thought a moment, took another sip, and leaned back. "Have you ever said or done something that you knew was wrong the moment it happened, but you let it go? Later, you regret it, but the longer you don't go make it right, the harder it becomes until you would choose death instead?"

Stone thought about his life that precluded much chance of that magnitude of regret. "No, but I know what you mean."

Bernie winced as he took another sip. "God, I wish that kid would get me some decent Scotch instead of this paint thinner." He sipped again and set it down, fortified. He looked over at Stone. "That's my white whale named Molly."

"When?"

He raised a frail wrinkled hand and wiped his brow back over his thinning hair. "Oh, I think she must have been about four or five when Madeline left, and it was about a year later when I yelled at her and her mother."

Stone was aghast. "You yelled? That's it?"

He nodded. "It wasn't the yelling, it's what I yelled. It

was evil, and it was wrong."

Stone shoved his hand out, palm up. "But surely—"

"I didn't take it back right away... but by the next day, year... whatever, it was just too much. That's when I quit shopping at the little store or talking to local people or as you put it, stopped."

Stone sat silent and waited. He could see the war. Everything was bubbling up, and the taste in the man's mouth must have tasted more like the dregs of a cesspool than mediocre Scotch.

Bernie heaved a huge sigh and collapsed in on himself. "I called her an idiot and an animal, two things nobody should call anybody. I felt afraid. I didn't know what to do when a child comes at you with arms spread for a hug. I screamed at her to keep away from me, and then I screamed at Ruby to keep her idiot animal away. It was horrible. I was the biggest, ugliest animal that little girl could have ever seen. Only humans can be that ugly." Bernie looked up and realized whom he was talking to... "You should know. You've seen the worst."

Stone raised his glass, and as he started to take a sip, he raised a knowing eyebrow. "And I have seen the best."

STONEHEART

BAER CHARLTON

25

The small yellow house set back from the street, behind the larger house. Stone sat on the motorcycle, listening to the tick of the cooling engine. For all the charges up San Juan Hill, as it were, courage in the face of battle, the gunny never thought he would show hesitation in approaching the door of two women. Stone realized he did not know what he was doing there other than to say a simple hello. Some battle planner he turned out to be.

"Hello." The flatness of her speech gave her away.

Stone startled. He had been so focused on the driveway that he had not heard her walk up. He knew she would not purposely sneak up on him. She was too open-spirited for that. "Hello, Molly." Stone did not need to turn around, but he did anyway. He swung his leg over the back of the motorcycle and stood up.

Molly looked at him with a tilted head, and then straightened as a large soft smile washed across her face. She stepped off the curb and buried her face in his chest, "Stone!" His arms hung briefly at his side, but as he was getting used to these shows of affection, Stone recovered and wrapped them around her shoulders and upper back. The evening air must have been heavy with pollen was his only explanation as to why his eyes were suddenly irritated with stinging water.

Molly released her hold and leaned back to look up. "Mama will be happy to see you." As she took Stone's hand and walked him across the street, she snuck a look back at the big black motorcycle. "I'm sure there is an old pot of coffee that has been stinking up the house for hours that we need help hiding. Is that your motorcycle? I really like motorcycles, but I've never ridden on one, so maybe one day you can give me a ride if it's okay with mama. Okay?"

Stone laughed. He had forgotten how rat-a-tat-tat she spoke. Molly's mind maybe did not go far, but it went just far enough in many directions. Stone smiled inwardly as it occurred to him that Molly's chatter reminded him of sitting around a hooch or barracks, listening to the different conversations of the squad. It had always felt like home to him—one piece of his former life that Stone missed.

Stone sat in the backyard looking up at the stars. The mug warm in his hand, and the cool twinkling of tiny lights overhead. He knew they were giant burning balls of gas too far away to grasp, but close enough to see and enjoy. No matter what part of the world he was in, one thing was constant—the stars. For Stone, they represented stability, even in transitory circumstances.

"They are beautiful, aren't they?" Ruby stepped out onto the patio as she slid the screen door shut. "I guess you have seen all the constellations, haven't you?"

"No, no I haven't." Stone turned to watch the woman

ease down onto the chaise lounge. "There are constellations over the North and South Pole that they say you almost have to be on the ice to see. Maybe someday I'll go do that." He chuckled. "It really sounds silly when I say it."

Ruby studied the man who walked through life with such a serious view. "Why, because it serves no higher purpose?"

"It just sounds so frivolous." Stone stared at the sky and a shooting star.

He smiled at a memory of his attempt at frivolity. "I took an R&R once. I was based in Italy, and we had to go into Rome just about every other day. So, when I took my R&R, I went to Paris for two weeks. The first day there, I walked about fifteen miles, the second day I walked almost twenty. The third day, I realized I was attacking Paris. My measure of enjoyment of this spectacularly beautiful center of culture was by how many miles I walked. So, after seeing the Louvre from the outside and Notre Dame from the outside, I walked around the Eiffel Tower. I walked from one end of the Champs Elysees to the other, and back. I walked through all the major parks, hiked up Mount Michelle, and even considered walking out to Versailles. Instead, I caught a hop back to base and just hung out there."

Ruby reached out and grabbed his arm. She was in horror but also saw the humor of it all. "How old were you?"

Stone thought back. "Thirty-two."

She laughed. "You should have stayed in Paris and gotten laid."

Stone's head snapped to look at her.

Ruby looked at him in mock horror. "What, you think I'm too old to remember being thirty-two? Did you ever live?"

"What kind of crack is that?"

"Stone, you were a marine. What about nineteen?"

"Vietnam."

"No R&R? No going down to Hong Kong and renting a little friend for the week?"

Stone turned away and sipped his coffee.

"Hah! I knew there was once a young Stone with a beating heart-on. Now, what about your twenty-first birthday?"

"San Francisco." Stone remembered his birthday in vivid detail.

Ruby smiled, ready to tease some more. "Anything special?"

"They took me off life support."

Horror washed through Ruby as she remembered whom she was talking to. "Stone, you don't play very fair."

Stone did not even smile. The long years did not exist. The taste and smell of Letterman Hospital persisted. "That day, it was pretty special. From what I'd been feeling for the last few weeks, having just an oxygen tube in your nose is as good as a whole bunch of drinks out with the buddies."

Ruby put her coffee mug down gently as she thought about the man. "So, just for argument's sake, you had a little fun in your late teens, and then that was it. No more good time... just run around the world protecting the innocent and killing the creeps."

Stone had never thought about his life in short

summation—but it almost fit. "Well, not so much in those terms, but yes. By the time I was a real sergeant, responsibility always overshadowed getting wild or going off and doing anything trivial."

"So you never lived off base?" Ruby shifted in her chair as she sipped her coffee. Her eyes watched the man over the rim.

"Once—I hated it. I rented an apartment overlooking the pool. It was August, and the pool was lined with women lying in the sun. I toured the place on a quiet Sunday morning. I moved in on a Wednesday, and then Friday night and Saturday came. It was nonstop noise."

Ruby laughed. "How long did you last?"

"I moved in on the twenty-sixth of August, and moved out the day after 9/11. Everyone was called back to the bases all over the world."

"Some experiment." Ruby turned sober as she looked in her mug and sipped her coffee. She thought how his freedom had just been another hell with a bad ending.

Stone gave her a moment to digest the meaning of his two weeks of civilian experience. "So where do you go from here?"

She quietly put her mug down on the small table and slowly ran her hands over her arms, thinking. Ruby looked at the stars and sucked her lower lip in around her teeth. Her one eyebrow and shoulder rose. "I really don't know." She leaned back in the chair with a deep sigh. "I've got thirty-two hours a week at Denny's, and I square away a gentleman's apartment twice a month. Molly has a counter job she hates at McDonalds for the twenty some hours a week they will hire a quote, 'person with challenges.' We get by. There was a little life insurance, but after burying

Hank, it only allowed us to move in here."

Stone read her face and voice. "And you hate working half time and so does Molly."

"Right."

Stone's movable eyebrow rose. "Explain, 'squaring away a gentleman's apartment'."

She laughed. "I guess that does sound kind of hanky-panky, doesn't it? But, no. Mike is a regional buyer of wood who exports or ships interstate to make products we don't here. Stuff like furniture or even hardwood boards.

"He's here about one or two nights a week, and then back on the road. He has three sets of luggage and they get packed exactly alike. He has four suits, in triplicate. Two dozen dress shirts, and on and on. When he comes home, he sets the bag on the stand and removes anything but the clothes and ditty bag. I take everything to the laundry, and restock his ditty bag. When it's re-packed, I stick it in the closet, in rotation with the other one. If for some reason he traveled twice in the week, he calls and lets me know. I sort out the two bags and make up one, and have the other cleaned.

"When I clean the apartment, I will gather the dirty clothes and go through the checklist of foodstuff. I drop off everything at the cleaners, do the shopping, and restock the apartment. When he comes home, he knows he has a clean apartment, clean clothes, and fully stocked cupboards, freezer, and bar. So if he was to ever bring someone home, he knows he doesn't have to pick up the old pizza boxes and underwear in the living room or change the sheets before asking if they want to stay the night."

"Wow." Stone's eyes were wide.

Ruby nodded with a smile. "I'll say. It's total mom

and ease of mind for only a grand or so a month."

Stone smirked "You get a grand for that?"

"No, silly, I said he was a smart man, not a push-over. I get five hundred, and the rest is his accounts at the various stores. I just clean and schlep, no keeping track of money."

Stone, ever the strategizing gunny wondered. "Okay, but what about long term? What about going back to Fall, rebuilding Mom & Dad's, or Mom & Molly's?"

Her head rolled back onto the cushion. "Oh, I wish. Molly would be waiting in the car before you finished telling her the idea. And, me... well, all of my memories, good or bad, are there. I like the sound of Mom & Molly's. Hank would have liked it, too. But the land and building weren't ours. We didn't even have insurance that would have rebuilt the structure. In fact, I'm not sure it was insurable as it was."

Stone nodded. "Being a logging cantina?"

Ruby's head rose off the cushion. "You knew about that?"

"I have my sources." He chuckled. "So why can't the landlord rebuild it?"

Her face turned dark. "He's not the sort of person that builds things. He just destroys."

"And calls little girls evil things?"

She furrowed her brow, and then her face exploded as if slapped. Her words slipped out in little more than a breath. "I had forgotten about that day." She looked up with total understanding. "It was you... you on the motorcycle that saved his life."

Stone studied her face and nodded gently.

"You..." Her head whipped around looking for

Molly, who was not there. Her voice lowered back to an almost whisper. "You've spoken to him."

Stone nodded again slowly. Leaning forward, he placed his mug down next to hers. "He's a tough nut to crack, but I guess I'm just harder headed. I can tell you that was one of the worst days of his life. If he could take anything back in his life… it would be having said those awful things, and not hugging Molly. That was a pivotal day for him."

Ruby hissed, "But he's still the man he is. He's not going to rebuild the café."

Stone shrugged. "Maybe not. Maybe the café needs to be down the road a bit. Maybe you just need a new landlord."

"What are you saying? There's no other café in the area, and if there was, it wouldn't be for sale now."

"And there is no building either." Stone leaned in. "All I'm asking is would you be up to doing it if it could be done?"

Ruby half laughed. "What would I do for a cook—you?"

Stone laughed a deep belly laugh. "It could be worse. I can at least burn an egg. We had a guy in Panama that could burn C-rats."

"What's a C-rat?"

Stone chuckled remembering the former company cook. "These days, they call them MREs, which means Meals Ready to Eat. The C-Rats, for Canned Rations, are individual rations used in the deep field or extreme cases when fresh or other canned food wasn't available."

"So I'm guessing that you don't or didn't need to cook anything, but this guy burned them?" Ruby laughed at the humor.

Stone fished his phone out of his pocket and scrolled through his address book. He looked at the record. "Hmm, too bad."

"What's it say?"

"Says he went to bed four hours ago, he's in Maryland. You don't want him as a cook or anything else, he runs a collection agency."

Ruby scrunched her face. "Don't usually need a bill collector for a nine-fifty lunch bill." She leaned over and put her hand on his holding the phone. "So, do you have a good cook in there?"

Stone looked at his watch and thumbed the screen. "As a matter of fact..." His thumb poked the record, and he became rewarded with the sound of a ringing phone.

"Hello?"

"Hi, Miriam, sorry about the late call, but is Spuds there?"

"Stone?"

"I'm sorry, yes. How are you?"

"We're taking everything one day at a time... but we're doing okay. We're moving back into the house now, and Jimmy was just putting away the poles." She chuckled. "We thought of growing beans on them, but who wants to harvest beans twenty feet in the air?"

Stone thought how good it was to hear her laugh.

Now she was shifted into lighter spirits. "How are you doing, Gunny? Where are you?"

"I'm fine, Miriam. I wintered over in Iowa, and now I'm in Medford."

The woman's voice tinkled from the phone's tiny speaker. Stone thought of a wind chime, melodious and happy. "There's a Medford in Iowa?"

"No, I'm here in Oregon. I need to ask James a few questions…"

"He just came in. Here he is." He heard Miriam hand off the phone. "It's Stone."

"Hey, Gunny, how's it hanging?"

"Looser than…" Then he remembered the derogatory ending to a fellow grunt's mother. "Hey, Spuds, I have an important question for you."

"Fire away, Gunny."

Stone smiled evilly. "Is it possible to burn a C-rat?"

"I wouldn't know, Gunny. I'm not a hundred and three years old like someone I know."

"Smart ass." Stone laughed. "Okay, let's take an MRE. Is it possible to make it acceptable for a general or an admiral to eat?"

"Am I cooking?" Stone could picture the young man leaning back against the kitchen counter, lord of his kitchen kingdom… wizard of the world of food.

"Of course."

Spuds became serious; the conversation was about food. "What country, and what conditions?"

"Here, in Fall, Oregon. You get a week to go shopping."

Spuds laughed. "Jeez. I thought you were asking a tough question. Why Fall? what's there besides ash and burned-out snags?"

Stone's voice turned into pure gunny. "The restaurant you're going to be cooking in."

"Okay, so it's a restaurant… and MREs for a general."

The gunny reassigned the restrictions. "Let's make it

harder, it's for an Admiral from the Pentagon."

"Okay, a prissy little fuck. Well, first..."

"Wait, tell this to Ruby, your new boss." Stone handed the phone to the surprised woman and leaned back with a self-satisfied smile.

Ruby waved her long hair out of the way and put the phone to her ear tilted so Stone could hear, too. "Hi... Spuds was it? I'm Ruby."

The stars twinkled like no other that Stone had seen before. The city sound was quite lulling, but as Ruby had eluded, still a city. Stone drifted in and out as he caught the short acknowledgments from a novice to Spuds weaving visions that would leave anyone hungry. Even if he were talking over a dinner of large lamb burgers in a place of white tablecloths and an owner with an infectious laugh and an English accent, Spuds could have you drooling, and ready to order whatever he was serving. Stone laid his head back and smiled as he thought, *I guess I'm becoming a foodie.*

BAER CHARLTON

26

The creaking door roused Stone from his slumber. In the dim light, Ruby stood in her bathrobe. Quietly, almost floating, she crossed the room on silent bare feet. She looked down at the man lying in her spare bed. A slim smile flickered across her face in the dark where he could not see. She knew the dark T-shirt he was sleeping in probably had four capital letters on the back, USMC. For some, adjusting to civilian life would take another whole lifetime. Quietly, he asked, "Ruby, what's wrong?"

Equally as quiet, she put her index finger to his lips. "Shh-shh-shh." She silenced him as her bathrobe slid from her shoulders to the floor. The short white satin slip glowed warmly in the moonlight falling through the window. "You don't need..." She shushed him again as she lifted the sheet and blankets and slid into his curved body, little spoon in the big spoon. Gently pulling his large arm over her like a familiar blanket, she assured him in a low throaty voice, "There is nothing here that will do either of us any harm. In fact, it will probably do us both a lot of good." The night folded over them as the big spoon relented and softened while the moonlight fell gently on the blankets and the couple.

In the soft predawn light, Ruby stirred. The deep gravel voice behind her offered a soft good morning as she sank just a smidge deeper into the bigger spoon. "Are you awake?"

"Not if you're thinking about going for a run," he grunted.

She chuckled, and then remembered he did run daily. "No. But I got to thinking. Is Stone your first name or last?"

"Last."

"Do you have a first name?" Ruby felt she needed to know.

The large arm slid tighter about her shoulder as Ruby felt his head burrow deeper into the pillow. She waited for the snoring to begin, but it never came. "Percival."

Her eyes rolled and looked at the top of her head as she recalled information. Her smile slid sideways as she too burrowed even deeper in the other pillow. "Percival... as in the search for the Holy Grail, it fits. You had a smart mother." Soon the breathing of both matched, slow and steady. The Oregon sun rose gently from behind the eastern mountains and started a new day.

STONEHEART

BAER CHARLTON

27

"Well, was she interested?"

"I think I have her attention." Stone eased himself down into the lounge chair across from the wheelchair. With the drapes drawn back, the hospital room filled with light. He noticed the book and recognized the cover. A small smile tugged at the scar side of Stone's face where it would not show, but his eyes started to sparkle. Pointing at the book, "How far have you gotten?"

Bernie held up the dragon book and looked at it with curiosity as if it had just appeared in his lap. "He's hurt in Normandy." Then looking up, he asked, "Did you leave this in here?"

"I read it, and I didn't see any reason to not leave it." Stone shrugged.

Bernie continued reading the page. "Hmm, it's not the little kid's book the cover suggests."

"Kind of hits a chord, doesn't it?"

The older man looked at Stone for any signs of mockery or sarcasm, but found none. He gently marked his place and laid it aside. "We'll see." Turning the chair, he started to roll, and then stopped. "You have that phone of yours?"

Stone nodded and fished it out and offered it to Bernie, who refused.

"You're going to need Daniel's phone number, so you might as well put it in there." Bernie gave him the information, and then accepted the phone as it rang the number. "Good morning, Sylvia. It's Bernie. I need to speak to Dan, please."

Bernie cupped his hand over the phone as if it were an old school phone, never realizing the pick-up microphone was still exposed. "Sylvia is Dan's mother. She never cut the apron strings, even after he got married..." He hurriedly put the phone back to his ear, "Yes, and a damn fine job you do of mothering, I mean looking after him as you do, dear." He rolled his eyes at being caught. "Yes, dear."

"Daniel, Bernie. Listen, I need you to pull together all the paperwork you need on the strip of commercial land in Fall for transferring the title." He listened. "Right, and bring it all over here to the hospital as soon as you can. We need to roll fast on this before I lose the fish of a buyer off my hook." Bernie looked at Stone with a wry smile and winked. "Correct, we're going to run a straight-up quitclaim deed on an all-cash sale. I found a mud-sucking carp who doesn't know how much ash he's buying. He probably thinks it's prime timber. Oh, and bring a notary so you can post it all after the sale. We'll see you when you get here." He handed the phone to Stone.

Stone chuckled as he slipped the phone back into his jacket. "Moss doesn't grow on you, does it?"

"Not when I have a stupid bleeding-heart fish on the hook." Bernie cackled. "It'll take him at least an hour to get here, so push me down to the cafeteria. I'm dying for some real coffee."

***

"MIS-ter Mynhoffer," The large nurse stood in the cafeteria doorway with her fists buried in her hips.

Stone giggled and almost sprayed his mouthful of coffee all over the table, and Mynhoffer leaked a small spray before he swallowed the rest. "Cheese it! It's the Butterfly. Quick, hide me." A giggling Bernie pulled on Stone's shirtsleeve and leaned behind him for protection.

The nurse in question strode over to the table and leaned over the two men as if they were arrant boys, which was not too far off the mark. "Bernie Mynhoffer, you know better than to be out in a public space like this in your condition. Besides, your lapdog, Daniel Davidson, is up in your room and most probably ready to check your colon with his nose." Message delivered, she spun around and marched off.

Stone looked at Bernie. "In your condition? What's wrong with public spaces?"

Bernie pouted at the retreating Amazon as he flapped his hand at Stone. "It's nothing. I'll tell you later. Just push me back so we can get this done."

Stone did not like being in the dark, but also knew he was no one to be lecturing anybody on minding the medical directives. He pushed in silence.

The afternoon sun was just starting to slant enough to shed light across the table under the window in the private room. The notary was all business. Stone did not think she said more than five words other than *"sign here, here, here, and here,"* and *"initial here, here, here, and here."*

As they were signing, the trumpets of DC gave her a

little start, but she kept on doing the business of clearing the signatures on the documents so she could leave the proceedings of a crazy old man and his friend.

From Ski:
What up?
From Stone:
Buying land. How much $$ do I have?
From Ski:
If serious — I have 2 ck
From Stone:
Ck
Can U swing a hammer?

Shuffling the paperwork into proper order, the man in the suit sounded almost ready to whine. Stone really was not much impressed, but he understood what they were doing was not in Bernie's or his lawyer's best interests.

"Just so I'm clear," pointing at the wrinkled one-dollar bill on the table between them. "For the whole and complete sum of one US dollar, you are quitclaim deeding to Stone a total of forty six acres of commercial property in Fall, Oregon."

Bernie nodded and finished. "As well as the full use of two hundred and fourteen adjoining acres to do with what he pleases and, if what he does with it pleases me, I will quitclaim the additional acreage to him as well."

The lawyer finished stuffing all the paperwork away in his briefcase. Closing the case, he leaned back in the chair. "Bernie, we have done some interesting things over the years…"

Bernie cut the lawyer short. "But none of them

benefited the general population of the area. Everything we have done has only benefited you and me. Don't you think it is about time we start giving back?"

The lawyer muttered, "I suppose."

"Stone here will need some help with this project from time to time, and I want you to help him. As long as you can, I want you to bill me or my estate, but when you can see your way clear, I would expect you to also start practicing some pro bono work, too." Bernie's one eyebrow rose as he looked into the lawyer's eyes and soul.

Exasperated by the old friend and client, the lawyer turned toward Stone. "Do you have any ideas as to what extent you want to develop the strip?"

Stone smiled. "I have some fog, but for right now, the three or four structures are the important ones to jump on. Down the road, I think some kind of farmer's market like Bernie was talking about. I saw a lot of different markets in other countries, and they all create a place for building community and that is what Fall is going to need the most in the next several years."

The lawyer stood and extended his hand. "Well, it's a hell of a different idea than I woke up with this morning, but I like it." They shook. "It was great meeting you. Bernie, you look really good for a man that's dying, so keep up what you're doing. Stone, we'll stay in touch," he inclined his head and left.

The two men sat looking at each other with silly self-satisfied grins. Bernie nodded at the drawer, but Stone shook his head. Reaching over for his jacket, he withdrew a bottle of eighteen year-old Scotch from the inner pocket. "I took the liberties this morning. I figured if you saw things my way, even at a fair market price for just the five acres, there wouldn't be any reason to be drinking paint stripper."

Bernie smiled and offered out the two glasses with no ice. At Stone's questioning look, he offered, "At eighteen, ice is sacrilegious."

Stone poured, put the bottle down, and laid the cap beside it.

Thinking a moment, Stone raised his glass. "Here's to building communities."

Bernie smiled. "I like the sound of that." Raising his glass higher, he added, "Hoorah."

They leaned back and sipped in friendship as they thought about what changes could happen in four short hours.

"Okay, Bernie, I'm going off shift." The large nurse stopped just inside the doorway, and then slowly walked over to the table. Lifting the bottle of Scotch, she read the label and slowly closed her eyes as she seemed to cave in on herself. She opened her eyes and gave the two men a stern look, spun on her heel and left. Less than one minute later, she returned and quietly placed another glass on the table, and in a low growl finished, "I'm going off shift. I will be back in less than ten minutes. Hide that damn bottle, but you best be keeping it close because I am not going anywhere until I hear just what the hell happened in here today."

True to her word, it was closer to eight minutes before she was back with her rolling desk chair she had taken from the nurses' station. Her moccasin clad feet, and beaded fringe leather jacket over her blue scrubs were as incongruous as a black woman with a Native American name, or someone larger than Stone with a name like

Butterfly, but there she sat and giggling like a schoolgirl as the two men explained their cockamamie plan.

"You know, when Fawn and Ed were looking at opening that clinic in Grants Pass, they had plans drawn up. I'll bet they would still have those plans, and with some expansion, it would probably handle that physical therapy gym you're talking about." She leaned back laughing with two dark hard apples for high cheeks. "Hell, whatever they have would beat out raising a pole barn."

Stone shook his head. "What's a pole barn? A barn to stick poles in or a Polish barn?"

Butterfly jerked forward and leaned toward Bernie. "Is this boy special?"

Bernie, who had been quiet for a while, just mumbled, "Nah, he's just not country... yet." He seemed a little out of breath.

The nurse and longtime friend leaned in closer. "How much did you drink?"

The patient gathered the strength to point at the glass, which still had at least a finger left of a two-finger pour.

She put her hand on his forehead, and then started to gather him up. "Help me get him on the bed, Stone." The two lifted the man who weighed less than he appeared.

Stone looked at the man who now seemed a bit small for the bed. Then he looked up at the nurse who had a very concerned look on her face as she shucked out of the leather jacket. The only thing she wore which did not plainly state "Nurse" were the beaded moccasins.

As Butterfly replaced the oxygen cannula into Bernie's nose and adjusted the oxygen flow, the soft whisper of a voice came from the pillow. "Tell him. He needs to know."

She gave Bernie an ugly look as if she had bitten a piece of rotting apple and had only found half of the worm. She looked at Stone and nodded. He followed her out into the hall. She turned to face the seemingly empty nurses' station. "Chelsi, I'm back on. Find Doctor Feelgood and get his ass here now. I don't care what or who he is doing at this hour, just get him here. Call over to the Red Cross. We need a unit of matched platelets and get that lazy flea biter up here toot sweet. I want a full work up and have the lab rush the B and counts." She waited a couple of heartbeats. "You hear me, Chelsi?"

"Yes, ma'am. Feelgood, platelets, and blood—STAT."

The Butterfly started to turn toward the cafeteria, and then the Hawk turned back. "And Andrew, you get your tongue out of Chelsie's territory and back to the third floor where you belong, or I will be having words with that sweet wonderful wife of yours."

A chagrined male voice answered, "Yes, ma'am. Right away, ma'am."

Butterfly stood with one fist buried in a slung-out hip. Staring at Stone, her eyes burned under the half-closed lids as she listened to rubber soled shoes hurrying down the hall on the other side of the wing. Looking through the walk-through, they caught a glimpse of a young man walking fast as he was pulling his scrub bottoms into place.

Butterfly gave Stone a disgusted knowing look. "I don't have to talk to my niece. She already knows what kind of a jerk she married. And what he doesn't know is that she only has twelve more units before she can sit for the bar and be a lawyer." She smiled with a satisfied smile, wide and toothy. Stone liked this woman more and more.

288

She would have made a great gunnery sergeant or master chief.

After she squared the blood tech away, Butterfly and Stone sat in the cafeteria talking. She explained Bernie's condition.

"So this pine cancer, it's fatal?" Stone was lost.

"No, not always, but it's nasty. Unlike a regular lung cancer, you have many things going on in a forest. Besides all of the pollens, there are the spores and molds. Throw in a few hundred fires over a lifetime, and you have some collected ash. Any of these can start the cancer, but the others see the shark-feed, and pile in."

"So, where is Bernie in all of this?"

Butterfly looked down the hall at a noise only she heard. "A month ago, when he was first told, he just walked away. He was just ready for the end. That is a little before you found him, and they probably won't be doing any serious investigation into the cause of that accident."

"I saw the tire tracks. They were straight off the curve. You couldn't have drawn a straighter line to that tree."

The nurse scowled. "Hmm, yeah, the last tree standing…"

"But what now?"

"It's a holding pattern. We're hoping for a lung transplant, but we can't start radiation or chemo because he's too weak for the transplant. So we throw the dice. The good news is his blood is type O, and no match easier made in heaven."

Stone's face was half surprised as it pulled on the scars. "Why a transplant? Isn't it a little radical?"

"More like conservative. All of the warring shit is in

his lungs. Remove that, and you're only dealing with the residual stuff. After that, organ rejection is a walk in the park— respectively speaking."

"Is there anything I can do?"

She gave him a good look, thinking long and hard as to what she could tell this man. Finally, throwing convention to the wind, she said, "You already have been doing it." Butterfly put her fingers up and started counting, "You got rid of the shit he was sneaking. You got him talking, and now you have given Bernie something to look forward to accomplishing. Hell, for a dying man, I haven't seen him so alive in the last twenty years."

She leaned in toward Stone. "But, between you, me, and the stump in the forest, you best be getting' on with that project. He's going to need something bigger than a hole in the ground to get him out of his bed soon, with or without new lungs."

Stone held up his finger. "Thanks for reminding me. I have a phone call to make before midnight in Florida."

The nurse stood up to leave. "No, you stay sitting. You and your phone have a lot of work to do. I'll be in with Bernie. Doctor Feelgood should already be there, and the lab should have called me by now. I'll be back up in a few, and check in with you on my way out." Stone watched her steam down the long hall. *Yup,* he thought, *A master chief, for sure.*

He listened to the rings and the third was interrupted. "Dammit Stone, you never call a girl, you never send a girl flowers, and now, in the middle of the night, you call right in the middle of a great movie."

Stone laughed. "Which one?"

"*Lawrence of Arabia.*"

"Ah, what the hell, Rusty, I hate to spoil it for you, but the Arabs did it."

The gravelly half-feminine laugh rattled through the phone. "How the hell have you been, mister? Last I heard you were burrowing into a snow bank in Minnesota or somewhere cold."

"Close, it was Iowa. Now I'm in Oregon... and I need your help."

"Good, because my new girlfriend, and I just got back from a cluster fuck in Haiti, and we are raring to go do some real damage somewhere."

"Haiti? Girlfriend? Hello? Did I dial some strange number?"

Rusty growled a laugh. "Honey, we are strange." They both laughed. "I went down to Haiti to do a build of two hundred homes. Because of one thing and another, three-quarters of the materials were stolen and resold on the black market. So, we built a total of nine homes that, when I left, had no wire in the walls and no pipes where they were needed. It was the most frustrating three months I have ever spent in my life."

"And the new woman in your life?"

"That is a mystery, which we'll have to wait until you meet my Angel. So, where do I set the GPS for this run?"

Stone gave up. "I would tell you Fall, Oregon, but it won't show up. Set it for Medford for now, and we'll talk in a few days."

Stone thought as he was about to hang up. One more tease— "Oh, Rusty, can you build four things at once?"

"Oh gawd, Stone, I'm going to have to beat you about the head and shoulders when I get there. Yes, I can do those micro-miniature projects. I built developments for a living."

"Okay, I guess I'm going to have to trust you then. Thanks, Rusty."

Rusty settled down. "Give me a week or so Stone. I'm getting older, and can't drive so far in a day."

"Roger that." Stone thumbed off the phone and leaned back, smiling.

Laughing, he decided to have some more fun.

From Stone:
When you are finished with that,
Can you swing a hammer?

The trumpets sounded before he placed the phone on the table.

From Admiral:
Are you serious?
This I want to watch.

From Ski:
Is a frog's asshole watertight?

From Stone:
You two have any time off coming?

From Ski:
We have to talk to our boss right now
Will call in morning

From Stone:
Tell the POTUS I said hi

STONEHEART

BAER CHARLTON

28

The late spring rains beat on the large showroom windows. Slim wondered if the clouds were more connected to his life than the meteorologists might know. Any other year, he would be sitting in this window like a kid in a candy store choosing between this truck body, ooh, and maybe the red one over there. The blue one looked like it had more room in the sleeper, but then again, did he really need any more room?

A phone rang and Slim languidly turned his head to look back into the sales office. Nobody seemed to be jumping on the phones. Then Slim realized his leg was vibrating as the old school phone jangle came from his pocket. The one ringtone Slim did not think he would ever hear.

Slim fished the phone from his pocket on the third ring. "Stone?"

"Hey, Slim, how is the hauling business?" Stone greeted.

"Hmm," Slim pondered what to tell a man he had met only one morning almost two years before. "A lot has happened since I met you, son."

"Slim, I'm sitting down, and having coffee. What's going on?"

"Whall, you remember my sister and her husband had the truck stop we ate at."

Stone nodded through the phone. "Ellie and some suave dark Italian named Harold. Yes, I not only remember them, but I just tried to call the truck stop. They only told me there were new owners, and they couldn't talk about the past owners. What the hell happened out there?"

Slim took a deep sigh and dove in. "Harold had been dying of liver cancer. He just didn't know it until he was so tired he couldn't even pull a short four-hour shift without taking a two-hour nap. Ellie knew, but some guys are just a little hard headed. So, she sold the stop to one of the big chains. They went home and then down to Key Largo and just waited until he just didn't wake up one morning. If I didn't already know my sis was a saint all these years putting up with me, she nailed her claim to that there barn door for sure now."

"So, now what, Slim? You sound like you're at a truck stop now."

Slim looked out the window. His voice was years and miles away. "Dealer. son, truck dealer."

"Time to buy a new rig?"

Slim's focus wandered down the line-up of new trucks. "Nope, time to hang it all up. With the truck stop being what it is, and regulations, insurance, carrier weights, run sheets, fuel costs, the lack of decent Smokey's on the road, crazy drivers, and not a decent meal from here to Omaha... Whall, it just stopped being fun. So I'm selling, not buying this time."

Stone could feel the lead in the man's heart. Somehow, he knew the man should not be left on that battlefield—no man left behind. "Dang, Slim, that is the worst luck—just when I needed a trucker I could depend on."

"Whall, Stone, I appreciate the vote of confidence, but I'm sure there are other drivers... out there..." Slim's eyes tracked a restored Peterbilt driving by the window. The sun was sparkling off fresh chrome details—not too many, just enough. The candy apple red paint had the look you only saw on trucks in the late seventies. It was the paint job that screamed *Owner-Operator* with pride. The kind of rig Slim had seen in the early days and had only dreamed about driving.

"Slim... Slim, did I lose you?" Stone could hear the breathing and truck noises, just not his friend.

"No... no... I'm here, Stone." He diverted his eyes to the highway so he could concentrate. "Just got distracted for a moment."

"She'd better have had some great long legs there, Slim... you about fell off the earth," Stone joked.

Slim ripped out one of his trademark belly laughs. "Oh, she had better than long legs, she has a large front-end, if you know what I mean." He laughed so hard he almost coughed up a lung, and snuck another quick lustful look at the cherry in the lot. *Who would need Viagra with a rig like that?*

Slim remembered the phone. "So what kind of hauling do you all need there, Stone?"

"I don't know, but it all has to come to Oregon. I haven't located anything yet, but it's going to be a wide variety of stuff, like building materials, and large tents, maybe a motorcycle or two. What do you need to haul that kind of stuff?"

The lifelong trucker weighed the information. "Whall, I reckon, most of that would be flatbed stuff. If you haul it all this summer, it can all be flatbed stuff. Even the motorcycles can tolerate a little rain... It's just when the lightning starts, you might want to pull the rider inside."

They both laughed as the owner of the dealership walked up with paperwork. "Stone, I have some paperwork to go through. Randy is about to try his semi-annual screw me and then try to rob me blind while I'm in the throes of a new truck-smell orgasm. He just doesn't know that I've been fakin' it all these years." The brunt of the joke smiled at the old humor, which went back to one of the first trucks he ever sold to Slim.

"Tell him to leave some for me, Slim. And think about how I can get these materials from the East Coast to Oregon, with several stops on the way."

Slim signed off. "Ten-four, good buddy. I'll catch you on the flip side."

The dealer tapped the stack of paperwork on the table and then started thumbing through as if he were looking for one certain item. Slim let him do his dance. It was all part of the same dog and pony show they had done for the past few decades. Over the dealer's shoulder, Slim watched as one of the yard hawks made just as much of a deal. Innocently, the worker slowly worked backing the red truck into a slot where it directly faced the owner's office window. If it had been for general sale, he would have parked it way down the line to face the sales office windows instead.

A slow sad smile crept across the large man's left

cheek. "Cut the crap, Randy." The man stopped and looked up like an innocent spring lamb. "We go back too far. I know every trick you have ever pulled and have driven some the shittiest deals you have ever forced on me. The only thing worse you could have done was force me to marry that skank sister of yours."

The man smiled at the mention of his younger sister who Slim had dated in high school and went on to be Miss Arkansas and marry one of the more respected bankers in their hometown. He gave Slim his blank stare of innocence. "Why, whatever do you mean, Slim?"

Slim leaned in and growled, "There is a cherry bomb sitting out there, and your yard hawk just stuck a sign on that says 'Slim's'. I know you. You had them parade it by a few minutes ago, and now this."

The man did not have to turn around. He knew exactly where it was parked because the slot had stayed vacant, held on the overcrowded lot for over a week, waiting for this moment. His finger slid through the pile of paper to the last sheet. Putting it on top, he began the bullet points as he knew his audience would be looking at the merchandise. "The shell is original 1969, but everything else is a Peterbilt 579 XRT."

"There's no such thing as an XRT." Slim snapped, catching his good friend in a lie.

"Excellent Retirement Truck." Randy calmly looked down and continued, hiding his small smile. "It has a state of the art instrument cluster, including a Ryan storm scope so you can get the ninety-four layers of lacquer under cover before the hail tap dances on your hood. The sleeper has been stretched to include a wide-screen TV with a ground-plane satellite dish, Bose surround sound in both cabins, wet bar, a commode and a high capacity six-head sauna-shower. The custom machined fifth wheel has a full run of tracking." He fished out a large photo and flipped it over for Slim to see. The standard grease slots had been filled in, and new ones cut, spelling out *Not For Hire.*

Slim lowered one eye and looked through the eyebrows of the other. The dealer smiled and leaned back in his large padded chair. Knitting his fingers together behind his head. "Okay, I lied about the shower, but the rest is all there." He spun around in the chair to gaze on the object of their mutual admiration. In hushed tones of pure reverence, he related the rest of the story. "She was coming across the auction over in KC. She had been built as a parade queen, but near the very end, the guy lost everything in a tornado. I knew he'd get raped if it went on the block, so I ran out to talk to the old boy. I made him the offer he needed, he pulled it from the field, and I drove it back. We put the last few things on it, and now it's ready to go."

Slim thought about the deal and the years he and Randy had danced with each other since school. "What did you give him?"

"I gave him twenty-eight, and I sent him a couple of old trucks I needed to get rid of. All total, I'm into her thirty-three."

Slim nodded gently, acknowledging the information. "How big is the stake going through my heart?"

"Thirty-five."

Slim thought about the paltry two grand spread. "What about the two rigs you sent him?"

Randy looked across the desk at his oldest and closest friend. "What part of 'I needed to get rid of' did you not understand?"

Slim thought about his longtime friend and almost brother-in-law. "I'll need a trailer, too."

"You have two trailers."

"I need a flatbed."

"You don't drive a flatbed."

"I just started."

Randy was one of Slim's oldest friends. If there was anything to know about Slim, Randy knew it, especially if it had anything to do with his trucks.

Randy gave Slim a hard stare. "Since when?"

Slim looked at his watch, "Whall," he drawled, leaning back in his catbird seat, "I figure it's been at least three or four minutes."

They held deadpan stares, neither daring to blink. "What?"

"I need a full with twins on the back. Triple would be better, with matching cat back."

The man ran his fingers through his sandy graying hair, then reached over to his phone and dialed some numbers. "Danny, do we still have that high-medium bridge-weight triple-axle Dane out back?" He waited. "Great, move it to the paint shop, and pimp it to match the red Pete. And Danny, I want all new shoes full around, this is the last run at Slim, and I'm not gonna have him jacking his jaw out on the interstate about how he got screwed one last time."

Hanging up the phone, he turned to Slim. "It's a forty-eight and should be ready for anything other than a D-9 cat. I'll throw in a full set of tarps, bangs, and cinches. I'll take your rig with the two trailers and…" He looked at another sheet in the stack, and rolled his eyes up to see the calculator in his mind, "eighteen thousand."

Slim knew the man had left no margin in there for any profit. He also knew, with their history, it was not for him to question what the man wanted to do. "How soon?"

Randy rolled his eyes and looked at information about his business that was never on paper. "Give me a couple of weeks on the paint, and we'll make sure it's ready for anything you want to do with it."

Slim shifted in his chair. The deal was done. "It sounds like a run to the east and then off to Oregon."

Randy smiled. "She'll almost break a sweat."

They rose up shaking hands. The two familiar hands formed a longtime fit. "You have a car I can borrow until the Cherry Bomb is ready?"

"Well, I'd loan you my Porsche if you knew how to drive a stick." He fished his keys from his pocket. "Oops, hmm, drove the Caddie today. You're in luck." Smiling, he handed him the wad of keys.

"I don't need the house keys," starting to remove the car key.

Randy frowned. "Then where are you going to stay?"

Slim smiled evilly. "I might stay at your place, but I have a set of my own."

"Where did you get a set?"

"From your wife," Slim locked him in another deadpan contest.

Randy blinked. The old salesman knew he had just been sucker punched by his best friend. His smile smeared to one side.

Slim smiled at the old joke between the two men and their wives. "I'll go on down to Key Largo and shack in with Ellie. Maybe I'll work on my tan."

The dealer walked him out. "Well, you know where everything is, and the spare room is always made up and never used. Just call Toni before you walk in on her naked or something."

They shook with all four hands in a ball. "I'll see you in a couple of weeks. Call me when it's done, and I'll be right back."

Slim slid into the soft seat of the big car. Pulling the phone out, he paired it to the hands-free and called Stone. "I have a flatbed truck and a driver for y'all. They'll be available in about two or three weeks."

Stone boomed back through the car's speakers in stereo. "Sounds great, Slim. I'll give you a call when I know what needs to be coming and from where, then you can direct the truck driver from there, or you're welcome to fly out and be part of what we're doing."

Slim smiled. "Oh—not just no, but hell no—this man will never fly. Just give me a call."

"So where are you going to be?"

Slim laughed. "I've got a big car, and I'm headed for Fat City—Key Largo. I'm going down to shack in with my sister for a while. We need to do some jawing about life and moving on."

"Take care of your family, Slim. I'll be in touch." Stone hung up, and started poking his phone.

From Stone:
Have truck & driver in 2 wks
From Ski:
Have tents, and a few other things

Slim wheeled the large car as if it were a micro-mini

car. Surprising a Toyota as he nosed the large car out onto the boulevard, Slim headed for the interstate. Casually, as he watched the rearview mirror, his right hand slid down between the two large seats. His fingers curled around the handle of the forty-four Magnum Bulldog pistol. Without looking, he knew it was loaded with custom hot loads, and full metal-jacketed slugs for deep penetration.

Slim smiled as he thought about habits and how they can define people. Turning on the radio, he poked the fourth setting button—his favorite radio station. As he turned on to the on-ramp, he goosed the big V-8 engine and relaxed into the soft deep-cushioned seat. He chuckled to himself as the car slid into the third lane of the freeway he thought *some things just never change.*

STONEHEART

BAER CHARLTON

29

The man looked out the large door. The street was quiet, almost no traffic. Behind him, the mechanic dropped the outside case shielding the primary chain on the Harley. The cool gray eyes danced from the street to windows, trash bins, anything that might move or hide anything that could move, or be a threat. The body had returned from the war, but the war had never left the mind. His hearing only partially focused on the movements of the strong slender fingers of the mechanic.

Max looked up and over her shoulder. She knew that stance, had seen it dozens of times with dozens of returning bodies. Max gave him the bad news in a gentle voice. "It's time for a new primary, and you have two teeth missing on the main drive sprocket."

He nodded, looking back at the mechanic who had recently become a friend. "Go ahead, Max. Any idea about how long?"

"Give me a couple of hours." She straightened up to her full six-foot and then some. "Before you walk off, let me check the stock."

Max stopped and pulled the phone out of her back

pocket, looking at the caller ID. "Yeah Gunny?" She listened, nodding as she walked over to the man in the doorway. "Here, Stone, I need to check some stuff, so you talk to him." She handed the phone to the man with the long black hair. "Talk to him."

"This is Osiel."

Max's ponytail flipped a low arc as she spun to walk deeper into the shop, leaving the two men to talk things over. She already knew she and Peanut were in. She smiled and pulled the items needed. *Heck, a chance to go camping with a bunch of old and new friends, what's not to like?*

"Sure, pulling wire for a house or commercial is all the same. Circuits are bigger, and the gauge is thicker, but wiring is wiring. Count me in, I'll just tell the union hall I'm on vacation."

Max showed the man the parts and a thumbs-up. He nodded. "Sure, just let me know a few days out, and I'll head your way. I even have my own framing hammer and nail-bender belt."

Osiel turned and smiled at Max, nudging his chin with a questioning look on his face. She mouthed back quietly, "Hoorah." He silently chuckled. "Yeah, and I guess I could stick a gun to Max's head and force her to come along, too. Sure. Okay, we'll talk soon." He hung up the phone and returned it to the mechanic. "It sounds like one hell of a project."

She laughed. "Osiel, you missed the last one, this is not a project. This is going to be one hell of a party. I just wonder if Jeannie and Elvis will be there."

"Elvis?"

"Seeing is believing, my good man." Max turned back to the bike. "If I'm lyin', I'm dyin'. Now go get some lunch or something. I have work to do." Max flipped the long ponytail to her back, sat down on the mechanic's crawler, and smiled as she adjusted her dog-pawed sports bra.

***

Two thousand miles away a phone rang on the wall. Above the phone was a large rotating red light that had come from the top of a state trooper's patrol car. The bright red light flashed around the walls. The three-fingered hand finished pushing the board through the large noisy shaper, reached down, and shut the machine off. The hook that on most days substituted for a right hand reached for the belt and tapped the remote that turned off the howling dust collector. The man spun on his feet and tapped one of many small remote triggers about the shop.

"Howling Dog Woodworks," the man answered the distant phone, which was now on speaker. He leaned his fleshy butt against the edge of the large cast iron table of the shaper.

"Is that howling coming from scratching your nuts with a sharp hook?" The high-pitched voice tinkled with a slight metallic trace from the speaker.

"Tinkerbelle, does your mommy know you're making obscene phone calls to a dirty old man that's standing buck nekkid in his woodshed?"

"Only wood you'll ever raise again, old man."

"Sweetie, if I didn't love ya before, I'd marry you all over again."

"I might not be as drunk the second time and probably just say no, so we could live in sin instead of the middle of the Ozarks."

"So, is lunch ready?"

"No, I still have my panties on, but you have an email that Herb forwarded to you from a Ski. Looks like there is something... yada, yada, blah, blah... looks like we're taking a trip to Oregon."

"What's in Oregon?" He gently scratched behind his ear with the hook. The old scar still itched every once in a while, even after twenty-some years. The doctors said that the nerves may knit one by one for the rest of his life, but Somalia was fresh in his mind every day.

"Do I have to send you to the vet to get you checked again? Trees are in Oregon and someone named Gunnery Sergeant Stone."

The man's head snapped up and looked at the phone. "Did you just say Sergeant Stone?"

"I didn't stutter, honey."

He rocked his butt off the cool metal and stood. "Honey, we're taking that honeymoon I've always promised you. Call the storage and have them pull the RV out and prep it. I'll be in and call Herb back."

"So who is this Stone guy? I haven't been able to get you past the big muddy for love nor money."

"Make me a special lunch, and I'll tell you after. It's a long story."

"Okay, big Hammer, I'm a taking the panties off rat now... lunch in ten minutes."

He was already turning off all of the breakers. "Put the black lace ones back on, and I'll be there in three."

"Oh, honey, you really are a dreamer."

The man pulled the large barn door across and locked it. Turning, he made his way across the five acres on one foot, and one finely carved wooden peg—the best advertisement he had ever spent time doing. His mind was not on the large woman in the orchid print muumuu now bustling about the kitchen making the noon meal. As he walked up the pine-needle strewn forest path, his mind was stuck in a bombed out school, thousands of miles away and twenty years before, and a sergeant who had saved his life by a simple mistake.

The speakerphone at the office was warm from the long conversation between the two old Marines. "So we're just showing up and doing whatever there is to do?"

Herb chided his friend. "Squirrel, I'm sure if you call this yeoman, Ski, she could fill you in a little better. But you hung up on her a couple of years ago, so I'm not sure that it would be better if maybe I call her."

The woodworker ran his hand over his head. "Nah, my screw-up, I should fix it."

Herb acquiesced. "Whatever flips your boards, Squirrel."

"Well, hell, Herb, I was thinking that if they really are building stuff out there in the forest, it might be a handy thing to bring my portable sawmill. If they have logs, I can run them down to boards for something like siding. The worst would be I have to just drag it home again unused."

Herb thought about all of the raw wood. "I could drag my portable shop along, too. You never know." He thought a moment. "If they have trees, maybe I could turn some green bowls to bring back to finish later. It would at least help with the fuel."

Squirrel shifted the conversation's gears. "Yeah, fuel. What are you getting with that pusher of yours?"

"Just the RV, I get almost seven, but with the trailer, I'll be good to average six."

The two continued to talk about their favorite

subjects— their RVs and travel. They were always ready for a little road trip. The wives stayed happy and would swap riding off together in one or the other bus, or just throw the men out and it would be a girl bus and boy bus. Either way, the four were content to be on the road no matter what the reason.

From Ski:
Eight Field tents in Omaha
Yours 4 duration
1 - Complete Mess for battalion –
thought U might want.
Shower trailers on way
Happy to be on the road, no matter what the reason.

From Stone:
Thx – send address
Truck on way

From Ski:
Better B big truck

From Stone:
Driver big 2

From Ski:
I know?

From Stone:
No
But he makes my hug feel small

From Ski:
Jeannie bringing Elvis?

From Stone:
OMG – I have 2 run 2
***

"Slim?"

"Stone, I have you on speaker in my new truck. What's hanging?"

Stone laughed. "I have three more addresses, and they are almost in a line on your way."

"Just tell me the cities, and what I'm doing, Stone. Then send the addresses and info to my new email address and it will load directly into my truck's route-master."

"Slim, I'm not even going to pretend that I might know what you just said, and I'm not even sure it wasn't dirty."

"Come on, Stone." The big driver laughed. "You have to keep up with this stuff or the kids will end up running the country."

"Oh, hell, Slim, they already do. Okay, here is what you're doing. First, there is a nun you need to pick up in Des Moines. Her name is Stella, and she's like a sister to me."

Slim laughed at the pun. "I'm sure she'll be like a sister to me, too. Good thing I have a jump seat in this rig, Ellie is coming, too."

Stone considered the ramifications of the news. "I thought she was retired in the Keys or something?"

"Retired from working her ass off, but that didn't mean she gave up her class A driver's license? She and I would have been team drivers if it weren't for Harold and the truck stop."

"What about sleeping? Isn't it a little tight with three

people?"

"Why, the good sister can have the third sleep shift, with the two of us drivers, there isn't much reason to stop except for food, fuel, and a shower."

Stone stumbled. "What about…"

Slim laughed as he led the truck right onto an on-ramp. "The only thing my new sleeper doesn't have is a shower."

"Okay, Slim, I'm sure you and Ellie can teach Stella things. She's had it worse but she is a mother superior now."

"We'll say grace. So you said three stops. What are the other two?"

Stone pictured the map in his mind. "After you get Stella, then it's just a short hop to Omaha, Nebraska for your main load. It's about twenty-five tons of tents and field commissary. Eight full company barrack tents in total at the National Guard base are assigned to an Admiral Mike Woodford. All of the paperwork is done and you're expected.

"Next, you have a longer run and south a bit to Salt Lake City. I need you to swing by and see my Harley doctor. She has some stuff that needs to come out, probably a bike or two. If it's too much for you to haul, she'll just have to drive them herself, but I think they were bringing a camper or something."

Slim signaled and slid the truck over a lane. "Ten-four, we're about two hours out of Chicago, and then it's two up to Milwaukee. From there, Ellie can drive, and we can be on the good sister's doorstep in the early light. Did you want me to pick up any cheese while I'm in Wisconsin?"

"Slim, around here, Wisconsin product is called contraband. Just bring the stuff on the list and whatever comes up at the stops, and we'll be good."

"Ten-four, Stone, we're gone."

***

The admiral grabbed his briefcase and hat as he walked out of his inner office. His new yeoman was sitting at her desk. She glanced up briefly and silently returned to her work. Her eyes sparkled from staring into the monitor and entering notations of troop movements and fleet status. The mountain of information, which flowed daily through his office, was a three-person job, but with cutbacks, he was restricted to only a single ensign. "What's the count, Captain?"

"Not counting the shock troops, I have a rough three hundred and seventy-four."

The admiral turned to where Ski stood with her new bars on her lapel. "And have we heard from the base commander at Pendleton?"

Ski gave the admiral the situation report seemingly from the top of her head. "No, sir. He's on field maneuvers, and he's with the Red Team's Ninja contingency. But his second said that what we propose is an interesting field exercise. They also have a complement of engineers who might want in on this. He said that there are some old guys that go back to the Seabee days, and they would probably want to trade in some R&R time for a part in the party, too." She swung around to face the admiral and smiled. "I'd say that this maneuver is getting nicely out of control, sir."

He smiled at the thought of a small town in southern Oregon about to be invaded by many hundreds of retired and active personnel. All of them there to give to the community and area, something they had had before, as well as something they had been needing for a long time.

The admiral thought a moment. "What day is D-Day?"

"Wednesday. The shock force will fly in from the carrier shortly after dawn and attack the tents and commissary. The commissary and food storage units should all be functioning and ready to stock by noon. The supply trucks are slated for 1500 hours. The convoy is targeting to arrive the next afternoon. We believe that we will have a full green light for 0800 on Friday. The foundations were poured this morning at 0600 Pacific Time. I understand that all the pours went well."

"And we are scheduled for…"

Ski snapped out their itinerary. "Tuesday morning at 0520, we will land in Seattle at 0645 Pacific Time, and be on base by noon. We won't miss the kick off, sir."

"Good." He turned back to his yeoman grinding her way through the mind-numbing numbers and data. "Ensign, don't stay late. It'll be there tomorrow."

The young ensign blushed. "No, sir. I mean, yes, sir. I'll leave when the captain leaves, sir."

The admiral looked at his watch and saw the hands collected at the ten. Turning to the new captain, he said, "Go home soon, Ski."

As Ski was staring into her monitor, she raised her two fingers to her forehead and gave the admiral her best offhand Brownie salute. He smiled and left before she gave him a command.

STONEHEART

BAER CHARLTON

30

Stone, Trent, and Ruby surveyed the forms full of setting concrete. They looked small and ineffectual surrounded by the twenty acres of cleared land. Beyond the graded and smoothed beds, as well as the graveled parking areas, there was nothing but gray ground, black trunks and in the distance, more gray hills. Stone's memory of the deep forest that had surrounded and hidden the small town was now gone. Each day they arrived on site, Stone thought he would be prepared for the shock, and each day it would take him back to another set of nightmares.

Stone looked down the road to where the village still stood. There were trucks and a car at the gas station, people coming and going. The new paint on the buildings was doing a good job at hiding the scorch marks and a few places blistered from the heat. Stone stood watching the life that kept going.

Trent cleared his throat. "We know that in a few years, there will be low growth of green across the valley. In another ten years, the reprod, 'new trees' to you, will be up about twenty feet. In thirty years, there will be harvestable forest and, in fifty, we'll all be dead, but there

BAER CHARLTON

will be large-board trees. Life goes on, Stone. It's one of the big things that make us different from the city folk, we look at life, and they only see possessions."

"But that forest wasn't a possession." Stone stood with his hand stuck out at the destruction, and sounded just a little strident. "It was a beautiful swath of trees. People worked there, animals lived there..." His voice began to rise.

Ruby stepped over, gently took his hand to guide it to her chest as she leaned into him. "Yes, and we know it's more than you see. We grew up here. This forest was here when our parents were children, but it wasn't always. This isn't like a war zone. Stone, this is part of our life. Just the same as Hank and LaLonnie not being here anymore, it's all a cycle of a circle. Everything is born, it grows, and then it dies. Sometimes, it is small like a moth or a mosquito, and other times, it is huge like the Biscuit Fire. One acre or one million acres, if you look at the ashes, it's horrible, but if you look back or forward, it's just a part."

Stone stuttered, "B-but... but it... it just doesn't make sense."

Trent shrugged a shoulder and pulled a small sad smile across his face. His right hand swept from his back pocket up and onto the top of his head, removing the Timbers' ball cap in the motion, "I guess it's just a case of not throwing the hammer."

Stone gave him a hard look. "The what?"

Ruby laughed and patted Stone on the shoulder and arm. "The hammer. It's an old story. And if I'm going to talk about my grandfather, I need some coffee." She wandered over to the car and opened the trunk.

Trent laughed. "You packing a thermos in there,

320

Ruby?"

"Oh, Trent, I should have Stone wash your mouth out with soap for swearing like that." She raised the lid on what looked like a large cooler, and began to lift out strange items. Pulling on some pivoting legs, she pulled a stand of sorts to its almost four-foot height. Next, she placed a burner ring and hose, topped with a large capacity coffee percolator urn. Nodding to Trent, she directed him to the car door. "For your tasteless joke, you can get the water out of the backseat and start filling the urn."

She unzipped a fresh bag of ground coffee, and the aroma hit Stone in the memory box. "That smells like the roasters in east Africa." The scent was one of the few good memories Stone had about his time in the area.

Ruby smiled, "It is mostly Tanzania tea berries, with a bit of Sumatra for body."

"Well, you have one fan right here, and the next one will be working in that building there." Stone pointed, indicating the third foundation. "You might have to figure out how to pipe it over to Mary Margaret so she doesn't wear out your new door."

Ruby smiled over her shoulder as her hands kept working. "From what you have told me of the girl, she can wear out my door any day she wants."

A large bulldozer headed their way. Stone watched in fascination as the driver skewed its blade to push dirt to the side as it ran along a very large trench. Within a few minutes, the large pile of dirt, and the large trench were one—a flat field with two miles of poly-pipe coils spread out for over two hundred yards.

"Wow." Stone turned to Trent. "And that pipe with water in it will end up heating all of these buildings?"

"Same as my house," Trent replied. "All the geothermal does is supply the basic heat, which around here, happens to be warm at 58° because we're close to some lava beds or something. In the community building, they are going to put in a big heat pump, which takes the heat from the ground, and squeezes it to make 120° heat. It goes into the radiant pipes in all the floors, and that heats the buildings. The cost is about a quarter what it would cost to do it with propane or oil."

"That's pretty amazing."

Trent watched the large dozer clean its work as he explained the heating system. "The Romans had it all through Rome, and they stole the idea from the Greeks who got it from the Chinese."

"Gentlemen, we have coffee. Trent, bring your boys in. I brought enough for everyone."

Later, they sat on the tailgate of Trent's truck, looking over the foundations and Stone remembered. "So now that we have the coffee, what is with the hammer?"

Ruby groaned and laughed at the same time. She took a sip and settled her butt just a little firmer on the tailgate. "My grandfather had a wonderful saying when things were just beyond your control, but you still need to rail against the storm, inequity, or even a bent nail. He was from the old country and had many quirks. There was one saying that made no sense to me as a little girl, but for some reason, it did sound right. He used to say in his thickest burr, 'Och, the suffering of it all, but for the chance, if they had only thrown the hammer.'

"I asked my Gran what it meant. She just patted me on the head and said, 'He's just talking back at the wind.' So I let it go, but I loved the saying because Pops, in my heart, was Pops the most, when he was repeating that meaningless old saw."

Ruby leaned forward with her story. "When I was a senior in high school, and about to graduate as the first in our family to do so, Pops came to me and sat me down to have a serious chat. Any time he was about to spend more money than the cost of a stick of gum, it was time for a serious chat to talk over the disbursement of riches and princely sums."

Ruby's voice began to show some deeper emotions as she continued. "He asked me, 'what would you deeply wish for, if the paying of it were of no worries?' That isn't to say he would buy me what I wanted, but it was just that he wanted to know what I wanted. The knowing was supposed to be enough. Pops knew he wanted a Chevrolet, but just knowing it was enough for him to keep fixing the De Soto, which died almost the same week he did. Pops just kept patching and mending, and all the while, knowing he really wanted that Chevy, which for him, was enough.

"So there we sat. Pops thinking I would want something that he would never buy." Ruby drew a heavy sigh, and her voice began to quiver over the thought of her past. "And me wanting only one thing from Pop's other than his kindness and the occasional hug that he bestowed as often as he made a dime squeal. I asked him the real meaning of that saying of his—what was the throwing of the hammer.

"He thought long and hard. He wasn't a man to be pushed lightly or rapidly into what he was about to do. After at least a couple of minutes of Pops wringing his hands and rubbing the face, he was ready. As he told it, a few centuries ago…" Ruby paused in her story.

BAER CHARLTON

Stone's mouth hung open. "Centuries?"

Ruby continued. "I know, I know. Remember, he was from the old country, and time and history are like yesterday to them.

"So, a few centuries ago, the small kingdoms were engaged in constant warfare. The people eventually grew tired of warring, so they decided to have a mock battle or competition to prove their manhood. The winner would rule the entire collective kingdom for a year until they held the games again to choose the king for the next year. Today, we know them as the Highland Games, and today, they are just that—games. But this particular year, it would decide many things, including what to call the entire island.

"So it came down to the last two clans in the grueling elimination—the Scoots, and our clan, the Haags. The competitions were tough, and the men were tougher. It wasn't like today where people had to get up on Monday and go to work at the office, so the games took days, maybe even weeks, and they were tiring.

"It was down to the final competition, and it was up to the Haags to make the choice as to the last game. To make things worse, as the games progressed, because of one thing or another, a game would be eliminated from the choices. Therefore, with the final game, the choices were down to the pike throw, a twenty-five pound javelin, or the hammer throw, a thirty-eight pound stone on the end of a large rope the length of a man's arm.

"The pike is thrown from one end of a field to the other where your opponent is standing, and the goal is to throw it three times. The contestant who throws the pike past his opponent two out of three times is the winner and

324

champion. If both throw all three successfully, then they step back three paces and try again until they have a winner.

"The hammer is swung three times back and forth between the contestant's legs, and then swung over a pole above the head of the thrower. The trick is to throw as straight up as possible in order to get the most height. You have to be swift and nimble as well because the stone was coming back down very quickly. So you needed to jump out of the way, or you weren't going to work on Monday.

"So... the great champion of the Haag clan decided the pike was the best of his talents, and a sure win. It was pikes at forty paces to start.

"The Scoot champion had a great arm on him. Bless his heart... he also cared about his fellow man, which was the undoing of the Haags. They paced off the field of competition, each man traversing what they expected was twenty strides, if they could count. Who knows what really happened that day, but what they did know was that the Scoot champion let go a great effort, but at the last second, slipped ever so slightly.

"When he saw what he had done, and assessed the path of the pike, he yelled a warning to the Haag champion, who happened to be a wee bit deaf. So when it was critical that the Haag be shading his vision to see the pike that was headed right for him, he instead put his hand up to his ear and asked: *'Eh?'*"

"Killed him." Stone laughed.

Ruby drove her finger into the palm of her hand for effect. "Pinned his head to the ground like a butterfly in a pin case."

Stone laughed with an open mouth of awe. "So the

Scoots won, and that is why it's called Scootland... I mean Scotland?"

Laughing she snapped the towel across his chest. "Oh, hell no. The war broke out before his body flopped a third time off the wee heather. They fought tooth and nail for another hundred years in a senseless loss of lives and property."

"But... if they had only thrown the hammer..."

Trent nodded. "Now you're getting it."

Stone offered, for his own clarity, "Sometimes you try to do the right things, but for the twist of fate, it all can go so very wrong. But it's not really anything you had control of, like Bernie's crew just trying to make some repairs, and..." he said as he spread his hand out across the gray landscape, "and now everyone hates him for starting the fire."

She shook her head as she cocked back the one side of her mouth. "Sadly, that is one of the hardest lessons to learn."

Trent added, "Or sometimes hard to make up for... but selling you the property was a good start. As long as you didn't overpay."

Stone looked at his mug before taking a sip. "Oh, I didn't overpay."

As they sat sipping on their coffee, Stone's phone rang. "Stone."

A voice from Stone's past drove a stake of ice through his heart. "Gunny, we have three tanks, a water buffalo, and fourteen dancing girls lined up next to a gas station in some fire zone called Fall. Where do you want us to lay down suppressive fire?"

Stone froze. Ruby could feel his arm muscles tighten,

and his body became a solid block, "Stone? Stone, it's Ruby... Listen, it's okay... Stone talk to me." She grabbed the phone. "Who the hell is this?" she barked. She stood looking into a deathly white face.

"Ma'am, I'm sorry, but the name is Riley, Pete Riley, ma'am. They called me Squirrel, I didn't mean no harm."

"Squirrel, we have a situation here. I'll have to call you back." She hung up the phone and stuck it in her back pocket. "Stone, honey, can you hear me?"

In a voice that felt more like last night's whisper than anything resembling speech, "He's dead. I saw the body."

"Squirrel?"

Stone nodded.

"Honey, dead men don't make phone calls. But when I get my hands..."

"Maybe I can help." The bald black man with Clark Kent glasses clad in Hawaiian shirt and shorts walked up. "Hi, ma'am, my name is Shay, John Shay. They all called me Tweeter."

She reached out her right hand but left the other hand on Stone's chest. "Ruby, John, Tweeter... whatever," She waved her hand to clear the air. "What the hell is going on?"

"Well, ma'am, we have a problem." Turning to face Stone. "We have someone with us that Stone had every right to think was dead. In fact, he should be."

Tweeter took both of Stone's shoulders in his hands. "It's okay Gunny. Squirrel really is alive, and if we hadn't put him in that cold box, he would have died. The hypothermia caused a little damage, but it saved his life."

The reverend grimaced at the stupid look on his former sergeant's face. "I know. It was a shock to me too when he and Wolfman showed up at a RV campsite with their wives. I thought I was having flashbacks and Nadine would have to either shoot me or take me to the hospital. But, he's here, here now... and he wants to help if you'll let him... It's your call, Gunny."

Stone drew a sharp deep breath. Tweeter and Ruby could both see him compartmentalizing the information. He chose his only defense. "We have fresh coffee."

"Yes, sir, I'll bring him up." He started off, and then turned. "We have five RVs, a thirty-foot portable sawmill, and a portable wood shop. Where do you want us?"

Trent stepped in. "I've got this." Sticking his hand out, he walked the man off. "Tweeter, was it? I'm Trent. I'll be the ramrod for securing everyone. We graveled these three acres down this way to park trucks and RVs and anything else we need access to." They walked south toward the town of a single gas station.

Stone and Ruby watched them go. She nudged her hip at his thigh. "Did I ever tell you that I didn't ever want to wake up from this dream?"

Dazed, Stone looked down south where a large line of trucks and RV's were lined up well past the gas station. "This isn't what I imagined either."

"What did you imagine?" She felt the hardness in her back pocket begin to vibrate. "And just how many people do you know and are in that little pocket of magic?"

The gunny shrugged. Grimacing with a stupid smile of innocence, he answered the phone. "This is Stone. Where are you at, and what do you need?"

"Gunny, this is Loadmaster Pele. I have a load which I'm about to dump on your location. Please clear the field to your east of anybody or anything that may get hurt."

"Say what?"

"Sir, you have a double load coming your way in five, four, three, two, load away. Stand by for second drop in three minutes."

Stone turned to face the east as his hand and phone slowly slid down, and he looked up. There in the sky about two thousand feet above him was a C-130 Hercules with nine large containers falling as their chutes were opening. This was really turning into one very crazy day.

As Stone and Ruby watched the large heavy containers land as softly as an elephant jumping from a two-story building, his phone rang again. He raised the phone as he slid the face to answer. "Bombing Range, what have you got for me now?"

"Stone, it's Slim. I have an overweight load of tents and other stuff, including a very large hug or three for my son. Where do you want the load?"

"Oh, shit, Slim, I don't know. Come on down though, we're being bombed, and the coffee is on and hot. Are you in Fall?"

"Rogers on that. We're sliding past a line of about sixty RVs and a gas station. Some guy named Trench or Tenth just gave me the green light to move up the line."

"Pull into the large parking lot about two hundred yards ahead on your right. Hurry up, or you'll miss all of the bombs."

Stone heard the beep and switched to the next call, "Stone. Let me guess… you got lost."

The sound that greeted Stone was not the thunder from inside a diesel truck. It was the hurricane from the load deck of a large cargo airplane with its ass-end hanging open. "Gunny, this is Loadmaster Charlie Delta Nine, look up and to your south. Merry Christmas. Wish I could come and play, but I'm due back in the Sandbox in ninety-seven hours, and I still want to see my wife and girl. Delta Company sends you their best from Bagram." Stone could hear the jump klaxon go off as the man hung up.

Stone got a lump in his throat as he turned and pointed out the trail of dots falling from the tail of the large airplane high above. In the parking lot, a candy apple red truck screamed into the parking lot. Slim and the women opened the doors and stood on the running boards watching the mass of parachutes open and drifting toward the field.

Ruby leaned into Stone. "Now I see why you little boys like to play army so much. You play with big fun toys, do fun stuff like jumping out of perfectly good airplanes, throw expensive stuff all over the ground, and expect someone else to pick it up. It's all so exciting."

The first jumper landed about twenty feet in front of them. Unbuckling his harness, he pulled in his chute and walked over. The man was almost as old as Stone and his face had suffered only a little less over the years. "Jump Master said 'the man standing point would probably be Gunny Stone.'" Stone nodded, as the sergeant saluted. "Master Sergeant Trapper Tyler. My brother Pace, served with you in Vietnam in '72. I understand you paid him a visit over the winter." He offered his hand. "I just wanted to personally thank you on behalf of my family for seeing he got home and checking in on him."

Stone could not speak, but as he shook the man's hand, he could feel the name, rough etched on the smooth black stone under his fingertips on that foggy night. He croaked back as the tears ran down his cheek, "The honor was all mine. It was the least I could do. He was a fine sergeant, and probably why I survived."

"We'll talk later, sir, but right now, we have some tents to get up." Turning to Slim who was walking up, he pointed out the lay of the field. "As I was coming down, I couldn't miss your rig and the tents. I mapped it out. If you can put your rig facing this way between those two hump boxes, as soon as we get them moved, we can pull everything off and be good to go."

Slim two-finger saluted the sergeant. "I'll be on that, son, just as soon as I take care of this." He turned to Stone and was already crying.

Stone folded him into his arms. "This is one thing, Slim, everybody out here hugs. If I have to get used to it, so do you. I take it that everything is good now with Osiel."

Slim unfolded his arms, nodded, and could only mouth out the words 'thank you.' Turning, he was off to his new truck with the gold lettering and a logo of an exploding firework on the side. As Stella and Ellie walked up, they were shaking their heads and laughing. Stella gave Stone a big hug and a kiss on the cheek. "Don't tell the Pope. That was from Trina. They won't make it. The little one is down with a bad cough, and Bugs is just not up to the drive." She looked around. "But you do seem to be putting on quite the party." She then turned to Ruby. "You must be Ruby. Stone has told us nothing about you, so it must be all true, don't ya know. I'm Stella, and don't let me ever hear you calling me Mother Superior or Sister. And this lovely lady is Ellie. I adopted her as the sister my parents would never let me have."

"Hello, Ellie. Stone has told me a lot about what little

he knows. I hear we both lost our Harolds about the same time." The women hugged.

Talking to no one in particular, Stone wandered off toward the highway, "I'm going to go help Trent." He made it to the highway and looked down the road to where a handful of men in white helmets with Military Police armbands were directing the traffic of a very long motorcade of RVs and other campers, trucks, and cars. Occasionally, one did not turn into the parking area and continued toward the coast.

The phone rang and was at his ear before Stone realized he was responding. The gunny caught the name on the phone just as he answered. "Ski, where the hell have you been? We have a war zone here, and it just keeps getting crazier. What the…"

"Stone, can you stop the white car, please?" Ski asked.

Stone looked down the road at a little white car slowly coming around the trucks. Without thinking, he stuck his arm up and watched as the car ground to a full stop. Then he heard the choppers. Turning in disbelief, he was greeted by four HUS-1 Seahorse helicopters landing on the highway. The little white Toyota crept up next to Stone, and the man looked at the choppers, and then Stone. "Whoa, dude. Like, what's going on…? Are we, like, being invaded or something?"

Stone, feeling a little frisky with a need to be exerting some kind of control, turned his most serious face to the guy and reported. "Sir, this is a major DEA offensive to clean up the entire region of pot growers, tree huggers, bunny humpers, and deer kissers."

The young man's eyes grew abnormally large as he

slowly curved a U-turn in the road. "Dude, don't tell 'em I was here, okay?"

Stone pantomimed zipping his lip. He was not laughing while watching the man race away at the blinding speed of about seven miles per hour. As Stone chuckled, he became distracted by the sound of a C-47 Shithook. The double bladed helicopter could lift almost everything, and in Stone's experience, it usually did.

Landing in the field, the tail dropped and a soft-field forklift left the bay followed by several guys in navy dungarees. The Sea Bees had arrived.

Stone dropped his face, laughing, into his left hand. "Oh, balls of fire, it's an invasion."

"Say, sailor, new in town?" A female voice squealed.

Stone's head snapped up as he spun around just in time to catch a bubbly blonde followed by a brown and black flash. Jeannie wrapped her legs around his waist. She was about to choke Stone to death as Ruby walked up, followed by Rusty. "See, Ruby, I told you he was a slut. Leave him in the middle of a highway and he attracts blondes and dogs like a magnet."

Jeannie did not give up any territory. Still hanging on Stone, she stuck out her hand. "Hi, Ruby, I'm Jeannie and this is Elvis." Just then, a white streak raced past. "And that forty-five mile per hour couch potato is Angel, Rusty's new girlfriend." The white greyhound returned to Rusty's side and licked at Elvis's nose.

Rusty peeled Jeannie off the poor man and gave him a hug, saying softly, "Thank you for having me here. But what the fuck were you thinking when you invited the entire third fleet to invade Oregon?"

Stone laughed and had to hold on to his friend.

"Honest, Rusty, I thought just you, me, and a few friends. You know, have a few beers, and throw a few nails at a log, the usual." He looked up at the short redhead approaching in the flight suit. "Uh, oh, here comes the real instigator."

Rusty let go and turned around. "Oh shit, this little thing is the omnipotent Ski? This is the person who puts fear into your bowels so you have to change outhouses in the middle of the day. The know-all, sees-all, and be all you can be?"

Ski slung a hip out and buried a small fist in it. "That would be Captain Omnipotent to you, Rusty... It is Rusty, isn't it?"

Stone recoiled in mock horror. "Oh, God, they made her a captain. What were the idiots in the Pentagon thinking?"

The gathering settled back around the coffee and a large table, which had miraculously appeared from out of a box, a truck, or somewhere. Stone noticed a convoy parked on the far side of what was rapidly becoming a tent city, the eight big tents in the foreground, and several clusters between there, and the convoy. Everywhere he looked people appeared with vehicles. Still more helicopters had migrated from the highway to the far field. He gave a stink eye to the short redhead who just shrugged and raised her hands. "Things just... escalated."

Stone looked at his phone and the number displayed Medford. He showed it to Ruby, and they stepped away from the confusion.

"Stone, this is Butterfly. I thought you would want to know. We brought him out of the coma late this morning. He's doing fine, and you can probably visit him this evening for about five minutes. I think he would like that, and it would be good for his spirit too."

"Thanks, Butterfly. I'm in Fall right now, but should be there about seven."

"We'll see you then. Oh, and Stone?"

"Yes, ma'am?"

"You might consider bringing that woman. I prayed on it, and I have a feeling that they both need this."

Stone looked at Ruby who had been listening in, and she nodded. "She says she'll be there, too. We'll see you then."

As he hung up, Ruby looked around at everything happening on the eighty acres. "We need to get some movies of all of this." Stone noticed her eyes were sparkling wet.

He snorted. "Great idea, but where are we going to get a movie camera?"

Ruby looked at him, and then started laughing. "Nobody showed you anything about your phone, did they?" Ruby reached for the phone and in three moves, she was taking movies. "Help me up on top of this truck so I can get a birds-eye view."

Stone looked at her, and then started laughing, "Nobody showed you anything about this circus that just blew into town, did they?" He pointed at the helicopters standing idle in the field.

She laughed and slapped him on the chest like a schoolgirl. "You know how to hot-wire one of those?"

"No, and I don't know how to drive them either, but I bet I might be able to get us a ride." He smiled, and they started walking as Stone found his gunny voice, "Ski, we need a chopper flight."

The redhead laughed, as she jabbed her elbow into the arm of the other redhead. "I'm on it, boss man." Rusty just giggled.

Jeannie jumped up and held out her phone. "I want to take movies, too." Stone's arm waved her to catch up, and she danced after them as they headed out to what had become a helicopter parking lot.

In the distance, they could see one of the rear rotors spinning up as the long arms began to swing—the power of Ski at work. Ruby laughed at whatever comment Stone had made just as Jeannie caught up with them.

Watching the three, Trent sat down with a coffee mug next to Rusty. As much to himself as anyone else, he muttered, "There goes a force to be reckoned with."

Rusty looked at the three, then over to where Ski was getting to know Stella. Turning back to Trent who had watched Rusty's selection of view, she asked, "Which one?"

The thin ex-logger contractor raised an eyebrow as he thought about that truth, and sipped his coffee. Swallowing, he pursed his lower lip, and finished with, "True."

Rusty lifted the computer pad from her lap and went back to moving the large plot map around. Trent leaned over and pointed out things the two contractors were watching for. In the distance, the helicopter lifted sluggishly off, passing overhead as it began its aerial tour of the controlled chaos of the first day as over a thousand people and their equipment invaded the job site en masse.

STONEHEART

BAER CHARLTON

31

"Did you have any idea that this much was going to happen?" Ruby screamed over the roar of the rotors and wind.

Stone marveled at what looked a lot like a military base in any number of countries that he had called home. He just shook his head. "I just mentioned it to Ski, and asked Rusty to come ramrod for Trent." Stone's eyes widened and he threw up his hands, pointing out at the overflowing of 80 acres of people, machines, vehicles, helicopters, and a full convoy of Hummers and trucks. He looked hopelessly at Ruby and smiled.

She leaned into his shoulder. "Molly is going to be overwhelmed. But she is going to love it." Ruby leaned across the open area and yelled at Jeannie. "Molly is my daughter."

Whether Jeannie could hear or not, it didn't matter. She just smiled and nodded as she kept filming the scenes and emailing the clips to Rusty's laptop. Stone grinned because the two had become quite a team. Then he laughed It didn't hurt that Angel was a cute girl for Elvis either.

BAER CHARLTON

The intercom broke in Stone's helmet. "Sir, I just got word that you need a hop to Medford hospital, and we could refuel at the airport. Are we good to go?"

Stone looked at Ruby and then back at the pilot. "Chief, who authorized the hop?"

The copilot held up his cell phone. Stone thought *I should have known.* Stone tapped the side of his helmet as he looked at Ruby. She nodded that she had also heard. He mouthed, "Where's Molly?"

Ruby looked at her watch and thought. Looking up, she yelled at Stone, "Work."

Stone keyed the throat mike. "What is the ETA to Medford, Chief?"

"Twenty minutes unless you're in a hurry, Gunny."

"We have a slight detour. Do you know the area?"

"Tell me where you want to go. We can look it up on the phone and plot it by GPS. But I can't put it down in the parking lot of the Lone Tree Bar and Grill, we were eighty-sixed from there last month."

Stone laughed at the thought of taking a Blackhawk helicopter to a bar. "No bar, Chief. We're just going to pick up a drive-through order, and then kidnap the counter girl."

"Our kind of sortie, sir," The pilot looked back with a lecherous smile. "If you know the phone number, we can call it from here when we're five out."

The gunny asserted as Stone reined in the flyboys. "We have the number. Just hold the hormones. We have her mother on board."

The copilot chimed in, "This wouldn't be the famous Molly that we are kidnapping, would it, sir?"

Stone looked to the man in the right seat. "One and

the same, son. Do you know her?"

"She served the best biscuits and gravy in the world, sir. But it's her smile that is worth the drive up from Brookings, sir."

"What's your name son?"

"Hobbaker, sir, Tommy Hobbaker."

Ruby pulled on Stone's shirt, so he showed her where the throat mike key was for the passengers. "Tommy, are you Tiger's boy?"

He laughed. "The one and the same, ma'am."

"Well, when you get home, kick your father in the butt, and hug your momma. Tell her Ruby said she's a saint, but she needs to come up and join the circus."

"I saw my uncle's RV parked in the third row near the east end, ma'am. When they get the cook tent up and running, my guess is, she'll be in the thick of it." The co-pilot cleared the gauges and windows as he scanned the sky around them. "My guess is that dad is bringing up the truck with a self-loading arm. I heard tell a call went out for logs to make siding."

They all sat back and enjoyed the ride over the mountains. Out of respect, the pilot had swung south enough to clear the burn area, and they were now over the mountains of tall Douglas fir. Jeannie had finally put on a helmet to mitigate most of the noise but had not stopped filming and sending the clips. Stone guessed that Rusty was getting an almost blow-by-blow view of their travel.

A smile tugged at the side of Stone's face. The last time he had been in an open door of an aircraft was leaving the Sandbox. The difference of the terrain and the circumstances were as different as the way he now viewed his life. Stone thought about seeing out of both eyes, and feeling at peace—the ride was just a ride. He looked toward the north and recognized the configuration of the off-ramp leading down into Grants Pass.

The radio crackled as the pilot came through the helmet speakers. "Gunny, we have provisional access to the airspace. I have a young lady on the phone. She is ready to take our order for a car-side delivery. Key your mikes and place your orders. The grub is on us, sir."

Five minutes later, a Josephine County Sheriff car stood by a cleared part of the shopping center's parking lot. The young woman stood next to him with a big smile as she watched her mother wave from the large door of the helicopter. As the chopper touched down, Stone jumped out with an extra helmet and ran bent over to Molly.

"Here, put this on. It will make it quieter, and you won't get your hair blown off your head. You just quit your job." Molly looked at Stone with large shocked eyes. "We'll tell them later, or the sheriff can tell them now."

Stone shoved a hundred-dollar bill in the officer's hand. "Go have lunch on us, and tell them we kidnapped Molly. We aren't bringing her back. They will have to come to Fall to see her." He checked Molly's helmet and they started for the helicopter. Turning back, he looked at the laughing officer. "Thanks for clearing the space." The officer just saluted as they dashed for the chopper and lifted off. He would tell his grandkids about this one.

The budding filmmaker shouted over the noise, "Hi, Molly, my name is Jeannie."

STONEHEART

BAER CHARLTON

32

The clear plastic oxygen tent cast a hazy surreal appearance to the shadow of a man behind—more like a dark blotch on the white linens, and the voice more like a light breeze of yesterday than the forceful man Stone had talked to just a month ago. Stone questioned if the man was alive, or even awake. Only the face was visible, half submerged in the pillows. Silent images wandered across the television screen. As Stone glanced back and forth from the man to the television, he got a strong feeling that the images were of an invasion or a very hot build of a base in a far-off time and land.

"Where the large tents and convoy is…" Stone leaned closer to hear over the hiss of the oxygen, "that would be nice… large field of grass for games… backstop or two." Stone could feel the strain of talking on the man's low strength.

"We can talk about it in a few weeks." Stone urged the man to rest. "We just wanted you to see what was going on out there."

The screen went dark, and the young man in the scrubs looked up from the laptop. "Sir, that is all she sent and what I pulled off your phone."

"Thanks, Jody. I appreciate you being able to do this

for us and Bernie," Stone showed his gratitude.

"No problem, sir. I do stuff like this in my sleep. I'll clean this all up, and put it together. Rusty has my FTP link, and they will be sending me everything from the site. Tonight, I'll set up a group contribution page and then anyone can dump stuff. Eventually, we'll have a record of everything anyone is filming. It's gonna be off the hook." The kid stood and put his feet back into his red clogs. "As I get things put together, I'll feed them to Bernie here. Or maybe I'll just tap into the hospital cable and set up one of the dead channels and loop it for anyone to see."

Butterfly bounced her bottom off the wall she had been leaning against in the darkened room. "I know I want to watch what is going on out there," she looked at the monitor, "but for right now, I'm going to run you kids out of here. I need to have some serious quiet time with my boyfriend here."

Bernie managed to speak. "Stone?"

Stone turned, as the rest left the room. "Yeah, Bernie," he approached the tented bed.

"Thank you for bringing Ruby and Molly." He breathed a few deep, for him, breaths. "I didn't know what to say... to them... but I'm glad... you did."

Stone thought about the twenty-some years this man had been in a prison of his own making and was now in another. He was working hard to make amends. "Bernie, you did fine tonight. You did just fine. Each road starts with a small step. It sounds like a stupid platitude, but I can tell you the road and steps are real. When you get down the road, it is only then that you can look back at that first scary step and know that it was hard, but worth it." He put his hand up to the plastic sheet. "We both have a lot of work to do. You do yours here, by being good and help Butterfly help you." The man on the other side raised his hand to the plastic and they touched fingers. Nothing needed to be said.

Stone turned, and Butterfly gave him a hug. Stone froze for a second then molded to the other body. "I guess I'm getting used to these."

Butterfly chuckled. "And you best never get out of practice." She pushed him back and smiled. "Thank you for bringing them both." She turned then and walked Stone toward the door, continuing too quietly for the man in the bed to hear. "I don't know what is up about the young woman..."

"Molly."

"Molly. But I do think whatever it is, or was, this will be good for him."

Stone looked back over her shoulder, then at her dark eyes. He bit at his lip and nodded. Patting her on the shoulder, he turned to the door, quietly admonishing, "Take care of my friend."

At the end of the hall, Stone joined the two women. "I'm taking the hop back out. We'd drop you off, but I don't think the neighborhood could handle the Blackhawk landing on your street. I would just take you back out, but I think Molly needs some different clothes."

"Can I just burn this uniform?"

Ruby laughed. "Soon, honey, soon." She turned to Stone. "What is the game plan?"

"Well, off the top of my head, we have a thousand hungry people to feed three times a day. I don't know what is really set up, but I do know that Spuds and his mother are out there now, so there is something. It also looked like someone was moving in a battalion canteen, so as long as there is food stocked, they will be fed. But could it really be the same without the Molly and Ruby show?"

Ruby looked at her daughter, and the smile on her face said it all. Looking back at Stone she slowly wagged her head. "No, no it wouldn't. Give us a couple of days and we'll be out."

They all hugged until the elevator came. As Ruby and Molly turned in the elevator, Ruby frowned. "Where are we going to sleep, in the car?"

Stone laughed. "Of course not. You get to bunk in with me... and about five-hundred other people in the tents." The door closed on the horror on the two faces, and the laughing face of the man who had been there all of his life. Turning toward the stairs to the roof helipad, he chuckled to himself, *it's fun, just like a coed dorm.*

From Ski:
Losing light – sit-rep

From Stone:
Got caught in Love Fest.
Send condoms

From Ski:
Bring Jeannie back. Elvis jealous
Admiral 45 min out
Rusty called Powwow at 2100

From Stone:
Helo back
On way

STONEHEART

BAER CHARLTON

33

The top of the tent slowly rose and fell with the wind. Stone knew it was dark green, but his mind saw desert sand. Stone was just thankful he was seeing it all with both eyes. On a cognitive level, the gunny knew he was safe, but the side of his mind that was running wild took him back down bad roads, dark streets, and dangerous paths. They lead up back alleyways, down hillsides and through the muck, goo, and fetid waterways stinking of rot and death.

The gunny could feel the wounds and insults to his flesh crawling across most of his body. A piece of him held on to where he was now. The rest of him was sucked back to the Sandbox, back to Somalia, back to Panama, back to Grenada, back to Croatia, back to Columbia until he was back to one particular night in the jungle of Vietnam. The dark green canopy overhead was filled with tiny sounds that did not fit into the jungle night surrounding him. Every one of his buddies was sweating from the heat, and the fear creeping across their skin like the centipedes, lizards, spiders, and worse. The average age of his company was twenty. The average age of his squad was nineteen.

Stone never saw the canopy light up in his dreams. Instead, his dreams filled with the cold river of fear that snaked its way to the hot center point in his bowels where the single round from an AK-47 passed through his stomach, and out his back. The unstopped round had become a half-inch mushrooming mass of lead, which removed half of the radioman's head, leaving chunks of brain and bone where the workings of a radio had been a second before.

As Stone passed out from the intense pain, the radioman fell on top of him, and the jungle ignited in a gathering cluster of three large barrels of Foo Gas igniting and focused on their dug-in position. The Vietcong never even checked for survivors. The scorched-earth nature of the explosive-delivered napalm had turned everything into last month's forgotten pot roast. Crispy and charred with an overbearing stench of seared hair, rubber-soled boots, and cooked off meat.

Out of the night, Stone could hear the screams of his buddies. He could do nothing but listen. Young boys that should have been riding around in their cars with their left elbows stuck out the window, one finger driving, and the right arm around their girl, driving slow in the night, listening to the radio turned down low, the lights of the dashboard softly lighting the small girl's hand on a denim-clad leg.

"Gunny…" the screams he wished would go away.

"Stone," the ones that would haunt his nights, fill his pillow and sheets with sweat.

"Stone," sounds of screams from young men who

sounded like women.

The hand reached out of the shimmering jungle and gently rested on his chest with a slight shake. "Stone." The voice whispered again. "Stone... wake-up."

The night blurred and as his eyes focused. He could make out the shape of curly dark hair but the face was hidden.

"Stone, sorry to wake you, but you were having a nightmare." The woman thought a moment. "I'm sorry. I guess you have them all the time."

Stone gently leveraged himself up on the cot until he was on his right elbow. Blinking and trying to make things out in the dark. "Ellie?"

"No, honey, my name is Ruth. Ruth Anne Timkins, I used to live in the house behind the Black Hog Motel. I lost my house the night..." She choked.

Stone reached out and put his hand on her arm. "LaLonnie." She nodded. He gently rubbed her arm, then she broke down and fell into his chest, and he held her as she cried. Stone thought about how the fire had taken so much from so many people in so many places. It was not always only war that brought nightmares.

Finally, Ruth sat up wiping her palm and back of her hand across her face. She sniffled to clear the airway and a shudder of her body shook it all back into composure. Stone watched and marveled at the resilience of this woman who obviously lived a life in the middle of hard times.

She pinched her nose with her thumb and side of her finger, then letting go, sniffed one last time, deep and loud. Then turning, Ruth placed her hand on his chest again. Restarting her purpose, "First, thank you for your kindness, for the night you sat up with LaLonnie, and everything else. Thank you."

He nodded. "It was my pleasure. I learned a lot in that short night with her. She must have been an amazing friend."

"She was. But that's not what I'm here for." Bending down and picking something up off the floor, she sat up. "We need your help." She picked up a biscuit off the plate. "Here, open, and take a bite."

His nose became the first to be tantalized. He had smelled that aroma before. He just could not place it. Suddenly, Stone's mouth was full of the best biscuits he had ever tasted. As the gunny mushed it around in his mouth, his entire being exploded in the heaven of strawberries. Strawberries... like a fresh spring morning— dew barely evaporated, still cool from the night, strawberries. Strawberries like he had never tasted before.

"Wum budda ham boo dum?"

The woman nodded and clenched her lips in a self-satisfied grin. "Yeah, that's what I said. I guess that's a two-thumbs and a tummy up for serving these this morning."

She bit a small bite of the second half and shoved the rest in his mouth before he could say anything more. She stood and giggled. "Oh, and Rusty said move your ass before it turns to grass and she has to come in and play power lawnmower. Breakfast is in ten minutes." She looked out into the field where a Seahorse reached its destination. "Your ride just landed, and if you are lucky, they can be convinced that they are hungry, too." She turned and was out of the tent.

Stone reached down for his pants as several other

mounds in the night began the transition to the early shift. He fished his phone out of his pocket and read the time. 0412 AM He smirked as he put it back in his pocket and began putting on his boots. *At least nobody is blowing Revelry.*

The trumpets turned his thought to a lie. He closed his eyes as he muttered, "Doesn't that woman ever sleep?"

He checked the text as he headed for the large line of outhouses and the shower trailers.

From Rusty:
We need to talk before you
go fishing or something

Five hugs and as many slaps on the back later, Stone sat down in front of the two people who knew what was going on—if not the ringmasters of the overall circus. Trent was shoveling a biscuit dripping with strawberry freezer jam into his mouth as Rusty was just getting off the phone. A hand dropped on Stone's shoulder, and a large plate filled with eggs, bacon, biscuits, and jam, landed in front of him. Stone looked up and smiled. "How the hell are you, Spuds?"

"Hanging with the wind and trying to keep up with the ladies."

"How are the legs?"

Spuds smiled as he sat down. "Doing pretty good, or better than I would have thought. I've been pulling pretty much three four-hour shifts each day for these four weeks, and the right one is only a problem on the third shift. But I had Mary Margaret look at the nub, and she said that I have a flap growing that needs to be scaled back as soon as we can take some time off and get up to the surgeon in P-town."

"So an eight-hour day wouldn't be a problem?" Stone bit into one of the biscuits loaded with freezer jam and fresh butter. His eyes closed reflexively and his face relaxed.

Spuds laughed. "I know. Ruby's baking soda biscuits combined with that killer freezer jam Stella and Ellie have been putting up... Oh my glory, I just know I died out there somewhere and am now living in heaven. Of course, you know the secret is in the flavor bomb of the Oregon strawberry."

Stone opened one eye and sized up the rail-thin young man whose pants always seemed to be ready to slide right off. "You could use some more biscuits and jam." He poked the kid's belly.

Standing back up, Spuds slapped Stone on the shoulder. "Maybe next year when I'm relaxing or something." Turning to the other two, he continued. "Trent, Rusty, can I get either of you two anything more?"

Trent just puffed out his cheeks and rolled his eyes. Rusty laughed and looked up at the kid. "No, honey. We all know where the coffee urn is. We're fine, thank you."

"Well, if you need anything, just give a holler..." and looking about the now filling mess tent, he turned back, "before it gets busy." He laughed then walked off with his stylish roll as he rocked from one aluminum leg to the other.

"Did someone say coffee?" Molly bubbled down the long table with a fresh pot in each hand.

"Mmurf," Stone gulped and looked at the last mouthful in his mug. Swallowing it and the mouthful of biscuit, he held out the empty mug. "And how is the sunshine of my life this morning?"

Trent looked up and mock growled. "Stand in line there, sailor. I saw her first."

Rusty laughed at the boyish in-fighting. "Settle down boys and back off." She draped a protective arm around a giggling Molly's waist. "She promised on Thursdays she would be my sunshine."

Molly giggled harder, looking down with big eyes. "Is that true, Aunt Rusty?"

"I don't care who thinks they get you for sunshine, but they'll just have to wait until I'm finished with you."

Ruby wandered up, powdered in flour and wiping her hands on her apron. "Molly, sweetie, someone found a donation can again. They're over there in the corner. Would you go talk to them and get them to knock it off."

Molly rolled her big eyes as her shoulders drooped and her body sagged even a bit much for an overblown performance on a middle school stage. "Oh, why do they dooooo that?" Then perking back up to her usual self, she set down one of the coffee pots. "I've got it, Mom. I'm all over it like a chicken on a June bug."

Ruby gave a soft single chuckle as she watched her favorite person in the world walk through a sea of people. They had all been strangers a few weeks ago. Now it turned into a touch here, a smile and kind word there, a name, a hug, and a 'how are you this morning,' as she focused on the job at hand. "Where did she get that?"

"The June bug thing? You can blame that one on Rusty," Stone laughed.

"I am highly offended, offended I said. I never…" The redhead sat with a gaping mouth and wide twinkling eyes of mock horror.

"Yes, you did," Ruby snapped with a wink. "It's Thursday, so we get to blame it all on you today." She noticed Trent silently watching Molly. "You see it too, don't you?"

Trent turned around and looked at his oldest friend. "Molly just never had the sky to soar in before. She was never allowed out of the yard, but the sky came to her." He turned back to admire her smooth flow through the crowd. The girl had matured into a young woman in the few weeks. He sighed. "She is amazing." Looking back at Ruby, he said, "I thought Molly couldn't surprise us any more than the day she got off that bus and walked back into work."

Ruby grumbled up a lump in her throat and spoke with a deeper forced tone. "Speaking of work, y'all are keeping me from my biscuits."

Stone laughed. "Oh god, where is Slim? He needs to know he has another sister." A towel snapped with a cloud of flour on his back as she walked away.

"Don't you be trash-talking about my twin sister none."

As a pilot in a pickle suit walked up, Rusty cut him off and pointed at a chair. "Sit. I need him for about five minutes. You can have another cup of coffee or a biscuit or something. But right now, I need him." The pilot saluted, and then smiled at his partner as they took seats silently under the watchful eye of the husky woman with the red hair.

Turning to Stone, she swiveled her computer tablet around with the map of the construction displayed on the screen. Pointing to the different structures as she walked through the situation report, Rusty ran down the week's progress. "We turned on the north half of the clinic last night, and Trent will be going over the punch-list of things to fix this morning with Osiel. The guys from Cascade Electric should be heating up the southern half as well as the physical therapy center this morning.

"The solar guys only have houses three and four to tie in, and the grid will be at a full four-hundred and sixty kilowatts at peak. The power company has a crew here for the entire week to watch the grid-tie and make sure it's all flowing the way it's supposed to. Osiel and Trent are going to put some test loads on and that will take care of all that.

"The houses are pretty much in finish stages, and Ruby's house will be getting the primer rolled today and some of the paint by this evening. Two and four are up for mud and tape today, and the mystery manor is still in sheet rocking.

"Most of the pickle-suits are off playing games this week…"

Stone rumbled. "They're called maneuvers."

"Well, I don't care if they call them butt scratching in the deep forest, but the boys and girls club have been out of our hair all week, but they will be back tonight. So, we will be having a full house. The problem is… we have two busloads of Mennonites arriving sometime this afternoon, along with nine trucks of timber frame for the café and community center. I just don't have anywhere to sleep them."

Stone sighed as he ran his right hand over his face. "Bivouac the troops out in the field. The fresh sod is going to feel like heaven compared to what they have been doing this last week. Just make sure the shower trailers are fully up and stocked, and they'll be singing your praises. They're big kids now. Besides, if anyone complains, they can always eat burnt K-rats instead of biscuits."

Rusty looked hard at Stone. "Were you always this hard-nosed or are you just getting soft in your dotage?" They laughed softly, and then looked at Trent. "You got anything to add?"

Trent, who had been leaning his chin on his fists with his elbows splayed out on the table, sat up, and wiped the ball cap from his head. "Not much, unless she wants to come to work for me after this is over."

Rusty gave him a hard glare. "Not on your life honey. It has rained nine days since I got here, and that is about eight and a half too many."

Trent sucked in his lips into a tight line as his eyes rolled into his closing lids. "Your loss." Stone could tell the subject had become a running joke between the two. The total acceptance of Rusty as Trent's equal touched a warm spot in Stone's heart. Rusty had found a home if she wanted it, but it was not the home she had grown to know and love.

Trent turned reluctantly from the partner he had always yearned for and resumed telling Stone the situation report. "We have enough siding to finish out the done buildings, but we still need about nine thousand more feet for the café building. I have three self-loaders coming in this morning, and your buddy Squirrel, with that portable saw mill, just got some fresh blades in from Portland, so it looks like we will be in great shape at the end of the week to start putting up siding on the café."

Rusty continued the report. "On the monetary side, we have some bills which need to be paid on Monday."

"The funds for the payouts should be there today. Check later when the bank opens, and if the funds aren't there, get a hold of me or Ski. Anything else?"

The two shook their heads and Stone stood. "Then, I think I'm going to sea?" He looked over at the pilot, who nodded. The two sitting civilians saluted in unison, and smiled.

BAER CHARLTON

34

Long before the first rooster in the county had crowed, the quiet men in white long-sleeved shirts, black trousers with suspenders, and hobnailed boots had removed their straw hats, clenched their hands over their plates filled with biscuits, eggs and bacon, and sat for a moment of silent prayer. As they all looked up, the lead builder stood. "Brethren, let us pray on the work before us." As they all bowed their heads, everyone else in the large canteen tent joined them. "Heavenly Father, grace us this day. Guide our hands that our work is sure and true. Give us the strength to do the work that worships you. And, may we ask blessing on all who are here doing this kind work, and look after them as their lives move forward from this day. Amen." The answer came back in a hushed wave from each corner.

Then the usual tsunami of sound in the canteen washed over the full tent. The pickle pants and T-shirt troops passed through the mess line. Gathering a plate heaped with food, they passed out onto what had become known as The Gunny's Green. The large swath of grass had become a popular eating area with the military and those who joined them. On any given day that the military was on-site, the Green would fill with at least three-quarters of the diners. The blend of civilians and young troops shared lives and photos on phones back and forth. Numbers and email addresses were a regular exchange, and it was not unusual for Stone's phone to pass from one person bent on being in his phone to the next. Some were just making sure their information had been input correctly and completely. Others also left him notes that he had taken to reading before bed, but never deleting. Everything was saved, and synced for safekeeping, to a computer buried somewhere three-thousand miles away.

At seven, as the sun began flooding the site, a single diesel truck engine started up. Over the entire build site, there was near silence. People squatted on every rooftop, truck bed, or other advantageous viewing spots. The barn raisers stood on the floor where the new larger café would be. One by one, the huge timbers, squared trees, notched and tenoned to computer specifications, were lifted by a single crane and brought to the building floor. The hundreds, who had been dealing with four-inch framing nails, now marveled as giant wooden mauls delicately coaxed the three and four-hundred pound timbers into place. Tenons slid into the mortises, and along with kerf joints, were secured with one-inch thick dowels. The whole arch of giant timbers reached exactly from one side of the floor to the other. Depending on the age of the watcher, Lincoln Logs or Legos came to mind as the fitting and joining continued.

The arch, also called a bent, was complete. It

stretched nearly twenty-eight feet along the floor. The crane lowered a band toward the middle point of the structure. The whole form lay pried up to accept the band around the timbers in a figure-eight sling. Then, slowly, the whole bent lifted. As the top rose, the structure rotated on the two feet of the side timbers. Many ropes guided the placement of the structure's feet into the receiving sockets in the floor and foundation.

The only human sound was the leader quietly giving verbal nudges here and pushes there. The sound from his mouth, instantaneously translated into small twitches of hands, backs, feet, or the movement of the crane. The flow of the crane's movement was controlled by the barely perceptible hand movements that seemed slightly more than spasms from the director. There were many who watched, who understood the power of a thumb pushed sideways, or a sudden fist clench no matter where the hand was. Silent signals were the life-and-death communication of the military in the field, as well as many hand and arm signals among loggers. Each had their own shorthand, and the others quickly learned the silent shorthand of the timber frame builders.

Ruby stood in the middle of the alleyway between the commissary tent and one of the barracks. Four of the twelve bents stood erect. They connected to the others through the usage of beams called summers.

"I've got grub, but it's getting cold." Ruby did not have to yell. Within a hundred feet of her, six hundred people had been silently sitting or standing.

Stone slapped Slim and Osiel in the tummies and nodded toward what looked like the entire roofs of each of the buildings, sliding off in a waterfall of pickle pants and white or green T-shirts. Occasionally, there were jeans or the mud-yellow Carhartt bib overalls favored by the loggers and other locals. The three men had been relaxing on bales of straw stacked on the back of Slim's new Cherry Bomb. The straw was destined to be spread over the areas where several Boy Scout troops had been planting yearling trees. The straw would provide winter protection, keep the moisture in the ground, and help prevent erosion. Except for today, the bales made just the right kind of lounge chairs. Slim had even noted that Stone seemed to have acquired a taste for chewing on the straw and thought maybe he should take up farming.

"Well," Stone groaned at having to move as he rolled out of the makeshift chair and over the edge of the trailer, "I guess I need some food before I become skinny like Slim." He winked and smiled at Osiel.

"Dad never met a meal he didn't like." The younger man smiled and looked up at his father as he offered his hand.

Slim playfully slapped at the offered hand. "Do I look like I'm sitting up here all weak and puny like a waif kitten?" He slipped gracefully over the edge of the trailer and landed without a sound. "Now you go run along like a good boy. Give your auntie a hug on your way to wash those filthy hands. Lawd, I have no idea, nor do I ever want to know where you have been sticking those meat hooks of your'n. Now run along. I have man business with Stone here."

The younger rolled his eyes at Stone and walked on ahead. The older draped his large arm over Stone's shoulder, and smiling, turned his face to the sun and closed his eyes as they sauntered along the pathway.

"What did you need to talk about, Slim?"

"Shh, nuttin'. I'm just enjoying the sunshine, and the presence of the man who found my lost sheep."

Stone thought, and then just swallowed and kept walking. He could not have said anything if he wanted to.

The warm sun did feel good. It had the comforting feel of recovery and growth. As they passed between the clinic, and the soon to be finished café, Stone looked at the buildings, which were almost completed. The four houses were in a row stretching out toward what would become the baseball fields and general playfields.

A small grove of freshly transplanted thirty-foot maturing trees stood behind the houses. Included in this special tiny stand was one each of the four coastal trees of the Pacific Northwest: a dawn cedar, a Douglas fir, a giant sequoia redwood and a myrtle. Stone knew from talking to the local loggers that these four trees had a good chance of being there for a hundred years or more. But for right now, it was just good to see green in the area again.

As the two men lined up to enter the canteen, Stone's brow furrowed, and he looked back at the trees behind the houses. He started to think about the trees and the fact he had not ordered them. Next, he looked along the long wide concrete pathway and shrugged, perplexed. *When did two houses become four? Why does the path lead to an area for an addition?*

He fished his phone out of his pocket and started poking at the screen. Slim looked over and noticed how at-ease Stone had become with the new age of communication and smiled at the tool he had not known how to use only a short time ago.

BAER CHARLTON

From Stone:
We need 2 talk

From behind the dark netting of the tent wall, a familiar gravelly voice laughed. "Honey, give it a rest. Get some food and come on over. Trent and I have been wondering when you would notice the trees."

Slim laughed. "Some jungle scout you turned out to be. You don't blend in at all. They spotted you right off." Laughing, the two men entered the tent.

STONEHEART

BAER CHARLTON

35

"Well, other than looking like you're going to hold up a stagecoach, you are looking a hell of a lot better than the last time I saw you." Stone stood at the foot of the hospital bed.

The eyes crinkled around the top of the mask as Bernie smiled. "It looks like hard work suits you. Maybe you should get off your desk job and make those people let you swing a hammer for a while. Or maybe there is a latrine to dig?"

Stone turned toward Butterfly as she supervised the children playing for the first real time in a month. "He's feisty, too. What are you feeding him, Butterfly, beans?"

The nurse harrumphed and leveled an eye at the man lounging in the clean sheets. "Hmm, sassy too—but that comes from the green Jell-O he has been mooching off the cafeteria cart. I think the feisty is coming from the lack of a nice ice water enema."

Butterfly's eyes got huge as she mocked a look of shock. Turning, she rested her hand on Stone's shoulder as she leaned in toward him. "He looks good, but he is still only good for about ten minutes. If you are here in fifteen, I'll have to take drastic measures." She snapped her purple glove on her wrist. "And remember, don't touch him, and stay five feet back with them street clothes."

"Yes, ma'am." Stone gave her a two-finger salute.

"Don't ma'am me. I work for a living." She laughed her way out the door as Stone chuckled at the oldest sergeant's saying in the book.

Stone sat down to talk to the man in the bed. "I went over my bank account this morning."

Bernie watched Stone with a poker face. "Anything missing?"

"No, just the opposite. There was too much in the account."

The businessman thought a moment. "It sounds like a great bank to deal with. I wish my bank screwed up that way. Usually, there was less than I thought there should be."

Stone could see the eyes still crinkled around the mask. The man was definitely having fun at Stone's expense.

"I thought we had an agreement."

"We did, and still do. I directed the legal beagles to write the checks as you needed draws for the project. It was your mistake to assume that those funds be drawn all on your account. And we both know all about the word assume."

"But the building is going up on my land."

"Gawd," the man held his arm against his forehead. "Did you survive your whole career whining like that or just when they made you a gunny?"

Stone studied the man in the bed. His mind was

working overtime, but he was sure the very successful businessman's mind was running at a much faster clip than Stone's mind ever could. He searched the man's eyes for any avarice or duplicity.

"Look," the white mask fluffed. "What are you worried about? Do you think if you don't pay for everything, you somehow lose control of it?"

"Well, that has been buzzing around in my…"

"Stone, you know rifles, and how to kill people and all that—you did it all of your life. You have no idea about construction or the cost of beans. I've seen most of your bills and bills of lading. I know what you are paying for, and what never got charged. And maybe, it is time you know too.

"When you get back over there, you need to sit down with Trent and that gal, what's her name."

"Rusty."

"Rusty. You need to sit down with them and have them explain what is going on. I'm not the only person who sees the good in what you have brought to this area. You got charged $127 per thousand-foot unit for studs. That barely covers the trucking. The going rate for Trent is probably close to $480 or $520 FOB Roseburg. That wasn't because you're cute. That was from Dillard Pinkston, who had three sons that all went into the service. Two came home, but only one is actually here. He's hoping the doc you brought might give him at least half of his boy back.

"Your plumbing is coming from the son of a man who served in Vietnam, and then when they needed him in Desert Storm, he went and left a wife and son to fend for themselves. That was a short war but one week after the battles were through, his truck ran into a live Scud missile half buried in the sand. The only thing that came home was his dog tags, a purple heart, and a lot of heartache. He should have been home, but his uncle called him. We have an agreement. I am sticking to it. Nothing has changed. Well, one thing."

"What's that?"

"The sign for the café. I have some thoughts on that, and I think you would approve. From what you have told me, I'm pretty sure everyone else will approve, too."

"Okay, but I really feel sort of blindsided by being out of the loop."

They both looked at the door at the sound of a throat being cleared.

"I know I told you ten minutes, but the doc is on his way. So hustle it up."

Stone stood. "Thanks, Butterfly, but I was just leaving anyway. I can hear my ride returning." He cocked his head as if listening for the helicopter that either was or was not close.

Bernie pointed at him. "Just relax, and enjoy the ride. Everything is being taken care of. You have more than earned your stripes on this one. Now let me earn one or two for me."

Stone gave him a two-fingered civilian salute and turned for the door.

As he reached Butterfly, who was smiling and rolling her eyes, Bernie called out. "By the way, Stone..."

Stone turned.

Bernie poked at the oxygen tube in his nose. "I saw the pictures and video of those guys putting the little Christmas tree on the top of the timber-framed building.

What is that all about?"

"It's a timber frame and log cabin builder's thing. It means the structure is done. It's a kind of respect for the logs and the trees they came from. Maybe Trent can explain it better."

"Okay, thanks. Also, tell Rusty that I really like the website. Except there is one problem. The one camera that looks south got hit or something and looks right at the bright security light on the back of the gas station. It keeps me up at night. It should be watching the clinic instead."

Stone looked at Butterfly. She rolled her eyes again and told Stone quietly. "His TV is a big-ass computer monitor. He can't sleep more than about two hours, and he is awake most of the night. He looks at a few other things, but mostly he has the live building site feeds on all day and night."

Stone thought about the people or angels watching over his shoulder. Still looking at Butterfly, he answered. "Okay, Bernie, I'm all over it. We'll have you sleeping like a baby tonight." Quietly he growled to the nurse, "Slip him a mickey tonight."

Butterfly laughed as her body shook. Stone smiled. He liked having that kind of effect on people. He gave Butterfly a swift hug and barely escaped her swinging hand at his backside. He leaned into the door to the stair to the roof and disappeared.

Butterfly leaned against the doorjamb into the room looking at her patient who had his big-assed monitor turned back on. She knew the doctor would find him drifting in or out of sleep as he watched people working. She could tell that by the way the mask sat on his face there was a small smile hiding under the sterile white.

Deep in her heart, Butterfly knew Bernie was getting a better treatment than just medicine could provide. She pushed off the doorjamb and walked back toward the nurses' station.

STONEHEART

BAER CHARLTON

36

Rusty sat down across from Stone in the gathering gloom. The general construction was complete. The hordes of workers were gone. Only the final little stuff remained, so the crew was down to just a couple of electrical people and the finish carpenters. The mess tent was not much more than a sunshade of giant proportions. No more hundreds of rowdy workers in one door and out the other. The long tables, like the half a dozen barrack tents, stood empty, yet the coffee urn always stayed on and full.

Stone was going over the bills and looking up real pricing online with the laptop. As he found the differences, he made a notation in pencil on the bill's edge.

Rusty nodded her chin at the stack of bills as Stone looked at her. Stone put down the pencil and clasped his hands between his legs as he rocked forward, looking at the slips of paper. "I just don't get it, Rusty." He picked up a bill for lumber. "Why would anyone in business, when I'm willing to pay their full price, charge me less than the cost to just get it to me? This one for something called Romex wire. Osiel says that a great deal is about three times what they charged us. Why?"

Rusty reached out and laid her hands over Stone's to calm them. "Shh, shh, shh… Relax. You're getting wound up over something that you have no control over. As Ruby would say, 'you didn't throw the hammer.' They were probably asking why you saved Bernie. And then you turned around and started this?" Her arm lifted and waved expansively at the buildings, before she continued.

"They sat around their dinner tables and asked their wives why would some guy from somewhere else come and build us a clinic for the vets? Why does he care about a café that's run by a mentally retarded young woman and her mother? Who does he think he is saying that we needed a place for community meetings? Why would he care about us when our own elected politicians don't even care?" She stopped for the span of many breaths, and looked him in the eyes. "The answer is the same for someone paying for a stranger's breakfast. It is why there is Habitat for Humanity, a gold coin in a red kettle because a chubby guy in a Santa suit is ringing a bell hour after hour. There is no real answer. These are things… things that just are."

Rusty took his hands in hers. "Two years ago, I sat down next to a guy who didn't even know where he was going. You thought you were just looking around, but I'd seen that look before. I saw it in the mirror every day after my wife died. It's the look of lost. Not like when you are turn-the-wrong-way lost, but lost-your-soul lost. It's that kind of lost that sucks the life out of you. It tears at your sanity in little ways. And if it isn't set straight, it will leave you broken in the gutter.

"I was almost afraid to ask you if you wanted to help with that project there in the Smokies. But, after that breakfast, I knew that you were only lost because your compass had been taken away and you needed a new compass.

"All your life you have looked out for other people. It's no wonder you became a sergeant instead of an officer. They don't just look after the troops—the sergeants look after both. Yes, there are the rare exceptions, like Ski. She looks after you and Mike like you were her two boys. Sadly, I don't think she will understand that until he decides to retire. Then she will look up and realize she never seriously dated anyone, never got married, and never had kids. She will one day wake up, and she will have that same piece of paper in her hand that you had."

"DD-214, separation papers."

Rusty grumped, "Separation for you maybe, but for her, it will be a death sentence."

"How so?"

Rusty dropped her head and looked at him from the corner of her eye. "Think about it. Maybe she works hard, even gets a ship—big whoop. Maybe she works hard enough to even one day be an admiral like Mike. At the end of the day, she goes home to her brownstone in Georgetown, opens the door, turns on a light, turns the heat up, and what? Grabs a drink, and sits down in front of the TV and a cold dinner from the fridge?

"Mike goes home to... wait for it... his brother's wife. His children are, umm... strewn all over the globe, but they are... oh, that's right—his brother's daughters."

Stone frowned at his friend. "Why are you being so bitter?"

"Bitter? No, not bitter. Just here to kick that last piece of brains back up your ass so you see what is going on,

Gunny."

As she fluffed the stack of bills with her tough-skinned finger, she went on. "Those people didn't have this compass until you got here. This county... hell, this region didn't have a compass for compassion. You met them. They only had room for hatred. They hated the fact the forest was taken away. They hated that their jobs went up in smoke. Some probably hated that they had to cook for themselves, but they weren't stopping to mourn Ruby's husband or the other eighteen people who died around here. They didn't reach out to Ruby and Molly and ask them how they could help. They felt stung, and they were just kicking at the red ant nest, never thinking it might have been a bee, or just a sliver they had picked up in their pants from an hour before. They just needed to hate and kick. And then you came along."

She stopped talking and looked at him. His head hung down as he digested her words. She reached out and gently ran her hand over the bristles and down along the side of his head where all the scars were. Stone looked up, and his eyes were awash.

Rusty almost cried, too. She could tell there was a lot still bottled up for so long. Thoughts, feelings, and emotions that he still would not be able to name for many years. She held her hand on the side of his face. "You don't have to go there anymore, Stone. That life walked away from you and left you with only the best part. The part where you get to care about people... and the best is that they care about you, too."

He sniffed and wiped his eyes and nose on his T-shirt bottom. For the first time, Rusty realized it was a gray T-shirt, and she knew it had Team Molly written on the back instead of the usual four initials he had always worn. She smiled at his transformation.

"What? Do I have a booger on my face?"

The tough old broad chuckled at their relationship. "No, you're fine just the way you are."

Stone wiped at his face again and looked out through the mesh as if he could see down the road and around the bend about ten miles. "If I hadn't come back here at that moment... if I had been just fifteen minutes earlier, or a couple of hours later..."

"Why did you come back?"

"For the biscuits."

"Seriously?"

"Seriously." Stone looked her in the eyes while weighing the depth of their relationship, and what he could share. "I came back because of Molly."

"Molly?" Rusty froze. She waited.

He looked down and watched his finger draw squiggles on the papers. Sucking his lower lip between his teeth, Stone looked up and nodded. "Yeah, Molly."

They both took sips of coffee as they had a staring contest with hard eyes, taking each other's measure. Putting his mug down, the softer gunny continued. "You know that saying about 'out of the mouth of babes' and all that. Well, that's Molly. Only it's not really what she says, it's how she walks through the world. She has cares and worries, but she just strolls through and keeps the other stuff in her pocket."

Rusty's head cocked, and she was nodding slowly. "I never thought of it, but she kind of does that." She thought back through the last couple of months. "She really does."

"Well, that's what I came back for. I wanted to learn

how she does that. And her momma's biscuits were just a perk."

"Hmm, yeah, I've seen you and those biscuits."

Stone blushed. "Rusty, you are a dirty minded woman." He smiled and looked down like a five-year-old caught with his hand in the cookie jar. "It's not what you think."

"What I think is that you two have almost been connected at the hip since before I got here. I'm not complaining here... you could use a good woman. But if she wasn't such a sweetie, I don't think even Monkey Butt Jeannie could have gotten a hug in edgewise."

"We're just good friends."

"And?"

"And, nothing."

"So we moved Ruby and Molly into the first house this afternoon. Are you sleeping in... or out here in the big ol' lonely tent?"

Stone laughed, "Are you kidding? This would be the first time in forty years that I get a tent all to myself. I'm not passing on that opportunity."

"So you'd leave her to sleep alone."

Stone gave her a hard stare. "You really are a nasty minded woman. And don't get me wrong... I didn't say that like it was a bad thing." They both laughed. "I admit that there have been a few times, but really, it's not as serious as you think."

Stone looked down at his coffee. The little hamsters were spinning a wobbling wheel, but it was turning. The answer was not complete, but some of it was there for him to see.

He raised his mug, and took a sip then slowly licked

his lips.

"Stone?"

"Yeah, I'm here." His eyes had that drifty look as he looked up. "I guess we were both adrift, and we got lucky and each found a life raft who knows about the loss and the pain we were going through, even when we didn't know it was there."

They sat silent as Rusty thought through the revelation. "So you're not moving in?"

Stone smiled and shook his head. "I'm moving into Dawn Cedar."

"The third house is yours? That fourth one, Stoneheart, isn't yours? We've all been wondering who Dawn Cedar was for. Hell, I think there is a pool started on who was moving in."

"I've seen it. They are all wrong. I'm on the pool list, but I'm only there as a guest."

Rusty rolled her right shoulder where arthritis was setting in. "Then who is it for?"

Stone leaned back and smiled. "That, my redheaded friend, is for me to know and to remain on the shut-up list."

Stone stood. "I'm done for the night. Tomorrow early, Ruby and I are riding down into California, and we might be gone for a few days. Do you think I can leave you and Trent alone and not have you kill each other or run wild with the crew?"

"What's in California?"

"Just something I've been working on and I need Ruby's help."

Rusty knew she was not going to get anything more out of him and decided to let it go. She absently scratched behind her left ear. "Yeah, we're good. If anything comes up, I'll call. You two have a nice ride. How far down are you going?"

"Someplace called Ukeeah."

Rusty laughed at the screwed up pronunciation of the town. "Ukiah, it's an Indian name. Cute little place, you'll like it. If you have the time, run out to the coast to Mendocino. It's a living postcard. Ruby will know how to get out there. Get a room in a B&B and take an extra night. The hand off and ribbon cutting isn't for two more weeks anyway, so have some fun." Rusty closed the laptop and stood.

"I'll run it past Ruby. Thanks, Rusty." He gave the redhead a big hug. "You've been a great friend, and it's good to have someone I can talk to."

She patted him on the back. "Us girls gotta stick together."

A while later, as Stone lay in the quiet tent unable to sleep, he thought about the lifetime he had lived with hundreds of other guys in tents. This tent roof just hung on the pole, unmoving. Even through the mesh, Stone could see in the pools of lights dotting the project build area. Nothing was moving. There were no cars on the road, the gas station a quarter-mile away had closed an hour before, and only the security light was still on, probably keeping Bernie awake, too.

Stone thought about the silence. Even in the quiet of the desert, there were hundreds of personnel around making some kind of noise. His life had been filled with the noise of other people, and now there was nothing but silence. The fire had stripped the night air of even the sound of frogs or crickets.

The door latch snicked on the first house, the one they named Doug Fir because the Doug was the King in the logging of the coast. Stone strained to listen, and then he heard small, hesitant, bare feet. The hunched figure moved slowly down the aisle of cots. Finally, finding Stone it stopped. The large bundle of blankets and a pillow and her Mr. Donkey got laid out on a cot, and Molly climbed into bed.

"Goodnight, Stone," she whispered.

"Goodnight, Molly," he whispered back and she giggled.

They both lay there listening as the front door to Doug Fir, again, quietly snicked shut. This sound of padding bare feet was more self-assured. Ruby found the cot on the other side of Molly. Throwing out her bedding, she lay down. "It was too quiet in there."

Giggling, Molly repeated her good night.

Stone smiled. "Goodnight, Ruby."

"Goodnight, Molly. Goodnight, Stone. Goodnight, John Boy."

The three laughed softly and were soon asleep. Just before Stone drifted off, he looked up, and gazed across at Ruby, sleeping peacefully. A smiling Molly cuddled her Mr. Donkey. Stone did not have to see to know that it was there. Stone adjusted the pillow and rolled over, happy to be sharing the big lonely tent.

BAER CHARLTON

37

The tents began filling back up. The convoy was back, joined by four helicopters full of more pickle-suits. The National Guard electricians had helped Trent and Osiel's crew extend the hookups of the new RV Park to accommodate the overflow. Out in the lower field, Stone could make out the bright red Cherry Bomb parked next to Rusty's gold and black bus. Stone smiled as he heard the noise level rising in the canteen. Spuds, now in his comfort zone as chef, ordered the smooth flow of food from nine cooks in his tent kitchen kingdom.

Turning, Stone picked up another large gray tub of dirty dishes and moved toward the wash area before some shave-tail nineteen year old told him to sit and take a load off—again. *What is it with punk kids in pickle pants and their attitudes about gray hair?* He moved through the door into the steam bath of the washroom. The dark curls somewhat piled on the head of the woman looking into the maw of the industrial washer looked familiar, but the small rear end stuffed into the tiny white short-shorts did not.

Slim's sister slammed the door down on the washer and slapped the large red button. Turning, she saw Stone staring at her. She had seen that face on many men in her life, mostly on her late husband. She laughed as she leaned back against the stainless steel drain counter. Crossing her long, still good-looking legs, she smiled. "What's the matter, Stone? Never seen a gal in a pair of jump shorts before?"

Stone shook his head in confusion. "Jump shorts? What are jump shorts?"

Ellie laughed even harder. "It's a nasty old term our mama used to use. *Thems* is the kind of shorts that are so short, and so tight that a boy can only think about jumping 'em."

Ruby walked in at that moment with a matching shirt and shorts. "Y'all teaching Stone about the facts of life, Ellie?" She leaned up against the counter next to the other woman. Their arms found each other's waists, and they bonded like nesting salt and pepper shakers. If Stone did not know better, he would have thought they were sisters. The matching outfits almost made them look like twins.

Playfully, Stone set down the bus tray and turned on the gals who were having their fun at his expense. "I sure hope you didn't talk Molly into wearing that outfit, too. I don't think my heart could handle that much confusion."

"No, not Molly," Ruby teased looking coyly through her hanging bangs. "But we do have uniforms for Stella, Mary Margaret, and Jeannie when they get here this afternoon."

"Ah jeez... At least you have plenty of grunts out there to dig me a deep latrine when I blow a heart valve or something," Stone joked.

Ruby moved and put her hand on his chest. "I think you're safe for now, darlin'. Rusty said there weren't any jump shorts her size... but, we're still looking." She laughed, kissed him on the cheek, and turned back toward the kitchen area door. "Coming, Spuds!"

Giving Ellie a cold eye, but one of his crooked smiles, he turned and headed back out to the dining area to pull in another tray of dishes. With the camp filling back up, it became a never-ending circle of plates: clean plates to fill, serve, and return dirty. Stone knew he was just a cog in the works. In addition, Stone knew he just had his chain pulled by two of the best.

He thought about how much they must miss their two Hanks. Stone's large right hand pushed on the door as he walked back into the noise of two hundred people cycling through the tent for breakfast and catching up with new and old friends alike. With Spuds at the helm, the coffee was officially ready at Oh Dark Thirty, which lately had been creeping out as late as almost five. However, this morning the pans started to ring by half past three. The camp would be almost full by mid-afternoon, and the fire marshal would start turning a blind eye by dinner. Stone had a suspicion the dinner serving would see lines of people they had never even met.

He stopped for a second to watch the young woman with two coffee pots as she worked her magic with the troops and civilians alike. He wondered if he would ever stop enjoying the sound of her laugh, moving the young woman from diner to diner. Molly flowed with a kind word here, recognition there, asking if everything was okay and the interest she showed for each and every person at her tables.

Stone recognized the mirror image of her mother in the light two-finger touch on a patron's shoulder or elbow if Molly had both coffee pots. There was a pure talent

BAER CHARLTON

there, and it overshadowed anyone's first knee jerk reaction to seeing her only as a person with Down's Syndrome. That reaction just washed away with her wide smile, and their first sip of her coffee.

"She has really come into her ownership this summer." The gravel voice was as distinctive as it was soft and caring. Stone nodded as Rusty continued. "I wasn't sure she was the same person you had told me about when I met her this spring. She was shy and quiet. Everything you might expect from a girl like that." She leaned on her one good hip as the two watched with avuncular pride.

Stone started to talk, but had to clear his throat. "Yeah, but look at that little pocket rocket now. She'd make a damn fine sergeant."

Rusty laughed with agreement. "Yeah, wrangling three and four meals a day for a couple of thousand people for a couple of months can do that to you. That is, if it doesn't just drive you cow batty and running off into the forest."

Stone raised his one good eyebrow and looked at his friend. "Cow batty?"

Rusty did not even look at him for fear of laughing. Instead, she settled for slapping the back of her hand on his large chest. "Shut your front door, Stone," nodding, "cow batty."

"You're not going through that stage-of-life, are you, Rusty?"

She turned and leveled a half-open eye at him. "You know I can't."

Stone's eyes twinkled as he saw a dark figure come out of the third house. Turning to the redhead but preparing to make his escape. "Sure you can. It's called mental-pause."

Rusty swung, but only found air and a swinging door.

Stone slipped up next to Spuds in the kitchen area. "Listen, I need a special plate." He ticked off the foods he knew Butterfly would be looking for, and pointed her out to Spuds.

Spuds nodded. "I've got this, Gunny. She came by shortly after sunup and told me what she would need." He waved to her as she came in the other end of the kitchen. He put his other hand on Stone's shoulder. "We've got everything covered, and I do mean everything. You just worry about the ribbon cutting tomorrow. Everyone has their orders from Rusty, and we all have your back."

Stone swallowed. He had never felt like an extra piece of equipment before. He patted the young man on the back. "Thanks, Spuds. Oh, and is it true that we're having strawberry crepes tomorrow?"

"Don't push me, Stone. You're lucky I don't just slop you out some watery gruel and a hard crust of bug infested hardtack from a K-rat."

"Yum, crepes it is." They laughed as Stone ducked a spatula sweeping toward his head. Stone waved his fingers at Butterfly as he stepped out the back door. Then Stone looked at his phone.

From Ski:
Put on clean shirt. Company
We land in 5
Talk in Stone house?

From Stone:
Better B good

BAER CHARLTON

V Busy

From Admiral:
Get Un-busy

Stone looked at the new message and thought, *oh shit, what now?*

From pure reflex, the gunny lifted his left arm and sniffed his armpit. The scent was a blend of missed shower, combined with an early visit to the wood shop and a bucket of sawdust thrown on him. It was not wholly a bad smell, but he thought a fresh T-shirt might help and headed for the first house.

STONEHEART

BAER CHARLTON

38

"You're either crazy or just plain stupid. You cannot just float him in here as if he's somebody's mother just dropping in for a visit. Procedures exist for this kind of thing for a damn good reason." Stone was incredulous. The meeting around the antique dining table had just overheated to the realm of stupid. "Begging your pardon, Mr. Secretary, but you are a nobody here. You snuck in here for two days of the second week of the build when everything was crazy and thought nobody noticed."

The Secretary of the Navy bounced his index finger on the oak table. "That's not the point here…"

"Oh, but that is the point. You parked your blue four-door rental about fifty yards from the east end of the gas station's parking lot on Tuesday about 8:15 in the morning. You stupidly put on a white hard-hat. You walked to the corner, and then thought better and went back around through the RV Park and along where the convoy parked. You borrowed a belt and hammer from a heavyset redheaded woman who was handing out tools. You went with the team working on the second house, and then moved over to the clinic.

"I got the heads-up that you were here shortly before nine. You got busted because you had a commander's hard-hat on and didn't know how to use the tools in your belt, and you went AWOL from your assigned crew. You think you have a forgettable face, but to everyone in the Navy and Corps alike, your face is as forgettable as Ski's little peanut butt." Stone's left thumb waved backward at the now blushing captain. He leaned even closer into the verbal combat. "You had lunch with the eleven-thirty shifts because you didn't find any breakfast to your liking on the way over in the morning from Ashland.

"If you hadn't done anything stupid up until then, you went for the Olympics by choosing to sit with two people you knew, and who thought they had great disguises, too. At least the senator had been working here for three days... at the job he was assigned. The congressman wasn't quite as good as you—he showed up at ten, faked working as he nosed around with a white helmet and a clipboard. That stunt is going to cost him come Election Day. What he didn't know was that many phone cameras and one or two pads were filming his shenanigans. He is now referred to as Congressman Clipboard. There's no paperwork on site. Everything was digital, he stood out like an ignorant ass.

"But the three of you sitting there having lunch was the biggest screw-up of all. Three people you should have known or talked to asked to sit at your table. You three blew them off by telling them it was a private meeting. Well, you should have held the meeting in Washington, because you blew off the health director of the clinic, the owner of the café and community center, and the general contractor.

"Now you want to slide in here like you're the

fucking hero? And just to show what kind of stand-up guy you're going to drag the President of the United States in here for a three-minute guest appearance and what I'm sure is a full-blown photo-op just to show you have the biggest dick in the barracks?"

Stone leaned back in the chair, his eyes burning at the squirming Washington functionary.

The Secretary of the Navy tried to capture something of an upper hand by being gracious. "I apologize for his language, Captain…"

She cut him off. "Oh, no need, Mr. Secretary. Stone hasn't said anything offensive or untrue, as far as I'm concerned." Looking at the admiral for guidance, Ski got the secret go ahead with the running of a middle finger behind the ear that only she could see. "In fact, I think he has every right to be mad. What Stone didn't include was that you commandeered a military flight from Washington DC into Portland, and then a National Guard flight to Medford, all on the public's dime.

"This is the same public Stone has come back to help. He has spent time here. He didn't grow up here, but he knows how these people have lost everything: their forest, the jobs that were in the forest, jobs that supported those people, their homes, businesses, recreation, and tourist dollars. And now they will be asked to pay for not only yours, but also the congressmen's silly trips out here just because you three saw an easy way to capture some credit for caring.

"And tomorrow, you want to spend another five million dollars for a four-minute photo-op of you and POTUS pinning a piece of shit tin on a guy who will probably be wearing the uniform of the day—a T-shirt.

"Have you any idea just how stupid you and the President will look bent over this guy in a wheelchair doing something to his chest? It's going to look like a mugging. Because with you holding the chair so the victim can't get away, it will always look like the President is slugging him in the guts. No matter how you take the picture, the guy's chest is half a hand away from his guts.

"This event tomorrow is a very personal event. The people who will be helped by this clinic already served with honor, and then they were thrown back into the forest like a used washrag. These people have been ignored by the VA, Washington, you, the congressman, the senator, and yes, even by the admiral and me. We are all parts of a system that failed these people. Then Congress made budget cuts that took three-quarters of their livelihoods away and that was before the fire. A fire, I might add, that only cremated the walking dead.

"Only Stone saw the need to build this clinic. So he recruited some people to help. He didn't come to Congress and ask for the money, he reached down into his own pocket. However, when he came back, he found a lot more people that needed help. Again, it was Stone who reached out and found people to help. The only thing that came from Washington has been you and two jerks that didn't even stick around and do some real work for once.

"We've had over three thousand people come through here to help. Some could only give a few hours because they just drove by, but wanted to do something. Stone didn't know it, but we had a cash problem from the first days."

Ski glanced at Stone who sat frowning and shaking his head. "We had people just driving by or even coming out of their way to open their wallets, pull every bill out of it, and shove it in the hands of someone who might know where it needed to go."

Quietly Stone asked, "How much?"

The red hair whipped as she turned. "Check with Rusty, but I think it is already over $600,000 and growing." She turned back to the Secretary who was squirming uncomfortably on this small woman's skewer. She obviously also had a very long leash.

"Look, I know somewhere down deep, you thought you meant well. Nevertheless, the best thing you and the members of Congress could do now is first, wave off our boss. Then tomorrow, stand quietly in the crowd, and watch. Because this is about local people—not us, not the Navy, not Congress, or Washington, it is just the local people. This is what they did, for them. We were just blessed that we got to help. In addition, if you don't get it, Stone is an honorary one of them. As long as he wants it, this is his home." She sat back, finished.

The Secretary looked at the silent admiral. "Do you have anything to pile on to your boss, Admiral?"

The man who seemed at that moment more a 'Mike' than an admiral did. He pursed his lips, looking at the Secretary. "You're not married, are you, sir?"

The bureaucrat squirmed. "Working on my third and I hope last. It's been a tough go, but we have twelve years in so far. Why?"

The admiral waved his index finger at the gathering. "At this table, which one of you would be doing the talking? Which one would have the clearest view of the events and field of fire?"

The man started to answer, and then closed his mouth.

Slowly, he worked it out. He looked at Ski, then Stone and finally, back to the admiral. "Point taken." Then he turned to Ski. "So that's the way you would advise the President on down?"

"Yes sir."

The Secretary of the Navy turned back to Stone. "Stone?"

Stone leaned back in his seat, visually creating a separation from the Secretary and the small fireball. "Sir, I'm just a battered old war horse, but I do know the winning team at this table."

Resolved, the Secretary leaned back in his chair. Thinking, he finally looked up. "I guess I wasted a trip."

"No, sir," Ski assured. "You came out to witness some of the best this country has to offer. It's what we believe in, it's what we fight for to protect. We just don't get many opportunities to actually witness it happening. There was no FEMA, no Red Cross, and no whining about how the Fed wasn't coming to the rescue.

"This fire wasn't a sexy disaster like massive tornadoes or hurricanes in a major city. The destruction was complete and out in a region of the country forgotten by us back east and the media. And, without some trashed neighborhood to stand in front of or waist deep water to stand in, there is no photo-op. The same goes for all the people whose tornado or hurricane happened in their heads. There is nothing to film for the eleven o'clock news.

"Spuds is missing both legs, but has been putting out thousands of meals a day through the build. Sexy? Yeah, he is, but nobody wants to watch a gimp just throwing hash for twelve hours in a mess tent.

"There is Squirrel. He should have been dead in

Somalia." Ski pointed at the now smirking Stone. "In fact, the gunny thought he was. But, the guy and his wife drove from the east coast with his portable sawmill and turned out all the siding on these buildings single-handed, because the other is just a hook. Sexy? Only if you close your eyes and listen to him talk to the woman he worships.

"Are they getting paid to be here? No. Just the opposite, they have spent thousands of dollars to be here. All we can do is hug them and keep them steamed up on coffee."

The admiral offered his brand of olive leaf by adding, "And there are always those amazing biscuits and freezer jam."

The Secretary frowned. "Biscuits?"

A chagrined Stone held his head down as he typed into his phone. He raised one eye and looked across at a companion conspirator who was having a hard time not laughing and giving away what had happened all those weeks before.

Stone, tight-lipped, said, "I've got this."

From Stone:
Spuds, could U bring SECNAV
plate of fresh Bs with J

From Spuds:
Thru door in 2

"Other than being the short-order waiter, I'm not sure what I'm doing here." Stone started to rise.

The Secretary waved him back down. "Sit down, Stone. You're the most senior person in this room, and the most important."

Stone sat slowly as he eyed the most senior person in the Navy. "How do you figure, sir?"

The Secretary pointed at Ski. "She is the adjutant to the admiral who, in the scope of things, is my adjutant. I'm the adjutant to the President, and we all work for you, the citizens of the United States. That is why we all defer to you as 'sir'. The only person who gets in the middle of that chain of respect but not command, is a Congressional Medal of Honor recipient—even the President must stand and salute that person."

"So, you were here to keep the peace between the squabbling children, so to speak." Stone smiled at the admiral whose eyes were shifting back and forth to point to the other two.

A light knock sounded on the thick door before it swung open. Spuds entered and placed a large platter with steaming biscuits, butter, jam, and plates on the table. "Compliments of the new café, sir. Sorry for the old pancakes the other week, sir," Spuds smiled sheepishly, "a mean-spirited prank for all the C and K rats we ate in the Sandbox, sir."

The Secretary laughed. "So those stupid bib overalls didn't fool anyone, did they."

"Well, sir, around here, we remove the plastic label that says large, large, large, before we wash them. And, if you look around, running sandpaper on the knees doesn't fool anyone. It's the backside that gets glazed and worn down where your wallet sits year after year. The middle of the pocket gets black and glazed. It's the outline of the wallet that turns white with the abrasion. Begging your pardon, sir, but you just looked like a rube from the city, a big city, at that. But, if it is any comfort, your two-hour old pancakes probably tasted better than Congressman Clipboard's pancakes with strawberry sauce. The cayenne pepper probably wasn't what he was expecting the flavor to be." Spuds smiled.

"You're quite the one, aren't you, son?"

Spuds was shining with his position and authority. "Sir, there are three things you learn in the Navy or the Corp—never piss off the Executive Officer because he assigns duty. Next, always be on the good side of the Boats or the Gunny, because they make up the work details. Last, and most important, don't fuck with the cook."

The Secretary leaned to one side to get a better look at Spuds' aluminum legs.

Stone filled in the gap. "Spuds was due to rotate three days before. He would have been strolling down easy street or out driving around one finger on the wheel, with his elbow out the window, and his right arm around his girl. Orders from the SECNAV extended us all an extra six months. It wasn't on your watch, you just happen to step into the sights."

The Secretary took the measure of the young man on the aluminum legs. "You seem to have a good command of those legs."

"They do for now, sir, but as soon as Mary Margaret gets set up, she has some ideas about ones that will be more comfortable for me to stand on all day."

The older man smiled. "So, you're the cook. Are these biscuits yours, too?"

"I wish. Those are Ruby's claim to fame. The jam is a secret recipe of the nuns and Ellie. I just hack at the rest of the food."

Stone and Ski both coughed and chuckled at the young man's humility.

Ever the consummate political player, the man asked, "So, anything the SECNAV or Navy could do for you personally, son?"

Spuds understood the loaded nature of the question and waived it off. "I'd love to go to Paris and study cooking at the Cordon Bleu, but the skills would be a waste here in southern Oregon. So, for me personally, nothing that isn't already being taken care of by Stone here. But, there is more than a company's worth that could use the VA's help out here in the woods. We have access to a decent clinic in Medford, but several of these guys are dying of cancers and stuff they got in Vietnam with Agent Orange, like my uncle. The clinics in Medford or Roseburg aren't prepared to deal with all of that, so they have to go all the way up to Portland. But a lot of these guys, they can't even deal with going to the big city of Grants Pass or Roseburg, much less Medford or a real city like Portland. This is why Stone built the clinic out here in the sticks."

Stone noticed the frown of confusion on the Secretary's face. "Grants Pass is a town of about thirty thousand and Medford is about double that. Spuds mentioned his uncle who just died a couple of years ago. He had a hard time even being inside, much less go to a large town or city."

Spuds nodded. "Unc could come in and shower or eat with us, but he always slept out in the forest since he came home from Vietnam. If we ran the VA like Medicare, these guys could go to a local hospital or clinic, and for the extremes, something could be brought to them, like we'll have here."

STONEHEART

"Here?" The official frowned in confusion.

Stone explained the mission. "The clinic will be more like a tiny hospital. We will be able to get surgeons to come in and do the minor stuff for the guys like Spuds who grow extra skin on their stumps, which causes the cup to stop fitting right." Spuds raised the leg of his shorts to expose a band of duct tape securing his right leg.

With a nod at Spuds, Stone continued. "We have a four bed clinic, with round the clock care available and food. With a little extension, we could process chemotherapy and radiation on a limited scale. Doctors could donate some time, and we even have this house built with four bedrooms as a guest cottage. So they have a place to stay, we feed them, and they help our clients."

The Secretary took another bite of heaven and thought as he chewed. "How are you getting paid now?"

Stone thought about the question then smiled. "We haven't bought a cash register yet, but I'm sure something down the road will come up. But, then, I'm just a broken down old gunny on a motorcycle, running around the country visiting people. So, this is way above my pay grade. I just built a clinic, and they came, but I'm sure that Paul and Mary Margaret know what they are doing. If I was to hazard a guess, I'd say the good sisters are supporting Mary Margaret, and Paul is living on his VA pension."

Spuds waved and moved. "Gentlemen, Ski, it's been grand, but I have people to feed, and roasts to get in the ground. Mister Secretary, it's nice to have finally met you. Stick around for dinner. It's going to be a knock your socks off barbeque done up southern Oregon style."

The SECNAV wet his lower lip. "Roast beef is one

of my favorites."

"Oh, no, that is for lunch. We're going to have spotted owl, venison, possum, clams, crab, tuna, steelhead, salmon, and other road kill on the menu for dinner." He waved as he rocked his style of walking back out the door.

The Secretary chuckled. "Funny guy." And then he noticed that nobody else was laughing.

The sound of trumpets at a distance blew from both sides of the table.

From Rusty:
Stone, come now
We have trouble
Elvis is here

Stone looked up at Ski and noticed the smile was only on the side of her face the Secretary and the admiral could not see. "Did you get this, too?"

She stood up. "Yeah." She looked up from her phone. "Gentlemen, we have a crisis that Stone and I need to attend to. Please refrain from killing one another until I can watch and have refreshments at hand." She saluted and turned.

As Stone and Ski walked up the sidewalk toward the front of the clinic, they were both laughing. "Do you think it was dangerous leaving them alone?"

Ski waggled her hand "Eh, who cares? I've worked for both of them long enough. I'm ready for a change." She laughed even harder.

"Hey! Old man saggy butt!" Jeannie's voice trumpeted through the screen mesh of the tent as Elvis nosed open the door.

Stone laughed as he knelt down for a big tongue face wash and a hug from the Dobie. "Hey, monkey butt, you're early. You caught me before I could put on my pink running shorts."

Jeannie walked out of the mess tent dressed in what Stone now assumed was the uniform of the day. However, before he could make a smart crack, Mary Margaret and Stella followed in with closely matching shorts and tops. Stella's larger, baggy shorts were matched by Rusty's, but they all had the same laugh on Stone, as there were group hugs all around.

Ski hugged Jeannie and they both looked at Stone. "I guess I better go get in uniform, too. And here I had my heart set on the Elvis uniform." She faced and looked up to Jeannie. "I brought my doggie ears and sideburns."

BAER CHARLTON

39

Somewhere in all the confusion of massing several thousand people, the large parking lot was cleared of trucks, cars, and motorcycles. It was not the usual ribbon cutting. With speeches short and humor long, the gathering painted a canvas of camouflage, bib overalls, with many T-shirts commemorating different buildings. Old friends stood next to new old friends. Two dogs ran rampant as first Elvis then Angel did the chasing—everyone laughed, and no one cared. It was not a distraction, but part of the entertainment.

Rusty stood with Trent on the Cherry Bomb's flatbed trailer. There was a lot of reminiscing going on about how the summer had started. Rusty had gotten a lot of wolf whistles for her rendition of the jump shorts uniform, and Trent had made her blush by going down on one knee, and asking her to come to work for him.

The event was more like a large family or a clan picnic than a gathering of people from thirty-one different states, and all for their own personal reasons, but with one single focus. Stone sat on the steps of the café with Ruby and Molly and looked across the field of mostly people he had never known. About every fourth one emerged as a face he recognized, but they were intermingled with the many that came not from his many years in the military, but from the region's past. All of a sudden, his pocket vibrated.

From Ski:
U started this.

Stone laughed. Ruby leaned over and rested her chin on his shoulder. Molly leaned against his other side and poked him in the ribs, saying quietly, "It's true, Stone."

Stone put his arm around her small shoulders, and kissed the top of her head. "Maybe, but you served me that first cup of coffee."

From Stone:
Molly made me do it.

Molly laughed and playfully slapped his arm. Stone turned to a laughing Ruby. "Molly is beating on me again."

Ruby snorted and with a mock seriousness admonished them to behave. Up on the flatbed trailer, Trent was winding down and talking about the real person behind these buildings. Stone switched to another message board.

From Stone:
Start him coming.

Stone kissed Ruby on the cheek and stood up. His timing was military as Trent called his name and the crowd roared with applause and cheers. Stone recognized many company war whoops, and above all, a thunderous "Hoorah." Stone's hand moved from handshake to handshake, and pats on the gunny's back, as well as slapping a back or twenty, while he crossed the parking lot toward the trailer. He climbed up the ladder to stand on the back with Rusty and Trent, the cheering and noise grew. Stone hugged Rusty and then Trent, thanking each quietly in turn. Rusty gave him the microphone, and he walked to the edge of the trailer.

Three times, the gunny had raised the microphone to his face, and then could not talk. He wiped his face, and whispered to Rusty that it was dusty up there. The crowd waited silently. Finally, Stone cleared his throat and looked across the highway at one lone green tree, standing about five feet tall. He thought about how each morning, Spuds had carried two one-gallon jugs of water across the highway. Then, on two aluminum sticks, he scrambled up the slope to serve the little tree its morning water. By the second month, he was mixing the water half-and-half with old coffee from the night before. His explanation came across as pure Southern Oregon forest-raised—the Douglas fir likes the acid in the coffee.

Stone thought about the little tree growing strong across the highway. *How do you tell someone from New York City that a little Christmas tree on the west coast likes its morning coffee?*

Slowly, Stone raised the microphone to his mouth. "First, I'd like to thank our Uncle Sam for putting up with me for thirty-nine years and preparing me for this day." The laughter and clapping washed over him. "I've been in over two hundred fire fights on five continents and more countries than I want to remember, but there is nothing as scary as a crowd..." He stopped and collected his thoughts.

He looked to the café steps. The sea of people stood silent. Many had experienced Stone's stopping in the middle of a conversation, or had themselves or a loved one who did the same. He studied the café and slowly brought the microphone back. He spoke not with the booming authority of a gunnery sergeant, but the soft voice of a person who had been deeply moved. "Two years ago, I stopped for breakfast because a very good friend that I had met the night before told me I had to stop there for breakfast.

"I had no idea that I would never get to sit, talk, or share some Jack with LaLonnie again. Those few brief hours of conversation changed my life. She came out in the morning, and insisted I should stop at Mom & Dad's Café a few minutes down the road. Not just to stop, but to meet Ruby, Hank, and especially Molly. That's all she said. I had to stop and meet these three people. It was a simple thing."

Stone's vision shifted to where he knew Spuds would be leaning up against the light post at the corner of the sidewalks. He smiled to see Spuds' arm draped around the shoulder of his girl. Spuds's mother waved her fingers at Stone as she leaned into the son she was so proud of, and the man he had become.

Stone looked back at the crowd, his voice dropping a little deeper. "She made a simple suggestion. That suggestion was as life altering as an IED removing your legs. As simple and life altering by a sniper a hundred yards away, or a drunk in a car, taking away your ability to walk, replacing your feet with four wheels. These all are simple things, but they all alter your life. Mine just happened to be for the good.

"I did stop, and as I sat there in a rustic log cabin smelling of the forest, good food, and with people laughing and saying 'Hi', a young woman, barely more than a girl, came up and asked me the most important question that I have ever been asked in my life. Molly asked whether she needed to know me, or if I was just passing through.

"My life consisted of the Marine Corps. Everything I knew and called home was the Corps. Then at age fifty-seven, I was no longer a part of that life. They handed me a DD-214 form, and said, 'Go home,' except, I no longer had a home.

"So there I was, riding around the country on a motorcycle, just passing through." He raised his right arm and pointed toward Molly and Ruby. "Just passing through, until this little girl gave me a reason to have someone know who I was."

Stone paused to swallow some rocks, which choked his throat. "I told her with an opening line like that, I would definitely have to come back. So, I introduced myself... and swore that I would come back."

Someone near the back of the crowd yelled out, "We're glad you did, Stone."

Stone laughed. "I'm glad I did, too. But, I wasn't happy to see what happened while I was away. Yet, in a way, it was like the old saying about when a door closes, a window opens—or something like that.

"While I was away, we worked on the idea for this clinic. We didn't know where the clinic would be, but I'm glad it is here. And I'd like you to meet the new doctor and nurse who will run the clinic." He turned around where four large men lifted Paul and his chair up onto the trailer.

Mary Margaret, now dressed in a more conventional outfit of denim pants and shirt, walked up the stairs where they had been installed.

"This is Dr. Paul Hollis, and this beautiful young woman is Sister Mary Margaret. Now before any of you young bucks get any ideas, the 'Sister' part is her vocation, not just because she is black and a woman. But, if you want to be put in your place, join her for one of her daily ten miles of running. One of these years, we are going to teach her the American word *jogging*.

"Moving up the map is the next building, which is the community center and gym. Mary Margaret has told me she plans to offer morning exercise classes, and eventually yoga, or at least stretching classes. She also told me we would have ballroom dancing, but I think she was just teasing me about my way of dancing. I don't know what my buddy told her, but it wasn't me dancing—I think it was how I looked when I was on fire."

The crowd laughed with Stone as he gave up information about the past and his obvious scars with such endearing self-deprecation.

"Further along, we have the Café. Molly, would you come up here, dear?"

Ruby pushed Molly as she hesitated. She finally walked across the parking lot, winding her way through the crowd. Molly's smile never wavered and her steps proved sure. As she mounted the trailer and walked over to Stone, he put his arm around her shoulder.

"How do you feel today, Molly?"

"Fine."

"Do you know what day this is?"

"Saturday."

Stone laughed. "Yes, it is. But it is also a very important day."

She frowned slightly and looked up at him. "What?"

"Today is the first day of the rest of your life. Are you ready for that?"

Molly thought about the old saying but knew how it was true. "Okay."

Stone nodded his chin at the crowd. "Do you know who these people are?"

She thought, and then realized there was more to the question than can you name each person. "No, who are they?"

Stone smiled. "Customers... But not just any customers—hungry customers."

"Okay." She beamed.

Stone winked at the crowd. "But Molly, we have a problem."

"We do?"

"Yes, we do. Earlier, I tried going into the Café to turn on the lights and the stove, so we could serve these hungry people. Unfortunately, the door was locked. Do you have the key to the Café?"

Molly looked at her mother, as she said, "No... but maybe..." Ruby was shaking her head, and stood and turned out her pockets to show they were empty.

Molly turned back to Stone, and then turned around to look at Trent and Rusty. She looked back at Stone. "We don't have any keys."

Stone put his fist to his chin. "Hmm, maybe we have a problem... or, maybe we have a benefactor. Molly, do you know what a benefactor is?"

"No."

Stone turned Molly back toward the crowd, so she could not see Butterfly pushing a wheelchair toward the temporary stairs.

"A benefactor is someone like a guardian angel. They look after you or watch over you. Sometimes they do more than just watch. Sometimes they help in larger ways than you know."

Molly smiled brightly. "Like you."

"Well, yes and no. Sometimes to be the benefactor you want to be, you need some help. This benefactor has been around a long time, but he just hasn't been seen for a long time. Recently, he and I finally came to a meeting of the minds, and I asked him for some help. What I didn't know was that he needed my help to be the benefactor he wanted to be. So, we worked together. And now, I would like you to meet your old/new neighbor, Bernie."

The crowd grew silent. The locals knew who Stone was talking about, but their view of that name did not connect with what Stone was saying. The non-locals followed the locals' lead and stood waiting. Butterfly helped Bernie out of the wheelchair and up the few steps to the trailer. She stood holding the small cylinder of oxygen that connected with a clear hose to a cannula at his nose.

Bernie looked gaunt and a little shaky, but Stone could see the determination in his eyes. This had become something Bernie wanted to do, and nobody could do it for him. Stone snapped his fingers for a marine's attention, and then pointed at the wheelchair. In a second, it appeared on the trailer. Stone brought it up behind Bernie, and put his hand on Bernie's shoulder. Stone patted, and he could feel the resolve as the man slowly gave in to reality and sat down.

Rusty handed Bernie a microphone. The man's eyes had not left Molly. This was not for the crowd. This was entirely about Bernie, Molly, and making the world right, even if it was only a little place in southern Oregon. "Molly." The sound controller adjusted for the almost whisper of a voice. "When we met twenty years ago I wasn't a nice person. It was almost the worst day of my life. Now, I want you to know, that every single day since, I have remembered that day. I wasn't nice to you."

Molly just smiled, and stepped over and patted him on the shoulder. "It's okay. You were probably just a kid then. Kids can be very cruel sometimes." She nodded to reassure the man before her.

Bernie smiled and leaned back into the chair. "A couple of years ago, Stone and I met. He had strongly suggested I should drive down the road and have some biscuits and one of your smiles. I can see now, I should have listened to him then." He sat just breathing, and building his energy as Molly just smiled, and rubbed his shoulder.

"Molly, I understand you want to open the Café. However, there are a couple of things that need to happen. First, I think you might need a sign."

Everyone turned to look at the enshrouded sign on the tall post near the street. "What do you think we should call the new Café, Molly?"

She looked at him and shrugged her small shoulders.

Bernie took a whistle from his pocket and handed it to her. "I don't have enough breath to blow this, but maybe if you blow it long and hard, we might find out what kind of sign we have."

The infection of Christmas morning was bringing out

the little girl, and as she turned around, she leaned against Bernie, and her left arm slipped naturally around his shoulders. She took a deep breath and blew the whistle long, loud, and sharp. As the sound died, but for the echoes in the distant hills, the shroud wavered and then fell.

The new sign, which had quietly been installed in the middle of the night, stood atop the post, bright and new. Molly was stunned. Only six people in the world knew what the sign would say. Yet, Stone did not realize just how wonderfully right it would look. The Mom and Dad's had given way to the next generation. The crowd approved of Molly's Café, and Stone guessed it would be a hit.

Molly stuttered. "I... I don't know what to say, but somebody misspelled Mom and Dad." She turned around to look at Stone. "Is it really my Café?" She got a nod and a smile.

She turned back to Bernie, and found him dangling a set of keys from his fingers. Her eyes lit up even more as her mouth dropped open. Before either could think, she hugged him around the neck. She had no idea what curative power a simple act could have, but there were a few that did. "Thank you, Bernie."

"No. Thank you." He brought the microphone back up. "Now, as you know, you can't serve customers with a closed Café so, how about another of your super whistles."

She took a deep breath and blew the whistle again. On the sign, a tracing of neon lit up and read a matched image of what was now glowing in the window *We're Open Now* – the simple phrase she had repeated to her first customer of the day, every day, for many years.

"That looks great, Molly, but before we go eat lunch, we have some other business to do. Can you help me with this?" He handed her a larger set of keys. "These are the keys to the clinic. I want to welcome Doctor Hollis and nurse Mary Margaret to Fall, Oregon. They also have a new member of their team who is going to be the administrator. So, we need to give the keys to her. Could Stella Yoder come up here and take control of these, please?"

Stella's leaving Des Moines and the convent had been a tightly kept secret. She had decided that retirement was merely taking up what you love to do and going where you could do it best. As Stella walked up the steps, nothing belied her seventy-two years of age, except the gray winning the battle over the blond in her hair. Stella hugged Molly as she took the keys and stood next to Mary Margaret and Paul.

"Stella, these are the keys to the houses Sequoia, Dawn Cedar, as well as Stoneheart. The larger ring and set is for the clinic and the community center. There will be some more keys. They're more janitorial keys pertaining to the grassy field, the outbuilding, and sport house, but other than the keys to the Café, Ruby and Molly's house, and Doug Fir, you are the holder of the keys to the kingdom."

He turned to Molly again. "Molly, could I get you to give us one more super whistle?"

As she blew, the shroud over the lettering, standing proud over the building, fell to the ground below the sign. The sunlight shone blindingly off the polished brass letters, which spelled out 'The Hank & LaLonnie Health Clinic.'

Now the crowd was ready for an uncontrolled round of applause and cheering. Even Stone had not known about the sign. He turned his head to find Ruby had left her seat on the steps and was making her way through the crowd as it parted ahead of her.

She climbed up on the trailer. With tears in her eyes, she hugged Bernie around the neck. Quietly, for only Bernie to hear, "Thank you, Bernie, and welcome home."

He hugged her back. "It feels good to be back."

Ruby looked up at Stone and mouthed, *did you know about this?*

He shook his head and shrugged his shoulders. He did not know who made the decision, but he wholeheartedly approved. After all, even early into the project, they all knew it would be a clinic for more than just the vets.

"Stone," Bernie tried to look around, so Stone stepped out. "Stone, you have shared your plans with me, and I respect them. But I also want you to know about this envelope that I have in my hand." He wiggled a thick envelope. "Some on this trailer know that everything on these eighty acres is held in a trust inside the Stoneheart Foundation. This envelope contains the conformed copies of a land transfer of the eighty acres in which you bought from me at the agreed price, which you paid. Also, in this envelope are conformed copies of a quitclaim deed and land transfer of the remaining eighteen-hundred and seventy-three acres I owned in this valley. The Stoneheart Foundation, now for all intents and purposes, owns this valley. Take care of it wisely, and with the same heart you have exhibited to me, and here this summer," sticking out his hand, "and welcome home."

Stone stood stunned until Mary Margaret poked him in the ribs. He looked at the silent crowd, his mouth hanging open. Then one of the men he recognized from that day long ago when he saved Bernie's life, yelled out, "Ah, hell, Stone, hug him. It wouldn't be the first time, so you two might as well get used to it."

Stone laughed, and it broke the dam for the crowd. Turning, he smiled and hugged the now standing Bernie as if he were a delicate piece of china. He stood rocking as the two cried. Stone's eyes locked on the deep brown eyes of the giant wet face of Butterfly, Bernie's new private nurse.

BAER CHARLTON

40

"I sure hope someone got a good picture of Molly's face when she understood the Café belongs to her." The oxygen flowed into Bernie's nose as he stopped for a deep breath. "I want a large picture of it to put over our mantel." He reached over and put his hand over Butterfly's hand.

She smiled and covered it with her right hand. The two had become very close friends. Months of being within feet of each other for twelve-hour days had led to talking. The talking had started one-way only with the occasional question for clarification. The conversations had grown from occasional to constant, which eventually led to sharing. The hardened heart had slowly unfrozen and glacially started toward a shadow of what it had been in earlier years. With each visit from Stone, and then Stone with Ruby, Butterfly had watched the evolution of the man she had come to care about deeply.

As the conversation bounced around the room among the close friends, Butterfly watched Bernie's eyes and the color in his face. Her right hand slid ever so slightly back to the man's thin wrist. It was easy for her to find his pulse. Aware that she was checking, his face turned, the eyes drooped, Bernie smiled wanly and nodded his jaw to acknowledge that it was time.

"Stone," the nurse asked quietly.

Smiling at Rusty's joke, he turned toward Butterfly. Seeing her taking the man's pulse, and the way Bernie was sitting, he nodded and rose. "Well, folks, enough of this gold bricking." He stretched his arms and yawned. "Ruby and I have work in the Café. You three have the clinic to tour." He pointed toward Paul, Stella, and Mary Margaret. "Rusty, I don't care what you do, but Bernie is about two hours late for his nap. And he gets really bitchy when he misses his nap time." Stepping around to pass Bernie, Stone rested his hand on the man's shoulder, and leaned close, and spoke, "I'll check in this evening when I bring dinner."

The crowd shuffled out and split up on the sidewalk running the length of the four houses to where it led out toward the grass sports field. Stone and Ruby stopped to admire the row of low-lying craftsman bungalows. Each was unique by the style of a front porch, and the treatment of shingling or cladding. In the first location was Douglas Fir, Ruby and Molly's house. Its siding was the same raw edge of bark running the length of the clapboards that clad the Café and community building. Sequoia Redwood came second, sided with heart redwood. It had become the new home of Paul on the ground floor, with Mary Margaret and Stella each with a suite upstairs. The third house had been made for Bernie, with accommodations for the round-the-clock nursing. The front porch was deep, and well overhung to hold the large round table, which seated six. It also had the best view of the grassy field.

The sidewalk dipped, and swung back a way to reach the stone house. This was the guesthouse for anyone who visited, as well as the office of the Stoneheart Foundation. The outside walls were clad with fieldstone to represent that the heart that is cold as stone can change to become warm and welcoming on the inside.

Ruby smiled as she looked at the plaque on the column of the third house—Dawn Cedar. "I should have guessed the house was for him, and that tree is perfect. His family was always that way in the area—huge, majestic, and everlasting. I'm also glad he will finally get to be friends with Molly." Then she thought about what she and Stone had picked up in California. As they turned back toward the Café, she asked, "When do you plan to tell him?"

It took a few steps for Stone to realize what she was asking about. "Oh... let's leave it for a few days. When everything settles down. Then he won't be so wound up."

With the end of the ceremonies the day before, traffic in the Café was busy with a lot of breakfast overflow from the mess tent. Many just wanted to eat in the new Café they had all been instrumental in building. Others came to only sit at the new Coffee Congress table. The large horseshoe shaped table allowed for mass conversation, but Molly could enter the center and pour the lubricant that kept the jaws jacking. None other than a silent and listening Congressman Clipboard administered the morning's coffee. He had impressed many, as he not only listened, but then also took copious notes on his notepad still clipped to the board.

As lunch was winding down, Charlie and his service dog Trooper came in to say good-bye. At seventy-nine, Charlie had known Stone all of his life. He had served with Stone's father and been in the hospital having an appendectomy when Stone was born.

Stone hugged Charlie gently and sat him at a table close to the path he took while bussing the tables. Between trays, they could catch up. They spoke in the shorthand that they had used when Stone was a kid hanging around the motor pool as "Uncle" Charlie worked on and swore at the battered vehicles as they were returned to a working order.

Charlie was long past any swinging of hammers, but he had brought his motor pool chest of tools. He took a few of the marines and guardspersons aside to chide them as only an old sergeant could do. An area in the RV Park got a canopy for Charlie and Trooper. More than a few helpers joined them. It was obvious that the young Turks went there to learn from an original shade tree mechanic.

Trooper was a golden retriever/yellow lab mix, with a heartbeat slower than forty and a tail that never stopped wagging. Charlie encouraged people to socialize with Trooper, unlike most service dogs. Trooper's job was to smell Charlie for a blood sugar change so Charlie could test himself and administer his insulin as needed. Having been shot-up in Korea may not have triggered his condition, but it did not help that he had only half of his guts left. The slender man laughed that it was a form of liposuction d'guerre.

Stone had reached for the gray bus tray under the

counter, and then stepped back to lean against the copper-clad sideboard. Molly had hesitated, at first, to pet Angel and Elvis, as they were the first dogs she had ever really gotten to know. Their high energy may have scared her. Trooper sensed Molly's uncertainty, and he sat up to make it easier for her to reach him. Then he just sat there as she lightly touched his head.

Ruby strolled over and leaned with Stone. Her left fingers found the strand of hair that had gone AWOL, and pushed it back into the loose bun. Two strands on the other side took the chance to get even wilder. "I'll bet you a back rub the dog ends up with his head on her lap."

Stone hiccupped with a snort. "No bet. He's been doing it all month. But I'll still give you a back rub if you rub my feet."

"Deal, if you promise to do that thing by pressing your thumbs on my temples."

"Oh, then I get... um, a neck rub." Stone had to search for something in his world of not needing. His eyes never left Molly and Trooper.

"Well, if we're going that far, then I hope that hot tub is working tonight."

"You tried it last night, too?" Stone looked over and laughed. "You should have knocked on my door."

Ruby smiled coyly. "I didn't have the heart. The door was vibrating with each snore."

"Oh, shut the front door. I don't snore." The gunny laughed because it had become a running joke in the tents and now the house. All three—Stone, Ruby, and Molly—had very distinctive snores, not loud, just distinctive. Stone's attention returned to the young woman and the dog with his head in her lap. "I got Osiel on the hot tub first thing this morning. I think he had to run into Medford for a part."

Ruby poured them both a mug of coffee, and they stood with their backsides against the coolness of the metal counter as they watched Molly succumb to the will of Trooper. It became obvious her heart was melting, and Stone felt there might probably be a dog in the near future to become a big part of the complex of Café, homes, and clinic. He knew Paul had come from a family of dog owners, but Mary Margaret was in the same camp as Molly.

Ruby took a slow sip from her coffee. Swallowing, she leaned her head slightly toward Stone. "Did you ever have a dog?"

"There were tunnel dogs in Vietnam, and a few bomb dogs in Iraq." Stone's frame remained straight as he almost relaxed leaning up against the makeshift counter.

"No, I mean as a kid."

"Once," Stone sipped his coffee as he weighed the rest of the answer. "For a few hours," he finished.

Ruby turned to study the busboy and benefactor she knew almost nothing about. Weighing whether she actually wanted to know finally became overshadowed by the curiosity, which came from being a small-town girl knowing everyone. "For a few hours? What happened?"

Stone stood watching every little twitch to the golden dog's tail and every roll of his eyes. The dog was obviously trying to maintain a balance between his work and his new friend. This tension was mirrored in the young woman as she sat timidly stroking his head.

Stone took the last sip from his coffee mug and then stared into the bottom, seemingly for answers. In a distant voice, from a place long ago and almost forgotten, he spoke. "It was a Christmas present for my brother and me." He leaned forward and quietly placed the mug in the almost full bus tray.

Stone straightened up but Ruby could tell that his shoulders caved in ever so slightly to the memory. The old burns on his face had flushed for a moment then paled back to the usual color. She could sense the war deep inside of him as he fought to talk like a regular person in a casual banter, instead of the safe regimen of the chain of command. Ruby felt she might have overstepped.

"You don't have to..."

Stone shook his head. "No, it's okay. It's just that sometimes I don't know how to explain things, and I don't want them to come out wrong either." He turned to look at her.

Once again, she saw the small twitch just at the side of his eye. Once again, she wondered if it could just possibly be a tiny tattletale of fear. She reached out her hand to his arm. "You're among friends here, and you are very safe. There is nothing you could ever share that would be offensive. I may not understand some of the horrors you have seen in so many wars, but I damn sure have seen my share of things, too."

Stone examined Ruby's face, trusting, and then turned to look out the front windows. "Ever since they had gotten married, my father had known that my mother loved dark unsweetened almost pure chocolate. Therefore, every Christmas, he would get a couple of pounds, and leave a trail of little chunks on the floor near the tree. He called it Rudolf... er, droppings."

"Chocolate turds," she added to let him know he was on safe ground with any language.

He nodded as he snuck a glance at her. "Well, the year I was four, my brother Charlie was eight, one of the guys down at the base had a mess of puppies."

"What kind?"

Stone shrugged the one shoulder and nodded toward the dog now leaning its side against Molly's leg. "Golden fence jumper, probably."

Ruby nodded, also focused on the large dog and her daughter. A small smile worked on her tired face.

"So dad brought the puppy home late when he got off swing shift and stuck it under the tree, basket, and all. I'm sure there were a couple of other small presents he put out also, but the important thing for him was the chocolate trail of turds."

Ruby realized in horror where this story was going and reflectively braced her hand on his arm. "But pure chocolate is poisonous to dogs."

Slowly, the screw turned at the corner of Stone's mouth as he turned to face her. "We found that out the next morning." He paused for a deep breath. "The folks found me on the floor next to the basket wondering how I had somehow broken the new toy."

The silence was deafening as Ruby realized the horror visited on a small boy. Her shock-braced hand on his arm relaxed and turned to a soft comfort. "And you never had another dog."

"Animal," the Gunny corrected. Nodding toward the young woman as he bent forward and grabbed the bus tray, he straightened and started for the doors to the back. He looked at his boss. "Not even so much as a goldfish." He then looked toward the tableau of the young woman and dog. "She and I are in the same boat."

"That is a horrible story, Stone," she whispered huskily.

He shrugged his shoulder as if to say, yeah, but it's my story, and then pushed the gray bus tray against the swinging doors and was gone to wash dishes, leaving his boss to mull over the first of many horrors visited on the man. Ruby had thought that only war could be hell, not thinking that war could also be the possible stability in a life.

BAER CHARLTON

41

The dinner crowd had been nice and evenly light to moderate as Ruby and Stone left the Café in the good hands of Spuds and Molly. Spuds was teaching Molly the ins and outs of how they ordered supplies up to a week in advance. Molly was enjoying having a *brother.*

Ruby and Stone strolled slowly down the walk, each in their own thoughts.

"What do you think?"

Stone returned to reality. "About what?"

"James and Molly."

"Who?"

"Spuds."

Stone stopped. This revolved into a part of being a civilian he had never expected. "As in boyfriend /girlfriend, Spuds and Molly?" His mind raced. His military life had clear lines of do not fraternize with this group or that. Now those barriers might be blurred or nonexistent. "Is that allowed?"

Ruby recoiled as if he had slapped her. "Because she has Downs?"

Stone's face opened in shock and embarrassment. "Oh... I had forgotten that." Stone backed up a step as

BAER CHARLTON

Ruby's face went from shock to a concerned angry frown as it moved into his face. "What? I did... I mean... Well, I just don't see Molly that way."

"Then what did you mean?" Her voice was sharp and threatening, and Stone could feel the hovering menace just below the belt.

Stone backpedaled. "Well, for starters, they work together. But, more importantly, she's now his boss. It is fraternization one-way and sexual harassment the other. At least in the Corps it's defined that way. But you civilians make up your own damn rules as you go merrily down the road playing bungle in the jungle." Stone raised his eyebrow in the hope it would look a little disarming. "Back rub anyone?" he whimpered.

Ruby thought about it a moment. "Hmm, maybe in a minute. But right now, you are really afraid of me." She planted her hand flat on his chest. Ruby watched his face. She could tell he was mentally squirming. "I think I want to take that out for a spin for a moment."

"What do you mean by that?" Now Stone was worried that he may be in over his head.

She turned and resumed walking. "I'm thinking."

Ruby started walking along the pathway past the houses. The tribe was all but settled in for the night. Paul, Stella, and Mary Margaret would have gone to bed just after devotions at nine as they would all get up shortly before five in the morning. Stella would awaken for her lifelong devotions. Paul and Mary Margaret went for a short 5K run to warm her up for the real run to the lake, up over the ridge, and back for a grand round of ten grueling miles.

The third house would become silent by eight in the

evening as Bernie still slept upwards of sixteen hours a day. Ruby and Stone both knew the light in the eastern window belonged to Butterfly, sitting in her rocker, trying to read in a battle to stay awake. The few returned crickets and a frog made the night sound good.

Stone and Ruby came to the end of the sidewalk. They looked out across the huge acreage now known simply as The Field. The grass had returned lush from the coastal air and stretched over thirty acres. The RV Park had three lone campers. The sound of indefinable music ebbed and flowed across the field. One camper, or possibly all three were breaking the rules of noise after nine. Stone felt sure nobody really cared.

"Okay, I thought about it."

"What…"

"Shush," Ruby stuck an index finger in his face and tried to look stern. "No talking." She pointed out into the dark field. "You have sixty seconds to be in the middle of that field… When you get there, you had best be naked. I don't want no sweaty USMC T-shirt against my naked skin. For the next hour all I want is grass stains."

Stone blinked, and Ruby was gone. Twenty feet away, Stone saw her blouse, so he left his left boot there as well. The crickets and the owls were on their own.

As the first-night sliver of a moon rose shortly before midnight, Ruby traced the road map of the battle and surgical scars with her index finger. Her head rested comfortably in the saddle between his rib cage and navel. Stone's toes wiggled hello to her sparkling eyes. Ruby thought back on the months she could have had access to his body, but their friendship did not suffer from the few times they already shared a bed. If anything, their bond as friends had become stronger and more durable.

"Taking a trip down that road or just remembering the scenery?"

Her eyes slid shut as she smiled. "Just enjoying the scenery I have right now."

"I need to move my butt just a smidgen. I think there is a young blade of grass that wants to give me an annual." They both sat up laughing.

As Ruby leaned her back against his back for support, she looked north into the waste of the burned off forest. "Stone?"

"Um?"

"Have you ever played the game 'what if'?"

"It sounds like the game of regrets."

She poked the ribs snuggled behind her, knowing that she would not get any reaction, but at least an acknowledgment. "Not that kind. Not what if I hadn't done such and such... but what if I had been born a man?"

"Is this about Rusty or a game?"

Ruby slapped behind her and caught a palm-full of naked thigh. "Leave my sister out of this... but that is a solid point." Ruby turned and rolled over onto her back as she flipped one leg over him. Next, while leaning her breasts against Stone's back, she reached around to hug with her hands on his chest. Ruby's cheek lay against Stone's shoulder as her hands dropped and rested in his lap. "Rusty played the game and chose to act on his 'what ifs'. I'm just not sure if Rusty the man could comprehend what the challenges really were going to be for Rusty the woman."

Stone thought about the long talks, which seemed like a lifetime ago. He thought about how surreal Rusty had seemed back then, and how close to family she was now. "He knew... nevertheless, it didn't matter. There are some things in life where you just don't have a choice."

Ruby changed cheeks and looked over at the last trailer light wink out. "That's what I mean. It's just an exercise of alternate universes. Not about choices."

"So, what is the 'what if' that you've been mulling over?"

"What if you had been born a logger around here?"

"Were my grandfather and father loggers?"

"Of course."

"Then I guess I would be a logger until I died or got stoved up like that Taylor guy."

"Taylor? Seth Taylor? He's not stoved up. He had a D-8 Cat roll off a cliff on him. He's lucky to be alive."

"So, it's kind of like being a marine?"

"Well," she rubbed the short fuzz on his tummy. "Kind of, except for all the marching around, naps, and stuff... it's probably a little more dangerous in the forest though."

"Yeah, I heard those trees are armed and dangerous."

She slapped Stone on the side of his hip. "Talk to Spuds about how dangerous."

He looked over his shoulder. "I'm just teasing. Spuds and I have already had those talks. That's why I built the clinic here, and why it isn't just a VA clinic."

Ruby tensed as she looked over his shoulder. Stone's head snapped around and saw the shadow of a figure walking hurriedly along the sidewalk toward the field. "Uh oh," Ruby whispered. "Here comes mommy." She poked Stone in the ribs a few times to punctuate her words. "You are in deep doodoo, young man. Taking advantage of an innocent girl in the fresh grass on a moonless night."

Stone looked at the sky, and realized Ruby had known it was basically a moonless night all along.

"Stone, Ruby." Rusty's voice carried across the field. "I don't know if you are out there or not... even though I see a blouse, a boot, and a bra on the grass... but there are five helicopters headed your way, and you know what the field looks like when they light up their landing lights." She turned and started back toward the Café. Over her shoulder, Rusty leveled a parting shot. "I'm just saying."

Rusty smiled as she heard a muffled 'oh shit' from somewhere near the center of where the five helicopters would be in a few minutes. Down the valley, the pounding sound of rotors was becoming audible. Rusty chuckled softly as she walked through the back door of the community center. Her mind was on a 'what if' of her own, and it had to do with having not warned her friends. Sometimes it did an adult a lot of good to be caught at something society thinks only young people do.

Rusty stopped in the dark of the large open hall, as she could see through the open door into the Café. Standing quietly, she took in the scene. The tablet lay on the table where Molly was lazily finger-sliding pictures by as Spuds talked about each one. It did not matter what the pictures were. What made Rusty's chest swell and turn warm was the one arm draped across the young woman's shoulder. The angle of Molly's head, leaning comfortably into Spuds' chest, told Rusty all she needed to know about their relationship.

With a large smile, Rusty quietly retraced her steps back out the rear door of the center. She wiped the damp from her eyes as she stepped outside. She knew she would miss this special place in the world, but also realized it would always be a close second home. The night sky lit up as the five large Black Hawk helicopters positioned in front of the two figures in the field. Rusty thought *home could never be more exciting or strange.*

Rusty fished her phone out of her pocket as Jimmy Buffett started to sing...

From Stone:
Is coffee on?

From Rusty:
Are there grass stains on your knees?

The phone vibrated in Rusty's hand, and she shifted to the new message board that was coming from aboard one of the helicopters.

From Ski:
Any berry pie left?

From Rusty:
I'll rustle some up

BAER CHARLTON

42

Stella slid into the empty chair at the round table that had become the default staff table. "That was one of the busiest days of the most hectic weeks I ever want to experience again, you betcha."

Rusty leaned back in the captain's chair and eyed the retired nun. "Really? Seventy-eight people through the clinic, and that's busy?"

Molly strolled up behind Rusty and popped her on the head with her towel. "Rusty T. My Heart, your momma told you never to lean back in a chair that way. It isn't ladylike, and it weakens my chairs." The woman blushed and eased the chair back onto four legs, and hid her smile and chuckle deep in the mug of coffee.

Molly ignored the redhead and fawned over her new mother hen. "Stella, you look exhausted. I watched that parking lot, and you were hopping like a bunny in spring. Y'all want some coffee before you pass out?" The stream of brown liquid was already hitting the bottom of the freshly overturned mug. Stella just glowed at the attention of the young woman. "I've got some really great local blackberry pie I can have Spuds heat up before he turns in his apron for the night. With maybe a tiny scoop of the forbidden on top," she added, knowing Stella's weakness for ice cream.

"Molly, dear," she rested her hand on the young women's hip, "this is where that pie would go on me if I ate it, especially if I indulged in that creamy Tillamook Vanilla Ice. No, I'd better stick to maybe just a tiny salad without any dressing."

Molly looked at her and mothered the woman. "Oh, Stella, they have just been working you too hard over there. You betcha." She walked off toward the kitchen ordering window, singing out to Spuds. "Boyfriend, fire me a white on black with heat, yellow blanket on the pair." The slice of extra sharp cheddar cheese on top would mean Stella would have to take her lactose pill, but she would be in heaven thinking about growing up on the farm.

Sister Mary Margaret giggled. "That girl has a way, her way."

They all watched Molly move from table to table with the last diners of the night. "I just want some of that energy of hers." Rusty marveled. She turned to face Stella. "She and Millie put up a hundred and sixty plates before Spuds showed up for the lunch rush." They looked back at the topic of conversation as she pulled a plate of pie á la mode out of the window. "And look at her... you would think she just started her shift."

Stella chagrined at being put in her place about what busy is, smiled while raising her mug and took a sip and watched her slice of heaven delivered. "And where has she learned all of this sass talk? I almost expect her to start chewing and snapping gum."

Rusty laughed. "That would be Ellie's influence.

Don't expect the gum. Ellie doesn't chew gum. If you listen to Ellie, she has a theory about sass, charm, cute, and the volume of tips and return visits. That ol' bird is just downright scary when it comes to understanding human nature and how to make us tick to her drum."

Stella opened her eyes from the first bite of pie, ice cream, and cheese. "Speaking of forces of nature, where's Stone? I haven't seen him around all day, and I have a bone to pick with him about his noisy buddies and their house shaking mode of coming and going."

Rusty laughed at the description of the five new Black Hawks landing as a squad on the field the night before. Then she started to turn red at the memory.

Stella watched the freckles blend into the flush of her skin. She put her fork down and patted at her mouth with her napkin. "Alright, give."

Rusty looked around as if she was about to divulge the deepest dirt. "Last night, we were going over the books when a call came on the radio. Five transitioning helicopters needed a pit stop. Except there was a problem."

Mary Margaret asked, "Problem, with the helicopters? They sounded in very good health last night. Both when they landed and when they took off an hour later."

Rusty smiled slyly. "The problem wasn't mechanical, it was human. They had scanned the field way ahead for any animals needing to be shooed away. Only the two animals who showed up hot and sweaty in the infrared scope were human. There were bits and pieces of still slightly warm clothes spread in a trail from the houses. So they called to ask if someone could go shoo the animals away." Rusty was biting down on the tip of her tongue trying not to laugh. Mary Margaret remained busy translating everything in her head. Finally, the light went on, and her eyes got big. Rusty, Stella, and Paul all exploded in laughter at the awakening of the young nun.

The black face still could not hide the flush of blood as her face got even brighter and she remembered how the large helicopters landed at night. "Oh, that could have been very illuminating if they hadn't called ahead and just came in turning on those big bright lights."

Rusty smiled. "Luckily, I had the decks cleared by then."

"So, where are the truant twosome?" Paul asked.

"Touring a ship. The Essex is getting a new captain in a few months, and she decided to tag along on the ferrying operation of their new squadron of Black Hawks who are replacing the old Sea Horses."

Rusty smiled. "Being the kind of officer we all know her to be, she decided to treat the team to the best pie the coast had to offer. I don't think she'll ever have a problem coming on shore for an occasional good meal. In fact, the way those fliers went through what we had left, I'm not sure they are going to wait for her to take command."

"Did I hear you right? Ski is going to dump the Pentagon and take a command?"

Rusty swiveled to look at Spuds who was standing there with a small plate of berry pie himself. The man had gray-green bags under his eyes, but a smile on his face. Exhaustion seemed to be running through everyone, except Molly.

Rusty nodded. "Turns out the Admiral will be retiring soon, so she took the opportunity. Actually, I think that you, Ruby, and Ellie, corrupted the little thing. She now realizes there just isn't any good food to be had in DC. Everything worth eating is out here."

Spuds smiled. "Does that mean you'll be staying, too?"

Rusty laughed. "Oh, hell no, honey. I do my own cooking. I also thrive on trashy food. It fuels the monster in me. Oops," she stood up quickly, "speaking of monsters, I need to let the little girl out for an evening run on the field." Waving at everyone, she said, "I'll see y'all in the morning before we roll out."

"You're really going to leave?" Paul sounded dejected.

The redhead leaned over and gave him a hug as she kissed his cheek. "Paul, sweetie, you knew it was coming. I need to be in Oklahoma by next Monday. Besides, you know it just wouldn't have worked out between us. You're an ash blonde and I'm a redhead. You're natural, and I'm Clairol 147. It would be exciting for a while, but we'd just burn each other up like two comets."

Paul laughed and put his arm up to hug her head. "Oklahoma, huh? I know a really nice sleazy greasy spoon in the south end of Tulsa."

Rusty gave the man a hug. "I'll get that address from you in the morning. You had me at sleazy."

"You're not going to wait around to say good-bye to Stone and Ruby?" Stella frowned.

Rusty stepped over and with a toss of her head, leaned in and hugged Stella. Quietly, she assured the older nun, "I said good-bye to both of them last night when they left. I will always know where to find Ruby, Molly, and all of you... As for Stone, he and I are both rolling stones. But we have each other in our phones."

The tall thin runner stood up. Her eyes were awash in a stoic face. Rusty looked at the tall woman, smiled, and glanced over at Molly. As she moved in for the last hug of the night, she confessed to Mary Margaret, "Everyone had been watching Molly become a woman, but they missed the most amazing transformation standing in front of them. You have grown from wonderful to amazing. We should rename you Grace." They hung onto each other as they quietly wept.

"But Mary Margaret has always been my name."

Rusty held her back. "Is that true?" She looked at Stella.

Stella nodded. "She came to us with that name already. We thought it was strange that she didn't have a Somali name or even a Swahili name. She was always Mary Margaret. So when it came to take her vows, nobody ever thought about changing it."

"That may have fit her then, but she has become Grace."

The two stood in the casual side-hug of close friends. Never could anyone imagine two dissimilar people could become fast friends.

Paul coughed. "I'd vote for Fast Eddie... But it doesn't fit her... now."

"It's not too pre... pretend something?"

"Pretentious." Stella leaned back in her chair, studying the young woman, no longer the gawky little girl in her mind's eye.

"Stella, don't lean in my chair." Molly scolded as she walked up, drying her hands in her apron. "What am I missing? What's wrong?"

Rusty took Molly under the other arm and brought her in for a kiss on the cheek. "What is wrong is you were being missed while I was saying my good-byes. And Mary Margaret is thinking of changing her name."

Molly giggled at the kiss, and then her eyes got large as she looked around Rusty toward the nun. "Is that true, Mary Margaret?"

"Rusty thinks I should."

"But to what? You can't be Monkey Butt, because that is Jeannie's name."

Rusty ran her hand down Molly's hair, petting the last of the little girl who had become a woman over the summer. "Not a nickname honey, but her real name as a nun."

"But Mary Margaret is her name."

"That's the one she was born with, but when nuns take their vows to become nuns, they take a new name from the scriptures, the Bible. Now she is considering the name Grace."

The young woman thought about the name and looked at the other darker woman. "I like Grace, and you are, too. I've watched you take the shortcut down the hill across the street. You never fall."

"Grace has many meanings, honey. The one I was thinking of is about finding peace within one's self and creating that calm about you so others can heal."

Molly thought about the concept. "I like that one, too. But there's the prayer people say before they eat. That's a grace, too."

"Yes, it is."

"Well, Grace is that prayer, only people call it a blessing, because they are blessing the food. But Grace is our blessing. She is a blessing for all of us and the people who come to the clinic to heal." Molly sorted her thoughts about Grace aloud.

Stella looked though the milky cloud of her wet eyes, and in a wavering voice, settled the discussion with conviction. "I guess that's the definitive answer for you, Grace. Yah, I'll call Des Moines in the morning." She glanced at her watch. "Um, later this morning." She stood up, "and with that, I'm off to my chambers and bed."

Everyone's eyes turned toward the muffled sound of trumpets coming from Paul's lap. The man turned red about the ears and smiled as he picked up his phone and read the text.

From Stone:
We all like the name.
Give Grace our best
Home in a few days
Bringing new Doc

STONEHEART

BAER CHARLTON

43

"So, how is the new boy fitting in, Paul?"

The doctor wheeled up to the table and waved to Molly, pretending he was drinking from a mug. "Interestingly, quite well. Did you know that before joining the Navy, he had never been outside the boroughs of New York City?"

"Is that relevant to him fitting in?"

Molly put the coffee down and patted Paul on the shoulder. He thanked her as she went back to the cash register, and then turned back to Stone. "In a way, since getting here, he gets up at dawn and runs the other way from where Grace runs. He always finishes in the trees and likes taking walks in what used to be the forest. He says that he can feel the power of the new trees growing under the concrete layer of gray ash." Paul sipped at his coffee and leaned back. "I'm telling you, if I didn't know better, I would have thought he grew up here. The guy is a full-fledged, tree hugging, deer kissing, forest denizen."

Stone laughed and grabbed at his stomach. "No. Stop. It hurts."

"Oh, now there's a healthy laugh we don't see enough

of." Ruby slid into the chair next to Paul and across from Stone. She rested her hand on the doctor's arm. "What is your secret, oh Master?"

"We were just talking about our new nutcase, the tree squirrel."

Ruby's face feigned with horror. "Oh, for the grace of Mary Margaret, please don't nickname him Squirrel." She grew her eyes into a crazy look. "That would be just... nuts." She leaned back and started to sip her coffee as if nothing had happened. "And then you would have to explain the whole fuzzy tail."

The two men were holding their mouths and stomachs, faking throwing up at her terrible puns at the expense of a nice guy. Ruby continued, "But Ben is a nice guy... for a doctor, but a little strange... even for a shrink."

"You guys talking about my new main man?"

Stone leaned back and looked over his shoulder. "Good afternoon, Grace."

As the woman slid into a chair next to Stone, she leaned over and kissed him on the top of the head. "Don't worry ampendaye baba (dear uncle), you will always be my number one man." She crossed herself. "After Him, of course."

Ruby looked at the young woman with curiosity. This enigma entered her life as a quiet nun who ran almost naked every morning for about ten miles. Now, she was relaxed enough to wear a tank top and a sports bra over leggings and sandals, and joked with the men as if she were a regular girl ready for a date.

Ruby watched as she sipped some coffee, and while putting down her mug, she said, "So what is it that you like so much about Ben? What makes him your main man?"

The dark face became darker as the woman frowned and thought, but then relaxed. "I don't know... he just understands."

"Understands what?"

"Me. What I like... the running, the forest..."

Stone finished it. "The quiet."

Grace stopped and just looked at Stone. In only two words, he had perfectly illuminated the reason for her almost magical transformation. She sighed, "Yes."

Ruby leaned onto her elbows with her woven fingers nesting her chin. "Quiet?"

Stone looked down at his coffee. Wondering if he should share what he had known all along, but seemed hidden from all the rest—the true meaning behind Stoneheart.

Resolved, Stone looked up. "Yes... the quiet." Taking a sip of the coffee, Stone set it down and folded his arms on the table as he leaned in. The late afternoon sun slanting through the western windows made long square pools of late summer warmth on the wooden floors. Through the open windows, Stone could hear a few cars go by, but there was also a bird in one of the trees. Stone smiled to hear that another creature had found the oasis of peace and hoped it would stay to become a critical part of the healing process.

"Long ago, in a beautiful country, there was ugliness. Beauty can be found anywhere, even in the desert, but war—not only is it ugly, it is noisy. Not the kind of noise that is all the time, like in New York City, but the kind that is so jarring and makes so much impact that it tears your life apart and leaves nothing but the sound of war. Even in your sleep, there's still noise. It wears you out, and you're never refreshed. If the bullets don't kill your body, the noise of war still kills your soul. It batters at you nonstop until you withdraw into yourself and your heart turns to stone.

"But not only war. There are other things that do the same. A bad word spoken that haunts you until it consumes your life, a city that hammers at you, and then you get away, only to be hammered by other things like war. In the Navy, you don't see war the same, but for a shrink, he sees the aftermath. He saw the noise that was, and still is, in the minds of those who had the courage to ask for help. Still others find only a single way to turn the volume off, and that is what Ben is doing here. To help them turn down the volume, and not just turn it off.

"It is also why we brought him here. He didn't know it, but his tolerance for the noise was coming to an end. He needed the healing of quiet." Stone reached over and covered the slender black hand with his large white paw. "The same quiet Kidogo Mary (My little Mary) needed. The healing quiet I found on the motorcycle, and even more-so, the one night and breakfast here in Southern Oregon. Quiet."

Ruby looked at the deep black pool of the wet eyes as the nun leaned over and rested herself against the large arm of her benefactor. There had been a pool of something under the surface of all the buildings and gathering of people. Ruby had always known Stone would not be staying. It was not as if he had gathered in his own family, but instead, it had evolved gradually. Stone had brought this family here to do what he had always done, take care of others. Ski had told Ruby while aboard the ship that Stone would never be able to stop being the Gunnery Sergeant, because it was just who he was—a mother hen.

The atmosphere of quiet and healing traveled around the table as they all sat listening to the bird in the tree and the truth in their souls. The warm square sun-patched rugs shimmered in the late afternoon. The huge open ceiling with the giant timber framework gave a sense of a sanctuary of a church.

The sun was lower in the southern sky. The summer was over, and soon the fall would settle the temperature. Windows would close for the winter, and then the rain would start to wash the forest of the rest of the ash. The soil would become rich from the last generation of forest, the new would begin to push green through the cracks and duff and ash, and in the spring, the new green would also help heal the area. However, until then, there was the new growth of the community center, clinic, Café, and new neighbors. As Ruby absorbed it all, and the people at the table, she added... *and new family.*

Ellie stepped out of the office where she had been doing the books. Ruby had done her own books but had always hated that particular task. Ellie, on the other hand, did not like prepping the food so much, but liked the books. They really had found the other half of their bookends. Quietly she called, "I hate to interrupt y'all, but Ruby...?"

"Yeah, sis?"

"This is gonna sound silly, but, what all is a dorner?"

"A what?" She started to rise.

"I have a bill here for $428.57, for a dorner..."

Ruby fell back into the chair and started laughing hysterically. Now everyone wanted to know what it was.

Molly quietly walked over and took the receipt from the woman's hand. She glanced at it and stuck it back in Ellie's fingers. She looked at her mom and laughed. Kissing her new aunt on the cheek and patting the kiss. "Honey child, it's just nothin' but that big old dumb mixer."

"It's what?" Ellie looked back into the food prep area of the large kitchen where, on any given day, Ruby would bake up to six hundred biscuits. Then she looked back at Molly.

The young woman shifted from her southern mode to her imitation of Stella. "Ya, you betcha, it is nothing more than that big ol' dough-runner back there, doncha know." Molly kissed her on the cheek again and walked off. "Just ask me, I know everything," Then she looked back with a coy smile. "I own the joint." She laughed with her classic half laugh and half giggle as she sashayed back down the counter with the exaggerated hip swing of Jeannie, her Portland sister.

The table exploded with laughter at Ellie's stunned face, and Molly just being the New Molly—owner, and headline entertainment.

Ellie stalked over to the table and plopped down next to Ruby. "Explain how you get mixer out of dorner."

"It's dough-runner."

"Still don't make no sense."

"How do you spell dough?"

Ellie closed her eyes in confused resolution. "D-o-u-

..."

"No. How do you spell a female deer?"

"D-o-e."

Ruby tried to not laugh. "Okay... Now, if you only have half your teef, chew tobaccy, and wear your hat backwards... How do you spell doe?"

"D-o."

"Now, you've met Tyler."

Ellie frowned and shook her head, but still thinking through the literally thousands of people she had met in the last three months.

"Yes, you have. Freckles, about half the brains of a squirrel, chew stains down his bib-overalls, and feet the size of Slim's truck. He thought you were my twin brother..."

The light went on. "But I don't understand the runner part."

"He don't cook, but he knowed it was a runner." Ruby shot a goofy smile at Ellie as everyone else got the gist of a machine that ran.

Ellie's eyes got big as she caught the drift, and then closed them at the sheer backwoods of it all. "Oh gawd, I shoulda know'd. After all, I am an Arkey, and Slim is my brother."

Ruby stood up, patted Ellie on the shoulder, and gave her a hug. "It's okay, sis. We all have our crosses to bear. And some of us are lucky enough to get to bury a few." She looked over at Stone with a nod. "And Stone and I are going to go help someone else bury one right now. We'll be down with Bernie, but should be back up for supper. We'll call."

Stone looked up from his phone. "Butterfly says that

she will have him in the living room."

"Good, we'll stop by the house on the way down."

Ellie rose and hugged her new sister. "You kids take care of that man." She turned to Stone and hugged him. "If you weren't such a sinner, you'd be a saint, but we love ya just the same. Go help your friend."

Stone looked down at the trumpets in his hand.

From Butterfly:
He's ready.

STONEHEART

BAER CHARLTON

44

Bernie looked better than he probably had for years. He was smiling softly and draped comfortably in his chair. His demeanor was of one who had it all, yet had nothing. He had been at the top of the heap, and still had nothing. Now he had all but given it all away, and now had almost everything. He was a man at ease in the belly of a beast that was warm and caring.

Bernie's face turned toward the last of the warm afternoon sun. The light filtered through the sheers across his eyelids as his mind drifted and waited. Butterfly leaned her bulk against the rough-hewn timbers that made the archway from the entrance to the living room. She watched with a nurse's eye on his breathing, subconsciously counting his respiration. She knew his blood pressure was lower today than it had been in the last two weeks. Butterfly observed the way he held his feet in the socks that kept them warm. Even the length of his fingernails and hair were in her constant purview.

A smile crept upon her face. This is how the man should have been for years, comfortable with himself. She thought about her own husband. He had several years left of driving trucks through some of the worst the Pacific Northwest could throw at him, but she also knew that when he came home for a few days, he laid draped on a chair the same way she had taught Bernie.

She heard a scuffle of feet on the sidewalk outside. Two large steps and she quietly opened the door, saying nothing.

Stone frowned and mouthed, "Is he asleep?"

Butterfly smiled. "No he's just relaxed. Come on in. I'm making tea. Can I get you some, or would you like some coffee?"

Ruby stepped in and hugged the larger woman. "You are such a dear. It has been so long since I've had any that I think it would be wonderful to join you in tea. If it's Chamomile, then Stone will have some, too. He needs to sleep tonight."

"Actually, forget it. If you don't have Chamomile, then I will just have some water please." Stone leaned in for his hug and nuzzled his nose down into the woman's neck. "Umm, is that mountain juniper I smell?"

Butterfly pushed back and looked at him as she giggled. "Oh my gosh, you done turned into a logger on me."

"Is that Stone I hear?" Bernie rose from the chair and left his cane. As he walked a step, Ruby came across the room and hugged him.

"How are you doing today, Bernie?"

"Well, Ruby, I'd be full of piss and vinegar, but Miss Fussbudget over here makes me void every hour and won't serve me deep-fried cod with vinegar. So I'm just screwed and happy." They laughed as Bernie stuck out his hand. "Hello, Stone."

Stone waved the hand out of the way as he moved in for a hug. "If I have to get used to this, so do you," he growled in the man's ear.

Bernie laughed. "Once a pain-in-the-ass jerk, always a pain-in-the-ass jerk... eh, Stone?"

Stone held his fist up in the air in a salute. "Brothers to the end, Bernie."

Ruby rolled her eyes. "I'm helping you with the tea, Butterfly. This man's shit is too deep for me."

Butterfly held her fist up in a salute. "Amen to that, sista."

The sexes parted ways as Ruby passed the folder and bag to Stone.

Stone turned back. "We might want to talk about this up at the table, Bernie. Let me get your cane."

"Leave the cane. Just give me your arm."

The man took Stone's arm as they slowly moved toward the large black walnut dining table that Stone knew came from central Oregon. All of the wood in the houses came from nowhere but Oregon. From the myrtle wood or vertical grain heart Douglas fir for trim, to green oak, madrone, maple, walnut, dogwood, and catalpa for cabinets, chests, and furniture. Everything sourced and brought in. Stone never asked Bernie how he had sourced such a quantity of amazing craftsman-made furniture in such a short time, nor did he want to know how much it cost. Nothing looked or smelled as if it were brand new. From the trim on the cabinets to every piece of furniture, all had the look and feel of being in place, lovingly cared for, for a hundred years. All of it had showed up with an interior designer who had the schematics for the paint colors and furniture placement. Even Trent did not know

465

who she was or where she had come from, but Stone felt sure Trent would use her again if he needed a designer.

A while later, the remains of a berry pie lay in tiny pieces of crumbs at the bottom of the pan, four plates all but licked clean. The teapot had gone cold sitting untouched under the cozy. The afternoon sun was long gone. All that remained from the passed around box of tissues were four crumpled piles. The talking had wound down.

The hardest part had been telling the story of the car, driven up the Northern California coastal region on Highway 101 in the middle of the night. Fall was the one season of the year where large fires combined with the opening of hunting season. An early cold had driven the masses of deer down onto the flats, creating the perfect storm of events. Add in a little ground fog to the clash between three large deer and a brown Cadillac on a turn high above a deep bend in the river, and you have an auto accident that went unnoticed for several hours.

The insult to the injury had come somewhere in the river. The purse, or whatever she had been carrying her identification in, had gone missing. The registration for the car was in a closed post office box. The notice of the accident had returned to the Eureka office of the California Highway Patrol, and they turned everything over to the under-staffed sheriff station, which was too far under budget to pursue the notification any further.

Finally, Ruby opened the small bag and looked in. "She had a small watertight insulated lunch bucket."

Bernie leaned back with a small smile. "It was her purse for larger stuff. She loved that it was called a Playboy. She even had some bunny stickers on it. But you couldn't miss the red and white square bucket."

"Neither could the divers. One of the first ones brought it up. This was inside. Someone knew that it would be important eventually."

She pulled a small jewelry box out of the bag and set it down in front of Bernie.

Bernie looked at it but obviously, did not recognize it. He looked up at Ruby and shrugged. She just nudged her chin back at him to open it.

His hands trembled as he opened the box.

There were two wedding rings with a small note rolled up and running through the two. Bernie stared at the rings and the meaning of them. Slowly he withdrew the note and unrolled it.

Bernie, my dearest love,

There is no other man in the world I want to spend my life with.

With all of my heart, yes.

Maddie

Ruby pushed the tissue box across the table. Butterfly got up and retrieved two more boxes. Everyone laughed at the truth of the tissues.

As they gained control again, Ruby took a receipt out of the bag. "It appears she had gone down to San Francisco to have them custom-made. She was headed back when she hit the deer."

The man sat quietly as he stared at the rings in the box. They were not large or fancy, just a little different in the way they looked as if they were forged or beaten into shape. Bernie remembered a conversation when they were seniors just after he had given Maddie his graduation ring that did not even fit on her thumb. Therefore, like most girls of the time, she had put the ring on a chain around her neck.

"Bernie?"

"I th… I was just thinking. I think these are made from my graduation ring. It was so large that it wouldn't fit on any of her fingers, so she put it on a chain. One day she looked at it and said that all it was good for was to recast it into wedding rings."

He looked up at Ruby and then Stone. "So, she was coming back?"

Stone nodded. "It would appear so."

The man slumped in on himself. "All these years."

"Neither one of you ever stopped loving the other." Ruby reached for the box of tissues as Butterfly grabbed out a fast three or four. They laughed.

Gently, Bernie closed the box and gazed toward the Café. Smiling a small wrinkle of his lip, he pushed the box back across the table to Ruby.

"Bernie, she got them for you…"

"Yes, she did, but the reason gold is so precious is because it can be cast and recast many, many times, and it never gets lost. You hold on to those for me."

Bernie looked at Butterfly and they both smiled. Their many hours together had merged a lot of their thinking. He looked back at Ruby. "Most nights, we call the Café for food. It's after they close, but we know that Spuds and Molly are doing clean up, prepping, going over the books, or something. So we order something easy. Lately, they have walked it down to us together.

"Now, I'm not blind and neither is Butterfly… when we see her take his hand as they walk out of here, we know something is up… and it ain't balloons.

"So, when Spuds gets as smart as the girl he's holding hands with, you offer my Molly those rings. They are the best I have to offer... A lot of love is embedded in that gold." He pushed the tissue box back across the table, but it just sat in the middle. There was nothing else to be said.

The "Thanks, Bernie," sounded more of a croaked whisper. There was no voice left.

Bernie turned to Stone. "How did you find her?"

"Ski."

Bernie leaned back in the chair and rolled his eyes closed. "Man, what I could have done with a right hand like that. I wish that little girl would come to work for me.

"That little girl is going to be commanding the third largest ship in the world come next May, unless she opts for a light cruiser based out of Puget Sound."

Butterfly laughed. "We knew before you knew, but it didn't stop Bernie from propositioning her about a job that he doesn't have to give any more."

"Hey, for her, I'd start a new business."

"Let's just leave her to run the Navy. The world is safer for it."

Trumpets sounded and Stone and Ruby laughed. "There she is now."

From Spuds:
dinner @ 4?

"Spuds, he wants to know if we're ready for dinner."

Bernie laughed. "Quick! Hide the pie evidence and tell him to come ahead. The Café is closed, so tell them to join us. They're family, after all." He locked eyes with Ruby, and they both smiled warmly.

BAER CHARLTON

From Stone:
Bring dinner for 6
Ur family 2

The night air was silent as Ruby and Stone finally closed the door to Dawn Cedar. The evening had been a joy of family teases, friendly joking, and deeply felt sharing. The kind of family around a table Stone had never experienced. There was no talk of troop movements, reveals of a new sort of weapons, discussions of moves, or movements. Stone could tell their gentle talk had meaning for the people who had become attached and caring.

Stone had listened to the quiet in the hearts and voices. Stone heard the quiet, which only comes from the respite from the torment, worry, and uncertainty, a certain quietness of self-assurance that can only originate from within. He knew that from each of them, it had come from finally knowing, making peace, finding new friends, gathering strength through a collective, laying to rest old loves, and taking up new ones.

It was about recapturing driving during an early summer's night, with one finger on the wheel and an arm around your girl while the road wound out slowly ahead of you. The song playing on the radio happened to be just the one you needed and wanted to hear.

They stood looking at the thin line of a new moon rising over the hills. "What are you thinking?" Ruby leaned into his arm. Stone moved it out of the way and draped it over her shoulders. She snuggled into Stone's body and stuck her left hand down into his left rear pocket. Her right hand rested lightly on his chest.

"People."

"Which ones?"

"All of them. Take your pick. I have a phone full of them."

"Okay... Slim."

"I give him until about Thanksgiving. He'll have dropped about twenty pounds from eating bad food, and the big red truck will come rolling around the bend with a Christmas wreath on the front grill, and he'll be begging your new sister to take him home. Besides, this is where Osiel is—those three are all the family they have."

"Okay, you brought her up... Ellie."

Stone thought and heaved a huge sigh. "The truck stop wasn't her. She was there so she could see Slim all the time. Hank was the one who loved the diner, she just loved being near him. Irritating and abusing the customers was just a bonus. My guess... down the road, she'll come out of the back just to abuse Trent until he gives up and asks her out."

"Trent?" She stiffened and looked up at his chin. "You do know he's gay, don't you?"

He did not even flinch, but instead smiled that thin Stone grin. "No he isn't. He made you think that because he knew he could never have you." He looked down at her. "Trust me . . . he and Rusty got really close. If Rusty says he isn't gay, then he isn't gay. However, he is a marked man. He and Ellie just haven't figured that out yet. Or so Rusty says, and she's one smart fella."

"Molly?"

"She's going to be just fine. She still misses her dad, and so do you, but you both draw the healing from everyone else. You two will never lose the memories of him, and that is the best thing. From what I have heard from people, he was a great guy. I will always carry that one picture I have of him waving through the cook's window. He was in his own heaven. Hank loved what he did. He loved the people he worked with. He loved where he was and lived. You could rename that field out there Hank's Field and not one person would say you were wrong. It just isn't big enough to represent how big his love was for this place." Stone could feel her softly crying and then turned to wipe her eyes on his shirt.

"I didn't mean to make you sad."

"I'm not," Ruby sobbed then sniffed. "I'm just so happy that you see all of that. Six months ago, none of that was in place. I see all of it now, and you are in the middle. But you're also leaving in the morning... I just don't understand."

"Tiger stripes, I guess. All my life, I've fixed things and moved on."

"Yeah, you don't know shit either." Ruby laughed. "So what about Spuds and Molly?"

"I figure they either scare you on Halloween or give thanks in November."

"How do you figure that?"

"You do know that she isn't up there in her room." Stone jerked his thumb back at the house she and Molly shared. "I'm willing to bet there is a certain beat-up yellow van still parked down at the far end of the parking lot just past the clinic."

Ruby's head knocked against his chest. "Oh gawd."

"Hey, Spuds isn't stupid, and neither is Molly. She'll be home by one or two."

She was quiet as they walked slowly out toward the

edge of the sidewalk overlooking the field. "'Hank's Field, huh?"

"Has a certain ring to it."

They stood quiet in their own thoughts. An owl swooped by on silent wings. Other shadows flittered about. Stone now knew that they were small birds that ate as many night gnats out of the air as the bats.

"Now what are you thinking?"

"Two things, I'm wondering if there were any helicopters that might come landing tonight, and if Hank would mind if I put some grass stains on your cute bottom again."

She turned him around with the hand in his back pocket, and headed back the way they came. "Not tonight, buster. If I don't have to worry about my daughter hearing us, then I'm making good use out of the little black lacy thing I got in town a few months ago."

As they both started walking faster, there played the sound of trumpets.

Ruby dug in his pocket and pulled out the offending phone.

From Ski:
Got a moment?

Ruby typed, and Stone just laughed.

From Stone:
This is Ruby. Stone is busy tonight.
You can have him tomorrow…
Just not early.
Tonight he's mine.

BAER CHARLTON

So go to bed.

From Ski:
Yes momma,
Hugs all around.

.

STONEHEART

BAER CHARLTON

45

The trees were tall, dark, and lush. The gray of the highway was gritty and worn. The motorcycle chuffed gently at the side of the road. A stone's throw down the road, a doe peeked cautiously out from behind a tree, silently crossed the highway, and then bounded up the embankment and disappeared into the upper forest. The trees were rich with the sound of birds, searching for grubs in the bark, or just singing as the morning warmed.

The large bush moved as a hand pushed it aside. The boots felt strange after all the months in only running shoes. Somehow, the denim jeans felt a little stiffer than he remembered they had last spring. Stone looked north with longing, and then south with anticipation. For the first time in his life, he realized he had a choice about where he went next. From now on, no more orders, no more drifting. It was all his choice – him, the motorcycle, and the road.

The crickets vibrated in his pocket and he fished it out. Stone glanced at the name and growled with his early morning voice, "Hello Commander. Giving up texting?"

"Not a Commander yet, Stone, but I'm looking

forward to that greeting all too soon. This time, the question is longer than I want to text."

"What can I do for you on this joyous morning?"

Stone looked down the road as two fawns stepped timidly onto the highway and then bounced across and up the embankment to join their mother. His mouth dropped open in a wide smile.

"I'm sorry, what did you say? I was distracted by a couple of cute little deer."

"At your age, I hope you meant fawns."

"Two, they just crossed the highway in front of me. I don't ever want to get used to the joy of seeing that kind of thing."

"Then you better stay there. I don't think they have any of those moments in Sacramento."

"Hmm, I *am* headed south..."

"As you get closer, I'll text you where to go and who to see. We need you to testify about what you did with the clinic and all at Stoneheart. We have an admiral out there who wants to partner with the state of California to provide something similar in a couple of places."

"I need to be heading south soon before it gets cold in the passes. How long will this take?"

"It sounds like it's going to be just a deposition, so maybe only a day or two. If they need more later, they can fly you back out from wherever you are." She paused "Where are you headed, anyway?"

Stone thought about the question. "Going home?"

"Where's that?"

Stone laughed. "I'll tell you when I know." He poked the phone that had gone dead.

His hand rested on the warm helmet. He smiled at the

custom paintjob that one of the helicopter jockeys had airbrushed for him. The entire helmet looked like a large chunk of granite with a heart shaped hole carved into the back. Under the heart were incised the traditional words Semper Fi. He thought about what he had just told Ski. Smiling, Stone looked south as he fished the phone back out of his pocket.

> *From Stone:*
> *Where am I going, Sweet Cheeks?*

> *From Rusty:*
> *Be still my heart. Couch is made up.*
> *Head toward Tampa. 23 days*
> *We leave for Haiti for the winter*
> *Angel misses you*

> *From Stone:*
> *Angel misses Elvis*
> *But, I'll take a hug and kiss any day*
> *Soon*

A fourth deer peeked out and looked south as it watched the loud thrumming motorcycle disappear around the bend. The quiet settled back down around the section of forest. As the birds started to sing again, and the woodpecker went back to hammering at the tall pine, the deer stepped timidly onto the asphalt. Looking back at where it had been, it turned and bound forward into the new.

BAER CHARLTON

Author's Note

For some writers, this is where they bare their souls about plagiarizing... er, I mean, ripping their story from the headlines. I'm at the other end of the spectrum. When I wrote this book, there was very little being said about the invisibly wounded. In fact, very little was being said about the returning wounded at all.

The related stories of Bob Woodward (one of few reporters who got too close to their story and lived to tell about it), had gripped the nation, had the commiserate follow-ups, and the fact that he was back to work. Now we can move on. Bob, there are a lot of us that know what that really means.

Meanwhile, we had transitioned out of yet another country. The regimented retreat was news for almost a week. "Meanwhile, in further news... On Capitol Hill again today, Congress recessed for..."

I was in rewrites.

As Congress again took away, the funds that kept many timber rich counties running—while their permanently shuttered lumber mills—from a Federal shutdown of timber sales...

I was in final rewrites.

As my publisher was going over my edits, Congress pulled the funding on twenty-seven rural Veteran Administration medical clinics. Many of these were the only medical attention for the local vets who are now faced with hours of driving for just a doctor's visit.

As the publisher's deadline needed these final sheets, 51 forest fires gripped the West— devouring huge areas of forest, homes, businesses, jobs, and ancillary incomes, including the western edge of Yosemite National Park. The year 2013 will go down in the record books as one of those that other years, and their fires, will be compared to.

On a happy note, I was asked by one of my heroic beta readers if in my trips to Grants Pass, Oregon if I had ever been to a certain restaurant and met a waitress named Debra. The answer was no and no. One day, after the release of Stoneheart, I will have to do that. I understand that she and Molly have a lot in common.

So, no, I did not rip my story from the headlines, as it were. I wrote this book for all of the people that I have met or not met, through no fault of their own, and who made it back, but never have made it home. This book may not be a road map, but I would like to think that it could stand as a guidepost along the way.

There are many who have helped in this book. Most with ties to the military and cannot be thanked here. You know who you are, and once again, I thank you for your service, your sacrifices, and for caring that I "get it right."

To Leslie Root MD, Tony Colorito MD, and Roc Reed, Physical Therapist extraordinaire. Thank you for your knowledge, expertise, and the sharing when it counted most. More importantly, thank you for keeping me going. For Dr. James Cook, thank you for Letterman Hospital and your service.

To my beta readers who braved the raw pages, especially Pat Erickson who led me back to my soul and gave me the shovel I did not want but needed. To Shar Stacy who reminded me that this story was always about the people, and who kept me in touch with my sanity and humanity when the sleepless nights were at their worst. To

Mary and Paulette Stevens for helping me tell part of their story—the story of so many who have served in silence.

Fiction—is a trick. It can resemble true-life, but then in the end, after you have laughed, and cried, loved and hated, you can close the cover and say, "It was only a story." I will let you have that. It is your right as a reader. And you can leave now and hold on to that.

Real fiction is based in truth. The more truth and reality there is, the more compelling the story. My special thanks to Jeannie "Monkey Butt" for being very real, and a nice friend. And I would like to also extend thanks for Terry and Kathy, the owners of the Dockside, and for allowing me to use a great place, a great sandwich, and their waitress.

As for Elvis? Buddy, you're momma made me do it, but at least I gave you your own army to run with.

Portland is a great place to run. And if you're here in May, don't miss the Oregon Humane Society's Doggy Dash.

The other very real characters that are in this book are Traumatic Brain Injury (TBI), and Postraumatic Stress Disorder (PTSD). Luckily, we are starting to have a very real and very involved social conversation about both. The light being turned on the two has moved back and is now lighting up areas from the NFL, down to shaken baby syndrome, abused children, and victims of rape. We, as a society, have a very long conversation ahead of us. If the theory that one-in-five people in America are suffering from PTSD is true, then that is forty-million people. This book deals with a very small chunk of ice off that iceberg.

I hope there are warmer waters ahead for all concerned.

PTSD is treatable to a point. TBI is a training of work-arounds, but there is help. However, both require the patient to be able to get to the help. That is a treatment for the nation, which we need to work on together.

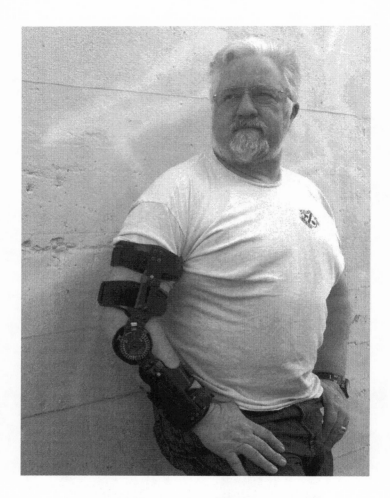

BAER CHARLTON

About Author

Baer Charlton graduated from UC Irvine with a degree in Social Anthropology, monkeyed around for a while, and then proceeded onward with a life of global travel, multi-disciplinary adventure and meeting the memorable array of characters he would come to describe in his writing. He has ridden things with gears, engines, and sails and made things with wood, leather and metal. He has been stitched back together more times than the average hockey team; his long-suffering wife and an assortment of cats and dogs have nursed him back to health after each surgery.

Baer knows a lot about a lot of things in this world; history flows through his veins and pours out of him at the slightest provocation. Do not ask him what you may think is a simple question, unless you have the time to hear a fascinating story.

Other books by Baer Charlton

The Very Littlest Dragon

Death on a Dime

Made in the USA
Charleston, SC
13 May 2014